PENGUIN BOOKS
The Viewing Platform

Ian Wedde was born in Blenheim, New Zealand, in 1946 and was brought up in East Pakistan (Bangladesh) and England, and attended the University of Auckland. He currently lives in Wellington, New Zealand. He has travelled widely in Europe, Asia, the Middle East and North America. He has won awards for both poetry and fiction and has held a number of writing and research fellowships and grants, most recently the Meridian Energy Katherine Mansfield Memorial Fellowship at Menton in France (2005) and a Fulbright Travel Award to the USA (2006). Between 1994 and 2004 he was head of art and visual culture at the Museum of New Zealand Te Papa Tongarewa. He now works as an independent writer and curator. His novel *Dick Seddon's Great Dive* was awarded the National Book Award for fiction in 1976, but it was *Symmes Hole* in 1986 that established him as a major voice in Pacific fiction. Described by the *NZ Listener* as 'a remarkable and even triumphant achievement', *Symmes Hole* also benchmarked Wedde's distinctive mode: a fusion of the novel and the essay. *The Viewing Platform* is Ian Wedde's fourth novel.

Also by Ian Wedde

Novels
Dick Seddon's Great Dive
Symmes Hole
Survival Arts

Short Stories
The Shirt Factory

Poetry
Homage to Matisse
Made Over: Poems
Earthly Sonnets for Carlos
Pathway to the Sea
Spells for Coming Out
Castaly
Georgicon
Driving into the Storm: Selected Poems
Tendering
The Drummer
The Commonplace Odes
Three Regrets and a Hymn to Beauty

Essays
How To Be Nowhere: Essays and Texts 1971–94
Making Ends Meet: Essays and Talks 1992–2004

Edited
The Penguin Book of New Zealand Verse
(with Harvey McQueen)
The Penguin Book of Contemporary New Zealand Poetry
– Nga Kupu Tuitohu o Aotearoa
(with Miriama Evans and Harvey McQueen)

Translation
Selected Poems of Mahmoud Darwish (with Fawwaz Tuqan)

The Viewing Platform

Ian Wedde

PENGUIN BOOKS

PENGUIN BOOKS
Published by the Penguin Group
Penguin Group (NZ), cnr Airborne and Rosedale Roads, Albany, Auckland 1310,
New Zealand (a division of Pearson New Zealand Ltd)
Penguin Group (USA) Inc., 375 Hudson Street, New York,
New York 10014, USA
Penguin Group (Canada), 90 Eglinton Avenue East, Suite 700, Toronto, Ontario,
M4P 2Y3, Canada (a division of Pearson Penguin Canada Inc.)
Penguin Books Ltd, 80 Strand, London, WC2R 0RL, England
Penguin Ireland, 25 St Stephen's Green, Dublin 2, Ireland
(a division of Penguin Books Ltd)
Penguin Group (Australia), 250 Camberwell Road, Camberwell, Victoria 3124,
Australia (a division of Pearson Australia Group Pty Ltd)
Penguin Books India Pvt Ltd, 11, Community Centre, Panchsheel Park,
New Delhi – 110 017, India
Penguin Books (South Africa) (Pty) Ltd, 24 Sturdee Avenue,
Rosebank, Johannesburg 2196, South Africa
Penguin Books Ltd, Registered Offices: 80 Strand, London,
WC2R 0RL, England

First published by Penguin Group (NZ), 2006

1 3 5 7 9 10 8 6 4 2

Copyright © Ian Wedde, 2006

The right of Ian Wedde to be identified as the author of this work in
terms of section 96 of the Copyright Act 1994 is hereby asserted.

Editorial Services by Michael Gifkins and Associates
Designed by Shaun Jury
Typeset by Egan Reid Ltd
Printed in Australia by McPherson's Printing Group

All rights reserved. Without limiting the rights under copyright reserved above,
no part of this publication may be reproduced, stored in or introduced into
a retrieval system, or transmitted, in any form or by any means (electronic,
mechanical, photocopying, recording or otherwise), without the prior written
permission of both the copyright owner and the above publisher of this book.

ISBN 978 0 14 302092 9
ISBN 0 14 302092 7

A catalogue record for this book is available
from the National Library of New Zealand.
www.penguin.co.nz

This book was written with the assistance of a project grant from Creative New Zealand in 2004 and the Meridian Energy Katherine Mansfield Memorial Fellowship in 2005.

Lalon says:
Fortunate are those who see!
Lalon Shah (1774–1890)

Contents

one	Executive Summary	9
two	Purity	14
three	Home	22
four	Identity	29
five	Lust	37
six	Authenticity	45
seven	Home	62
eight	Beauty	74
nine	Desire	87
ten	Adventure	91
eleven	Home	106
twelve	Hospitality	120
thirteen	Loneliness	147
fourteen	Purity	158
fifteen	Home	185
sixteen	Fear	193
seventeen	Identity	212
eighteen	Home	228

nineteen	Pride	247
twenty	Authenticity	260
twenty-one	Home	277
twenty-two	Loyalty	287
twenty-three	Beauty	302
twenty-four	Home and Adventure	308
twenty-five	Hospitality and Triumph	326
twenty-six	Doubt	337
twenty-seven	Viewing	341

one

Executive Summary

A delicate, seaweedy tang of effort was perceptible in the crisp atmosphere – the supple facilitator had worked hard at the group's primitive physical camaraderie. The little, emaciated woman in leg braces was breathing normally at the end of the exercises and had an expression of ironic enjoyment. The lean dandy did not take part ('Physical jerks?') and had not removed his dark glasses – he sat on the edge of a table with his trouser leg hitched up and a look of bored incredulity on his face. The dark, brilliantly smiling man from Bangladesh was the facilitator's equal in suppleness. There was a hefty blonde woman who participated heartily but without pleasure. A glamorous Maori woman arrived late, saw what was happening, and left again. She returned languidly when the 'physical jerks' had been stood down. The only athletic member of the group, whose tan gave him an outdoorsy look, went effortlessly through the assorted stretches, breathings and encounters as though he already knew them by heart.

Clean, bright, UV-filtered sunlight refreshed the decor of the cultural tourism workshop. Sunlight even 'flooded' the room: the view of the sparkling harbour blended the brilliance of air and water. The view infused the lucid contents of a water jug, in which ice-cubes tinkled and lemon slices floated. The workshop participants drank equally of liquid and illumination.

This was probably what the sponsors of the Cultural Tourism Initiative were hoping for, thought Nancy – nicknamed 'Ants' or 'Antsy' in the group's bonding sessions, despite its shifty efforts to circumvent the obvious. She had been tempted to suggest 'The Jerk' and solve their problem. She allowed the cool light to run down her quickly gulping throat and concealed her difficulty by a birdlike sipping. She managed this while dangling one crutch from her right forearm. She noticed the group averting its eyes from both her dexterity and her little swallows.

Neither the UV-filtered light nor the chlorinated and fluoride-treated water could be called natural in any exact sense, but at least the water had come straight from a tap, the light was sunlight and the view beyond the shining window was grand not just because of the mountains at its far end but also because of the city buildings that reared up raggedly in its foreground – a graph of glinting glass. Antsy put her own glass down with a quick movement that pre-empted her tremor and hid her irritation with the group's terms of reference. What was all this crap about natural beauty? She was herself a complex spectacle, at once prosthetic and primordial, composed almost equally of what little flesh tissue she retained and an array of implants and aids that allowed her to pump blood, walk, see, chew and, she guessed, think – not to mention the diverse pharmaceutical supports that sustained this complex equilibrium, this balance between the light and dark sides of consciousness.

The group paused in its activity while the museum's CEO, whose sensational necktie was also awash with watery sunlight, welcomed the newly assembled CTI team. He had the floor to himself. The night before, the welcoming cocktails had been shared with the Ministry of Tourism and the Ministry for Culture and Heritage. Then, it had been 'Hands-On', the notorious Minister of Tourism, who demanded the limelight. This was his baby. Next, the Associate Minister for Culture, dressed in bewildering purple flounces, had been drowned out as the guests, made bold by canapés and wine, began to shout.

Ants watched the museum's CEO narrow his eyes like a hunter or alpine explorer against the glare of New Zealand's famous hard, clear light as he spoke of the significance of tourism to the museum industry framed, as it were, by viewing the country's natural splendours.

This was a long bow that Ants had seen drawn to snapping point many times. Its current reissue, in the almost rinsed interior of the workshop suite, was no more banal than the others. However, the sparkling view out to the city's glass towers, the iridescent harbour and the distant, sombre mountains with their residual spring caps of snow, served as an autocue for the museum chief's speech, which decanted categories in and out of each other with the aplomb of a prize-winning cocktail barman. He had been briefed about the CTI team's key themes and wove purity, identity, authenticity, beauty, adventure and hospitality into his remarks. Ants began to count. Shifting his media-coached gaze from one team member to the next and not omitting the workshop's lithe facilitator, the museum chief used the word 'splendid' four times, 'natural' five, 'awesome' and 'spectacular' seven, 'sublime' eight and 'beautiful' fifteen. Twelve of the fifteen times he spoke the word 'beautiful' included eye contact with the lightly perspiring facilitator. Her gaze met his for the first nine, advanced to eyelash-fluttering for the next three and concluded demurely for the balance.

Ants doubted if the team members could see that the quiver of her lips was caused by amusement, not disability. Her amusement was not just at the CEO's mating display. The Absolutely Pure marketing guru William was not bothering to conceal his derision. He had declined to come dressed for workshop romping as the cravenly nicknamed 'Bill' but was showing bony ankles and feet in expensively branded socks. His packet of magic markers lay unopened next to his A3 note pad. But Ants watched him enjoy squeezing his plastic 'think-about-it' ball. He even pressed it to his mouth and inhaled its rubbery tang. The tourism ministry's Beauty portfolio specialist, Patricia, wittily nicknamed 'Cowpat', was watching the CEO flirt with the leotarded facilitator. Her A3 pad was covered with bullet-pointed notes in assorted colours, but Ants had her down as the tough girl on the set. Her competent body was ready to workshop hard in comfortable, multi-zippered outdoor garments. She had the poker face of an old-school negotiator and was not wasting her time on trivia. Hinemoana, the team's manaakitanga and hospitality specialist, nicknamed 'Gloria', watched the CEO below voluptuously lowered eyelids. She was hungover and had poured much of the jug of water into herself. Her magic markers were arranged in a flower shape and she had hung her squeezy ball around her neck on its elastic band. It rested at the base of her throat like the bizarre feather corsage of an exotic bird. Joris, nicknamed 'Boris', the Dutch adventure tourism entrepreneur, had cornered Trade and Enterprise's venture capital broker the night before. This morning, he watched what was happening with the optimistic air of someone convinced the break was soon. He was wearing his own branded 'Good-2-Go: We Add Venture' adventure-wear and had drawn a succinct, effortless graph on his A3 pad showing the relationship between demand-side danger and supply-side safety in parallel with demand-side risk and supply-side thrill. The Bangladeshi team-member, Mohammed Baul Biswas, nickname 'Biz', watched everything with a meaningless, brilliant smile. Ants had seen Biswas shovel his magic markers and plastic 'think-about-it' ball back into his 'Up-Keep' workshop tote bag. She could tell that the man had kids. Biswas was neat and spruce – his responsibility for the CTI theme of Purity struck Ants as bizarrely appropriate. When he drank from his glass of shining water, his trim moustache lifted from white teeth and the folded handkerchief with which he wiped his smiling lips was neatly pressed.

Biswas dabbed his moustache and resumed his smile for the benefit of the museum CEO, whose final phrases were hushed and apostolic. The CTI team's mission would establish international research benchmarks. The view from here was promising, suggested the CEO, combining prophecy with a lingering appraisal of the workshop facilitator, whose body was knotted at the hips into an intriguing cross-folding of legs. William emitted a barking laugh disguised as a cough. The team would leave with the godspeed of all those for whom viewing went beyond crass consumption of the spectacular and into a realm of spirit.

That took 'spectacular' up to eight, in the same category as 'sublime', counted Antsy. The minority term 'spirit' had made its only appearance. Across the room, Antsy's team-mate Gloria raised eyelids weighted with the previous evening's wine. Her expression, as she looked at the museum's director above her incongruously gaudy throat ornament, was professionally noncommittal. Perhaps it was weary. When she looked across at Ants, she seemed to smile, though her lips did not move. A complicit softening of her expression warmed the space of chilly light between them. When Gloria winked, Ants experienced a moment of velvety darkness, as though the cheerfully illuminated workshop room had been extinguished for a split second during which a parallel universe of black nothing and unlit nowhere had opened up and she had been there, in the dark, at the same time as here in the fresh light of hope and godspeed.

two

Purity

Thin gauzy veils of pure khati white water hang before the huge black fortresses of rock, sundor! So spectacular-beautiful, Grade 1 Attraction (G1A)! Biswas recoils from a thought of the Kaaba. And then (Allah!) recoils even further, flinches back from an image of the great haj crowd of pilgrims swirling around the holy mount. Confused in his mind now about this beauty and the lines of campervans and rental cars crawling in a procession down the mountainside, like a haj, and these Orientals with the car doors open on the side of the road and their mouths opening and closing in excited talk beneath video cameras, very expensive ones, maybe why not pick one up cheap on the way home in Kuala Lumpur, Keshamoni love it? Or plasma-screen TV?

And now the Cow woman's hot thigh in the pant with zips to make it longer or shorter, what would the short look like? Maybe lassi or rice pudding, maybe one day he will find out, would he like to? Now the zipped-up cow yoghurt mishti doy thigh is pressing against Biswas in the back seat of the mini-bus as it goes down the mountainside, feeling sick, what does she want? 'Okay Biz? Having a ball?' This is her joke, no? 'Name is respect for Baul poets.' 'Oh, whoops, sorry.' Still laughing, so why bother? She cares for the under zip warm pudding kheer and mod on her breath after drinking in the bars.

'Awesome, isn't it, Biz?' Patricia is her real name. Biswas does not understand the joke in Cowpat but retains Cow. Does he want to think of Krishna's milkmaids?

'It is indeed very beautiful, yes, Pat, wonderful asset.'

'Nothing like it in Bangladesh, Biz, right? Water's all flat. Ours goes vertical. Typical, really. Pack of skites.'

'Skites?'

'Boasting. Big-noting. Mountains with bloody great egos. Sell themselves. "Absolutely Pure".' A vindictive tone enters Cowpat's voice – her sturdy thigh tenses. 'How easy is *that*?'

'Absolutely Pure,' repeats Biswas uneasily. 'Masterpiece of engineering, obhiman!' Yes, indeed. GIA. But the cataracts and sky-high walls of wet black rock fill him with fear, why? Skites? Blasphemy? Foolishness? Heads with video cameras coming out of windows?

'We are a watery people. We have a great love of water. The village pond. And many of us living on boats. We have much respect for the water. Policy Plank (PP) for Bangladesh Rural Advancement Committee (BRAC). You like I show you.' He would like to show Cow people with raised, prayer hands in the shining river at full moon, in chait. But then, he would also not like to show her this.

'But the floods? Shocking I hear. Dreadful. Thousands?'

'Very bad sometimes.' The vista skids across his eyes. Biswas is grinning with nausea and his thigh begins to jig next to Cow's – he switches the comforting vibration to the other side. 'But what we know, this you can't control, natural forces, isn't it?' He tries a word: 'Prakriti.' He waves at cataracts falling down sheer precipices.

'But. Thousands? Acts of God, I suppose. You'd say.'

In his bowel a pain turns slowly, like a hand. It is connected to the heat against his thigh, which he moves away. The pain remains. How can Biswas explain to Cow that floods are the everlasting wealth of shonar Bangla? The flood that took his mother, father, wife and unborn child? That almost took Keshamoni, whose muddy hair he feels tangled around his left hand? Flood noise under the rain roaring on the polythene roof? Ma, baba, gone quick – not a sound. A splinter of bamboo driven through the palm of his right hand.

Didn't see Parveen go. Roof with polythene collapsing when Keshamoni's brown, muddy head rose from the water next to his left hand. Wrenching a turn of the slimy hair around his wrist while the bamboo dagger drove through his right hand. He should wash. He should pray. His cellphone has rung reminding him to pray. Maybe he is carsick – the minibus swoops around a hairpin corner cut into the slippery mountain. The empty abyss flies past the cold window glass. Icy air of hell rushing up from the pit.

And then.

And then, he is thinking, inside the dazzle of his smile and the frantic jig of his thigh, you also can't control, but I am not telling you, why a woman in Satkhira Ashashuni upazila is walking five kilometres for drinking water and another from my Pankhali village carrying her child because her others drowned in the salty shrimp gher? When she went out to get unsalty water? This I am not telling you. This is not GIA.

Biswas pictures his barii mukhi homesick carsick pain as a lonely hand searching for another one to hold. It is holding hands with his path-swept Pankhali home village and also with thick, brown Dhaka city petrol-air. Haj family name – holding on to that. Holding Mecca. Holding the bamboo flood platform. Holding Keshamoni's long hair. Holding Kuala Lumpur-Dhaka International Bangladeshi check-in and 100 plasma-screen TVs on baggage trolleys. He is laughing because he is sad. He is angry because he is laughing. He is laughing because it is easier than explaining to Cow.

'Wouldn't have thought it was all that funny, Biz?' He covers his mouth, his Banglawood smile, his snigger ('So sorry, Pat'), and quells his dancing thigh. 'Or am I missing something, Biz?'

Yes, missing. He directs his waning grin forward at a vista of forest as the mini-bus enters a valley whose trees are called beaches, why? He is also not telling her how the imams cry out to each other through crackly loudspeakers all across the city in the dark before dawn. Then the black crows caw-cawing and the dogs yelping along the alleys. While the beautiful light, thick like butter dhal with dust and petrol, not thin like this cold light – how morning light comes pouring down all over the house roof-top after his washing and prayer. And not telling Cow about the park near posh Gulshan with the lake and rich young men and women holding hands with flowers but not really quite touching, how lovely. About washing his lunghi at the pond-ghat in Pankhali.

Biswas swallows back not sickness but a sadness that is also angry. The sweet young bouquet lovers by pea-green Gulshan Lake water with palms and dusty mango trees and blazing marigolds with the smell of water in their dry dirt make him angry-sad. And the unwholesome chill of the mini-bus window.

Therefore he hopes that the unsmiling look he turns towards Cow (she does not move her thigh) is his 'look' Keshamoni calls it, squealing and running away.

'Perhaps you are coming to my room,' he suggests, 'tonight. We can get better acquainted. Check out my Project Concept Proposal (PCP).'

'Well, well. Biz! Thought you'd never ask. My pleasure.'

The mini-bus parks among campervans and the group follows a conga-line of tourists to 'the Chasm'. From a viewing platform above the thickly sluicing Cleddau torrent, Biswas gazes with disgust at a smooth, foam-rimmed orifice through which a pistoning muscle of pure water thrusts itself without pause, watched by many videos. He watches the sturdy, alternating march and shift of Cow's buttocks ahead of him in zipper pants through which he can see her underwear. She also has her little video camera and is always taking, taking, taking.

It is wet and cold under the dripping beaches. Always, sound of water. Biswas holds thoughts of the Pankhali salt gher woman in his sad-angry heart.

The water is still pouring away in his mind in the mini-bus, he is thinking Pankhali woman, also little Keshamoni on the flood platform, her muddy hair around his hand, when there before them is the black mountain thrusting up from its own reflection in the water. It is just like he has seen it how-many times? So-many times in brochures, tour guides, postcards, CTI briefing kit and inflight magazine between Kuala Lumpur and Auckland. Must-see spectacular, never-to-be-forgotten, natural wonder of the world, World Heritage Site (WHS).

This is famous Mitre Peak. How does Mohammed Baul Biswas know? Is a Cultural Tourism Operator (CTO). Is the United Nations Development Programme (UNDP) counterpart scholarship. Is a Parjatan Bangladesh Tourism operative. What doesn't Biswas do? Paedophile road-trips, resale cellphone, porno DVD, running guns to Bandarban. Parjatan Bangladesh Tourism slogan: 'Get here before the tourists do!' Yes, say the business associates of Mohammed Biswas, laughing, and what about conversion to Islam of George Bush Jnr? This is an image the Bangladeshi CTO has been prepared for, like Taj Mahal, Yosemite, Sydney opera-house, Niagara Falls, giraffe-necks against sunsets on Animal Planet TV, white-sand-with-coconut-palm and bikini bosoms. Is a Global Cultural Asset (GCA), a destination, grade-one Value Adding Potential (VAP), see how they do it. Now, 'Get here before the tourists do!' is not funny any more. Now, with water roaring in his ears and lassi-thigh acting no-problem see-you-later, Mitre Peak fills Biswas with horror. There GCA Mitre Peak rises, true, from its reflection in mirror water, but like a black tooth or spike, terrible and poised to strike.

'There she is.' The mini-bus driver, Stan, puts a cigarette in his mouth. 'A beauty, every time. Can't go past her.' Stan lights up and encourages his first exhale to re-enter the vehicle. 'Pub's over the road. Half an hour. Time for a quick one.'

Biswas wants to wash but not in this impious water, he wants to pray but not in the presence of the black tooth. He imagines a black Dhaka crow flying across dusty-thick, not-too-hot basanto sunset with prey in its claws, rat or kitten. Then he makes his Elusive Bird fly across the view of Mitre Peak. It flies through Stan's cigarette smoke where he stands at the foreshore admiring her for the umpteenth time.

'Quite a beauty isn't she, Mr Biswas? Reckon they think so.'

'Who think so, Stan?' The others have gone to the pub over the road. Biswas tries to decipher the tented humps at the edge of the car park. Why nobody is selling anything down here? At home, boys selling cellphones out of sportsbags, paper cones of peanuts, raw cucumber and carrot slices, thermos chai, Bic lighters, garlands of marigolds on Saraswati puja and bunches of roses or rose-heads pinned in heart shapes on Valentine's Day. Here, only what-are-they-doing?

The humps are two khaki people, a video tripod. Cloud drifts across the pointy summit of Mitre Peak blushed with end-of-day pink. Then the rosy cloud drifts on and the black fang is revealed, only one of its kind, worth waiting all afternoon for.

'Awesome, I'd say, wouldn't you, Babs?'

'Just awesome, Frank.'

'Ke-argh, Babs!'

'Ke-argh, Frank.'

Biswas watches the khaki American videoists wade through footage from National Geographic Channel. 'Ke-argh, Stan?'

'She's a native bird, Mr Biswas, cheeky sods, probably see some in the morning.'

Cheeky sods? Biswas watches the elderly videoists pack their equipment in the Kea campervan. Okay, very good Brand Value (BV) native bird camper! The Elusive Bird might be laughing 'Okay Biz!' as the American Kea leaves the car park through the Way In.

Stan also is laughing scornfully with gusting coughs past a fresh cigarette. From the pub comes thudding music and shrieking voices when the door opens. Biswas scouts along the darkening shore towards the lights of the tour-boat terminal. What is my Primary Objective (PO), my Key Performance Indicator (KPI), Biswas mocks himself? What, indeed, at last, come to nitty-gritty, am I doing, ponders Biswas? He retreats to shadows where he can wait without being seen to be waiting.

Same everywhere, thinks Biswas, backing into a slithery flax-bush and jumping out again. Tourist Pilgrim Uniform, like the Cow's zipping pants – TPU! Made-in-Bangladesh TPU! Kea campervans, rental cars, Globus, Real Adventure coaches, Chasm viewing platform, Christchurch International Airport. Tourist pilgrim haj uniform made in Bangladesh! Get there before the tourists do! Before George Bush Jnr becomes a Bangla Bai mullah!

But not nani and appa in morning Reeboks showing under saris while morning walking just-a-little-bit-faster around Gulshan Lake, adjusting hair-cling of saris while fresh Reeboks working little-bit-hard below. He imagines them in pants like Cow's, short-zipped, or running!

He does not want Stan to hear him laughing by himself in the slithery shadows of the car park. Mod-shouting bursts from the bar behind shiny, unpleasant bushes. Biswas moves towards the ferry terminal.

Na, what are we doing to clean the path? Amader moto manush hoyo na, manusher moto manush hoyo, God bless our trade and God bless our golden shonar Bangla! There is money to be made! Manufacture TPU, what comes back? India has Raj history, Thailand has sex, Europe has the Eiffel Tower, England has the Queen, USA has Disneyland, New Zealand has Absolutely Pure. What is Bangladesh's niche?

Hartal bombings, laughs Biswas, sounding like his cawing crow. The dark tour boats are grinding against their jetties. No one is sleeping in the coach park windbreaks.

PBCP-Red Flag cadre shootouts, Rapid Action Battalion (RAB) crossfire? Prawn gher not-to-drinking-water from Satkhira Ashashuni? Malaria, rabies, cholera? Diarrhoea? Biswas has read about these in the International Travel Alerts (TAs). Bangladesh Experience? This is a Destination? Floods, snakebites, kidnappings, these are Attractions? Tourist haj zipping up and come to see?

Angry crow pecking at his thoughts. Dacoit-miscreant child sex, Kidney Ravi's organ trade, pharmaceuticals, brothel-islands down by Barisal?

Booming music from the bar across the road. The pink light has gone and the black Fang is metal against metal, a fearful thing.

Slum tours.

Where, croaks the obdurate Biswas crow, is the International Travel Alert for this Fang? It is like this, kaka-uncle, caws the gouging crow. Clean the path. Attend: this pure water that makes you feel sick, kaka, this Absolutely Pure that makes you angry when Cow says, 'Beauty, beautiful, beaut,' when she says, 'Having a ball,' this Beauty that frightens you – these are signs for you to clean the path to your Point of Difference (PoD), isn't it?

'Point-of-Difference,' Biswas enunciates elaborately, mocking the words with the prim articulation of his lips, teeth and moustache. The last syllable of the phrase makes him grin or snarl at the world-famous black mountain. He is a glint of teeth against the landscaped plantings of hardy wetland bushes, at the edge of the street lights, by the deserted terminal.

three

Home

The bar's interior is loud with the exhilarated roar of Happy Hour kayakers. But at the table where the wee Aussie and the voluptuous Maori have been paired, two silences have fallen in quick succession. The first followed Nancy's answer to a question about Krishna's milkmaids. No one else in the team knew what Mr Biswas was talking about at the workshop. He seemed to be relating tourism to Lord Krishna's fondness for fun-loving milkmaids – a suggestion William looked forward to seeing 'fleshed out' in a business-plan to turn flagship scenic hotels into brothels. But Nancy has another explanation: it is all about the erotics of nature refined through art. With the exception of Hinemoana, the CTI team members drift to other topics and move away.

Hinemoana suspects there's more droll humour in the little Aussie than she's getting credit for. But the second silence follows Hinemoana's question about where Ants comes from. Nancy, Antsy or just plain Ants has a way of driving silence ahead of her babbly replies to questions she thinks are too easy to be left to idle conversation. Ants moves jerkily through the social exchanges of her conversation. This is because, for Antsy, easy questions are usually the hard ones that have hidden layers – conversational flip-flops that a keen professional mind can really get down to business on and do some work.

'So – Antsy – where do you come from? Where's home?'
Silence – the little beak beginning to quiver. Oh shit, thinks Gloria. Call me Gloria. Relax, girlfriend. Antsy's

getting-started silences are way too deep for most people. This one's way too deep for Gloria, who takes her glass to the bar. Returning with her nose in an expensive New Zealand pinot noir, Gloria finds Ants's reply ready.

'No, actually, I think it's a really simple question, Ants,' says Gloria, affably, brooking no nonsense, withdrawing her relishing nostrils from the glass and taking a mouth-filling swig of sensational wine. Over Antsy's hunched shoulders, past the pale blue, blinking, acetylene gaze of the clever, fidgety Aussie, she can see that the blackboard list of decent available bar-treats is dwindling. The hunk in the rugby league shirt with the sleeves ripped off-of chewable biceps, the one who got cheeky with her over putting the expensive wine on the project tab ('Must be a choice manaakitanga, eh, sis?') is standing on a chair wiping away the new season whitebait fritters, manuka-cured high-country salmon and mountain-thyme cervena. Good grief, it's only just dark! Who else is here? Who's eating? Who else can afford that? Whose lunch went to 6 p.m.? Which Department's down here as well? Who's getting stroked?

The stud catches her looking and does an excellent bun-flex before stepping down from the chair.

'No, but I mean, "Where do I *come* from?" isn't answered by me saying "Australia", or, kind of closing in, "Sydney", or, you know, "Cultural Studies at UNSW". Not given the job we have to do. The stretch you and I have as a team, Gloria.'

'Talk to me about stretch, girl,' suggests Gloria, watching the bar stud return to his station.

'I see this as a unique challenge. I'm excited!' Ants dips to her wine like a hummingbird. 'It's not really about nation, or profession, those kinds of legitimations? Remember all that bullshit we got told back at the beginning? The Minister, those guys? They beg our kinds of questions. I see you seeing that, Gloria. We can unpack this.'

'I can unpack that,' groans Gloria.

'Because, of course,' Ants rushes on, 'any one of those dumb question-beggers is itself a set of under-read conditions. Like, my "Australia" as a white, Jewish immigrant, professional intellectual whose only insecurity is the loss of peer esteem on an international conference circuit.' Ants giggles and pauses to sip.

Gloria looks at the little Aussie with growing affection. The kid's a wreck but she's a wee battler. 'You hungry?' asks Gloria. Antsy's tiny beak dips back to her wine – perhaps she's disappointed. 'Sorry, kid,' says Gloria. 'This girl's got to eat before she can think. Krishna's milkmaids, white Australian guilt, big stuff needs fuel.'

What's left? The range of 'gourmet burgers', forget about it. Mussels in coconut milk and kaffir lime? Of course – has to be there: the plate of breads and 'dips'. Not on your life. Dips, dips, dips – a girl's life could be ruled. That and the lately fashionable mini-wonton with fishy dipping sauce. Ministry catering. Only good thing – put your sticky fingers on the sleeve of the Kaiwhakahaere Matua's Armani, see his eyes go very slowly to the place.

'So, your case is different from what?' Gloria has her repertoire of blunt strategies. To the studly barman who looks more Fijian than Ngai Tahu, she semaphores French fries with mayonnaise, better be Belgian mayonnaise, too, bro' – her fingers measuring fries, her luxuriously pouting, lipsticked mouth accepting their oily saltiness. Gloria's chin-tilt answers his put-it-on-the-tab? See how easy it can be? Home's where you can talk to people without saying a word.

Ants is still stuck in her silence. 'Let me guess,' persists Gloria. 'You want to say, "Different from Aboriginal people", probably, something like that. Or different from wogs, or different from some fresh-off-the-boat or other, Vietnamese or whatever. You're all the bloody same, you white Aussies – can't come straight out with it. Jeez, Ants – you're an Aussie chick, not an Abbo, you live in Potts Point or somewhere else cool, and you teach, what was it?' Gloria lets Ants's silence take its time.

'Diaspora studies . . .'

'Don't tell me – it's complicated, too.' Gloria grabs big Cowpat as she goes by with sloshing beer glasses. 'Come here, Cowpat. We need help with this one. Home. Where is it. What is it. You usually have the answers.'

'Ask William,' says Cowpat maliciously, keeping her course steady. 'I think it's got something to do with the place they post power bills to. But he probably knows better. He usually does.'

Ants sips her fine wine with tremblingly extruded lips. Gloria gives her hand a pat. The bowl of French fries arrives.

'Help us out here, bro',' she says to the stud. 'The little Aussie and me are having a conversation about home. Should be simple, right? Let me guess: you're a coconut, right? One of those frangipani fellas?'

'Nah, mate. Ngapuhi – down here to spy on these rich Ngai Tahu. See how they take money off flash Maori like you? How about another wine?'

Gloria regards the man with merry appreciation. 'See, Ants, this fella's got it down. He's from Rawene or somewhere like that. Some no-hoper deadshit place. They're trying to figure out how to make sweet oranges into P.'

The barman chortles. 'Let me guess – Ngati Stinkbomb. Everybody else got the microwave, but your lot are still cooking spuds in hot mud, I'll bet. Ngati Tourbus.' He takes Gloria's empty glass and departs.

'Wrong, as it goes,' says Gloria, watching him slide through the crowd. 'We're probably cousins. Why doesn't that surprise me?'

'Order some more, why don't we?' says William, reaching over. 'Then we can eat all of these. Excellent idea, Hinemoana.'

Gloria smacks his thin fingers aside. 'Only if you answer

a question. And keep it to Hine. You sound like our HR manager.'

'I will call you that, because the fully rounded name suits you,' says William, who is drunk on boutique micro-brewed pilsner. 'And God knows you need one. An HR manager, not a fully rounded name. Or another glass of, Christ, don't tell me.'

'You ask him, Antsy,' says Gloria. 'I just want to wring his scrawny turkey neck when he gets pissed and smart-aleck. Every night, actually.'

'Go on, ask me a difficult, searching, intellectual question. Ask many,' says William, around a mouthful of fries. Mayonnaise runs down the scowl-line at the corner of his mouth.

'So, this is where the interesting conversation moves to,' says Joris, also arriving. 'And these look, kind of, like Belgian potato fries: why those Walloons get so fat. Why they have to come here to walk in the mountains, make me rich.'

William is staring at Ants. 'Nancy, isn't it. From Australia. The fortunate country.'

'What Gloria and I were talking about,' says Antsy, 'but not really getting to the bottom of, you know, because it's one of the tough ones . . .'

'Let me guess,' says William. 'You were discussing the issue of indigeneity. Does it mean anything outside of strategic planning documents written by consultants whose cousins are service-providers of indigenous content or venture capitalists wishing to attract government quid-pro-quo, the mission statements of corporates wishing to despoil natural resources owned by native peoples, the statement of intent objectives of the state sector, or the whingeing argot of the United Nations? Answer number one: only if you're not. Answer number two: no, anyway.' William emits a yelping, hyena-like laugh.

'We could possibly go there,' says Antsy, after a silence in which William downs his beer in successive, nervous tilts of the glass – his Adam's apple, white and stippled with an imperfect shave, like the parson's nose of a plucked chicken, seems to act as a syringe, plunging down at the loaded swallows of zingy, hoppy fluid.

'No we couldn't,' says Gloria. 'This is one of his favourite party tricks. Make him save it until we're all sick of each other. Then we can all kill him. It can be an indigenous ritual.'

Hectic spots of colour have appeared on Antsy's cheeks. She has enjoyed William's performance. Now she seems to be taunting him. 'But it's a part of it, wouldn't you say, Bill?'

'William,' says William.

'The question was, Bill, where do you come from? Where are you when you're at home? What kind of condition is that, really? Because it's complex, isn't it, Bill? It's not a simple issue, Bill. I guess we'll all be tackling it, on the road, during the next couple of weeks. The vectors, the tensions, the semiotic. The routes and roots. That's with an "ou" and an "oo".' Antsy's mocking lips make wee tubes which she extends towards William, as though offering to kiss him.

'Oh well,' says Gloria. 'I tried.'

'Home,' says William, ominously. 'Where am I when I'm there?'

'For me,' says Cowpat, elbowing in, 'it's the three "f's". Home is.'

'Friends, family . . .' begins Joris, with an optimistic lilt.

'Furniture?' suggests William.

'Fed, fucked and financial,' concludes Pat. 'Does me.'

'You revolt me, Patricia,' says William. 'A member of senior management. Someone under the harsh spotlight of accountability. Someone we all look up to. Or rather, someone we all look down from. An eminence. A viewing platform, no less, to slip into the mission jargon. Someone who shows us where to look, what to see, and how to explain it to people. 'Fed, fucked and financial.' And here are the crème de la crème of the region's strategic thinkers and one of our finest goes down at the gross fleshly hurdle of base animal gratification. Well, thank God is all I can say. For a moment, there, Patricia, I thought you were going to transcend form. Remember the team-building? I was a flame-person. I drew a picture. Now I've got Joris, a water-bearer. It's Hinemoana and Nancy, it's Patricia and our esteemed Asian subcontinental Mr Mohammed Baul Biswas. Miss him terribly. Wonder if he knows what he's in for. This is "home", friends. Off we go, two-by-two. The National Identity ark, and the fourth "p". Guess.'

'Piss off, Dick,' says Cowpat. 'You are a. And it was "f", not "p".'

'Policy,' enunciates William carefully. He tips his glass but it is empty. 'The place you don't have to be in to have arrived. Where we all are. Not one foot on the ground, the lot of us. Policy-people. At home in it. Aspirationalists. Flame-people, bridge-builders, water-bearers, I don't know, fucking what was it? Fellow-travellers I don't remember. Somebody toss me the squeezy rubber ball. Magic markers. Let's make a nice picture. Let's all rub each other's necks. It's okay to cry. Home is where it's okay to cry.'

At last, Nancy surprises the fidgeting group by laughing – an extended, nocturnal hooting, high-pitched, almost eerie. For a moment, the racket in the bar seems to dip in volume, as though her laughter's exotic pitch penetrates the impervious self-absorption of the happy hour.

four

Identity

'So – are we good, Bill?' Boris whacks Bill on the shoulder.

'Never better, and it's William.' William is hung-over and haunted by a memory of the twitching Nancy's mocking laughter the night before. William's timid nickname represents a group capitulation to the improbability of bar-room intimacy in his case. He probably made a fool of himself. The group also fell silent and moved on those several days ago at the meet-and-greet organised by the Department of Tourism (DoT) at the national museum. There was a grand, sun-setting view of the empty harbour, all form and bugger-all content as usual, and an equivalent air of groomed insincerity emanating from the museum's senior management assembled to greet the team on the site of the country's newest tourist magnet. William experienced the team's loss of nicknaming nerve and rapid departure from his viewing platform before the vapid vista and the equally vapid official conversation, with mixed satisfaction and melancholy, and downed his expensive New Zealand wine with a hacking laugh.

And why the fuck do these krauts, all right these fucking tulip-munchers, have to keep trying to say things like 'Are we good?', 'Cool, man?', 'Sweet?' and 'Kia ora?' as though they are practising a lesson in the correct pronunciation of vernacular expressions? 'Are we good!'

'Good to go?'

'Good to go, *Joris*.' William refuses to use the nicknames. He utters Joris's real name emphatically, looking his *buddy* straight in the eyes, challenging him to get kind of pally any time soon. Joris, whom the group has dubbed Boris – Joris Boris looks back lightly smiling and unafraid but not bland. It is in the entrepreneur's eyes, that quiet glint of crystalline, glacial substance. What age could he be, wonders William, not for the first time, trying to nurture his irritation. That smooth, light tan, those incurious, unblinking eyes, that flopping fall of light brown hair, those *teeth*, not to mention the air of lithe health despite cigarettes and frequent coffee: late thirties? Early forties? Does that give him time to get this fucking rich?

The age question has begun to torment William not just because he feels dishevelled, teeth and hair awry, with Joris around; but the frugality of Joris's identity makes him distraught. His cellphone has its own unobtrusive pocket and his dark glasses come to rest above his smooth, golden-tanned forehead. How he crosses his ankles and stretches out his long legs. The way he does not gulp his beer and lets the glass rest untouched on the table, while William begins to melt down internally, willing him to pick the fucking thing up and drink it. The way his cigarette smoking is unhurried and unfurtive, how the smoking does not make him stink, or if it does, makes him smell aromatic not stale. How his frank gaze doesn't pass judgement. His chattiness with all and sundry, and not least his spectacular success as company director of 'Good-2-Go Tours' (of course, 'We Add Venture to your Experience') in New Zealand, North America and Asia. Not to mention his polite rebuffs to the sexual hints of the desirable young women and men to whose outdoor experience he has promised to add venture. All of this, even especially the hair whose looseness falling across one eye adapts equally well to a good elemental drenching as to being windblown (and there are, in fact, a few salt-and-peppery flecks of grey in it at the temples) – all of this fills the *Bill* that chokes on his own timidly liberating nickname with vile and, after only a few days on the mini-bus, besotted envy.

This envy has much to do with the completely consistent

tranche of identity markers and brand values with which *Boris* conveys his confident sense of himself. That said, the man's physical grace fills William with gnawing resentment of the historical roll of the fucking dice that has added so much venture to Joris's already privileged experience.

And, that said, *Bill*, that is the William who would like venture to be added to his own experience, thinks more and more often about the loosely elegant, substantial heft of the Netherlander's dick inside the light cladding of his adventure sportswear.

'Oh look, it's Old Bonky,' says Joris, with the uplifting inflection of a man needing to get lightness into the silence that followed his first attempt to start a conversation.

And yes, it is 'Old Bonky' the kea, a core attraction in the lodge's car park. Old Bonky features in marketing material where he appears both as a native bird and as the Department of Conservation's avatar.

In his role as DoC spokesbird, the speech balloon twisting from Old Bonky's sardonic beak says, 'Please don't feed me,' and at his feet lie sandwiches, apples, hot-dogs and lollies in twisted-up paper, with red crosses slashed across them. Behind Old Bonky appears a snow-capped mountain range of immense, purely glittering icy peaks against a sky of aquamarine blue whose effect is to make you think of water fit to breathe, water so pure you could drown in it and still live, indeed enhance your rinsed health – you could freeze to death and emerge better, crisper and fresher than in your inferior brand-name life.

Yes, gloats William, snapping the wristband of his Rolex, an Absolutely Pure mountain range. One of mine. And you still want to beat me up about misanthropy, eugenic grossness, Eurocentrism and monoculturalism? Why, ripostes William, as if talking to a sceptical *Bill*, the Prime Minister herself, whose identity vigilance, her own and the nation's, is legendary, has appeared before a gigantic banner of the mountain range and Absolutely Pure slogan before taking off to the World Sustainability Summit in Johannesburg! You want cultural diversity, go to Sylhet and get shot by a rabid mullah with a home-made pipe-gun! Go visit Mohammed Baul Biswas!

The other things the brochures show Old Bonky doing involve low-level vandalism. There are humorous cartoon images of Bonky ripping the rubber sealant from around car windscreens, tearing off windscreen wipers, flaying daypacks and gutting tents. 'Don't tempt me!' admonishes Bonky in the pamphlets and campervan park signs.

Old Bonky is stalking the lodge car park, which is filled with a ranked fleet of Kea campervans. Perhaps he means to do mischief – William hopes so. But no – he has a clump of river-bleached tree-root tendrils which he is dragging, squawking and strutting, among the tourist facilities. Bonky plunges his scissoring beak among the shredding filaments. His behaviour is at once savage and beseeching.

'Oh, look,' says Joris, lightly. 'He's fucking it.'

So it seems – Old Bonky's nickname becomes clear at this point. So does the audience for which the crafty kea is fashioning his performance. Between the parked campervans branded with Bonky advances the darkly shining snout of the elderly Americans' video camera. Bonky ducks and weaves among the vehicles, dragging his fetish.

'Not there, Frank. Over there! See him?'

'Okay, I got him, Babs, I got him good.'

But Bonky, with a supercilious, rocking, sideways strut, disappears down the aisles of his fleet. This time, he leaves his dishevelled toy in the clear space ahead of the vans. His bright-eyed head appears between vehicles. He shrieks and curses, he flaps ostentatiously to the roof of a van and jumps from sight again, he struts into view and withdraws, he sprints with outstretched under-crimsoned wings across the space where his sex toy lies abandoned – but he does not offer himself to the video camera.

The Americans' patience, thinks William, is admirable but

will go unrewarded. This bird knows what he is doing.

'Smart bird,' says Joris. 'Bet you ten bucks he gets what he wants, Bill.'

'And that would be, Joris?'

'Is an outlaw. He makes them break the law. You watch. This I've seen before.'

The car park is peaceful for a time. Dazed honeymooners emerge from their mobile homes. From the lodge office comes the murmuring sound of a cricket commentary. That would be pleasant, grieves William – to be alone, at peace, on a folding chair, distinctly himself among the anonymous crowd, at the Basin Reserve, watching the delicate thuggery and stylishly reserved ostentation of a cricket test match. Some unpleasant children are squabbling about packets of chicken- or BBQ-flavoured potato chips. One of them snatches the BBQ-flavoured ones and runs shrieking towards the river. The other jams handfuls of the chicken variety in its mouth, truculently daring William to react. Of course, the river – there is also, as always, the sound of it, here, sluicing over its bed of smoothed rocks.

'See? What I tell you, Bill?'

'What is it now, Joris?'

Boris Joris points a languid finger at the elderly Americans. The woman, Babs, is walking with lowered head towards the lodge verandah. Old Bonky has noticed: he now poses serenely at the edge of the amphitheatre where his ragged lure lies in the epicentre of the video's viewfinder.

Babs returns with unobtrusive steps to the scene.

'Watch, Bill,' urges Joris confidently. 'This is good.'

'What's good about it, Joris?'

'Why you don't call me Boris like everybody else, Bill? I like it. Is friendly.'

'Because you're not a fucking Russian, Joris,' says William with venom that Joris Boris does not notice. He gently seizes William by the forearm. An electric shock shoots up into William's head.

Babs nonchalantly places a substantial club sandwich – a four-decker with ham, cheese and assorted salads – on the asphalt next to Old Bonky's sex object.

'Tsk, tsk,' says Joris, just loud enough for the Americans to hear. But the elderly videoists are focused on their task. Boris's slender, brown fingers grip William's arm. Yes indeed, agrees William, feeling chilled gooseflesh rise startlingly all over his body and the coolness of sweat beading his upper lip, here comes Old Bonky now, with a swagger in his gait, straight to the sandwich next to his ramshackle lure.

The Americans' video camera emits a soft, erotic whirr and Old Bonky lifts the bulky sandwich to his beak in one accomplished set of claws. He makes no sound – the taunting bird is gone. His depravity is compliant. Where before he strutted, ravishing his bait, now he deals with little fuss to the fruits of his performance. As he scissors off a slice and ruminates it in his discriminating beak, deftly shedding translucent morsels of gristle with his black tongue, the Americans emit muffled cries of triumph. Soon, the sandwich is gone and the kea also, dragging his river-bleached tangle of roots.

'May we see?' asks Joris politely, bringing the shuddering William with him with his lightly gripping hand. They gaze together at the video camera's LCD screen, at the enterprising parrot relishing his four-tier luxury club sandwich before a neat vista of Kea campervans with, at the base of a blue rubbish bin, the yellow wrapper of Chick'n Lick'n Potato Chips.

'We got him, Babs.'

'Got him good, Frank.'

'A very handsome fellow,' agrees Joris, drolly. 'Nice view.'

But William is speechless. An unexpected grief has welled up in his emphysemic chest. A loneliness, or something like a shame, has infected the icy triumph of his Absolutely Pure campaign whose uncompromising rigour has been his greatest pride. He longs, with a sensation at the corners of his eyes like tears springing, for the kea to be flying free across that brilliant vista which is his inheritance. He would like to repatriate Old Bonky from the shabby, mendacious space of the car park – to make his stalwart wing-flap and reckless, laughing cry fill the cold space with exultation, where now instead he drags his forlorn equipment past the sluggish brand-travesties of himself. He would like to kiss Boris on the mouth.

Heavy-hearted, William sees big Patricia slowly walking the length of the lodge verandah. He thinks he might like to go and talk to her. Her blunt pragmatism, her few words, her odd, catapulted clots of conversation, her intelligence, her dislike of him. This could cheer him up. But she, too, seems a little craven – there is a kind of capitulation in her lowered head.

'Well, that was fun, Bill,' says Boris Joris. 'Now we start survey of environmental impacts of adventure promotions, yes? Adventure and Identity.'

William thinks he might prefer to sleep. To sleep deeply, dreamlessly, almost without breathing, his legs stretched out in fresh Egyptian cotton pyjamas, his fingers resting, cool and unclenched, above the coverlet. His eyelids, while tissue-papery and almost transparent, will gently dim the light he keeps on in the hallway of his flat – his night dashes, panicky and half asleep, disoriented by simple things like the need to piss, are a worry he manages. To be wearing muffling Bilsom ear plugs, the nice blue ones. The thought of working exhausts him. The thought of Joris's hand on his arm, the possibility that he might put it there again and the glimpse of a lightly sculpted penis-rim against the fabric of Boris Joris's monsoon pants, also exhaust William. They fill him with a kind of pleasant dread.

'Adventure and Identity.' William tries to retain his sceptical hauteur but can feel a 'Bill' kind of smile, something new and unusual, prising his almost compliant lips off his teeth. 'It does have a ring to it, Joris.' He tries a 'Bill' joke: 'It's very us, Boris.'

A small dog, restrained by one of the disagreeable children, goes past and seems to be returning 'Bill's' grimace. 'When you're smiling,' lilts a crooner in 'Bill's' mind, 'the whole world smiles with you.'

'Let's get it on, Bill,' says Joris – serenely, impeccably, humourlessly malapropic.

William feels his grudging quotation marks lift away from 'Bill' like little wings. They fly away like liberated birds, into the free air. He feels Bill step clear of William's brand-tormented doubt. Joris cheerfully smacks him across the side of the head and Bill loves it.

five

Lust

A light meal. No more to drink. A hot shower and a damn decent squirt of a girl's no-nonsense CK1. Fresh undies and nice baggy cotton pants from Untouched World ('Fashion, Homeware, Beauty') – great campaign, up there with the Country Road mob. Liked the matching horse and woman's coat with tussock behind. The stainless steel thermos flask and merino wool collar on the man. She brushed her teeth with Sensodyne. There was a slight hint of mosquito coil smoke in the verandah air as she walked firmly along – a bit local, maybe a touch of ti-tree? Distinctly excellent. Sound of river. From the backpacker's kitchen came the also-rivery sound of foreign languages. Pat heard French, German, Japanese, Italian, Portuguese, excellent. And the cynical, ingratiating inflections of the all-male Canadian kayaking squad from Vancouver Island.

'"Wild at Heart"? But, like, what does that *mean*? It's an airport, for Chrissakes.'

'Yeah, and it's got that *Lord of the Rings* . . .'

'That Gollum.'

'Right, right, that Gollum, like, hanging right over the terminal building?'

'So, you think, it's Gollum who's "Wild at Heart"?'

'Who gives a fuck. Nobody's thinking. Hey, here's one: "Southern, Naturally". See that? Somewhere back up the road. What's that, moonshine?'

'"Big River Town". How many of them we seen. Take out the franchise.'

'No, no, *this* one: "Switch On To Huntly". That asshole place?'

'Someone shot at us from the riverbank?'

'That one – the power station. Phew, now that's *smart*, man.'

Fresh, healthy, nasal, Canadian laughter.

Product testing, a bit of anecdotal – nothing's wasted. But Pat's mood had been depressed just a little bit by the cynical Canadians when she knocked on Biz's door. He, too, appeared subdued. Or maybe it was just his good manners. He had some project folders arranged neatly on the Formica table. He was wearing a . . .?

'We're calling it "lunghi", Pat. Is man's dress. Very comfortable-informal. Traditional, na?'

His thin, hairy ankles. His shoes neatly by the door. Pat took hers off.

He made some tea. He told a joke: 'Are you come-for-table? No, I am come-for-tea.' She laughed. He confessed to being little-bit homesick. She listened closely for wife references – none so far. Everything very neat and tidy – cups and saucers, teabags, a pair of black socks and boxer undies drying over the top of the shower-stall – he'd closed the intimate door, shutting out the view of his personal hygiene. He confessed to being confused about their project brief: 'Purity and Beauty'. No one had explained to him that he would be working with a team of tourism experts. Always making jokes, isn't it.

'I'm not sure I'm understanding, Pat. Is difficult for me. Lot of people wanting me to make the difference. Lot of money. Is making me worry. Feeling little bit lost-for-words, isn't it.' Then he clammed up on that front.

She got the feeling that the Biz whose dangerous, snake-eyed look had thrilled her a bit earlier on in their thigh-pressing mini-bus twin-seater had gone away somewhere else. Change of heart, maybe. Same old. Story of her life. He'd neatly combed down his hair – his room had a slightly cinnamony smell. She wanted to sniff his hair – was it there, the cinnamon? A darkly pungent pomade? What made Pat horny was men she didn't know and who didn't know her – she didn't mind admitting that. Men she knew bored her witless. They had the familiar male faults. They were often silly, even the ones she liked. She worked with far too many of them. They were mostly like big kids. She liked new, dodgy faults.

There was something dodgy about the black Biz stare. He had elegant, old-fashioned handwriting. His plain cotton shirt was very neatly pressed – his lithe wrists emerged from crisply buttoned cuffs. His fingernails were trimmed. He had a roam cellphone which called him when it was time to pray. He'd been pouring tea when someone called from Khulna ('Is Khulna calling, isn't it, sorry-pardon-one-moment') then Biz got pissed-off and shouted madly, then he shut himself in his bathroom with the washing. More shouting. He came out with that seriously, majorly installed smile. Fixed in place like a cattle stop. But looking sick and pallid under his dark skin. Good teeth, though, good but completely rigid with the nice moustache. Flash Travel Mate notebook computer, infrared and Bluetooth, webcam too. Packet of sharpened pencils from the Up-Keep team building. A 'water-bearer', from memory, solved the micro-economy team challenge – attends to the basics. Let's hope so. Let's hope he can. He took a drink of tea as though biting the cup.

A cute little carpet.

'Oh, right, prayer mat, I see.'

Don't give up yet. Thin, black, rail-like, hairy shins sticking out of the lunghi when he sat down opposite her on a sensible, stackable kitchen chair. His expression and manner so nice and polite, although . . . Fabulous smile, but . . . Little plate of wine biscuits. Quite sweet. But his hands trembled when he passed them to her.

Pat had been noticing that the Biz smile was definitely of the wind-up got-stuck variety. Something very strange going on behind those black eyes. And then, whoops, another cellphone call, another retreat to the boy's washing room, more yelling and the scary, snake-eyed look came back out with him all at once and he began to rave on. What happened to Mr Nice Guy? Mr Wine Biscuits? Mr 'Are-you-come-for-table'? Wildly pushing the neat folders around on the table. His PCP. His fucking KPI, his, whatever, BRAC? Picking the cellphone up, putting it down. Hitching at the lunghi. Pretty crazy, really. Over here, Biz. Hel-lo?

If here in land of tourist haj we got water so pure you see Travel Advisory?

'Come again, Biz?' Not the faintest what he was on about, but Pat leaned across all at once and sniffed his thick, black, cinnamony hair. No, she didn't, of course – not really. 'Not sure I'm following you, Biz.' And there she was, getting good and wet, with the fucking 'come-for-tea', the wine biscuit and the prayer mat. Jesus wept.

Purusha male making soul together with Prakriti nature-female, isn't it? Man of heart, can't-catch bird. Is my bird, bird may fly out.

'Air has weakened the cage, Pat.' Biswas knocked emphatically, emotionally, at his bony chest. 'Is Murshid, isn't it, is my Guide.' His narrow thigh began to jig within the lunghi.

'That's the name of your company, the Guide? Nice – simple. Got a confidence-building ring to it.' Pat reached out a hand and felt the tensioned leanness of the agitated Bangladeshi's thigh, the springiness of wiry hair under cotton. She didn't really, of course. Christ knows she was hot to. He'd been going on about a bird, quite poetic. No idea what he was saying, though. It didn't sound like a come-on.

How can the Bird sit down? Its pole has collapsed! I am wondering, I am getting-sick! A wild bird cannot be tamed!

'Feeling quite queer, Pat!'

I'll say. But the mad look in his eyes began to glisten with tears, somehow his neatly plastered-down hair was ruffled up – Pat guessed Biswas was really talking about feeling lonely. Poor bugger. She hoped so. She stepped (of course not) across the space between their practical kitchen chairs and lowered herself astride the quivering, rail-like thigh.

How can Unknown Bird go into the cage and out again?

'How to seize it, Pat, cage made with green bamboo, may be falling apart any-day.'

'So your company – the Guide – it does eco-tours? Nature kind of stuff? Trekking, jungle, animals – native birds, Biz?' Pat wondered if her face was flushing, if the curse of hearty mottling was lighting her neck up like a sex beacon. 'Elephants? Bengal tigers?' Slipping out of the Untouched Worlds and fresh undies. She wished. 'Village homestays?' It got harder for a girl to talk past the swelling in her throat. 'You'd be needing a guide, I imagine.' Lifting the lunghi off Biz's dark, fuzzy leg, slotting herself back down on the hard, jigging rail. 'Got any marketing material, Biz? Must be a hard one, what with floods etcetera. That we hear about all the time. And the various sicknesses.' Gripping, if only.

Faith, prayer, fasting, alms – all in shariat, isn't it. This is Guide, keeping us afloat. Also prophet name Noah.

'Everybody know, Pat. Noah's flooding.'

'Interesting, Biz – you have good old Noah as well? "Keeping you afloat", I like that. Come in handy, I reckon. What with the . . .' Try to stop saying the word 'flood', getting the wrong kind of response.

'Got Noah, got Adam, got Jesus, got Mohammed.'

What to do? Mixed milk with cow urine, isn't it – ghee for worship eaten by a pi-dog. Made a mess of life.

'Come on Biz, can't be all bad. Someone you're missing? Got a lovely wife at home, some wee kiddies, a fiancée?' Turning around, working her rump back towards him, feeling the long, slender, cinnamony organ slide in. 'Big family, probably?' Talk about flooding, good grief.

'Only one, Pat, thank you – Keshamoni, my little sister. Fifteen years. Teacher-trainee. Others all gone, isn't it. All drowned.'

No one goes into another's grave – going in alone. From greed coming sin, from sin death. Facing me are enormous waves. Catch wind! Control fire! Water without clouds? Changing clouds into water is act of creation. From dryness pours out sweetness. Water is life of creation – water washes away sin. Aliph, lam, mim – Allah, words, Prophet. Nobody understanding lam-words, too-hard, 90,000 words through Prophet, 30,000 in shariat-law, 60,000 not understanding, isn't it! At night sun shines, during day lamp burning, but still can't see. At side of heaven new flower-blossom on tree of light, my Prophet, Mohammed! Still can't see! What to do, Keshamoni?

'My Keshamoni!' – an animal howl suddenly pulled Biswas's lips back off his teeth. Then huge tears flooded down his nicely shaved cheeks. Snatching handfuls of tissues.

'Oh, Biz, I'm sorry. What's happened?' And then Pat did, really, put her hand out and touch the man's quivering forearm. Ran it down his arm and felt the smooth welt of a scar on the back of his hand.

'Never mind, not-to-worry, Pat, sorry, really sorry, maybe working tomorrow? Bit tired, see?' Head down, Biswas neatly rearranged the folders, pencils, cups and plate of biscuits on his lodge unit's Formica table-top after blowing his nose in an aloe vera-impregnated tissue. 'People telephoning, very bad people, Pat, bad news, bad timing, Pat. And PCP, Pat, having difficulty, isn't it. Got to finish.'

Whatever had got to him, she saw then how ruthlessly he capped it. How he sucked the crazy heat back inside himself and shut himself around it. The soft palm of her hand remembered the obdurate, steely hardness of his thin forearm, the slick gristle of scar tissue.

'Got to finish, isn't it. "Purity Beauty", Allah!' Brand-new scorn. The tearing-up eyes suddenly hot and dry again – that hard look, ferocious, aggressive, scary. 'Is too pure, Pat.'

'I beg your pardon?'

'Is too pure. Is too much "Absolutely Pure". How can this be?'

That sounded like goodnight to Pat.

From outside in the car and campervan park came the sudden scrape of gravel, the decelerating growl of an expensive car and the shrieks of a partying crowd – Pat heard Hinemoana's rich contralto laughter, lubricated with fine food and wine, the slamming of car doors, sounds of staggering on steps, more unabashed laughter.

Pat put her shoes on. The phone rang again – a dial-tone cheerfully imitating the William Tell Overture. Biswas didn't move to answer it – his dry, hot, black look waiting for her to go. Not a word. She went. Couldn't get out of the place fast enough. Talk about feeling a fool.

In the morning, thoroughly bad-tempered, underslept and unfucked, Pat sees William and Joris – Bill and Boris – in the car park. They seem to be having fun, for some reason. Boris impersonates a bird. He flaps around the car park on stork-like legs. There's something completely unconvincing about his laughter – the performance of someone with no sense of humour. Pat's had enough of them, birds and team-members, and she doesn't really want to be noticed. Hardly slept a bloody wink after the lovely social evening with Wild Bird, too pure, Prakriti nature-female bloody having-a-Ball, fuck me sideways! What was all that about? Raving lunatic. 'We-can-get-better-acquainted' not bloody likely. And not a sign of him this morning – nowhere to be seen. Good riddance.

A small, wiry-haired dog goes wheezing urgently by on a leash held by an overweight, sullen child. The dog's snout and jaws are restrained in a black Velcro'd tube. Nonetheless, it manages to maintain a tight, ingratiating, clenched grin, as if apologising for violence it can't commit.

William's laughing, though through clenched teeth. This is unusual in itself. But unlike Joris he has his sense of humour, however bitter and twisted. Pat's sick of William's idea of what's funny, too, but that goes way back. And then Cowpat sees Joris Boris playfully slap William Bill across the side of the head – William looks delighted. He doesn't play-slap Boris back, though.

There are thin cataracts spilling down the precipice on the other side of the river ('Too pure?'), the sound of river water rushing over its smoothed boulder-bed, the melodiously repetitive songs of a pair of tui in the nearby patch of bush between the lodge and the road, the sociable, droning sound of a cricket commentary (must be getting late in the morning), the joshing ring of Boris Joris's optimistic voice.

'Let's get it on, Bill!'

William's expression, at once appalled, thrilled and bashful.

And a memory, vivid despite the fact that nothing at all had happened, not a chance, of the freshly-showered, tensile scratching of the thin Bangladeshi's high-strung, dancing thigh and the lubricious glide of his long, un-lunghied member between her thighs.

It's a memory that's fading all the more quickly because Pat's sent it to the place reserved for its kind, a kind of virus vault in her mind where disappointments are disarmed, where they become jokes first and finally a kind of sediment, something that's settled thickly along the base of her past life, which she doesn't disturb because she leaves it alone and doesn't look back.

Pat walks briskly down the driveway of the lodge, away from people, away from the comfortable drone of the cricket commentary, away from the humourless sound of Boris being a bird, away from a chance encounter with Mr Baul Biswas, to get some video footage of the slender cataracts. From a picturesque bridge a little way up the road, she hauls the little beauties in with her zoom.

six

Authenticity

Dry mouth, blurred vision, tinnitus, nervousness. Endocrine effects like changes in libido – hardly what you would notice in a skinny little progressive neuropathic muscular atrophy victim. Nancy's hangover is from a nightly dose of amitriptyline, brand name Elavil.

Hinemoana's is from pinot noir and Laphroaig.

There is always a system, figures Nancy: get the big categories sorted out first. Then dig down, unpack, interrogate. Look for what is hidden, coded, for what has been overmantled, superseded, subjected to the wilful amnesias of power, history and gender, the 'regimes of truth', the territories. Look for what is fading, going out of the frame, getting invisible, becoming silent, zooming back into the brilliant micro-bit star of data before its eclipse.

This is a familiar morning exercise. Other people do push-ups or go swimming. Nancy pushes her mind up the same hill every morning, she makes it swim in the world. Everything streams complexly through her – she focuses all her effort on perfecting a calm filtering system, a way of soothing the stampedes of significance.

Because of her heavy orthopaedic shoes and the stringy twist in her stiff knee, Nancy is in the aisle seat with her silly legs stuck out and she looks across Gloria's sumptuously somnolent profile at the signage, billboards, iconography and leisure architectures of the tourist vista. They go storming by, mixed in with astonishing landscapes and a barrage of crappy, semi-rural suburbias, too fast to capture in detail. But Nancy's attention is vibrating with the effort – her lips pointing and sipping at the meanings as they fly into the bus past Gloria's motionless silhouette. She pushes Hinemoana's nickname into the traffic. She pushes her own new one in there, too. Get them working. Gloria and Ants. Antsy and Gloria. Gloria is good, she is glorious. The profile is completely gorgeous, at once haughty and smooth, with a swooping, authoritarian nose and voluptuously fleshed lips. Gloria hardly ever takes her dark glasses off. When she does, Ants sees eyes that are big, kind of muddy, sometimes bloodshot. They are glorious, they are Gloria's. Gloria's glorious profile is reflected in the mini-bus window through which Antsy is peering at the flashing-past signs and the reflection in Gloria's dark glasses is re-reflected there too. Antsy's bony head and her large, blue, blinking eyes are reflected in the window next to Gloria against the tearing-past view. Layers, layers, layers. Everything is frantic and immobile at the same time. She is vibrating in one place while this hurricane of signs batters at her thoughts and shakes up the hollow cavities, balancing devices and direction-finding tubes inside her head.

'You're so calm,' says Ants, quivering.

'I'm so hung-over, sister,' drones Gloria. 'Boy, those Iwi Development Corporation fellas can get competitive. Matariki syrah, girlfriend, mutton-bird and then they uncork the Laphroaig. In the conference room, catered. And they'd only just finished their lunch, too. Cleaned out the pub.' Gloria lifts a bottle of pure mountain spring water to her fine lips and sends a killer squirt down her throat. 'Relationships, decisions, progress.' Her hand falls back in her lap, snapping down the bottle's cap. 'Coffee would be so excellent, not much chance out here. But hey. It's all work.'

'Work,' echoes Ants.

Gloria hears the rebuke. 'Listen, girl, I know you were up half the night scribbling away, Miss Team. Manaakitanga. Hospitality. Tell you about it. What tradition's all about, darling. I had to be there.' A perfect beat. 'Loved it.' She drops a limp, warm hand on Antsy's bony knee. 'Stick around, we'll fatten you up, girl.' Well, that's not going to happen. Gloria's comforting hand says she knows it, too. 'Tell me stuff, Ants. I need a little time. Have mercy.'

The 327 bus ride between Bondi Junction and Edgecliff Station is what Nancy always remembers and always tries not to remember. When she thinks about it, usually when she is on some other bus somewhere else and always, now, when she has her 'stork legs' stuck out somehow or other in front of her, she remembers the sticky, exhausting Sydney heat in February and she tries not to remember the way her mum's lovely, dark, crinkly hair got wet behind her ears – how perspiration beaded on top of her foundation make-up. She remembers how her dad's shirt got wet across his knobbly shoulders and she tries not to remember how he worked at giving the impression he was not used to riding on the bus. She remembers the big trees in Woollahra and tries not to remember her mum making disparaging comparisons with 'scruffy' Bondi. She remembers these things because she can't help it and because they are magnets that have attracted many fragments – because her life after the 327 bus ride has gone on being about the ride and the huge swarm of fragments, of meanings and puzzles, that went on getting stuck to it, the first time first and then year after year – 'stork legs', high foot arches, 'slapping' gait. 'Sudden involuntary bursts of laughter or crying.'

They took the bus, not the car, because she was going to have to get used to taking the bus by herself. As if she could not get used to taking the bus by herself by taking it by herself. They took the bus to Woollahra because the Wolper Jewish Hospital was there. Her dad wanted the Wolper Hospital in Woollahra because it was Jewish. What made the hospital 'Jewish'? It was founded in 1948, by Jews – some founders were Survivors, like them, like her mum and dad: just kids then. Was its medicine 'Jewish'? It, they, would understand her, said her dad. Would it, they, understand her 'stork legs', asked Nancy?

Were her 'stork legs' Jewish?

Turned out the disease that gave her 'stork legs' was probably hereditary. Did that make it a 'Jewish' disease? What about her so-called eating disorder? Would that be understood better by 'it, them' – the successors of philanthropic Holocaust Survivors who founded the Wolper Hospital twelve years before she was born?

What about the 'sudden involuntary bursts of laughter or crying'? Were they hereditary, too? When did her mum and dad do them, these 'sudden involuntary bursts of laughter or crying' – or whichever one of them had passed the hereditary laughing and crying on to her? She would like to know, Nancy told them, on the 327, because then she could watch, the way they watched her.

Nancy did not want to remember most of this running argument, not all of which took place on the 327 bus between Bondi and Edgecliff, because it was funny, now, and laughing at her mother and father did not feel disloyal to them now so much as unfaithful to her own pain then.

'It's no laughing matter,' her dad insisted fairly often, using an Australian phrase he had learned, and she had to agree, it had not been, for her. But as for them . . .

'It's so much nicer,' her mum insisted, dabbing the perspiration from her forehead, 'than Bondi.'

'Nicer.' Nancy deliberately flattened the question into a retort.

'It's got more trees. It's got commemorative plantings.'

'For dogs to piss on.'

'As a matter of fact,' her dad said, 'it's got a trial dog off-leash scheme.' He thought of a joke. 'Bondi's got a piss-head off-leash scheme.'

'It's got Garden Awards,' her mum persisted. 'Including a Best Waterwise Garden Award.'

'I suppose that's connected to the pissing dogs?'

'It's no laughing matter,' her dad rebuked her. All the same, they had a bit of a laugh. They wanted to cheer her up. Her mum and dad laughed a little bit more when Nancy wanted to know if having a Small Sculpture Prize worth $13,000 (for dogs to piss on), an Award for Reconciliation (to piss on Eora people) and a Woollahra Philharmonic Orchestra (to piss on the Bondi Pavilion) were going to help the Wolper Jewish Hospital understand her 'stork legs'. They laughed, but they cried, too. That was probably where she got it from, Nancy suggested. The laughing and crying.

'You know what your trouble is?' her mum suggested back. 'You're just too clever. Too clever for your own good.' She stopped laughing and crying at that point. Nancy felt bad and took her hand. Her mum's hand was sullen and humid and lay inertly in Nancy's grasp for a while. Then it gave Nancy's hand a squeeze. But things got worse on the way home.

Were the doctors seriously suggesting that habitual leg crossing and wearing high boots was a cause of peroneal nerve dysfunction, if that's what she had? She wore high boots because they were what girls wore but also because they helped to hide and support her weak legs, which she crossed because you just did but also because it took the weight off her feet. One at a time. Without showing her pants. Or was it because she was anorexic, if she was, or was she thin because she couldn't swallow? Was not swallowing a hereditary, Jewish disease?

'Don't tell me,' ranted Nancy, on the return 327 bus. They liked the idea of Lou Gehrig's disease better than Charcot-Marie-Tooth disease or Landry-Guillain-Barré syndrome, because Lou Gehrig sounded more Jewish? They would rather she had Lou Gehrig because he was family? Also, didn't the nice doctors say that Guillain-Barré could be caused by herpes and AIDS? By swine flu vaccination? Was there a Jewish vaccination against swine flu? Did they give it to her when she was little? Was that what made her condition hereditary? The anti-swine Jewish vaccine?

The bus was crowded at the end of the day but they rode all the way to Bondi Junction with people staring at Nancy and caught the also crowded train home from there. Her mum and dad just let her rave on. They did not interrupt her even when her ranting turned into weeping. They said nothing when her weeping made her stop ranting. She could see her weeping reflection in the train window as it rushed through sunset towards Cronulla, the birthplace of Elle MacPherson, the great new Australian beach babe, and the sight of herself weeping made her weep even more. Elle MacPherson's image was suddenly everywhere in Cronulla, including the Rydges Sydney Cronulla hotel, which was also filled with her lookalikes. Nancy's dad called them the Hells. He was the hotel's marketing and promotions manager and they lived in an apartment with a view of Cronulla Beach and Gunnamatta Bay. He did the Melbourne Cup Lunch on the Beach and the Australia Day Opera on the Beach. The Opera on the Beach was his homage to Salzburg and, secretly, his revenge on the Nazi persecution of the Vienna Philharmonic. He held the weeping Nancy's arm gently as they crossed the hotel foyer to the elevator. Her high boots clattered on the marble floor. Nancy's mum had begun to weep on the train as well, but she stopped in the hotel foyer. Nancy continued to weep. An Elle MacPherson lookalike had been married in the Forby Sutherland Room and a mob of drunk guests pursued her to the hotel steps, where a limousine was waiting with white satin ribbons about a furlong in length. Nancy's dad shut the door of their apartment and took his daughter in his arms. This was when she stopped weeping, after the first visit to Wolper Jewish Hospital way over in Woollahra. The apartment was air-conditioned and she felt the tears shrivel and freeze on her face. Her dad smelled of the sweat that the long bus and train rides had extracted from him and she could feel his heart knocking against her in his bony chest. His breath whistled a bit in his nostrils, which were often too full of dense, untrimmed hair. Under the smell of his sweat, his shirt retained a slight perfume of the hotel laundry, like very hot linen.

'Now you know how to catch the bus,' he said. 'To Woollahra. Where they've got the Philharmonic Orchestra. Next, we show you how to get to Vienna, where they've got a better one. But first, just catch the bus a few times, kid, okay? And not the performance. This was enough. This was impressive, but once is enough. You're going to scare the Hells, otherwise. You're going to, anyway, but different, okay? By being clever, darling. Because you are.'

Wolper Jewish Hospital
8 Trelawney Street
Woollahra NSW 2025
AUSTRALIA

Everybody who had reason to know the address of the Wolper Jewish Hospital also had reasons why 'Trelawney Street' just kept on being significant and spooling out meanings. Probably not everybody studied them. Not everybody knowingly, with stubborn laughter and tears, collected the meanings of the 327 bus ride from Bondi Junction to Edgecliff. For Nancy, the collecting began with her dad's smell of sweat, the damp hair behind her mother's lovely little pale ears, her own 'stork legs' and the 1001 jokes about crossing those legs for Lou Gehrig. About Charcot-Marie-Tooth crossing her legs for Lou Gehrig.

'That was my nickname then – "The Tooth",' puffs Nancy, running out of breath and resting. Past Gloria's sombre profile, she can see her own pallid reflection in the window of the Cultural Tourism Initiative mini-bus. Gloria's reflection is there too, substantial and immobile. A landscape rich with signage is tearing past behind them both.

'Man,' says Gloria, pushing air out of her lips to show she is impressed. 'But now you're "Ants", okay? I can't deal with The Tooth. Too scary.'

These were the collected jokes that defended Nancy against the Hells and that got her to the University of Vienna. They got her to concerts by the Vienna Philharmonic in the Musikverein where she wept thinking about her dad's hotel-laundered shirts and their sad smell of a hundred scorched sheets. They got her to the University of California in Santa Cruz where she did her doctorate in the History of Consciousness programme and where she was when her mum died of heart failure, emphysema and other complications of heavy smoking, but not of hereditary Charcot-Marie-Tooth disease. She sat on a brown, late-summer hill above the campus whose purpose was camouflaged in its groves of redwoods and oaks and wept thinking about the fine bone-china rims of her mum's little ears, the crinkly hair wet behind them on the 327 bus approaching the leafy streets of Woollahra, Trelawney Street lined with fine trees, the Wolper Jewish Hospital camouflaged in its commemorative plantings.

'Now you tell me, Ants,' sighs Gloria. 'That bus – that's home. Isn't it? That old 327? Where's it now, girl?'

'Right here, I guess,' thinks Nancy, surprising herself. This is when Gloria's big head turns slowly to face her – the reflection of a fall of heavy curls is what Nancy's pale little face now intersects, against the rushing vista of the scenic route.

'And your dad?' asks Gloria, face-on.

'Remarried,' says the little mouth at the edge of its crazily speeding tangle of black curls, through which flashes of light, road signs and natural features are streaming. 'A Hell, actually. Quite a spectacular one, with big tits.' Nancy surprises herself again by laughing again. 'The old goat.'

Gloria's silence is full of a question.

'So, no,' finishes Nancy, feeling a bit more like Ants than she had before. 'No sign of Charcot-Marie-Tooth. Skinny as a rake, yes, but the old boy still goes swimming in the surf at Cronulla Beach and he drives new Jaguars in order to revenge himself on Nazi cars.' Antsy's little sniffle is hardly a 'sudden, involuntary burst of crying', but she sits back in her seat and blows her nose. She composes herself by thinking about the team's in-bus jokes about Travel Alerts, which Mr Biswas got them started on. A TA for homesickness? How can she be homesick for the bus when she is on it? Every morning of every day, she makes her mind climb over the barrier that the night-before's dose of Elavil – her nightly 'evil' – has built around thinking. She makes it go up the hill and look around.

It is not as if the less time you have left the less stuff you have to process. It works the other way. The less time you have on the bus and the fewer post-evil mornings you have in which to push your mind up the hill into the world, the more, the thicker, the faster it all gets. There is a destination down the road somewhere that is getting so dense and heavy with content it must, one day, simply stop the flow. Everything will be stopping there. There will be a single meaning and a single word for it. And at the moment you say the word – as your mouth takes a special, cooing shape from it, like a kiss – everything will stop, forever. It will be the end.

'Home,' whispers Antsy. But the bus keeps tearing towards the moment when Stan can have his cigarette break, somewhere with clean public toilets, refreshments, a view of water, trees and mountains, a viewing platform.

Gloria's heavy hand returns to Antsy's knee as if summoned by the word 'home'.

That is why you should not say it until the time is right. 'Fed, fucked and financial,' remembers Antsy and titters. Gloria's hand gives her knee a squeeze and returns, like a hibernating animal headachy with sunlight, to its own lap.

'Tell you what,' murmurs Gloria. 'When this gig's over, I'll take you back to my place. Meet the hard-case cousins. Travel Alert for the family of my koro, Uncle Mat.'

'I'd like that,' whispers Ants. Beyond the bus window

everything is already compacting – the scenic attractions, the natural wonders, the glory, the emptiness, the great distances, the huge sky, the whistling, chilly wind. It is packing down.

'It's okay, Ants, darling, you can talk to me. Just don't mind if I keep very still.'

Okay, here's what her post-evil brain has been looking at. Eighty viewing platforms so far on this stretch, all named something. 'The Lower Hollyford', 'The Divide', 'The Mirror Lakes'. The compliant, anxious, compulsive crowds of viewers. Gazing into the mirrors of the 'mirror lakes', seeing what? The viewing platforms of the tourist leisure vehicles themselves, the mobile platforms, the beetling, economy-model rental cars, the swaying campervans, ranking their viewing windscreens obediently next to the singular signage. Looking at? Looking for? Looking because?

'Remember Moeraki?'

At the Moeraki Boulders, the mobile viewing platforms were in a van park by a restaurant and gift shop whose architecture mimed the iconic boulders. The viewers were photographing each other on the viewing platform, adopting kung-fu or surfing poses against the glittering, sunlit ocean, photographing the lofty platform and the humping, grey, boulder-like restaurant and gift shop.

'Horse-piss coffee,' remembers Gloria.

Far below, the Moeraki Boulders themselves appeared distant and sullen – trivial, next to the rich text of the service-providing facility, the Moeraki Boulder brand.

'Everything packs down into the brand,' thinks Ants. 'It's the new authenticity.'

'Toi iho™,' mumbles Gloria. She removes her dark glasses and bugs her eyes above a luxuriously unfurled tongue.

A field of nibbling, domesticated deer converge on the trail of hay chucked from a trailer. A billboard of a snowy mountain peak rears up among them, whipping Antsy's head around as it flies past. There are actual mountains in the distance, a far cordillera, flashing with snow and ice. The billboard is advertising 'Everest' tents, sleeping-bags, thermal tops and polyprene hats.

'A Himalayan mountain at home in New Zealand,' Ants theorises.

'If you say so.'

The Everest stuff is manufactured in Bangladesh. Its name is the home word for where supplementary feed lies scattered on fields of tamely grazing deer. Where smoke rises from the chimney of the farmhouse where the big-handed farmer with the crinkly eyes of a mountaineer will soon go for a hot cup of tea.

'From Darjeeling,' suggests Gloria.

The farmer is at home in this word, it clads him in a homely garment of manly nationhood — though it points to a mountain he will never see.

Now Ants is enjoying herself again.

'I mean it,' mutters Gloria, squirting more mountain water down her throat. 'Share it all with me. Remember, we're a team. But gently, okay?'

Antsy's birdy laughter makes it hard for her to swallow and not swallowing makes it hard to talk. She waves a hand at the vistas flashing by: paddocks of docile deer, glimpses of lakes framed in foothills and the arty repoussoir of forest, the encircling cordillera of distant, snowy peaks.

A finger-post arrows past. 'Wilderness Road,' croaks Ants, shaking her team-mate.

'The Oasis,' suggests Gloria, waving at a Tex-Mex motel branded with a date palm and minaret, before a tough view of teal-grey glacial water rimmed with scummy sand. 'The Duck Inn. Homestay.' But she doesn't seem to like the deer farmer at home on Mount Everest, the wilderness with a road in it, the desert comfort stop sullen with too much glacial water, the feebly quacking pun, the home that isn't.

The mini-bus stops by the lake and Stan's first urgent smoke blows back inside. 'She's not a bad little audio-visual, takes about half an hour. Won an award.'

'Coffee.' Gloria may be angry about something. Biswas has travelled in the front next to Stan, hidden in dark glasses and a peaked All Blacks cap. He walks towards the lake. Bill crouches over Boris's elegant lighter and then they stroll like boulevardiers towards the multimedia theatre. Pat heads off in the opposite direction from Biswas. She videos the Tourist Information kiosk.

'Here's the thing,' says Gloria. 'And you won't hear me say, "from a Maori perspective" again, probably. Everybody gets the "Oasis" thing. But for me, maybe, there's another layer. I'll tell you about it.'

A Globus tour empties into the coffee shop, whose speciality is 'home-baked Cervena pies'.

'What's that?'

'Four dollars.'

'No, I want to know what it *is*.'

'A pie.'

'Yes, but what kind of a pie.'

'Cervena.'

'And what's that?'

'Like I said – four dollars.'

'Hospitality,' says Gloria. 'Manaakitanga. And look at all this stuff – outdoor gear from Bangladesh, "Southern naturally" woolly jumpers made in Fiji, Taiwanese fishing tackle and postcards printed in Hong Kong. Isn't this the world?' The Globus party niggles at the dialects of the food and beverage outlet. 'Just hold that thought, Ants,' warns Gloria. 'I can hear it growing there. What I was going to say, *manaakitanga*. Whose hospitality lets the wilderness road go there in the first place? Or did someone just place an order? See, that's what happens to me, though I live in the world just like you. With the Fijian natural wool jumpers knitted by Indian descendants of indentured labour out of sheep that get woolly on land colonial pastoralists stole off Maori.' Gloria's look tells Ants it's not her turn at the moment.

'Sorry,' she says. 'That's a bit bloody high and mighty. But something else.' Gloria's watching the tourists. 'What about these local chicks? Like, "Here's the pie now give me the fuckin' four bucks," right? What do you expect, an invitation to my home? Meet my unemployed boyfriend who's stoned out of his tree by morning-tea time? See, they don't want to serve. But the tour-bus people want to be served. That's their deal. They want "wilderness road", exactly like it says: some wilderness *with* a road. So, you see.' Gloria doesn't finish her sentence – she carefully swallows coffee. 'Don't get me started,' she says.

Behind them, arguments have broken out. 'What do you mean, you don't know what animal a "cervena" is?'

'Okay,' says Gloria to the quiet-as-a-mouse Antsy. 'This is good coffee. Another thing. Nothing against taking money, money is good, absolutely excellent, money. Bring it on. But you have to be clear when it's "wilderness road" money, know what I mean? Because it's not manaakitanga, it's something else.'

Gloria pauses. One of the Globusers drops a home-baked cervena pie in a rubbish bin.

'Don't tell me it's "meat". When we have a right to know what kind of meat.'

'When you come and stay up home,' says Gloria, 'that won't be a "homestay" and what you get from Uncle Mat's mob will be manaakitanga, not to mention what I'll warn you about later.'

'My randy old dad used to say,' ventures Ants carefully, 'that making a home in a hotel was like having a honeymoon in a furniture saleroom.'

'What was it like?'

'Rich people, hookers, conventioneers. I wasn't allowed to use the pool. Didn't have the body for it, anyway. They'd all have jumped out and taken a hygienic shower. The Filipina maids were sweet. That was my neighbourhood.'

'So you know,' says Gloria. 'The locals aren't grateful

enough. The locals are like these chicks here: "Four dollars."'

Gloria pauses again – she's sizing Antsy up. 'You're not feeling too flash, are you, girl? Want to tell me about it?'

'Can I talk to you about road signs?' asks Antsy. Gloria's dark glasses have clouds speeding across them, but it is sheltered by the coffee shop and not chilly. Even so, Ants is shivering.

'Come on, girl. We're this team. What are you trying to say?'

Antsy rushes on. 'You can't mistake the official, national signage, which is black and white road signs like Wilderness Road, there is also green and yellow Department of Conservation signage, which says things like Scenic Reserve, and there is brown and white heritage signage pointing to Historic Battle Sites and stuff.'

'This is true,' says Gloria. 'Can't argue with that.'

'All of these are about central authority and shared meaning. They narrate democratic compliance.'

'Purchased with my tax,' Gloria suggests, getting interested. The clouds in her glasses are replaced by twin reflections of the little Aussie's face.

'Exactly,' agree the eager little faces. 'They tell us that these are the correct names, Gloria. These are reliable directions, the real world. You can live safely in this world. This is a world where people can believe they're alive.' Ants moistens her busy tongue with cool coffee while not saying the last thought in her talk about road signs, the thought Gloria's waiting patiently for.

'I'm dying, Gloria,' says Antsy. 'I know this because I've got a killer disease. But I also know it because nothing's very real any more. Everything's kind of spooky.'

A ginger cat comes to Gloria and Ants's table with its tail confidently hoisted. Gloria expertly agitates the fur at the stem of the cat's tail with a scritchy red fingernail – the cat stands on tiptoe. Then it jumps onto Gloria's lap.

'I kind of guessed it,' says Gloria, making the cat purr

and dribble. It kneads at her sumptuous thighs. 'I'm really sorry, darling.'

'It's okay,' says Ants. 'And then, the other stuff's better.'

'What other stuff, Ants?'

'The giant fruit, the big concrete sheep, that kind of stuff.'

'I'm sorry?'

'The stuff that's trying to be different, not the same. That airport that's wild at heart. It's a lot less spooky.' The cat pushes its cheeks against Gloria's jaw, making her laugh. Maybe she's also laughing at Ants. 'Makes me feel more alive.' Antsy is trying to finish. 'Not so lame.' She ends with a wee joke. The cat ascends to the table-top. It licks the remaining cream from Gloria's slice of nice, clove-flavoured strudel. Then they both look past Ants at the café.

'And then I says, "Who cares what kind of fuckin' animal – animals have rights, too. How'd you like to end up in a fuckin' pie."'

'Right – how they think we feel, vegetarians.'

Now the cat jumps from the table and runs into the café where the vegetarian waitresses are laughing loudly and they give it the venison pie from the rubbish bin. Ants and Gloria sit in silence. They are smiling at Antsy's lame joke, the vegetarians, the cat. Ants is also smiling because it feels good to have said to Gloria what she never says to anyone. When she thinks these thoughts, she usually lets them run on past the big signs and into places that are not spooky at all, like handwritten signs for honey and firewood along the roadsides, like the signs made by kids selling bunches of spring jonquils out of coloured plastic buckets, like the amateur bed-and-breakfast signs with hand-painted pictures of nice pillows saying 'Zzzzzz', like the Thyme Out herbalist garden sign, like the signwriting for the Oasis Motel with its date palm and minaret and even like the no trespassing sign on the five-bar gate in the Hollyford Valley, the one with the skull and crossbones: 'Privit kep oute'.

'Thank you for listening to my rave,' says Ants.

'I feel special – thank you, girl,' replies Gloria.

'It comes and goes, but mostly it goes, it goes on going. It's like I'm disappearing, Gloria, a wee bit at a time. Not very Australian, most of us go on getting bigger and bigger and more red. One day I'll be a semi-colon or something.' The hooty sounds of her laughter stop abruptly when Gloria leans across the table and kisses her right on the wee tube of her laughing lips.

Biswas has washed his hands and feet in the lake, has rinsed his mouth there and is now praying, holding the lobes of his ears, lowering himself to touch his forehead to the hem of the mat against a backdrop of golden leaf-buds on spring willows around the lake. Bill and Boris are eating colourful ice-creams on a park bench next to a scenic reserve sign with a crossed-out dog crouching to shit. Pat is pretending to be asleep in the back of the mini-bus.

Stan's found a second-hand art catalogue in the opportunity shop by the Thai restaurant and has propped it up on the steering wheel – his cigarette hand hangs outside the van's window, entering furtively to turn the pages and make up the distance to his lips. The reproductions of paintings are faithful to the region's austere, lemony, freeze-dried and sun-baked, desiccated landscapes of tussock and granite, the braided, gravelly riverbeds and the weathered red shearing sheds. From time to time, the paintings include the harshly blonde, almost bleached-white hillocky haunch, breast and shining hair of a woman. She's been inserted into the hills or framed in windows through which the landscape is visible, or she is supine on beds beyond which the arid vista appears through wide French doors or patio screens.

She reminds Stan of the Prakriti thing Mr Biswas has been telling him about. Real old stuff.

'That's all very well,' says Gloria, settling in. 'But don't forget, the name of the place your painter's turned into Antsy's mate Elle MacPherson's arse is about eleven human generations old back from 1900.'

'Here we go again,' says Stan. 'And what's so special about 1900?' He turns the catalogue's golden pages – rotating them sideways to admire the painter's skill, the woman's horizon.

'That was when the trout got here and ate up the local fishes.'

Stan's a bit flummoxed as well as annoyed. 'What's that got to do with painting?'

'Yeah,' says Ants. 'And leave our Elle out of it. She's virtually my stepmother.'

'What's wrong with trout?' Stan wants to know.

'Trout's fine with me, Stan,' Gloria soothes him. 'Salmon even better. But they didn't just eat up all the Maori fish, they gobbled up Rakaihautu and his name as well. Who remembers the names he thought of five hundred years ago? Nowheres. They go with the wilderness roads. Roads to nowhere.' Stan silently turns a couple of blonde pages. 'Sorry,' says Gloria. 'Weird Maori shit.' She pauses. 'Sorry for saying sorry.'

'Whatever,' says Stan, expelling his last smoke and closing the catalogue with reverence. 'She's still bloody marvellous. Art.'

'She's still bloody waiting to go,' says Cowpat from the back. 'Where's our mad mullah got to? Our two fancy boys?'

seven

Home

When Joris finishes telling his story about the stacked-up rabbit hutches his father kept in the tiny yard of their tenement in post-war Rotterdam, and how the rabbits bred at a tremendous rate (Boris Joris, laughing, mimes little rabbits popping out and hopping with small hops inside little hutches, bumping their heads and grimacing), and how he, that is Boris's father, built wainscots to line Joris and his brother's room to keep the seeping damp away from their beds (Boris mimes pulling up a coverlet over his chin and chatters his teeth), and how he, that is Boris's father, used to tell them what they were eating was chicken and the rabbits had run away (Boris mimes big rabbits hopping away with immense hops across the tableload of beer glasses), and how the kids believed him as hard as they could because they were hungry and the chicken was really delicious, chopped up in bits, with gravy and dumplings and kool from the narrow tenement garden plots down along the railway line (Boris mimes shovelling rabbit-chicken into his childhood mouth and wiping gravy off his chin), which they mostly had one Sunday every month after kerk (Joris Boris mimes a wide, accepting, ingenuous, conspiratorial, childish smile, and takes an un-Joris like, hurried swallow of his beer), and how last time he, that is me, Joris, went back to the old neighbourhood the whole, but the whole, place was gone, even the streets (Joris mimes a devastating catastrophe with a sweep of his arm that almost knocks over the beer glasses on the table), it had been wiped out, but completely wiped out, and a new Philips light-industrial communications complex was there, mostly automated, he'd watched a new, smoothly gliding almost silent bus pick up a factory gate shelter-full of Muslim women in headscarves and pale green Philips overalls (Boris mimes women looking out of face-covering scarves), and what he'd wanted to be able to imagine was his father, a very short little man, worked all his life on the Rotterdam docks, coming back on his bicycle from the allotment garden by the railway line with a little sack of vegetables for the family but also for feeding the rabbits furiously breeding in the hutches in the tenement's damp yard (Boris Joris mimes a little man pedalling joyfully home and, with one cupped hand mounting another, rabbits fucking) – when Joris finishes his story, elegantly wiping some beer-foam off his lips with the side of one finger, but smiling with a certain glistening, almost-drunk emotion nonetheless – when the rest of the table realises that he's, finally, finished, everyone turns to look at William.

William will have a malicious, even sadistic, riposte ready-prepared with which to respond to Joris's, to Boris's emotional tale about his childhood home.

William's nasty joke will be along the lines of, 'If your father was such a short little man, how come he bred a streak like you, Joris – is there something else going on here, among the rabbits, all that rabbity breeding in the Rotterdam tenements?'

But the William who now consents to being called Bill and even colours-up a bit as though flattered by the name's rebranding, disappoints them by saying, 'So that makes you how old, Boris?'

Even Joris seems deflated by this response. 'That makes me fifty-eight years, Bill,' he says. His brief emotional glisten quickly evaporates: he drinks beer with a stylishly frugal lick of his top lip. 'Was late nineteen-forties, early fifties. Was hard times, Bill,' he adds, with his characteristically neutral good cheer, as though the hard times were now another experience commodity, even another adventure. 'Then we come to New Zealand.'

'What Bill wants to know,' Cowpat finds the gap, 'is how come you're so stunningly youthfully good-looking, Boris, when you're actually about the same age as him? Probably older.'

'Adventure,' says Boris smoothly. He might even now be bored. Bored, even, with his father's monthly look of chagrin as he lifted the lid from the Sunday goulash of stewed rabbit and said, as always, 'Ah, chicken! Overheerlijk!'

Out on the terrace, where Stan can smoke and Biswas doesn't have to be close to the mod-drinking, Stan's marvelling at the Bangladeshi's account of the sounds-like 'Bawl' belief that all life is female, though he's not following the connection with Krishna's sexily dancing milkmaids and the practice of sounds-like 'dehabad', which, if he's understanding Mr Biswas right, involves rooting without coming. For a start, how can you have rooting if everything's female and why wouldn't you come if the milkmaids are as hot as the Biswas mime of slinky swaying suggests they are?

Still, it's quite an interesting take on the art catalogue he's been showing Mr Biswas, especially the painting where the blonde sheila's bum is, any way you look at it, a tussocky hill. 'Look,' says Stan, moving the page into the light and indicating the technical finesse with which the artist has painted the fine down on her arse. 'She's a marvellous piece of work, all right.'

Biswas leans to look closely: this is maybe what Cow looks like inside zips? He has begun to think of her as a Krishna milkmaid — maybe to overcome anger that feels improper. Along the lakefront are radiant banks of beautiful-many-coloured flowers, 'Connie lupins', isn't it. Stan has told him this and explained about the 'beaches' trees. Biswas cannot even begin to understand how to believe the turquoise colour of the lake, the pink-like-rose-petal snow mountains far away, the Connies. What to do with this beauty that makes his teeth ache? Stan is smiling back at him with determined anticipation, wanting his response to the downy woman-hill and a bit worried about the Bangladeshi's milkmaid mime. Biswas carefully lets his own smile, within which his teeth are grinding horribly together, relax, little-bit, little-bit.

'And who is not immersed in sportive dalliance, Stan? This is what Lalon Shah say. In a famous Baul song-poetry.'

Stan's optimistic smile remains in place while he works this through.

'Who indeed, Mr Biswas.' Stan closes the catalogue – Biswas thinks he has maybe said something wrong. Stan's smile has closed with the catalogue. Biswas would like to talk to Stan about his Keshamoni problem – have to talk to someone, no? But Stan is getting up to go. 'Well, I'll wish you goodnight, Mr Biswas. She's a lovely night to be outside.' That blast of noise as Stan opens the terrace doors to the bar. A chant, sounds like, 'Baul, Baul, Baul!' flies out into the night from the team table, and is then cut off. Was Cow's voice, loudest. 'Baul?'

Is maybe Cow who can help. With Keshamoni. Very friendly counterpart, Cow. Not to be proud, Biswas admonishes himself. Is time to be building the bridges – he rehearses the Up-Keep workshop phrase. His behaviour has been impolite and ashamed.

Biswas gropes from the terrace into the darkness towards the place by the lake's edge where, earlier, he had looked at the crazy-making so-many colours of the Connie lupins. Saw Cow sitting down there all alone, looking at the Connies. He was astonished to see her shedding tears onto the video camera in her lap.

'What's mattering, Pat?'

'Go away, Biz.'

'Is beaut – sorry, Pat.'

'Yes, beautiful. Not beaut. But go away.'

Out there in the darkness, now, will be the Connies that are making Pat cry. 'One who keeps his Master's beauty in his meditation – what will he do when his death is decided?' Biswas sings the Baul songs of Lalon under his breath for luck – a high, quivering tenor, like a lake bird. Stumbling in the dark – where to find beauty? How to find beauty in darkness?

Back in the bar, Bill mimes Boris's silky swallow and empties his glass.
'Bill, Bill, Bill!'
He lifts his hand for silence.
Usually, William will say, 'It's simple,' and will watch with mixed satisfaction and desolation as his bitter truths haul down silence like a screen of armour-plated glass closing in the untouchable place where his rigour is on display. He will watch his audience press their soft vulnerable bodies and beseeching lips against his domain, occupied as much by his loneliness as by William. He will relish his loneliness and the superiority of which it is the stark brand, at the same time as he explores the familiar torment of his self-pity. He will know, again, that the unassailable brand of his loneliness and self-pity are what mark him as special. He will see them – that smugly voluptuous Hinemoana with her endless networks of nepotistic nose-rubbing, that gross Patricia whose barking confidence hides God knows what face-stuffing self-doubts behind the closed doors of her fussy, bachelor-girl flat, that boring Australian cripple Nancy whose every word has to hear its own citation before she can get it out of her mouth, and not least the bizarre Mr Biswas, whose neatness seems only to mask the boiling conflicts within – he will see them pressing themselves against his shining glass screen of difference and isolation, and then he will see them mouthing the usual curses and jeers and they will go away. It is then that William will usually laugh, raising his glass if he has one, saluting his own unbroken record of contempt.

William cannot see Joris's face against the glass. But Bill can see Boris over at the bar buying another round of drinks for Frank and Babs.

'It's not that simple,' says Bill, surprising himself.

William failed to go for the jugular over Joris's rabbit story and, come to think of it, he sat licking a coloured ice-cream, in his good Italian coat, cheerful before a low view of Lake Te Anau. It was a view that seemed blanched by repetition, William's domain of dissociation, where, however, the day before, his own sallow cheeks had been crinkled by a simple, contented smile. What is happening to the view in which William's loneliness and pride usually appear like the haughty profiles of alps? What is happening to William? Whose are those old scowl lines that have twisted into a bashful smile? Why does he seem to be smiling in the direction of the suave Boris who is schmoozing the American videoists? Why doesn't he think it's simple any more?

'What's not that simple?' demands Pat, as if affronted by this travesty of the man she has assumed she will always dislike.

You have to imagine a vista – not a 'view', insists William – in which a certain kind of history resides. In which no comment is offered. Whose only history is the unjudging, amoral, value-free history of geology, if you can imagine geology without geologists and their careers. Or a history of botany, if you can imagine no one has ever intruded taxonomies to this place, or a history of the remorseless evolutions of animals, if you can imagine that without seeing Animal Planet in your mind's eye. Nothing has happened here except what the earth's forces have caused to happen, except what hot and cold, the seed-scattering winds and the remorseless fatalism of evolution have caused to happen. Here, in this vista, there is nothing to judge and there are no judgements, at least no moral or value judgements. There is no value. There is nothing to say and no way to say anything. This vista is not perceived and so it has no existence in narratives or images. It has not been colonised by the demeaning tales of hulking, mountain-forming demigods. It has not been squabbled over by competing scientific theories or the foundation myths of warring societies. It has not had professional career capital invested in it and it has not become a territory defended with all the atavistic turf-scratchings, disguised as theoretical and empirical rigour, of its actual wild denizens. It has not become drenched in and stained by human emotions. Its existence has not been modified by ideas of how it might be different, might be like somewhere else.

'Or like a painting, wouldn't you say, Stan?' Stan has joined the group and is chucking down a chilly pint as if to sluice out something nasty in a drain.

Like a painting in which the mountain is no longer a mountain but has become a woman, in which the lake must be wrapped in proper proscenium drapes of repoussoir forest. This vista has not, in short, become a *view* – William uses the word 'view' as if describing the nasty thing in Stan's drain. He imagines, instead, this view-less place as a not-seen place, an impeccable place, a place beyond judgement, above reproach, untouched by disappointments, ambitions, envies, satires, and the leprous concept of beauty.

'I could feel right at home there,' says William with the hint of his old smirk. William is back on form. Hinemoana Gloria glares but knows better than to barge in – she licks traces of mediocre pesto from her fingertips. The elderly American videoists are enjoying a hearty repast of burgers and fries and William's gaze shifts in their direction and in the direction of Joris. They all seem to be miming slipping and falling over. Joris grabs Frank by the shoulder, pretending to hold himself up on a slippery surface. Frank pretends to fall and grabs Babs, who pretends that he has knocked her over. They are all laughing, Joris with expert insincerity.

Pat is subdued tonight, but William's bitter story of home has cheered her up: his nastiness is familiar. 'Just never going to get past it, are you William?' She semaphores jagged mountain peaks. 'The one-show pony.'

Nancy's silence might be the preparation of a response, might not.

Stan's offended – simple as that. 'Don't see what's so bloody wrong with a beaut view,' he challenges. He's had a couple of beers already.

'And then,' says the Bill who seems to have waited patiently for William to finish. Bill is looking across at Boris and the elderly Americans who now seem to be miming taking cleansing showers while sitting before their plates of burgers. Babs turns the fingers of one hand into a shower-rose while using the other to soap herself luxuriously under the armpits – Frank demonstrates how firmly she is braced on her chair by leaning his own hefty weight on it. Joris is raising his glass in a salute.

What about a place, on the other hand, asks Bill, where everything is judged, where everything is something else, where you feel the rising slime of history reaching to your nostrils? What about a place where your father expects you to be brilliant and respectful, your mother demands that you are good-looking and grateful and where the very air you breathe is thick with words about what has already happened, who has already done something, who has the right to an expert opinion, what quality is and how to know the real thing when you see it and how to see it, how to better yourself?

Your mother's leg stretches into this view. It is being depilated with a pinkish crème called Veet and the atmosphere is querulous with radio discussions of Issues. Your father, who is neither short nor a rabbit breeder, brings home quaking slabs of pinkish corned silverside that make you want to vomit and he asks if you've thought about shaving yet. Why? There's nothing worth shaving on William's cheeks. But of course, that's the point.

Into the lake of this lovely view, Bill's skinny, leek-like body dives clumsily; it emerges with a bathing-cap of slimy duckweed on its head and, while the picnicking audience laughs, breaks out in a prickly, red mosaic of duck-rash. 'Why are you covering up your legs with towels, Willie,' demands his mother. 'Use some Dimp if the sandies are getting to you.' But that's not it. If he uses Dimp he has to wash it off at once. If he gets sandy fingers he can't touch himself, let alone put on Dimp. How can he unwrap those legs, which are widely known as the Spags? How can he smile, when he sees the eyes of those he's smiling for drop to his snaggle fangs? How can he answer his father when he sounds stupid even to himself? What is he supposed to do when his mother's appraising gaze looks up and down his newly purchased suit and is followed by silence or a subject-change: 'I saw Frank and Minnie's boys today.' Yes, the ones who win yellow towels at swimming champs and are sleek in their slacks and team blazers. William plays a tune on the piano. His mother says, 'I hear Josh and Celia's boy's won a scholarship to the conservatorium in Sydney.' William is elected chair of the high-school Sceptics Club. His mother says, 'I hear John and Blanche's boy is going to law school.'

In the picture-window of this lovely view, at the bach, with the sea blue and sparkling out there beyond the sandy perimeter of scratchy buffalo grass, Bill's mother and father are discussing him, he can tell, as his glasses fall off when he puts the Moth's tiller over and capsizes into chilly water, punches up under the sail, chokes on bitter sea, struggles out into the clear. No, Bill cannot see them any more as he up-hauls again, but there they will be, in the picture-window, when he makes the beach at last. His father will not have run down to check on him. Yes, William did lose his new glasses when he tipped out. No, he had not tied them on with a lanyard. A *lanyard*. Think about it – all those idylls.

Years later, you go back there. You cannot find it – the view. The view of home with you in it. You cannot tell if it has gone, changed, or if you cannot remember it. Maybe it is just the scale: you were shorter then. The horizons and tops of things were at a whole different level. There are beach-front mansions with smoked glass and pilasters. Yes, there is still a children's playground with swings and slides. You realise you had better not hang about there feeling sentimental – in your city-slicker black clothes, your dark glasses. No, do not have a memorial swing with the local kids, do not reminisce with them about the time you jumped off the top with a home-made parachute. Their uncles and big brothers will be there within minutes to lynch you. This weird fucker, laughing his head off, chatting up the kids, swinging on the swings-and-slides, never seen him before round here. Fuck that, come on, boys.

'Home is the idyll,' says Bill. 'It's the place without rabbits and wainscots and creeping, or is it rising, damp. There's no pint-size dad on a bike. Home is where you can't, ever, be at home again. It's probably the place you never were. At home. It's the place you're glad is completely gone when you're stupid enough to try and go back one day. Home is what sets you free because you're not there any more. It's everyone's chance for their Great Escape.'

Joris wanders back – he's missed the big performance. 'I'm missing something? You all so quiet, something happen maybe? What, Bill's being a killjoy again?' He smacks Bill across the side of the head – a familiar gesture by now. Bill sips his beer. He seems calm rather than pleased with himself. The Americans are waving at Joris as they leave the bar – he waves back. Babs pretends to slip one more time – Frank pretends to catch her. Joris pretends to laugh.

'These are interesting people, Frank and Babs, from Fort Lauderdale,' says Joris into the team silence.

Only Ants is laughing. Bill watches her with interest, waiting for her to explain what is funny.

Home is where you go when you die. You were never at home in life. Antsy does not say this, it is not funny and it is not why she is laughing. She is laughing at the fabulous image of William under the sail, without glasses, nearly drowning, but still worrying about his mother and father watching.

But that is when Biswas enters the bar.

The whole place goes quiet this time because everybody knows you are not supposed to, but this foreign guy with the huge smile just walks in with about a truckload of Connie lupins. You can hardly see the smile for the Connie lupins he should not have picked, but it is there all right, simultaneously framed and covered up, highlighted and coyly revealed, by the immense armload of nodding, multicoloured lupins he carries in front of him towards the team's table.

'Pat. Is for you. I know you like Connies.'

The bar bursts into loud, sustained applause as Biswas piles the flowers in front of Cowpat. Wolf whistles, hoots, hand-clapping and the rhythmic male grunting and beer-glass banging that salute this as an excellent courtship gesture. And indeed, Pat's face turns as pink as a dominant hue of the flowers. The image Biswas had in mind was more like demure Gulshan Lake young lovers with long bouquets of moist-stemmed gladioli and pinwheel arrangements of fiery zinnias and appa big sister watching not-too-far-away. His smile begins to set.

'Come on Biz, get these out of here. What's this about.' Pat frogmarches the man and his immense bouquet from the bar – a pandemonium of whistles and glass banging.

'Gee, are we ready for this, team?' enquires Gloria. 'It seems we're entering phase two ahead of schedule. This will get intense.'

The bar's buoyant atmosphere seems to thin, to become oxygen-depleted, following the exit of the bouquet, the smile, the blush. William Bill is looking around. He feels both appalled by his sadness and exalted by his relief. No gesture will be this grand again tonight. It may be that the other lovers in the bar, and those who wish to be lovers, feel judged and diminished by the moment. There it was, thinks Bill – a view as gorgeous as any you will see anywhere in the world, a clear sky with almost frosty spring stars and a trail of newly risen moonlight on the lake, the stony lake-marge soft with toppling, heavy flowers, and you might as well, all of you, the whole lot of you, have stayed at fucking home.

eight

Beauty

But of course good old Pat was always going to be the base – good old dependable Pat. We won't say the bottom. Of the human pyramid. She's heard and overheard a lot of them, the bottom jokes. Nothing like a solid bottom to stop things going pear-shaped – where are you, Pat? We can rely on Patricia to get to the bottom of this.

What kind of a dimwit team gets built climbing on top of itself – but it happens all the time, anyway. The workshop facilitator, who had no bottom at all, had been chirpily unaware of the brutal metaphor she was constructing as she urged the CTI team members to climb on top.

Pat pushes the bewildered Biswas ahead of her towards her room. If she's angry, why is she almost laughing? And if it's funny, why is she on the brink of tears? Biswas sheds Connie lupins along the corridor but gives up trying to retrieve them. Good old Pat's big, dependable hand (a safe pair of hands) is planted firmly in the middle of his back. Her rage is pushing her forward as well. Like a big hand. She feels it urging her on, just a couple of clicks short of a major meltdown. Pushing big Pat, Cowpat, towards the door of her room, beyond which the rage can give up and turn into weeping.

Good old Pat's virtues. She gives the light-boned man in front of her a shove. Her *values*, like they'd said at the team-building. Reliable, dependable. Someone had used the word 'staunch', probably Hinemoana. Speaking of which. 'Straight', someone else had said. Probably William. What he'd meant was boring. You could tell he'd meant that because of the way he'd kept his sneery face extra expressionless. 'Solid', someone else had said, being a bit careful. And here's what no one had said: 'And built like a brick shithouse.' You're going to put that on the *top*? Of the pyramid?

In the whole team values session, in the 'Always Valued/ Mostly Valued/ Sometimes Valued/Sometimes Not Valued/ Hardly Valued/Never Valued' matrix of personal commitment to the team, good old Pat scored high on Decision Making, Power and Authority, Run Your Own Show and Working Under Pressure. Not bad on Working Alone, Work Friendships, Contact with the Public, Influence and Guide People, Work in Predictable Circumstances, Independence, Moral and Value Fulfilment and Troubleshooting.

Pretty much crapped right out on Create Innovative Solutions, Creative Artistry, Adventure and Risk, Seen as an Expert and Strong Theorist, Excitement, Demonstrate Innovation and Creative Self-expression.

The question at that point was: What does this score say about the Beautiful New Zealand portfolio at the Department of Tourism? DoT's beauty? Beauty, DoT? Her portfolio – an especially creative one. At least in principle. Given that it was about aesthetic issues. About . . . beauty?

The sleek Up-Keep team-building moderator had chided her gently. We don't protect ourselves in our jobs. We *realise* ourselves in them, Pat. Oh, thanks. The rest of the team had avoided eye-contact. Inside, she'd felt a familiar resignation. As if she didn't know the answer by now.

Warm and fluffy, small and feathered, unique and endangered, green and untouched, wild and spectacular, clean and green. These were her reliably twinned options. These were how beauty sold well. And these were how beauty sold DoT's products. Find me the thing that's warm and fluffy as well as small and feathered, that's unique and endangered and ekes out its survival in a green, untouched remnant of a wild, spectacular landscape within a clean, green island nation, and I'll fill your coach parks and viewing platforms, produce an accommodation crisis from backpacker across four star and cause a stock-run on residuals like Authentic Indigenous Craft. On toi iho™. And Natural Products, mostly sheepskins and honey.

And the word-derivatives of 'beauty' will be used in not less than eighty per cent of all Key Communication Objectives, no fewer than one out of five Cognitive Captions and no fewer than one out of three Affective Captions.

William's score went through the roof in all the creative, innovative and risk-taking value categories. Based on what? He glanced at her across the room and shrugged.

Hinemoana got a laugh out of the team and an obliging titter out of the Up-Keep moderator by asking what was wrong with describing big, muscly rugby league players as 'beautiful'. She pretty much wrapped her legs around the word when she said it.

Then they did the gender team challenges. With grades according to how you delegated authority, how long you spent planning, how long it took to execute your solution, how close to your proposal your solution was. Straight away, Patricia: team leader. Needless to say. They all just looked at her. Meanwhile, the slightly Asian moderator lowered herself in a supple sort of way to the floor without using her hands. Sat with her back very straight and her hips pushed forward writing notes. And nodding. She was a nodder – Pat could spot them a mile off. Compliant second-tier management material.

But, surprise, surprise. It was the wee Aussie who came up with the stroke of genius. Those tragic little high foot arches nobody wanted to look at outside the orthopaedic shoes, unusual upper body strength from the forearm crutches, light as a feather. Up she hopped to the top with one of the crutches as a reinforcing extension held by Hinemoana.

The 'boys' team (William) lodged a formal objection: use of prop. Solution had to employ *either* bodies *or* equipment but not both. Nancy argued (and won): not a prop, prosthesis. Fully a part of her.

The lithe Asiany woman upcoiled herself without using her hands again and commented, from her notes. That while Pat was the natural leader, she was able to empower another team-member to come up with the innovative idea (well done, Pat).

In other words, bossy not bright.

Then, as her dreamily smiling male assistant changed the CD to relaxing pan-pipey music and refilled the jellybean saucers, the leotarded moderator awarded the 'girls' team its prize.

'Though of course,' she beamed. Knowing they were expecting the joke. 'There are no losers. Let's just say the girls outwitted the boys. As usual. Not surprised, are we, girls?' She had a script, she stuck to it. Fortunately the museum was footing the bill for this crap.

The boys' solution consisted of stacked furniture. With a hook made from a coat hanger fixed to the end of a metal strut detached from one of the big-sheets-of-paper holders. Joris did it, mostly. Superconfident. It didn't work. He waved the failure away with a graceful shrug. Biswas was completely demented. Not a clue. Head-rolls, mad smiles. William did his best to look bored. Of course.

And the prize? Neck massages. From the boys' team. 'Down on the floor, everyone. Down you go! Don't be shy! There's a long journey ahead!' Down she coiled, the leotard, straight-backed, knees out. While her dreamily smiling assistant, Phillipe or something, took some deep breaths. Began to palpate the woman's shoulders with his eyes closed. While making a deep humming sound. Good grief.

William's expression a treat. Hands frozen above the crippled Aussie. Joris right into it, no problem. Hinemoana making the most of it, as usual. 'Good man, Joris. Harder, man. Yes, there. Oh, baby.'

And then. Having got herself down to the floor (using hands, both of them) she heard a polite huff of minor effort from the Biswas nostrils as he lowered himself behind her.

Couple of sharp cracks from his knee joints. And then his fingers went to work. Polite, delicate, respectful. Only word for it: expert. Strong, thin, *knowledgeable* fingers. That cinnamony smell from something, maybe aftershave or soap. These were fingers that could fold things. They could button shirts. Turn the pages of rice-papery books.

She imagined them reaching judiciously into foliage. Picking flowers. She thought of them as the kinds of fingers that could carefully pick, and hold, varieties of flowers. Make nice bunches of them. Precisely take out blemished petals, nip off dead blooms. Strongly twist off too-long stems. She imagined that head-on-one-side Biz look, that smile. As he looked at his handiwork. His handiwork. His handy work.

And now, this. The glorious lupins piled on, falling off, the table in good old Pat's unit. And the big, fat tears dumping out of her eyes.

'Pat, I'm sorry Pat, no, I'm not understand, what I'm doing wrong?'

Cowpat's tears just keep coming. Makes her madder than ever. Trying to tell him. Trying to yell her head off at him. And the sobs just smashing into the words. 'Don't? You? Understand?'

'No, Pat. Not.'

In the motel car park the drinkers are backing their cars out. Tooting their horns. Boasting. She hears Gloria's door slam next to her unit, the sound of music comes on, there are laughing voices. As usual, a party. A thump as someone sits heavily. And the bloody idiot just stands there with that look. With that look of amazement and horror on his face. Still holding half of the huge bale of bloody lupins.

Pat goes to her bathroom and drinks a glass of water. She splashes her face with the water. A few times. She imagines it still in the lake. Cool, aquamarine, stretching over to the mountains. Reflecting the mountains. The gravelly banks covered with Connie lupins. In the mirror, her face. Good grief, her face like a damn traffic accident.

Get a grip.

A polite knock at the door. 'Pat.' He tries the formal name. 'Patricia. Are you all-right? Am I helping?'

'Am I helping?' The bloated, teary face in the mirror. *Am I helping.* Pat doesn't will herself to smile. The smile appears. It's there. It's even amused. It comes from somewhere. From the voice she hears most days, often enough most days.

You have to laugh.
Nothing else for it, really.
What a joke.
You think that's funny.
Try this.

When Pat opens the bathroom door, her determination drives Biswas backwards into the motel room and the sofa with the dark brown raffia-type weave.

'What've you done with the flowers?'

He gestures at the open window. 'Out. Isn't it.'

'Oh, Mr Biswas.' Somehow, the formal name seems appropriate. 'We're going to have a cup of tea. Then we're going to have a nice talk. Okay?' Not 'Having-a-Ball-Biz'. Not any more.

'Okay, Patricia.' The smile, gone. 'I like that. Wanting to talk too.'

'Firstly, you're not meant to pick them, anyway. But never mind that. Secondly, you made me look a complete fool. Never mind that either. Thirdly, here's how the lupins got here. *Lupinus polyphyllus*: a tall originally blue and white flowered perennial from the west coast of America. Taken to the UK 1834. Hybridised with tree lupin and other species by George Russell to get the present range of colours. A feature of the coronation of George VI in 1937. The present occurrence in the high country is from a sowing by a farmer's wife, Connie someone, near Lake Tekapo, where we are now, in 1952. Hence called "Connie" lupin rather than "Russell" lupin.

'And fourthly, that's why. Connie's why I'm going to tell you a story. About Connie.'

'You're telling a story, Patricia?'

'That's right, Mr Biswas. Because it's the only way. It's the only way I know how to explain. What happened. How I feel. What's happening. What's happening to me. About beauty, Mr Biswas.'

'Beauty, Patricia.'

'That's right. My job. "Beautiful New Zealand".'

'New Zealand is very beautiful, Patricia.'

'Just listen.'

The neat Biswas moustache dips towards his cup of tea. He drinks appreciatively with quite loud slurping noises. His dark eyes are watching her over the cup. Funny how you notice things at certain times. He goes well with the coarse weave of the brown sofa. His eyes, the smooth dark skin of his face. His shirt of simple, patterned cotton.

'Once upon a time a bit over a hundred and fifty years ago there was a highland Scots shepherd called Jock Mackenzie. Only that probably wasn't his real name. Just what highland Scots shepherds got called.'

'Understanding. Like "Cowpat".'

'Not exactly. Never mind. Jock Mackenzie had a dog. A sheep dog. No, that's a dog that helps with sheep. It herds the sheep. The dog's name was Friday. Jock loved his dog Friday. They were always together. Loved his dog and loved his Bible. His Gaelic Bible, that's a special language. Not like Arabic, no, just the language his Bible was written in. Jock and Friday walked all around this country. The mountains, the river valleys, the mountain passes, and the big plains like this one where we are. This one's called the "Mackenzie Country". Because Jock and Friday found it. Should be called the Mackenzie and Friday Country. You can imagine them. In the snow and wind and rain, in the summer heat, walking up to the saddles of the ranges to see if there was any way through the mountains, walking along the stony riverbeds, walking through the dark, limestony gullies. Jock reading his Bible to Friday at night after they'd lit a fire and had something to eat. Had some sheep to eat, probably.

'It's beautiful country, isn't it? Big and bare and wild, and those blue lakes with the snowy mountains all around. Everyone thinks it's beautiful. William did an advertising campaign based on it. Absolutely Pure. They all went nuts over it, including the Prime Minister. Beautiful, pure, natural, unspoiled, all that kind of thing.

'Yes, I've noticed. Makes you feel strange. You get a bit worked up, I've seen that, Mr Biswas. Tell you what. Me too. Know why? Because it's lonely. It's so bloody lonely. Lonely, lonely, lonely. There's nothing. Nothing for bloody miles and miles except distance. Distance from what? From love, that's from what.

'I said, love.

'From love and everything that goes with it. Including sadness. Including anger and worry and loneliness again. Only it's a different sort of loneliness from empty distance loneliness. It's loneliness with love in it.

'It's how Friday would feel without Jock, out here. It's how Jock would feel without Friday. You think they thought this place was beautiful? I think they thought each other was beautiful. Jock's reading Friday the Bible in Gaelic, in the starry night, under one of those limestone bluffs, with enough firelight to see the book. Friday's watching Jock's whiskers move up and down while he talks to the book. That's what's beautiful.

'So, Jock and Friday found this plain. After the rough, stony, spikey hills and mountains and the narrow gullies with boulders big as houses and the snow and the flooding rivers. There it was, this wide, brown, grassy tussocky plain that just went for miles and miles, with a wall of snowy mountains all around it like a fortress. A safe place. Was it a beautiful place? It was full of Jock and Friday's love. It was huge, but they filled it up.'

'Yes, love, Patricia.' It seems that Biswas has been understanding. There's a hint of quiver in his expression. A moistness in the eyes.

As there is in Patricia's.

'Here's the sad bit. Jock got put in prison for stealing sheep. Maybe he did, maybe he didn't. Steal them. Sure, he and Friday had a feed now and again, but that wasn't it. They said Jock and Friday pinched a whole lot of sheep and took them out here to the Mackenzie Country. So Jock went to prison. Couldn't have his Gaelic Bible.'

'His book.'

'His book, yes. And couldn't have his dog. They took Friday away. And when Jock got pardoned and came out of prison he went looking for Friday. The dog he loved. The dog who made his world beautiful.'

'Finding lovely dog? Saving dog, yes?'

'Well, this is what I think. About the Connie lupins.'

'Connies?'

'Give it a try, Mr Biswas. You'll probably think I'm as mad as a meat-axe. Meat-axe. Never mind. This is a story I tell myself. When I come out here in spring. When the Connie lupins are flowering. When I look at William's tragic identity bloody loneliness and neurosis Absolutely Pure campaign. Never told anyone else. I'm probably telling you because you won't understand. Whatever. Maybe you will.

'I think Jock Mackenzie didn't die. That's what I think. I think he couldn't die until he'd found Friday. Not just that he refused to die – he couldn't. His love wouldn't let him. I think he was still walking all around here, looking for Friday, when Connie what'shername came and settled in the Mackenzie country in 1952. About a hundred years after Jock started looking for Friday out here.'

'Woman who planted the Connies.'

'That's right, Connie who planted the lupins. I think Connie was lonely. She was in the most beautiful place imaginable, but there was no love in it. She was lonely without love. Then one day she met Jock Mackenzie who'd been unable to die because he had so much love for his dog Friday that he just had to.

'Had to keep on.

'Keep on looking – are you all right Mr Biswas?'

'Is very sadness story, Patricia. Now I'm understanding. So sorry about the Connies.' Biswas gestures at the window through which he'd hurled his huge bouquet.

'Well, I don't know. Maybe it's not sad. Here's what I think. This is just my story. I think Connie whatsit fell in love with Jock Mackenzie's love for Friday. Maybe she fell in love with Jock, too. We have to call her Connie Lupins from now on, because that's what she becomes. Jock tells her, one night, by the fire he's lit out on the big open country hoping Friday will see it and come to have the Gaelic Bible read to him again. He tells her that the thing Friday liked next to listening to the Bible in Gaelic was smelling flowers. Jock thought it was because there were hardly any out here, and Friday, being the particularly intelligent dog he was, was greatly attracted to the flowers he did come across. He developed a special taste for them. He'd even get distracted from his sheep-herding work by a flower blooming somewhere in the thorny wilderness. Jock was worried that Friday had been lured from his own wild, bare country by the places with more flowers. Like the Sassenach towns. Sinful towns, Mr Biswas. Like the botanical gardens. Sorry, no, don't know where Gulshan is. Where Jock couldn't go, for fear they'd lock him up again. It was a worry that tormented Jock. Almost as much as the loneliness of his love for Friday.

'So what did Connie Lupins do? She planted flowers, lupins, all over the Mackenzie Country. To get Friday back.

'Excuse me.'

Pat goes to the bathroom to blow her nose. When she comes back, Biswas has his head in his hands. His shoulders are heaving. His sobs are moist, unrestrained, guttural, manly. 'My Keshamoni! Keshamoni!'

'Connie Lupins planted herself,' says Pat. Getting a grip. This thing's spiralled out of control. Didn't think it would have this kind of effect. 'She planted herself all over this country. She planted herself. She planted Connie Lupins for Jock Mackenzie and for Jock's love for Friday. She planted herself for Friday and his dog love for Jock and Jock's whiskers saying the Gaelic Bible. Under the stars, Mr Biswas. Under the beautiful stars.'

Somehow, faced with the Bangladeshi's humid quaking, Pat's ending seems lame. It peters out. She peters out. She feels a bit let down. Even silly.

'Mr Biswas? What's cashamoney? Sorry, it's just a story. Explains how I feel about all this beauty business. Why I went berserk about the lupins. But, cashamoney? Cash money? What are we talking about? You've got a money problem?'

Biswas raises his head – his grief is clear. 'Sorry, Patricia. Thanks, Patricia. Thanks for the talking. Is very good. Very good. I'm understanding. Is about love. Sorry for weeping.'

'So. Right-oh. What's this cash thing?' Let down would be putting it mildly. How Pat feels right now.

'No. Yes.'

'Try "yes", Mr Biswas. Let's not beat about the bush.' Pat sees despair make Biswas grin. 'Never mind "beat about the bush". Cash? Yes?'

'Yes. Is my little sister. Is Keshamoni. Is my Keshamoni. They taking her, Pat. Patricia. Abducting her, my Keshamoni, my little Keshamoni. Wanting ransom cash. Dacoit, Pat, miscreants, wanting cash for Keshamoni.' As she has before, Pat sees Biswas wrestle himself into hot, glaring control. He shakes out a carefully folded handkerchief and wipes his eyes and face. He needs to make his meaning clear. He blows his nose into the handkerchief. What Biswas says next flies out of the sound and effort of his ferocious nose-blowing. It is a noise not like speech but like a honking roar, a bellow, a trumpeting. 'For sex, Pat. For dacoit sex trading, putting

Keshamoni in brothel, in videos. My little Keshamoni. They take her, Pat. I need cash.' His lips have spread clear away from his gums, which are a dark purple colour, from which his white teeth stick out. 'Yes! Cash!'

Biswas stands up. He bashes his neat fists against his bony, echoing chest. He grips his hair and lifts it violently away from his head. He pounds himself on the head. He smacks one open hand against his heart. His eyes are now dry, but filmed over with a cataract-like opacity, as though all he can see is what he is imagining. What he is imagining happening to Keshamoni. His teeth show but not in his familiar smile of fixed, uncertain charm – now his top lip has lifted from his teeth which are thrust forward in an animal snarl. His neck has become a ropey column of sinews where blood pulsates.

'This is my love,' he says, with a gnashing movement of his jaws. His spit flies into Pat's face. 'This my homesickness, my *loneliness*, Pat. This. This, this, this. My loneliness beauty! My beauty. My beautiful Keshamoni. This, Pat.'

There is a globe of love in the heavens; where is the owner? Who can I ask about this? The earth produces nutritious fruits and nuts, the sky produces rain and it never ceases to flow. The sun and moon bring about creation, they are the guardians of that globe, and so they should be. Favoured and blessed are those who have been enriched. Favoured and blessed are dealings in trade. I have not seen the place where all this happens. Lalon says, my life has been lived in vain.

Biswas sings like his hands. His singing is neat. It folds the little turns of melody neatly. He sings in a high voice, with little quavers, with his eyes squeezed shut.

Then, 'Ma'adh Allah! Ma'adh Allah!' He beats his breast again.

Pat doesn't understand the language he's singing in. But she understands the tears that once again flow from under his clenched eyelids. She understands the terrible control that makes his voice perform the little, delicate turns and folds of the singing. What it costs him not to trumpet and scream again like an enraged animal. Why he grips his emotion tightly and twists it into a delicate song she understands better than the word 'beauty'. The word that is supposed to be the meaning of her life.

nine

Desire

Despite its overexcited portal, which combined themes of mountains, rivers and crashing surf done in a frozen tableau of painted, sculptural forms with skis, kayaks and surfboards poking out of it, the interior of the multimedia cinema was warm, suffused with comfortable, rosy light and soothed by a generic, repetitive musical hum with a muffled heartbeat bass thump.

William sank gratefully into his comfortable, moulded seat. Yes, Boris had begun to pitch to him, something about adventure profit margins where supply-side danger experience thresholds sink and demand-side age client thresholds rise. The multimedia staff knew Boris – he even smacked one of them, a young tanned woman, very lightly on the side of the head, and stopped behind to chat.

Bill did not want to admit it, but Joris's lightly erotic, no-special-favours sociability had started to get on his nerves. He had begun to feel disgruntled, even pouty. The formal intimacy of their buddy relationship was one thing, on the 'demand-side', but could there not be more – exclusivity? On the fucking 'supply-side'? The word 'exclusivity' came grudgingly to him and made him wince.

William slumped low in his theatre seat, tenting his ears inside the warm, heavy fabric of his Italian greatcoat. At the same time, the same thoughts made Bill wonder impatiently when Boris was going to come and join him in the comfortable seats. But meanwhile, the warm, rhythmic, salmony interior of the theatre soothed him. He felt a little drowsy. He brought the thumb of his right hand up to his lips, allowing his tongue to stroke the back of it, something he found comforting as well as an aid to thought. Then, all at once, the soothing soundtrack of the multimedia experience introduced a note of urgency and the lighting in the theatre began to obey a computerised synchronisation programme.

How many times, William thought petulantly, do they have to take me by the scruff of the neck and throw me against the wall of their fucking Wonderland? But Joris had now entered the theatre and there was new urgency in the suave Adventure Entrepreneur's voice as he leaned close across the arm of the adjoining seat.

Joris's warm, slightly feral breath in William's ear was insisting that no one was coming any more. No demand. His friends were telling him. The place was dying unless someone rammed a tour coach in backwards and delivered an audience that had been pre-programmed. Even, Bill, fucking sedated, know what I mean? Look: who's watching this shit?

Boris's hand urgently gripped Bill's stringy bicep.

We are, Boris, said a small, contented voice in Bill's head.

On the multiple wraparound screens in front of them a helicopter in a blizzard of exhilarating crystals debouched a grimacing extreme snowboarder whose terrifying velocity down a near-vertical slope of powder snow hurled him into a breathtaking abyss where he became an ecstatically smiling female paraglider skimming the sheer flank of a precipice above crashing white-water rapids far below, where she became a grim-faced male extreme kayaker plunging down a thickly muscled waterfall into boiling rapids, where he joined the furiously paddling crew of an inflatable white-water raft whose dreamlike passage down-river next allowed one paddler to morph into a grinning angler and land a handsome, glittering trout, another to suspend her nose above a glass of wine in a sunlight-dappled vineyard, and yet another (who had become a child) to be welcomed by a swaying, poi-swinging kapa haka group before an impressively carved wharenui on a stretch of crimson pohutukawa-flowered coast where, next, an extreme windsurfer flew high in the air through the breaking curl of an immense wave, before effortlessly beaching herself and, smiling straight-to-camera, being revealed, finally, as a sleekly wetsuited, blonde, glamorous and internationally famous New Zealand Olympic gold medallist.

'Welcome to Our Adventure,' she said, shaking salty hair from her eyes.

And that was the Introduction, because, next, the theatre seats themselves began to vibrate and twist, simulating the movements of extended replays of the adventures already summarised.

The moist plosives in Boris's urgent talk into Bill's ear were, themselves, like details of the strenuously thrilling, spine-tingling experiences on-screen. Bill also felt his body shaken lightly, on occasions enjoyably jarred by the hydraulic, synchronised seating, while his left ear was pleasantly bombarded by Boris's warm, spitty breath, lightly scented with Snifters. While Boris fiercely gripped Bill's goose-fleshed upper arm. While Boris emphatically pointed out the obvious, that no one who did this shit for real was here watching this shit, that the whole shit thing had cost a shit-fucking fortune, he knew, Joris knew, because he'd invested a shitload in this shit, and you know what the mistake is? Bill? That's so obvious? What do you think?

Bill realised, then, as the screen action shifted into a new, unexpected underwater domain with helpless crayfish being wrenched from rocky cracks, that he would have to get his thumb out of his mouth. If he wanted to reply to Boris.

He felt Boris's hand withdraw from his arm. The enjoyable sensation of Boris's humid, angrily beseeching voice in his ear was withdrawn. People in wetsuits were mingling with seals and dolphins. A whale heaved its glistening hump massively into view above the queasily undulating surface of the ocean. The sun set on a tranquil beach. A driftwood barbecue flickered. A city with an illuminated tower glittered in the night distance. His theatre seat stopped quivering.

Bill took his thumb from his mouth as the dreamlike, pinkish ambience returned to the theatre and the music resumed its soothing heartbeat. He saw that Joris was watching him, twisted impatiently sideways in his seat, his expression of agreeable, nondescript equanimity replaced, for the moment William caught it, by a look that had seemed briefly malicious or spiteful.

But then, 'Never mind,' Boris said, lightly. And if he had not been feeling so nice just then, Bill might even have suspected Boris of being droll when he next suggested an ice-cream. To complete the experience.

'Because it's been fun, wouldn't you say, Willy?'

Bill had to make a muscular effort to speak past the dumb, sedated memory of his thumb in his mouth. His reply to Boris emerged thickly, a bit slurred, almost paralysed by the numbing impact of gratification at being called Willy.

'Yes, please, Boris.'

ten

Adventure

'Right-oh,' says Stan a bit ominously, firing his last smoke for a while into the ornamental flax bordering the motel car park. 'This morning she's Aoraki Mount Cook. A real beauty.' He says the portmanteau name 'Aoraki Mount Cook' with a practised elision that gets it out of quotation marks. But he's just about had a bloody gutsful of his busload of wankers whingeing on about the views after pissing up nightly in bars on the project tab. That Bangladeshi Biswas bloke climbs up next to him in the front again – Stan reckons there might be something a bit murky about him. Once again he's got the dark glasses and the All Blacks cap on. But this morning he's not saying much, for a change. Probably because he made a dick of himself last night with the big sheila from DoT.

Can't say the same for Joris. A small party of ageing Japanese tourists wearing bits and pieces of serious alpine tramping gear mixed in with woolly cardigans and tan loafers is mustering daypacks and sheepskin seat-covers by another mini-bus at the motel entrance. The logo on the side of the bus is an amalgam of white-water rapids, snow and a surfer breaking left all stretched into a single, blurred motion. The wind-whipped text powering through the picture along the side of the mini-bus reads: 'Good-2-Go: Add Venture Tours'.

'Mine, mine!' shouts Joris, pointing at the tour party. He grabs William by the arm. 'My people!' The young Japanese woman helping the Good-2-Go tour looks across at the CTI bus – Joris ducks down.

Bill looks at 'my people'. He doesn't say anything: this is unusual, thinks Joris. Maybe he's thinking about the day before yesterday: the multimedia. This was perhaps strange, maybe weird. This silence: Joris leaves his hand on Bill's arm while he explores the silence a bit. Perhaps Bill's changing, he's coming around? Starting to hear what Joris is saying? Maybe it's time for another business talk?

Probably, what the silence means: this looks really, really stupid, the Japanese adventure tour with old people. Fair enough, that's a valid criticism: but. The Add Venture tour people assist each other into the bus dropping hats and spectacles and Stan accelerates bad-temperedly into the stream of campervans leaving Tekapo. But: this 'but' is what we have to think about. But what? Fair enough: the team doesn't say very much about his, Joris's business. Because, be honest now: what's to say? We're going to have a professional team discussion about elderly Japanese tourists in alpine survival gear lifting each other into Joris's Add Venture mini-bus? Sure, he can see how this looks. Demand-side-wise. Fair comment.

True enough, work it out. Simple: Identity and Adventure. As the adventure threshold sinks, the age threshold rises. This cuts into merchandise margins. See: Bill can understand this. Probably: he's thinking about it right now. Because, too, you have to factor in: disposable income, tour culture, economy of effort and the merchandise margins. Not to mention the world political/medical situation. Scandinavians, Canadians: they don't want to bunch up. Hard to organise. Already got too much gear. Not easy enough to terrify. They quite like scary Travel Alerts: this is, remember, anecdotal, qualitative research only. Even the fat Walloons. Back at Milford those Canadian kayak bastards told Joris that protesting Maoris shot at them on the river near Huntly. You believe that? The Canadians convince themselves, Joris understands that much. This make the adventurous Canadians happy. Was probably somebody blowing up willows. Out-of-season duck shooting. Happens all the time. But: they don't want to believe this. Not scary enough!

But: what.

'You're thinking, Bill?' Boris lifts his hand from Bill's arm. It's still clad in his expensive Italian greatcoat. Bill's a bit huddled up this morning. 'You're cold?'

'Not sure what you're asking,' says Bill, looking out the window at the vast, brown Mackenzie Country basin with its scattered outbreaks of absurdly anomalous, colourful, flaunting Connie lupins. 'Are you suggesting there's a connection between my thinking and my body temperature, Boris?'

'Always the joke, eh, Bill?' Get him out of the damn coat, thinks Joris behind his agreeable smile. Get him out of the crazy Florsheim wing-tip shoes. Take off the Kashmir scarf. Change the wrapper, change the packaging, rebrand: maybe the contents will change, too. Have to do something!

But: what.

'You know what, Bill?' says Joris pleasantly.

'I find who and when easier to deal with,' says Bill. Doesn't sound like he's telling a joke, now. He's looking out the window: Joris watches some very small muscles moving at the base of his thin jaw. He's looking for a sign of Bill's smile, the downward groove by the corner of his mouth. 'Content, it's always the problem,' drones William in a schoolteacherish voice. 'Always too much of it, trying too hard, or not enough, no substance. The second part of Darwin's law, Boris. Sexual selection.'

Joris is certainly getting a weird vibe off Bill. Same as usual: they find him, Joris, sexually attractive. So what? What do they want him to do about this? Maybe something a bit weird happened in the multimedia, day before yesterday. Maybe this is just a weird guy. Anyway: usually this works, too. This usually helps. Usually he can make it help. So long as. So long as they don't get too uptight about it. Like that little Japanese tour cunt Seiko.

'Sexual selection, Bill?' Boris makes his voice sound interested but not really. 'You lost me, there. I was going to ask you. Something.'

William turns to face Joris. He is wearing very cool, very black, very lightweight dark glasses: can't see his eyes even a bit. 'Theory of evolution, Boris.' And he's saying 'Boris' all the time, now, too. See? It's happening: same as usual. 'Natural selection says use as little effort as possible and fit in with what's around you. Don't show off content. Think of stackable plastic furniture.' William enjoys his own joke: the skin at the edges of his concealed eyes crinkles and his lips turn downward.

Really: he looks sick. Or is it: unhappy? Can't tell the difference and Joris doesn't understand what he's talking about, but: 'stackable furniture' sounds interesting. But: what? Maybe we're moving in a direction, thinks Joris, as William continues like some kind of schoolteacher, like that scary one in Invercargill when Joris was a kid with his brother Willem in the high school, who used to say things like: 'The Dutch are known as an industrious, businesslike people,' looking straight at Joris and Willem with that completely unfriendly expression.

'But sexual selection,' says William, still crinkled, 'says make a lot of effort and make it show, stand out from what's around you, show off your content. Think Connie lupins, Boris, like the ones all over the place out there, like Mr Biswas. Last night. Natural selection conceals its skill. Sexual selection brags about its virtuosity.' The crinkles disappear. 'Not getting through, am I?'

'To be honest perfectly, Bill, you're way much too intellectual for me,' says Joris, sounding cheerful and unworried about this. 'I'm just a businesslike Dutchman.'

Bill looks at Boris with appreciation – this was a joke, surely? Or maybe not. 'Sure, Boris,' he says. 'Whatever. A very successful one, too. "My people". The adventurous nation of Joris. Your "demand-side". You were going to ask something. I interrupted. You were going to ask what?'

'Exactly: what, Bill. What comes next? There has to be a plan: a theory for what comes next.'

'This is a very, very big question, Boris – how far are we travelling today?'

'Aoraki Mount Cook.' Joris pauses: Bill's just made a joke? He smacks Bill across the side of the head. 'Always joking, Bill. What I mean is, what comes next, adventure-wise? Always, there's a "what" to think about. The next adventure.'

'The next big thing,' says William.

'See, what I do,' explains Joris, 'I dress up people it's easy to frighten in survival gear, send them somewhere safe, no risks for me. I don't mind telling you this, okay? Only risk is, they're not frightened. Then they complain, Bill,' says Joris, sounding quite upset. 'Bad word-of-mouth. Or, worse, they want refunds.' See: now Bill's getting interested. This works better than at the multimedia. Maybe he thinks it's funny. 'Know who's worst, Bill?'

'You mean who doesn't get frightened enough and wants their money back?'

'Completely: it's the Dutch, Bill.' Boris goes to smack William around the side of the head again, but this time he ducks and takes off his expensive dark glasses. 'Absolutely the worst, Bill. Then the Germans. But the Dutch, think about it. Flat, Bill, not like Germany with alps. Completely flat country. Nothing to fall off. So: why?'

See: now Bill's laughing. So: what's so funny about that?

'So, what's the next big thing, is that it, Boris? Next big adventure for flat-earth people? Hard-to-scare flat people? You're asking me?' Bill's out-of-character enjoyment and mirth are attracting the attention of the team – Hinemoana's joke-expecting face appears over the back of her seat, the Biswas peaked All Blacks cap swivels anxiously around from the front. 'You're asking me, Boris?'

'You, Bill. Because you're the best at this stuff. The brand guru. How we can brand terror, Bill? This is the.' Cowpat coughs warningly in the back seat as Joris swerves out of the CTI conflict of interest contract. 'Let's think about the next big thing,' suggests Joris.

'Boris, for Jesus Christ's sake, in case you hadn't noticed, I'm as good as agoraphobic. This must be one of your key tools, Boris. In your terror arsenal. The travelator at O'Hare airport, Chicago, Boris, I was screaming the moment I got on because that was when the end of it began to come towards me. Took six strong diving instructors from the Great Barrier Reef, Queensland, to get me off. This was the international Tourism and Ecology conference two years ago. Ask our Patricia back there. They're still talking about William and the O'Hare travelator. It was the highlight.' William can't help himself. 'That, and Patricia's paper on Branding with Beauty.'

Joris feels the warmth of triumph spread across the entire surface of his body. See: he's changing, Bill is. 'Exactly, Bill. What I mean. You understand fear.' Joris warmly clenches the cloth of William's woollen coat-sleeve in one tanned, smooth hand. 'Is why you wear this, isn't it, Bill? These shoes. Out here, in the wilderness.'

'"Wilderness", Boris?'

'Whatever, Bill. Know what I mean. This is what makes you the best.'

'The best what, Boris?'

'Identity, Bill. And Adventure. How to show it, how to make it real. How to make it frightening.'

He does know this – he does! Joris watches William's laughter suddenly slide back again under the tight, thin skin of his face. He knows. He knows but he's hiding: it's not the pure and the beautiful in his great 'Absolutely Pure' campaign. *It's the fear*. How to make all that pure beauty bullshit look really, really frightening. The fools don't notice. The fear: just sneaks in there. Then they buy Good-2-Go survival parkas.

This is worth money! This is worth geweldig money, Joris, m'n goed zoon. God damn: what do I have to *do*!

Okay, okay: the conflict of interest, confidentiality and non-disclosure clauses in the contract. No interpersonnel business deals, only reports: individual paired-buddy thematic reports, the consolidated team report which Pat will edit. Okay: the executive summary, William has to co-write with Hinemoana to 'sustain the bicultural perspective'. 'Making Cultural Tourism Futures: a Comparative Study.' Blah blah blah. What about now? Okay: 'reports to be the commissioned intellectual property of major funder DoT with subsidiary project-share rights subcontracted to UNDP and Bangladesh Parjatan Corporation/Tourism Bangladesh, New Zealand Trade and Enterprise, the national museum and other local authorities and funding agencies'! Neuken! Fuk! This is a way to do business? Something comes out of that fucken stew?

So: what next? Just keep on. Whatever it takes. Because you only get one chance, Joris, m'n knaap: and this is it.

At the Lake Pukaki scenic lookout, Stan parks aggressively before the grand view up the lake across bizarrely turquoise water to the splendid horizon of upthrusting mountain peaks, including the iconic Aoraki Mount Cook. He waves his arm at this spectacular view, because why bother with these bastards, and walks off lighting a cigarette.

Joris stands at the edge of the viewing platform. What the people who wrote his CTI contract don't know: got to make a shit heap of money. And: there's no fear in this view. His Add Venture mini-bus arrives. The elderly Japanese adventurists begin to video each other in extreme survival parkas and holding alpine tramping poles, with Aoraki Mount Cook in the blue distance. Joris avoids Seiko, a young Japanese guide. Got an attitude: highjack the Jap tours, little cunt, maybe. He sits on a boulder below the scenic lookout.

Look, how simple! Feel small, get lost, get cold, get lonely, die. Absolutely Pure. No one can survive there! Frank and Babs, from Fort Lauderdale, Florida, guess what: afraid of falling over! Surprise surprise! What: falling over in the wilderness? In the scary mountains? Having an adventure experience? No, falling over in the bathroom! The neuken! Fuk! Bathroom!

Joris captures his screaming anti-social laughter with cupped hands over his face. The sound that escapes between his abseiler's fingers resembles the falsetto, feeble keening of someone who's finally lost hope of survival in the primeval wilderness.

Biswas is praying on his mat by the lake, on a smooth patch of grey gravel. The turquoise water laps close to his head. A campervan of three swarthy men has parked near the team bus. The men are dressed in brand-new Southern Naturally woollen sweaters. They stand, smoking cigarettes and looking down at Mohammed Baul Biswas. Their arrogance, especially the hauteur of a thickset man whose wavy hair glistens with oil, is directed at him. One of them flicks his cigarette butt in the Bangladeshi's direction. Another spits. They enjoy a joke while studying the DoT logo on the side of the CTI team mini-bus.

That night, in the lounge adjoining the functions room of the hotel where Hands-On, the Minister for Tourism, is hosting a reception for the project team, the same arrogant men have to be told to go outside to smoke. They are told several times by different members of the hotel staff whom they stare at with provocatively not-understanding looks. Finally they leave, but they do not go outside to smoke next to the bronze statue of Sir Edmund Hillary.

After a mihimihi by the tumuaki of the Iwi Development Corporation and a waiata in which Gloria joins, the Minister for Tourism unclasps his hands from their formal resting place across the groin of his trousers and hopes that the team has been enjoying itself and the splendid hospitality of New Zealand Aotearoa's hospitality industry. Because hospitality is our business and we want you to feel hospital – at home. We are a mature industry with a proud history of hospitality. Remember the icons: Thorpe Talbot's guide to hot springs *A Month in Hot Water*, 1872, sounds all right doesn't it, the nineteenth century's answer to the jacuzzi; the first Hermitage, 1884, nothing like a bit of fresh air even then to get the appetites revved up; the Grand Hotel in Rotorua, 1895, slapping on a bit of hot mud still popular, said to have a number of beneficial effects, can well imagine, must try it one day; Maggie Papakura and the Duke of Cornwall, 1901, and beautiful women are still one of our prime assets. The Minister coughs deprecatingly at his own risqué jokes and corrects the gender balance: The Tourist Department guides at Mount Cook around 1914 – what a good-looking bunch: the famous Peter Graham, Frank Milne, looked great in a suit and tie with climbing boots, a match for the tumuaki here, you must tell me where you get your suits, tumuaki. Wonder what Freda du Faur thought about the dress code on the top of Mount Cook with Peter Graham in 1910? Pretty cold up there. The great Rodolph Wigley's 'Height of Happiness' campaign for this very place in 1927, the modern concept of the naughty weekend, no I didn't say that. The New Zealand Railways 'Wonder Country' campaign, still works for us, getting on for a century later. What a proud history, what a rich history. What a contribution to our nation. But there is potential for us to grow, in particular to grow in partnership with our tangata whenua, our indigenous people of the land. Because this is what makes us special and unique as a destination. This and our beautiful landscape. Because the Maori are distinguished for their hospitality, and I know they will have done everything to make you feel at home in this beautiful landscape that we are blessed to share. 'Enjoy the manaakitanga and the kai,' says the Minister, with rehearsed confidence. 'We are looking forward to your words of visionary advice and to cooperating with our professional friends in the burgeoning hospitality business. And now without further adieu. Make yourselves at home. I know I'm going to.'

'"Without further *adieu*",' quotes a delighted William, who has winced his way through the speech while beginning to drink seriously.

'Praise God, that gorgeous man can *dress*,' marvels Gloria, leaving the Development Corporation tumuaki wrangling an indigeneity conversation with Biswas. 'And this is not bad, either.' She directs a plate of dinky wee whitebait fritters on toothpicks towards Ants. 'But just you wait till we get out to the Coast – I'll show you whitebait fritters the size of dinner plates for a fraction the price. Get some . . .' She motheringly inserts a fritter in Ants's mouth instead of saying, 'flesh on those bones', but Ants hears it and obediently snaps her wee jaws shut on the morsel.

'What's really needed,' says Cowpat to the Minister, whose attention has begun to wander from the professional business of the evening, 'is an entrepreneurial innovation venture capital fund. Specifically for new concept development in the tourism industry. Seeding money. Spending delegated to portfolio managers. Conceptual cross-fertilisation with unlike cultures. Right now, our innovation-response time is lagging. Behind.'

'Give me an example,' says Hands-On, whose manner with the catering staff might seem overfamiliar to some.

'Beauty.' Pat forges ahead. 'It's a concept whose values are changing, even eroding. Rapidly. In a world where.'

'Behind whom,' says the Minister.

'Bangladesh, would be one interesting example,' tries Pat.

'You're telling me it would, Patricia, though "interesting" is not a word I see surviving on the report page and please, dear, don't give me an action plan with impoverished partners in it,' says Hands-On, departing with his glass towards an attractive hospitality professional.

'What, man, you're telling me your indigenous hill tribes are resisting the financial benefits of tourism?' The DC tumuaki is grappling with the Biswas analysis.

'Armed resistance, isn't it. Smuggling AK47 from Bandarban

to Rangamati. And resisting eco-park.' The Bangladeshi's attention flits back and forth to the adjacent lounge from which the sullen group of dark smokers has been evicted.

Then there is the evening's highlight moment when Hands-On and Patricia walk firmly and even hastily from the room. The brief silence in which the functions room door sighs shut behind them has been caused by the sounds of breaking glass and angry shrieks. 'I don't fucking care if he's the fucking Minister of the fucking . . .'

'See: feels different, doesn't it, Bill?' asks Boris, much later. Bill's very, very drunk. Boris has him kitted out in Good-2-Go franchise survival gear. 'Feels like a different you, doesn't it, Bill? A new one. Ready for an adventure. Next big thing, Bill.'

'So. How do I look?' slurs William.

Try: straight ahead, thinks Joris. When he says the thought aloud, Bill doesn't think it's funny. Bill isn't thinking anything.

When Joris smacks William across the side of his head this time his glasses fly off and he falls sideways onto the divan. Joris picks the glasses up but doesn't bother giving them to William because he's passed out. A tiny thread of blood runs from his nose. Look: pathetic. Bill's skinny white feet extend from the cuffs of quick-drying, lightweight, wind-proof overpants. His open mouth is nestled on the sleeve of his red Gore-Tex parka. Joris drops William's expensive glasses on the coffee table from waist height and goes out carelessly slamming the door and leaving the light on.

In the morning, rain is promised but the project team walks up the scenic Hooker Valley in thin sunshine. Joris watches the newly packaged William in his red, Good-2-Go alpine adventure gear. William's gait is bandy because of the swaddling pants. His feet in strong boots strike down at the uneven rocks. His arms swing stiffly in the new parka.

'Didn't even take it off last night,' Bill confessed wretchedly at the assembly point. First time anyone had seen his bleak, grey stubble. Boris was closely shaved and shining. 'I know,' he laughed. 'You passed out, Bill! Right there on your sofa! Fresh air soon fix you up.'

How do I look.

It's true, m'n knaap: he's different. Different, maybe changing: good, excellent.

The well-formed path meanders among boulders and spiky Spaniards, pretending to be a stony mountain track. It is bordered by dry-stone walls pretending to be the piled-up edges of screes or water-courses. Joris watches the padded-out Bill walking along: feeling safe, you can tell. How? He's walking like he's *inside* the clothes: inside the shelter. Got his frightened body inside a shell. He's feeling this difference.

All around, the grey and white mountains, glaciers, screes and snowfields rear up and crowd in. They overhang with huge black and white bulks, their cloud-whipped, icy peaks pierce into enormous space and distance. The sky is blue, grey, full of blowing, freezing white clouds. The plants are harsh, savage, able to withstand extremes. Their flowers rise above the brutal, olive-green foliage on thick, scaly stems. In places, the tussocky grass has been flattened by immense weights of snow. There is a memorial cairn to climbers who have perished in these mountains. The eulogies praise their love of wildness and daring and are confident that they are at rest where they chose to be. There are distant cracking and thundering sounds of avalanches, of gigantic, unmeasurable forces. The chilly wind, with spits of icy sleet, is blowing out of a huge nowhere.

Bill walks bulkily through this, his arms and legs moving stiffly. His armour is a bright, warm red, and his body feels warm and braced inside it, as though in flexible, heated pipes. His feet, in stiff, light boots, are impervious where they strike the jagged stones of the path. His alpine walking poles steady him.

Then the path descends to a narrow swing-bridge over the rushing river. Joris watches William's body language change: sees him look around secretly for the reactions of the team. No one else reacts. Feel the fear you fuk. Joris wants to hit him: hit him really hard. Feel it: then keep going. He puts a hand on the small of William's back: it's stiff, like a plank. William crosses the bridge with the short, halting steps of a marionette. At the other side, the look Bill turns back at Boris is weak, triumphant, like after sex.

How do I look?

The river foams, white, over rocks. In the distance, above the head of the valley, the sky is glaring and blue, the mountains black in shadow on one side and dazzling in icy sunlight on the other. Bill's boots make the rocks clank and clash together like metal. They crunch down on sharp gravel. The harsh plants begin to include alpine flowers: there are fleshy white blooms rising from thick green leaves. A narrow boardwalk snakes across wet tundra: Bill's dainty, precarious footsteps become more stride-like. Joris takes his discreet hand from the back of Bill's parka. At the second swing-bridge, higher and narrower than the first, Joris does not put his hand on Bill's jacket and Bill does not look back over his shoulder on the other side. Some cold rain falls, making the path into a little creek. When it clears, the rocks and dark-coloured plants are shining and the air around the looming precipices and snowfields, the blue sky itself and the streaming and billowing clouds high in it among the immense peaks, seem to have been refocused. Steam is rising from Bill's walking body, and the air that he sucks into his hot lungs is cool and clean.

Joris can see this: he can see that the soft, weak body inside the Good-2-Go padded shell is feeling okay and this is very good: this is going to make a change.

Mist descends, it enters Bill's lungs and makes him cough, it collects in his nostrils and fogs his dark glasses. When the mist lifts, the project team has reached the grim desolation of the terminal moraine lake. They stand at its grey edge, breathing the ancient chill of filthy ice and thick, slaty liquid. Clanking slips of gravel rattle into the water from the crumbling scree walls of the valley. Strange growths of brownish ice sprout and sway in the turgid brew. The fresh snow of the mountain is distant now, measured by the bleak foreground. The team's steaming breaths impersonate the rising breath of the waters, cold, poisonous, sad, unspectacular.

'Know what this makes me think of?' Gloria's face is vivid with sweat – she turns her back on the dismal moraine.

'Stalin,' suggests William. He can't make the joke go any further, into landscape gardening, say. His body is warm and safe but he is shocked by this nightmare arrival.

'Coffee,' says Gloria, cheerfully, 'is what I'm reminded of. Bacon and eggs. Then, more coffee. Out of here, guys. Back to the four-star whare.'

In the flowery alpine meadow on the way back, on the artfully sinuous boardwalk, Joris sees his people approaching from the other direction. This is, maybe: not good. Not such good timing. The mostly elderly Japanese Good-2-Go: Add Venture tourists are advancing with caution along the wire-netted, non-slip surface of the elevated path. They're clad in Joris's red, high-quality franchised survival gear and they're grappling with alpine walking poles and video cameras. Still good margins on the survival gear but: declining sales. Low danger and rising age thresholds: looking like shit for longer term sustainability. Harder and harder to move volume: push profit above cash flow.

Coming in front is Seiko. The project team and the inching-forward elderly Japanese prepare to pass each other. 'Boss man,' Seiko says tauntingly. 'Good morning to you! How is the adventure weather up ahead!' An excited male voice crackles on her hand-held.

Joris keeps his manner light, flirtatious, amusing. 'This is my number-one guide, Seiko, like the watch: always comes on time.' He allows the bantering hint of innuendo to enliven his tone. 'Fully trained, the best at her job.' Bill's not laughing. 'So: checking the weather conditions, is it, Seiko? Mountain forecast? Avalanche warnings?' This is their in-house joke: part of the adventure experience script. He can see Bill paying attention but pretending not to: be careful, Joris warns himself.

'Absolutely right, boss,' says Seiko, translating for her nodding group while directing the excited, crackly male voice on her radio-phone towards Joris. 'Is my best weather man. Right now he's telling me what I'm missing.' Then, what Joris has dreaded: Seiko puts her ungloved thumb slowly in her mouth and withdraws it again, slowly. Gives a glistening thumbs-up sign. 'What you're missing, too, boss,' she says: little cunt. 'Have a nice day, everyone.'

Nodding konitchiwas, the courteous Japanese edge past. Their courtesy extends to not noticing William, who has suddenly lurched from the track and fallen to his waterproofed knees in the ecologically vulnerable heathers, alpine grasses and Mount Cook lilies of the soaking meadow to the side of the raised boardwalk. He retches miserably and uncontrollably, ejecting a dreadful, burning bile of envy and shame. That glistening, taunting thumb sliding out of Seiko's mouth.

How do I look? mocks the icy, furious mimic in Joris's head.

'Oh, whoops,' he says affably, while the project team measures its scant compassion for William against Hinemoana's dream of hot breakfasts. 'Looks like poor old Bill got altitude sickness.'

eleven

Home

The scenic attraction – the glacier! – has gone. The signs point to what is not there and therefore to what you can't see but they also point to what you could have seen fifty years ago!

This is what goes on amusing Antsy in the bar of the Glacier Hotel – the new one! Because the old one is not there any more either! The new one that points to the old one you are not in! Ants returns to her joke like a retrieving dog to its owner. She comes puffing back to it after silences that get shorter each time. The glaciers themselves have withdrawn, groaning and creaking, up the valleys they have created, their own brutal tracks or traces, the signs of themselves, and they are now reached, if at all, past a whole series of signage announcements (white on red). Their barefaced optimism keeps Antsy tittering.

'Wasn't it just great?' mimics Antsy. 'In 1954 you could have seen the glacier but now you can't! Is that fun, or what? And look! Now you can't see it in 1964 either! Or 1980! Here and now you can't see the glacier in 1954, 1960 and 1980! Talk about authentic! Talk about adding value!'

For that matter – and as a bonus – you can't see the Glacier Hotel that burnt down in 1954, when the glacier you can't see in 1954 was still there because it was still 1954 – the hotel that the celebrated alpinists Alex and Peter Graham struggled to keep alive, the same debonair guides who got Antsy's vertically compelled compatriot, the cat-like Aussie, Freda du Faur, to the top of Mount Cook in 1910 wearing, if the commemorative photograph in the bar is to be believed, suits and ties. But you can't see the dashing Alex and Peter Graham, or the aquiline Freda du Faur either, because it's not 1910 or 1954 any more, and they're not there any more, like the glacier isn't there any more!

Ants's titters are being shared by Bill, who, after a time of sullen resistance inside his Good-2-Go jacket, enjoyed the day's joke during their excursion to the timid, retiring ice.

'Iced,' says Bill with relish. 'Peter, Alex, Freda – chilled.'

'It is a new kind of monument!' suggests Ants. 'Or even a new kind of memorial. It is certainly a new kind of monu-mentality – a monumental absence! Or, in fact, a monumental suite of absences!'

'A tranche of AWOL's,' Bill contributes.

'1954 is absent! The glacier is absent! Peter and Alex and Freda are absent! The Glacier Hotel is absent! It is a whole new kind of visitor experience!'

'Time, an ever-moving stream. The illusion. The dharma.' Bill pretends to be a priest, a sadhu, a monk.

'We invite you to experience the absence of 1954 and everything that was present in it!' Antsy rushes on. 'Right here, on the site of this monument! That you can't see! This wonderful monument which is, of course, a nowhere! It is this valley *empty* of ice, it is this bush *replacing* the hotel site, it is *memories* of flesh-and-blood Peter and Alex and Freda! And how do you know where to find the monument to these not-here-nesses? How do you know where to *be* in order to *not be* in 1954? Read the sign!'

'The shadow,' says Bill, raising his glass. 'The spectre!'

'Go girl,' says Gloria a little carefully, keeping an eye on the skinny, chirping Aussie. Gloria is being frugal with her wine tonight and she has made a sullen blankness cover her face. Her air of patient menace is making Antsy babble. There is a light dew of perspiration above Gloria's heavy lips. Her eyelids are lowered over her carnelian eyes and she is counting the steady rhythm of a thought, slowly, with one red fingernail on top of the polished granite bar.

'You okay, Glor?' asks Ants.

'Glaciated,' enunciates Bill with relish. He is drinking soda water tonight but shapes the word with the self-congratulatory concentration of a drunk. 'Cryogenicised.' He lifts his glass of fizzing water and rattles its ice cubes. 'The Big Chill,' he salutes. 'Here's to the Long Cold One!'

Ants and Bill clink glasses. A visible shiver races through Ants's little body.

But Bill is warm. He is warm in these different clothes, in his new brand, in his nickname, in Antsy's company. At the same time he is freezing in Joris's absence.

'So: what's funny?' Joris demanded, as the 'absent signified' jokes started up in the bus. His sharp elbow dug Bill in the ribs where he was leaning over the back of his seat towards Antsy. 'What you think I have to do every day? Sell danger to clients who want to be safe? To clients who want to be scared about what isn't there any more anyway, but want me to make them feel as if it is still there, dangerous, and that they do want it?'

'Come off it, Boris,' Ants admonished him as the bus followed the track of the absent glacier. 'It's not as if you don't know what's being exploited here.'

'This doesn't fuck you up? And isn't this the kind of problem this neuken team is working about? That the $300,000 a year geniuses like Bill are supposed to be cracking?' This thumb-sucker? Joris did not say 'thumb-sucker' but Bill saw a look of cold scorn on his smiling face.

'We were just joking, Boris,' he said.

'You think this is funny?'

In the car park before the walk up to the ice-fanged face of the retiring glacier, some of Old Bonky's relatives were plying their trade. Simultaneously an experience and its pimp, both indigenous and ethnographic, the trouping keas were hustling the attractions of themselves among the campervans. They were sharing picture frames with package tours against the backdrops of the scenic tour coaches, with the children of rental-car holidaymakers from Sweden, Great Britain, Australia and the USA, with backpackers from Germany and Argentina. They were accepting the furtive inducements of illegal baksheesh food. They were defending their patches.

'What about this, Boris?' asked Gloria. 'You think this is funny?'

'I think it's fucked,' said Joris.

'What would you know?' That was when Gloria walked to the edge of the stony car park as if she was getting away from herself, not from Joris. There was that time Uncle Mat was up a ladder at Waiomio fixing the guttering – there were lots of people at the marae and he looked down and saw his niece letting those guys from Whangaroa flirt with her – they were flicking at the hem of her dress. He came down the ladder and she saw the uh-oh look on his face, but he folded the ladder and walked past them. Didn't say anything and didn't need to. His presence stayed behind as Uncle Mat's stiff back went around the corner with the ladder on his bony shoulder – the Whangaroa guys tried to laugh him away, but he couldn't be laughed away, even when the actual Uncle Mat had deliberately walked away from himself and what he might have done to the kids from Whangaroa.

The next night she stood up with the others in the wharenui after Uncle's korero and sang Kawiti's takuate as Uncle had demanded, the one where her Ngati Hine ancestor lamented the divisions among Ngapuhi. That made her cry. 'Good job, too,' said Uncle. 'Get some sense.' 'Good riddance,' was what he said when she told him she was going to work in Wellington. 'Maybe that way you'll remember who's your whanau. Doubt it, though.' Old bugger. When he walked away from her that time he left behind the old man whose bony embrace, smell of Vicks vapour-rub and teary face never did leave. Every so often, he'd be there again. He was there in the glacier car park – way too far from home.

She could feel the scratchy woollen front of his workshirt and hear the whistle in his breathing.

Uncle Mat's in the bar, now, too. She can hear his screechy breath, just by her ear. This is how much he loves her – to be where he doesn't know anyone and where they're all talking shit. 'Like a ditch full of frogs.'

Good to have you back, koro, Gloria tells him. I missed you.

Biswas is not in the bar – though the dark, smoking men are. They are sprawled commandingly in the lounge area, arguing over balance sheets. One of them flaunts an illegal cigarette, waving it about high in the air with the tips of all the fingers of one hand. They are drinking tea from a tea service on a tray and using toothpicks to select sweetmeats from a box. They hunch together over the sweetmeats box, grinning and deciding, comparing notes in a guttural foreign language. No one is telling them not to smoke – here, as not at Aoraki Mount Cook, they seem to have smoking rights.

Joris is refilling their teacups and gesturing with Good-2-Go brochures.

'See?' His neat voice, pitched up at sales frequency, easily crosses the bar. 'What they don't see they don't miss?' The men are not offering him the treats in their box.

'You okay, Glor?' asks Pat. 'Gone a bit quiet. No party mates tonight?'

Uncle Mat's bronchial whistle – what he used to call his bat squeak. His morning cough, like the roosters up on the hill next to Ruapekapeka, Kawiti's bat cave. The old bat. Leave me alone, you old bat. Go home. No, don't leave me – don't you dare.

Gloria's look at Cowpat is long and careful. 'We could start with you, girl. What's going on?'

'You mean old Biswas? Bizzo? Balls?'

'I don't know – do I mean old Busy Balls?' Gloria makes a gesture of ebullient flowers – she spreads her arms, encircling something profligate and absurd. 'This was weird, the other night?'

Pat takes her time. She draws a long swallow from her tall glass of beer. She keeps Gloria in her sights. The way her head is shaking, you can't tell if it is denial or disbelief. 'He's very homesick, Mr Biswas,' says Pat, taking another substantial swallow. 'Beats me why. All those floods etcetera. Over there.'

'This,' Gloria reassembles the absurd armload, 'was *homesick*?'

'Mr Biswas has a little sister,' says Pat. 'He misses her.'

Gloria does the profligate flowers again, this time with a melodramatic quiver in her fingers and with arched brows. 'A *little sister*? This?'

Pat's glass is empty.

'Come on, girl. You can trust Gloria. Promise I won't tell anyone.'

Pat waves for refills. 'I'm a big girl, Glor.' Her smile is artful.

'So am I,' says Gloria. 'Doesn't mean I can't get spooked.'

'So – who's spooking you?' asks Pat. She is looking where Gloria is too, at the dark men grinning over their sweetmeats and the attendant Joris. 'Don't tell me it's our old mate Joris?' She samples her fresh drink – Gloria says nothing. 'Hell's teeth, Glor. You know better.'

'Of course I do, fool,' says Gloria. 'But I'll tell you what's spooking me.' Shut up, Uncle. 'I've got to do my job. Then I've also got to do Uncle Mat's job. Then I've got to do the Maori woman job.'

'Who's Uncle Mat when he's at home?'

Gloria ignores the question and she ignores Uncle's bat squeaks. 'I'm a fun girl,' says Gloria. 'And here I am, always the one who has to do the heavy stuff.'

'Your wee Aussie mate gives you a good run for your money.'

'You see the looks on their faces – "Uh-oh, here comes

Gloria again." They get the uh-oh look. Especially Stan. I really get up his nose.'

'I blame "Uncle Mat",' says Pat.

'You'd get on,' says Gloria. 'But no, he's not "a big girl". Skinny little bugger. You should see him go over a five-bar gate. Should have seen him.'

'No relation, clearly, then.' Pat is still watching Joris attending to the sweetmeat eaters. 'What's our entrepreneurial mate up to? May have to read his contract to him again.'

At the far side of the room, the smoking men have made a polite heap of Joris's brochures and pushed them away to one side of their tea table. They continue to grin as they select treats from their box and to make stabbing gestures at their balance sheets. Joris has a shruggy 'that's-okay' smile on his face – he's offering the men thin Dutch cigars, which they are also politely refusing.

'Like, from Indonesia, Brazil, Colombia and Cuba. Outside leaf from Indonesia, binder leaf is Javanese Besuki. Inside from Brazil, Indonesia, Cuba. The best, only.' Joris holds one of his Dutch cigars under his own nose and mimes ecstasy.

The large man with the slickly waved, oily hair turns his full gaze on Joris's enthusiasm. He looks at the slender, smiling man with the cigar under his silly nose. The extreme politeness of the dark man's expression is not matched by his flat intonation. 'Tum kaun ho?'

'I'm sorry?' says Joris.

'Who you are?'

'Everest,' says Antsy – she and Bill are playing their new chain-branding game about what is not there.

'On top of the world,' finesses Bill.

'Lady Bowen Falls.' Ants clinks her glass on Bill's.

'Breakneck.'

'God almighty, Glor,' says Pat, surveying her team. 'Think we can pull this one off?'

Gloria takes a frugal sip of her excellent wine.

'Come on, Glor,' says Pat. 'You know me. No "uh-oh" here.'

'See, here's the thing.' Gloria turns herself on full bore. 'Every night so far this trip, which is not any different from a dozen other trips you and I've done, most of them with very fine objectives and an excellent team of gifted people – every night, Pat, there's only been one game in town with this mob. I'm sure you've noticed.' Gloria adds the last phrase with perfunctory politeness – she has no intention of stopping while Pat agrees or disagrees with anything. 'Our brainy little Ocker cobber's dying, Pat, and all she can really think about is going home. Not back home to some wee flat full of academic cultural studies journals, but dying. Going home. Guess how she thinks about the bus ride and where it's going? The views out the window?'

'Shit,' says Pat. 'She told you this?'

Gloria doesn't stop. 'Our other intellectual mate over there has spent his whole grown-up life trying to impress the parents, long dead, who wouldn't ever let him feel at home when he was there and only a poor little kid. Fucked him up big time. What's more, in case you hadn't noticed, he's got a serious crush on our entrepreneurial Dutch friend, why? Because Joris makes it all look effortless, like it would've had to be if poor wee Willie was ever going to make his parents let him feel at home. What about that tragic sailing boat story, Pat? Jesus wept. Too late to get home now, poor sod.' Gloria sips and Pat keeps quiet. 'Okay, so what about our sexy Dutch friend? He had a home once, a beauty, in Holland. But when they left, when he was so young he doesn't *really* remember it, only the family stories about it, he had to go on and on pretending that emotional rabbit was chicken. Poor bugger – only home he's got now is success that's pet rabbit dressed as chicken dinner. The man's a psycho. Speak of the devil.'

Joris joins them at the bar. 'Gora kutte se bara hai,' he says, cheerfully. 'That means a horse is larger than a dog, in Urdu.'

'I think,' suggests Pat, 'it's probably an insult, Boris.'

'You think so?' Boris has an armful of Good-2-Go brochures.

'And,' says Pat, 'you're not meant to be doing that, Joris. Trading.'

'Moving right along.' Gloria's glass is, finally, empty and she waves for a fresh one. 'Poor Mr Biswas, you say he's homesick. I think he knows what his home is, but there's something majorly fucked-up going on there and you're not talking about it. You know something, don't you? That we don't?'

'What about me?' asks Pat, ignoring the Biswas probe.

'You, Pat? Like you said early on: fed, fucked and financial. Don't look back. No regrets. Yep, you're a big girl, but you're a lonely big girl.'

Pat ignores this as well. 'And you – Hinemoana?'

'I'll tell you what.' This time Gloria takes a substantial mouthful of her wine. 'I listen to you jokers rabbiting on, excuse me Joris, about signs to what's not there, and then I watch the bloody keas begging in the car park at the glacier. I listen to a load of bullshit about hospitality from the Minister of feeling-up-the-waitresses, and so on and bloody on, and I think, Where are you, Hinemoana? Get your bloody feet back on the ground, girl.'

Joris smacks his sheaf of brochures on the bar and loudly orders a drink.

'Uh-oh,' says Gloria, sipping.

'Don't stop now,' says Pat. 'Just when you're getting to the juicy bit.'

'What bit's that?' Ants and Bill have stopped their 'absent signifieds' game and Antsy crutches herself closer. 'What's juicy?'

Gloria's rant gives off physical heat – a dew of moisture glistens above her lip. 'Every night, guys, all we really talk about is home. Home. After a few drinks, home, what is it? Where are we when we're there, at home? How to get back there, home? What's this all about?'

'Home, home on the range,' croons Bill.

'Shut up, Bill.' Joris's smile is amiably nasty. 'Is not funny.'

'Here's what I think, anyway,' says Gloria, softly. The effort of restraint makes her breathless. 'Every day we drive somewhere. We drive past clotheslines with nappies on. We whizz past old places with hay in them. We meet people in towns who're going home somewhere else after they've served our lunch. Every inch of the highway is someone's home. Every scenic view, every historic place. Is or was. Sometimes you can't see the signs to it because they aren't on signposts. And often you can't see the homes because they're inside people. Living people, dead people, doesn't matter. Alive or dead, it's all the same.'

Joris is loudly ordering another drink.

'I see dead people,' mouths William – but silently.

'You can't view these places!' Gloria's voice makes a melodrama of the word 'view' – she lifts it up like a trophy in the bar decorated with tremendous images of toppling ice and primeval forests. 'Because they're not out there to look at. They're in here!' Gloria presses her trembling, operatic fists into herself below her breasts. 'There's nothing "out there".' She is breathless. 'Also,' she allows herself a prima donna-ish sip of wine, and dabs her top lip with a hanky, 'also, 1954's not in the past, either. But that's another story.'

'Those bastards,' says Joris, quaffing smoothly. 'Know what?' He notices the silence. 'What, I'm interrupting something?'

'Don't tell me,' pants Gloria, allowing Joris to terminate her outburst. 'They want to open kebab franchises?'

'You guessed this?' Joris is impressed.

'I overheard this,' says Gloria. 'What, Boris, you don't like kebabs?'

'No,' says Joris, 'I mean, yeah, I like kebabs fine. But they don't like adventure.'

'Falafel Tours.' Bill tries a joke.

Antsy's lips are pursed as though she is about to whistle, but she doesn't.

'Whoa, fellas, don't all look at me,' says Gloria. 'I'm done. Hinemoana's weird spooky Maori shit.' She lifts her wine glass – its fresh rim wears the carmine trace of her absent lips. 'Talk amongst yourselves, team.'

In the lounge room of his hotel suite, Mohammed Baul Biswas has been home. He is calm. He looks calmly at the luxurious room. His mouth is fresh, though it has vomited. It is fresh because he washed it out three times before praying. As is proper. Indeed, today, he has prayed six times not five, but the sixth was necessary. He chewed a piece of cinnamon stick after washing his mouth and praying. Now, he ejects the chewed cinnamon carefully into the palm of his hand and, walking to the bathroom, drops it into the toilet.

Biswas does not like to sit on this toilet and he has perfected a technique of holding himself above it by using the disabled handles. He has bought himself a plastic mug decorated with a picture of a kiwi, to use as a lota, for washing after relieving himself. Biswas does not like that there is a toilet in the washing place but he is glad to understand the use of the bidet.

In the bathroom mirror his face is calm, but he splashes it with fresh water one more time. He is disgusted by the plug that keeps used water in the basin and his splashing wets the floor. He combs his hair again, holding the comb in the fingers of his right hand and following it with the palm of his left hand. His palm oily now with Ayurvedic henna oil, Natural brand. He washes his hands and rinses the comb also. He plucks loose hairs from it with a tissue and drops the tissue in the waste container by the hand basin. Putting his comb back in the cabinet above the hand basin, with hair oil and shaving tools.

Biswas looks at the bathroom. It has five taps but, really, it has nine taps. Because four of them producing both hot and cold water. The flushing tap for the toilet only producing cold water, but the taps for the bath, shower, hand basin and bidet all producing hot as well as cold water. The bath also has jacuzzi nozzles at the sides and, as well as using all the taps in the bathroom, Biswas has tried the jacuzzi jets of water mixed with air.

There is a retractable washing line above the bath and on it Biswas has hung the lunghi and the shirt in which he vomited. Next to the vomiting lunghi and shirt he has hung his boxer shorts and the pair of white athletic socks he wears with the boots Joris gave him. Biswas does not like these boots as they are complicated to take off and put back on again and they make the simple, cleansing routines of namaz clumsy when they should be soothing. Also, they smell – he keeps them in a plastic bag on the suitcase rack in the foyer near the door of his suite.

The bathroom has two mirrors, but really five. Because mirror above the hand basin is in three parts, so you can see to the sides of your face and in addition there is a small magnifying mirror on a retractable stem that you can use to look up your nose or closely at your skin.

The fifth mirror is a large, floor-to-ceiling one that you see yourself in when getting out of shower. Feeling quite playful at that moment before his cellphone rang, Biswas posed for himself, smiling shyly, naked, with the shower cap on his head for a joke. His thin, dark, hairy body looked familiar and though his family had always washed modestly at the village ghat with their lunghis or saris on, Biswas recognised in his own naked body's reflection the familiar, frugal shape of his family's body. He took off the shower cap and touched his right hand to his heart.

When he first entered this bathroom, the most splendid on the trip so far, he turned on all the taps and stood there in the middle of the white-tiled floor listening to the sound of the water pouring away. Then he used the toilet and the bidet, he shaved in the hand basin with hot tap running and then took a bath with jacuzzi-jets. Then washing his hair in the shower and rinsing his body after jacuzzi bath.

It was after this and after putting on a fresh lunghi and shirt that his cellphone rang and Mohammed Baul Biswas went home.

Now he returns to the lounge room of his suite and stands in the middle of it. Smelling of soap. He looks at the sepia-coloured historical photographs of the glacier that is no longer there and imagines that the soap smell comes from the melted ice. On the low, glass-topped coffee table there are brochures for helicopter and aeroplane rides for the glacier that remains. Also brochures for walking on glacier and climbing walls of ice – the brochures show people in red adventure garments, like Good-2-Go, waiting in queues to climb up ice cliffs using ice picks.

There is a large television set that Biswas has not tried and a cable decoder box for it. In the bedroom, which has an enormous bed that almost suffocated Biswas when he tried it, there is another television and cable decoder facing the bed and there is also a radio with an alarm clock. In the lounge, whose walls are covered in cream paper with leaf patterns, there is a minibar with soft drinks, wine, beer, and small bottles of whisky and gin. There is a microwave oven and there is a hot-water jug with sachets of tea, coffee and Milo. There are biscuits, nuts, sugar and salted pretzels.

There are three telephones in the suite: one in the bedroom, one in the lounge and a third telephone in the bathroom. Biswas was astonished to find a telephone there, with toilet and washing together. But it was his own cellphone that rang, summoning Mohammed Baul Biswas home.

Is true, doubtless, Key Performance Indicator, thinks Biswas so calmly he can smell the soap scent going in and out of his nostrils many times. His calmly nodding head makes the leaf shapes on the wallpaper move up and down in his eyes. True: life is female. What am I, Mohammed Baul Biswas, descendant of haj family, without Prakriti? Without you, my sister. My bird, my soul, can't fly without you, my little Keshamoni. My soul bird.

On the tiny screen of his cellphone appeared Keshamoni facing the camera that has sent Biswas this picture of her. Her naked legs thin and girl-gangly, hands held together before her private part, little too-young breasts like lemons, skinny ribs. Hair uncovered and untidy, not like Keshamoni. Keshamoni's beautiful hair. And sad look on face. Eyes not looking. Biswas knew this awkward body though he had never seen it. Never wanted to look at it and never wanted to see again.

In the sad-shame picture of Keshamoni, Biswas saw the modest body of his family, all gone except Keshamoni. And then he dropped the cellphone to run to the bathroom, he made the picture of Keshamoni go away from his mind. He made his Secret Bird, his black Dhaka crow, his soul man, fly into the small screen in his mind, spreading its wings across the screen. Making him calm as he vomited many times into the toilet, as he held himself steady with the disabled handles. Hearing the flush of the toilet's cold tap wash away the picture of Keshamoni's shame eyes not looking at him. *Not here, dada, my big brother – this is not Keshamoni, Keshamoni is not here.*

'No, my little Keshamoni,' Biswas says calmly to his Invisible Bird, while the wallpaper flowers go up and down in his eyes and the scent of soap goes in and out of his nostrils – 'Keshamoni is not there.'

twelve

Hospitality

Yes, it is difficult – very difficult, agrees the hotel manager. This is a young dark woman whose accent Pat files as professionally laundered. The woman herself Pat classifies as monogrammed. Talk about feeling like an old warhorse. All the same, old warhorse Pat knows how to stand still and breathe through her nose. The old warhorse can see that the newly monogrammed manager is just the kind of product the industry wants. Points on the board.

Sunshine's just what the industry wants, too. Tweety birds. Nice smell of blossom. The glassy façade of the hotel sparkles. So do the manager's spectacles. Maybe the blossomy smell is her. Pat's visualising school exercise books with neat underlining in coloured ink. 'Have a nice day.'

The manager holds the hotel's damage report in one hand. Her gesture both presents and disclaims it. Two rows down and a bit left of 'Have a nice day', the 'Do we have a problem?' smile neatly filed. She knows where to find the smile. She knows how to get it out. Put it on. Her smile's professionalism is a match for the warhorse smile on Pat's face. Tremendous number of busy hotel staff suddenly needing to reorganise brochure holders behind the manager. Behind the shining, UV-tinted windows of the hotel lobby. Excellent views of Pat and the manager, who are smiling. And of Mr Biswas, who isn't.

'Sorry. Was accident.' He's a lot more interested in the kebabers than in Ms Have-a-Nice-Day-Do-We-Have-a-Problem?

By the hotel entrance, two of the kebab franchisers are loading large suitcases into their rental van. The big, shiny-headed one is directing them while yelling at a cellphone held at arm's length. Waving a cigarette around. From time to time they all stare towards Biswas, who is staring back. No doubt about it – Biswas is the big view this morning. And the sky's blue: it's a crisp, marketable day. A beaut viewing day.

The slim, well-groomed hospitality manager does not need to hear the flat inflection in Pat's no-nonsense statement to appreciate:

'. . . that the Cultural Tourism Initiative (CTI) project team is made up of high-quality officers and consultants. That it has the support of significant government agencies and NGOs. Not to mention international sponsors. That it is the result of unprecedented cooperation between rival Major Regional Initiatives (MRIs). That it is a project of national strategic . . .'

Pat's paused at this point, because Ms Don't-Hesitate-to-Ask now folds the hotel's damage report inside its satiny cover with a logo of a glacial fissure in icy, crystalline blue and white. Ms Not-a-Problem does this while looking Pat in the eye – her own eyes are not even slightly modified by the lenses in her glasses and Pat guesses these may be cosmetic. Ms Not-Another-Word tucks the complaints folder under an arm that looks fit, with a crisp gesture of unchipped fingernails that shows she understands how the hotel's best interests will be served. She makes a considered management decision. It's good to see – Pat gives her a warhorse-type approving smile. Though under the circumstances, Ms We'll-Take-Care-of-It is unlikely to read about herself in the CTI report.

Stan leans against the open driver's door of the team's minibus. Between intakes of smoke his lips purse in a soundless whistle, suggesting a deep thought process switched to idle. He doesn't have much to say lately, driving the group through some of the most spectacular bloody scenery on this earth:

the dark, casually sloping shoulders of mountainous misty bush through the cascade-threaded Haast, the Strachan Range, the Fox – beauties. Nature's masterpieces.

'Was accident.' This was the Bangladeshi's calm explanation for all the smashed mirrors in his suite's bathroom. Hardly bloody likely. It wasn't just Stan who heard Pat and the hotel manager's silences daring each other, but Biswas had nothing more to say. He was watching the big yelping man light a fresh cigarette and not help the other two heave what looked like a portable gas spit into the van.

Today, Biswas is wearing a plain, dark-grey, lightweight suit with a buttoned-up grey-and-black checked shirt and a pair of polished, black slip-on shoes. His appearance is unobtrusively formal and even grave. Gone are the All Blacks cap, the sagging jeans and Joris's complementary walking boots, the Taiwanese Red Sox windcheater, the eager, locked-in smile. The smile has gone – not a hint of it all morning.

'Yes, it's a difficult situation,' says Pat finally. The 'hugely experienced' (William's joke) CTI project manager is wearing backpacker-type garments and maintaining eye-contact with the hotel manager, who is wearing something dark from Scotties and an enamel lapel pin with the blue and white glacial fissure motif.

'Yes, very difficult,' smiles the hotel manager, folding the damage report under a tense bicep. 'But we're in the business of resolving difficulties, after all. If we can't . . .'

'Who can?' finishes Pat. The charade is over, thank you very much. She knows that the manager will semi-conceal the incident. How much she'll reveal will depend on what's best for her career.

The three swarthy men by the hotel entrance have finished loading their van with the large items of luggage, including the portable spit. Two of them are now leaning against the van in the pleasant sunshine, smoking and looking around at the surroundings and, regularly, at Biswas. They are wearing identical Southern Naturally cream cable-knit sweaters with zip-up polo necks and brown ziggurat patterns across the chest. The third, the bulky man with a military-style moustache and shiny, pomaded hair, has been staring at Biswas while shouting at his cellphone or bossing his assistants. Now he turns his back on the CTI project team and lifts the thick hair from the crown of his head with one hand while talking urgently, secretly, into his phone. Dropping his hair, he violently smacks the roof of the van.

The hotel manager passes them on her way back inside – the bulky man hoists his moustache up his cheeks. He executes a small bow, holding the cellphone at arm's length.

'Come on, Stan,' says Pat. 'Get us the fuck out of here.'

Biswas is the last to enter the bus. He ducks his groomed head as he makes his way carefully to the seat beside Pat in the back.

'Don't ask,' says Pat to the team. 'Not yet, anyway.' She closes her eyes as the bus pulls out on to the highway. 'Let's get on with the job.' The silence in the bus exaggerates the wrecked sounds of what it speeds past – an empty cattle truck with a loose, crashing tailgate dribbling liquid shit, a pile-driver at a bridge construction site, a helicopter battering the air at a scenic tours landing pad. 'Get us Morning Report, will you, Stan?' requests Pat. 'Hands-On's being interviewed about us. About his pet project.' Biswas sits very still – no sign of jigging thigh this morning. He looks straight ahead. 'If only he knew, Hands-On,' says Pat and wishes she hadn't – the look Biswas turns on her is calm and without remorse. *Was accident?*

'. . . our greatest assets,' says the Minister unctuously, on the van's radio.

'But,' says the interviewer.

How do we know tourists want to be herded around the place looking at views? *Exactly! And we need answers.* And are we going to get them, Minister?

The mini-bus crosses impressive rivers on interesting,

unique and well-signposted wooden bridges. It skirts lakes reflecting towering primeval forests in mirror water and edges around weedy land grudgingly cleared for farming and scruffily marked by rotting sheds, rusting corrugated iron and desultory cattle – a human landscape whose survival seems doomed by scenery.

'. . . growth industry.'

'But.'

Are we a customer service culture? *Hospitality – a core national value.* And we know this how, Minister? *Exactly.*

There are many scenic reserves – they feel almost end-to-end. The CTI bus skims a frontier not of actual wilderness but of the idea of wilderness. The patterns of wind- and cloud-orchestrated purple shadow that sweep hugely across the surfaces of the landscape and rush across the windows of the speeding mini-bus resemble the lighting effects of a spectacular son-et-lumière.

'The CTI team's brief . . .'

'I hear, Minister, that the brief includes such high-level concepts as purity and beauty.'

Absolutely correct! I'd have to say, Minister. *What's wrong with philosophy?* Issues of accountability. *A close watch.* Junket? *International professionals.* From . . . Bangladesh? *Development challenges.*

Biswas gives the impression of listening but probably not to the radio. Almost inaudible, high-pitched hums of song vibrate from time to time behind his calm expression. From time to time he nods, but not at either the Minister or the radio host.

'He especially wanted the team to listen to this,' observes Pat, unnecessarily – no one is talking. 'Hands-On did.' As far as the interviewer is concerned, the whole thing is a scam or a rort. Maybe the Minister was hoping the interviewer would kiss his arse. Or that the CTI team would send psychic waves of support. But the team is poleaxed by images and discussion concepts. By visitor experiences and audience focal points, by strategic opportunities, by key communication objectives, by secondary cognitive and affective objectives. By key performance indicators, points-of-difference, by value-adding potentials. Grade one assets and distinguishing brand values. Their eyesight stripped out by the many thousands of viewing platforms.

Now, while the Morning Report interviewer disembowels the project's political sponsor and while no one is looking at the calmly humming man who last night smashed all the mirrors in his luxury suite's bathroom, the CTI bus negotiates an ambiguous seam between forests that cannot be viewed at all and that may not exist (though they are always promised) and others that exist only because they can be viewed. The bus with its stunned observers glides between lakes that may or may not be dammed, or recreational, or reservoirs, and others whose tantalising inaccessibility is what makes them unspoiled. It threads itself through views of mountains and beaches whose existence as experience products is predicated on them being seen and consumed, an existence that renders the same mountains and beaches ghostly as the mini-bus leaves them behind – and fleetingly substantial when it stops.

Biswas emerges last from the public toilets. He is hiding his plastic lota toilet-mug in his jacket pocket. Stan is smoking next to the van and looking up at a scrap of blue sky above the towering horizon of giant rainforest trees. Ants has crutched herself nimbly to the edge of the bush – she is poking something in the weeds with her orthopaedic shoe while holding her nose. Gloria is asleep in the bus – she has bought a pillow with a leaping trout on it and she dozes cheek to cheek with the trophy fish. Pat is talking on her cellphone. Bill is sitting at a picnic table clicking the quick-view button on his digital camera. Boris is smoking one of his aromatic cigars on the other side of the road, looking back at the team bus as if getting it into another perspective – reframing or rebranding it.

'Team spirit?' Pat is reassuring her Minister. 'Not too bad, considering.'

'Considering what, exactly, Patricia?' The Minister is talking close to his mouthpiece back in Wellington – she can hear his swampy breathing. That means he doesn't have the desk speaker on and that means he's feeling a bit shaky.

Not your appalling interview, thinks Pat. 'It's been a tough trip, sir.' She thinks about the young hospitality manager back at the Glacier Hotel as she puts on her best talking-to-Hands-On voice. 'Breaking news', ha ha.

'Tough in what way?'

Here's what your policy advisors, including me, have told you about putting all your solution eggs in one problem basket, thinks Pat. Don't. 'Tough in that there has been a great deal of information to process within the ambitious framework you designed,' she says, visualising his glower of suspicion. 'Meanwhile, back on the bus, Minister.'

'You hold this one together, Pat,' says Hands-On. She can pretty much hear the responses to his Morning Report gutting piling up on the switchboard. He's practically got the telephone in his mouth.

Hold this one together – what does the silly bastard think she is? Pat might have expected William to relish the secrecy of a gossip-rich, mockable, mystery drama (Berserk Bangla!), but the bugger's in the process of reinventing himself as the kind of outdoorsy type he despises. He either is or is pretending to be dozing between the wings of his red adventurist's parka collar. Or he might be incubating himself into Bill. His new pal Joris looks straight ahead. Cheek muscles working furiously at his exotically scented gum, but he's got the slightly interested expression of someone in no particular hurry for the next experience. Bad news looking for a headline, thinks Pat. Then there's the resident team mortal coil. The little Aussie found a dead possum at the edge of the bush back at the rest stop. Started to say something twittery about 'a long way from home' but then shut up. Now her silence is somehow even quieter. Looking past Gloria out the window, blinking madly as if her eyeballs are getting peppered with information like gritty snow. Pat can see that dear old Gloria is holding Antsy's thin, cold little hand, bless her. Gloria's expression is peaceful – her lips loose and pouty, like the trout's on her pillow. Bet your life, though – that girl's getting spooked as well. Not all the partying in the world can shut her 'Uncle Mat' up.

What the team can't see is that having reached across to give his hand a secret, encouraging squeeze, Pat has found her own hand retained by the thin, warm fingers of the calmly humming Bangladeshi. His gesture feels semi-formal, at once courteous and emotional – undemanding, intimate, comforting – even, she would have to say, grateful. Pat can't remember if she has ever held hands like this.

Hold this one together.

'You will appreciate,' announces Pat as the mini-bus stops for lunch, 'that Mr Biswas and I have some matters to discuss. We'll be at the Shoganda.'

'Shoganda?' asks Biswas in a tone of wonder.

'Enjoy the whitebait,' says Pat. She leads him firmly away from the team. Biswas is moving like a sleepwalker, with stiff, uncertain steps. 'Shoganda,' says Pat. 'It's a Bangladeshi restaurant.'

'Is in Chittagong,' Biswas moans.

'If you say so,' says Pat. *Hold this one together.* 'But it's here too. On the West Coast of New Zealand.' She gives his stiff arm a bit of a shake. 'Come on, Mr Biswas – this is what we're dealing with. We're here, now. You've got to be here.' She gives him another shake. 'And stop humming.'

When he halts in the middle of the footpath, Biswas is facing Pat across the sparse, jostling flow of pedestrians. Behind her is a shop window with a selection of Swanndri workshirts, gumboots and chainsaws. There is a cattle-drench display featuring a grand, laminated image of lush green pasture with black-and-white Friesian cows. It has snowy mountains in the background. The expression on the Bangladeshi's face is not a smile – his teeth show in a kind of grimace, a leer of physical effort. He seems to be hoisting himself into this view.

The pub to which Gloria leads the rest of the project team is a dark place even by day. The publican is smoking at the bar. He turns on a couple of lights.

'Gidday, Hine. Long time no see.'
'How are you, Mitch?'
'Can't complain.'
'All set for a feed?'
'Janice is expecting you.'

There are no picture windows in this place. Its ambience is of nicotine chiaroscuro and its transactions are inward – across tables, food and drink. There is an old smell of coal smoke. If you do not know the place, you will not be able to see into its corners. Stan lights up. Nobody stops him. Antsy props her crutches against an empty chair – her face is a little smear of paleness, a tiny shine on the gloom.

Gloria makes a T-shape with her hands. 'Here's what I think, team.'

'So,' says Joris. 'This whatever, back earlier?'

'No, Boris.' Gloria props her time-out T on the table in front of him. 'We have lunch. We forget about Mr Biswas. Later for Mr Biswas. We leave that to Pat.'

'Why, you don't want to know?'

'When she's good and ready, Boris,' says Gloria.

'The memsahib,' suggests Bill. 'Taking up the brown man's burden.'

'Another joke, Bill, probably.' Joris smacks him. Bill puts his glasses back on and shifts to a chair next to Ants.

The day before, the team ate at a restaurant in an instant village built on the site of a tourist attraction. Its hospitality was highly polished, like its glassware, and its views were almost blinding. The whitebait omelette cost $40 and the glass of decent pinot gris $12. The side salad was a small selection of mesclun greens for an additional $5. The sound system played noodly elevator music. The omelette was small – 'I'll show you fritter,' said Gloria – though not as small as the mini-fritters Gloria poked tenderly into Antsy's wee, snapping mouth at the reception notorious for the Minister's indiscretion.

Sometimes Ants wakes up at night and is not sure if it is dark because it is night-time or because she has the drapes tightly closed. Back at Cronulla, just a kid, she kept her room in the Rydges Sydney Cronulla Hotel dark all the time, because outside it was all about the beach-babe Hells, her skinny, hairy, bronzed dad was out there on the beach after his swim, doing the exercises he invented himself, the groaning, fog-horning boys were out there with their board shorts hanging off their arse cracks at the back and their semi-hards at the front.

There was a kind of darkness around the stinky squashed possum back up the road where they stopped for a pee in the podocarp forest. The maggots that fell out of it when she pushed it with her shoe were luminous in its darkness. Ants has a sensation of being snow blind from the bombardment of stuff through the mini-bus window – blinking the light back as it flies into her face past Gloria's dark profile on its freeze-framed, leaping trout. Everything that seemed vivid and almost painful the day before is now folding back into darkness – homely, comforting, despite the foreign smell of old, burnt coal. If she opened her drapes a tiny crack back at the Cronulla Rydges, a searing hot shaft of sunshine would shoot across the room if it was daytime. At night, the rhythmic ticking of a red and yellow neon came in. Now, she knows that if she parts the shadow at the edges of the pub dining room, there will only be more darkness. The details of yesterday's lunch are fading into the margins of the pub's dim interior, an interior that Antsy can't read because she can't see past the yellow halo of light around the team's table.

Yesterday, there were three distinct kinds of architecture in the scenic attraction village. Ants read them out for the CTI team while they ate their $40 whitebait omelettes in the blinding restaurant with its conversation-stopping music.

The Department of Conservation building had low, dark green, undemonstrative qualities that marked it as ecologically responsible. 'The architectural equivalent of lowered, non-threatening eyes and a submissive neck offered to the overmastering bite of Nature,' crowed Antsy, laughing too much to eat. Then there was the architecturally themed building in which they were having lunch, within an arcaded cluster of retail outlets for craft items, greenstone treasures bearing the toi iho™ trademark of indigenous authenticity, lunch and expensive extreme-adventure clothing ('Mine!' shouted Joris).

'Its structure mimics the swooping upward, hair-standing-on-end appearance of all those palms out there!'

'Nikaus,' said Joris, adding, 'you have to know this stuff, right?'

'G1A,' suggested Biswas, wanting to join in – he tried to separate the whitebait from its egg, but then cut his omelette into four pieces and left it alone in a tidy stack.

'As though they've had a terrible fright!' Antsy gushed. 'The lunch bill, maybe! Or the themed attraction!' Her exhaustion had begun that morning with pushing her mind up its usual hill but had increased as the result of a walking expedition around the overthemed scenic attraction, which featured eroded rock formations and blowholes shooting seawater into the air from wave surges. Finally, there was the incoherent cluster of local food and beverage outlets, film processing booths and accommodation and kayaking agencies, whose signage jostled for attention on the footpath and whose rubbish bins spilled the discarded milkshake containers of school party coaches parked nearby. The kids pressed their noses and mouths to the windows of their buses – they waggled their tongues against the smeared glass.

One of them took his trousers down and pressed his arse to the window. The nikau palms' hair stood on end. Not far away along the footpath paved with facsimiles of worn coastal rock, the sea bellowed in its dark chimneys.

The whitebait fritters that arrive from the pub's kitchen are the size of dinner plates. They cost $8 each and the handle of beer that comes with them is $2. There is a basket of French fries and a bowl of ripped lettuce and chopped tomatoes for no extra charge. Mitch pokes the smelly coal fire in a pot-belly stove and returns on carpet-slippered feet to his ashtray at the bar. A racing commentary murmurs from a radio in the kitchen. When two more customers enter the gloom, Mitch turns on the racing channel on the TV set above the bar without being asked to and draws jugs of beer from his taps without being asked to either.

'Haere mai,' says Gloria. 'What'd I tell you? Home away from home.'

'Maybe,' thinks Joris, chewing with neatly flexing jaw muscles, 'people would come here for catching whitebait? Adventurously?'

'Maybe,' replies Gloria, 'people would come here for getting shot, Boris.'

'Maybe,' says William, whose mood has mellowed in the dim, comforting, coal-smoky bar, 'we could just stay here. Jump ship. Forget the whole fucking CTI bullshit thing.' He forks an immense mouthful of fritter into his jaws. 'I wonder what memsahib Pat and the naughty Bangladeshi are discussing?' His Adam's apple syringes beer down his throat.

'Not going there,' warns Gloria. She is keeping an eye on Antsy. 'What say, Ants – good tucker?'

Antsy picks at the fringes of her gigantic fritter – the little, white creatures spill out of it. Each individual, tiny, maggoty fry has a minuscule black eye the size of its head, as though seeing was all it needed to do as it swam into the fine mesh of its fate. The eye and the bait's thread of gut seem about the right size for Antsy's sustenance, one at a time, picked at and passed to her mouth in darkness – each one a tiny taste of something so close to completely invisible there is no point looking for it. Her little lips ponder these larval fragments of watery flavour, in which she discovers rivers where the waning salt of oceans and the sweetness of trailing littoral weeds mingle, the vegetable trace of forest-leafy silt, the minerals leached and vanished from mountains, the tang of breakers at the shoaling river mouth. All these memories of places and histories. All these pale fragments in the darkness. All these fading, blending, mingling things. In the amber, smoky light of the bar, she herself is almost invisible, a little half-profile effulgence. It is as though the transparent thinness of her corporeal sign, her wee material self threaded with a shrunken vestige of gut, her eyes that are like the dark, complete meaning of her consciousness – as though this little disappearing sign is indeed itself about to become only the faint taste of its presence.

Gloria eats with measured, expert, thoughtful consideration. 'Excellent, Mitch, as usual,' she says to the barman. 'Compliments to Janice.'

'Any time, Hine,' says Mitch. 'You know the rules, just let us know how many you got in tow.'

'Don't know what this lot did to deserve your excellent hospitality,' says Gloria. 'Miserable pack of Wellington bastards.'

'Anyways,' says the barman, 'always a bit of bait somewhere at the old Erewhon. At least you know the season, Hine,' he adds, implying that the pack of Wellington bastards doesn't. 'None of that frozen rubbish around here.'

'See,' says Bill, washing down his last mouthful of whitebait with the last of his beer, 'a theme. The freezing thing again. Something to hang our concept on.' He looks to Ants for help with his game. 'The icing on the cake.'

But the thought on Antsy's tasting lips pauses. 'What did he say the name of this place was, again?'

'Erewhon,' William says – he watches to see if Ants is playing. 'Know where that is?'

'It's nowhere,' say Antsy's little lips. The words are more a movement than a sound.

'Actually, it's not really here,' says Bill, peering at her. 'Just like everything else. Like the glaciers. The real Erewhon's way over yonder, on the side of a way-over-yonder-type mountain.' He watches Antsy's trembling fork lift another almost transparent fragment to her lips that are quivering to receive it – or to speak, or perhaps to breathe. 'It's Nowhere. But you knew that.' He leans in, to catch what she might be about to say. 'You said that?'

It sounds, then, as though Antsy asks to be excused, or whispers something quietly polite that has that meaning. *I need to go.* There her crutches are, propped on a chair.

'It's Nowhere spelled backwards,' says Bill unnecessarily, guessing she must know that as well and looking around to see where, in the gloom of the bar with its old smell of burning, ancient, compacted forests and its sepia light that also seems trapped and ancient – to see where the slight figure of Nancy has got to. Where on earth she can have gone?

Across town in the Shoganda Restaurant, Pat's been listening patiently to Mr Biswas. Talking about rain and rivers. Not that she entirely understands why yet.

'Now – Biswas – you have to tell me what's happening. If it's to do with your sister and the cash. Like you told me. Because I can't cover for you.' She sees the word 'cover' miss the mark – the eyebrows are preparing a question before Biswas asks it. 'The mirrors – that wasn't an accident, Biswas.'

'Yes – accident, Pat.'

Maybe she's not understanding 'accident', thinks Pat. This could take more time than she has. On the other hand. 'Just tell me, please, Mr Biswas.' Pat snaps a papadum into shards on her plate. 'Start at the beginning. Take your time.'

'Yes, thank you, Pat,' says Biswas. 'Thanking you very much.' Then there's a long silence that Pat leaves alone. Hard as that is. She nibbles at her chokputi. Biswas is also nibbling – he has a small plate of pungent dried fish and green chillies and he keeps his head down over it, picking the little fry up with his right hand. From time to time he sips water and wipes his lips neatly with his table napkin. When he's finished the fish snack, he waves the empty plate away. His gesture is curt and confident. Then he watches silently until Pat's finished her spicy chick peas. Again, the quick wave of dismissal. This is another Mohammed Baul Biswas, at home in his own manners. Then he begins to talk. He doesn't eat and talk. He talks as if he's completely thought out what he has to say.

On eighth day of chait, in the dry season, first month of Bangladesh year, April, Biswas can be washed of sins in the rivers, in moonlight, standing in the water, among crowds, praying.

'But have to save Keshamoni before chait absolutions. Before basanto finishes.' Biswas puts his palms together in front of his face. 'Have to, Pat.' He sips water. They are getting the important guest treatment – Pat can hear a lot of ordering about going on in the kitchen.

'Okay, Biswas,' says Pat, and regrets addressing him as what sounds like the nickname she's seen he hates. 'All right, then, Mr Biswas,' she corrects. 'So is this a deadline or something?' The word 'deadline' makes his eyebrows begin a question. 'Is this when?' He just waits for her. 'When you need the cash by?'

'No tourists going to Bangladesh,' says Biswas flatly. 'Only almost very few, isn't it.' It's not as though he's ignoring her. Right-oh, thinks Pat. This will go quicker if I keep my trap shut. 'So what is my KPI?' asks Biswas, with a faint smile. 'How to win UNDP cash, Pat? Because paying against Performance Measures, isn't it. To Bangladesh Parjatan Tourist Corporation.' Again the faint smile. 'Not to me.'

Biswas makes a skimming motion with his right hand – then he holds an imaginary weight. With his left hand he makes a lightweight, feathery gesture, almost like his dismissal of the empty plates. 'Not to me – to Parjatan, to government, to . . .' He hesitates, as if concerned not to give offence. 'To *consultants*, isn't it, Pat. You understand.' Again, the skimming gesture. 'Consultants.' Biswas pauses. The word 'consultant' is offensive to him – Pat hears it offered to her delicately, she hears it as a foreign word, the way Biswas heard 'accident', 'cover' and 'deadline'. The way something foreign about how she used the word 'flood' made his face close up and not because of losing his family in one. 'Sixty per cent!' asserts Biswas with a bit more vehemence. The skimming gesture turns into a slice.

How are we doing? Needs the cash before the rainy season some time after April. Gets paid against key performance indicators – getting tourists to Bangladesh. But loses sixty per cent to skimming. Bit of light being shed, finally.

What's more, Biswas indicates, making a map with articles on the restaurant table, not only can't you get tourists to come to Bangladesh, you can't get the foreigners who live there to get outside a place called Gulshan in Dhaka. Got a nice little lake. Got swimming pools. Tennis. Biswas hits a backhand shot. And the rich Bangladeshis in Gulshan only go on tourist trips in Bangladesh for free, for write-down payoffs for political and licensing favours, a share of the aid skim. With amas for the kids, with grandmothers and aunties, with the cook, with three SUVs in a convoy.

'Sixty per cent of *gross*!' Biswas assembles the gross complement of table-top items. 'Cops!' He removes a water glass. 'Army!' He takes out the knives and forks. 'Rapid Action Battalion (RAB)!' He pushes a plate aside. 'Upazila admin! Cardes! Dacoit!' Biswas lowers his voice mockingly. 'Bangladesh National Party (BNP)!' He pushes a small, high-necked vase with artificial jonquils in it to the side of the table. 'Parjatan national tourism corporation!' Away go the salt and pepper shakers. 'Protection!' The Biswas voice is still calm and methodical, but he's panting a little. A small dish of spicy condiment is all that remains. Biswas lifts it lovingly in his upraised fingers. He adores it, turning it from side to side, rocking his head. 'This is for Mohammed Baul Biswas. After KPI, Pat. Understanding?' Then the condiment dish set down hard – some drops of reddish oil spit out on the tablecloth. Biswas grips the hair on the left side of his head and wrenches his neck across. The skimming gesture returns as a slice as Biswas cuts his own throat. He leans across towards Pat. His dry fish breath is truly awful, but not as bad as the killer look in his eyes.

'Got it,' says Pat.

'Get here before the tourists do.' Biswas sits back. 'Get here before the tourists do, Pat. Parjatan.' His composure returns quickly. Again, the faint smile. 'So, you see, Pat.' He gestures for the meal's next course. 'Is very problem.'

Another long silence while the food is served. This time Biswas waits until the restaurant's Bangladeshi owner's out of the way. He uses a spoon and fork to eat the biryani and dhal he piles on his plate. He eats voraciously but without signs of enjoyment, as if satisfying his hunger is a task. He picks items of salad from the central dish with his fingers and crunches them up. He snaps off half a green chilli with his teeth bared and follows it with a long drink of water. He begins to talk again before finishing his plateful of food. He waves the plate away.

'How to get cash, Pat?' Pat keeps her attention on the excellent biryani, but Biswas is not expecting a response. He answers his own question. 'Black market. Smuggling. Fixing film crews into slums, army-controlled Hill Tracts, Bengal Tigers in Sundarbans, isn't it.' Biswas smiles, but Pat doesn't see any more sign of enjoyment than in his appetite for the lunch. 'Lovely paddy fields, Pat, very green. Lovely villages.' He makes a hosing gesture with both of his hands formed into tubes. 'Tube wells, Pat.'

Pat's audit, as she carefully shifts a cardamom shell to the side of her mouth and ejects it onto her fork, has collated a deadline, a performance measure problem and a funding issue. Biswas hasn't yet said straight out that he expects to pay whatever the kidnappers of Keshamoni want from his UNDP grant, but he's sailing very, very close. And now we're hearing about the ways to make real money. The kind of take-it-for-granted stuff Pat absolutely does not want to be hearing about. Not on your life. Then there's the way he's eating – businesslike, without pleasure. The arrogant manner with the nice restaurant owner, the expectation that she, Pat, will keep quiet!

This may be as good a time as any to break her silence. Pat puts her knife and fork down. Biswas is looking at her – not as though he expects her to say anything, but as if getting himself ready for the next bit.

'Road trips,' says Mohammed Baul Biswas. He says the phrase carefully and politely and watches her. It's as though he expects a reaction, as he did to the word 'consultants'.

'Listen,' begins Pat.

'Sorry, Pat. Got to say.' He leans across the table. 'Sex tourism.' He remembers his manners and covers his mouth as if what he has to say stinks. 'Paedophile road trips, Pat.' Pat feels her decision to speak up at last freeze into silence again. 'This is Bangladesh tourism, Pat.' When he takes his hand away from his mouth, Pat can see his lips trembling.

'Sorry, Mr Biswas,' says Pat. She feels chilled but is aware that her face has flushed. 'My turn to say "Got to say this". I know you're in a lot of trouble. But . . .'

Biswas ignores her again. 'Twenty lakh of thaka, Pat. Five hundred thousand New Zealand dollar, Pat. What they think I can . . .' Biswas gets his lips under control. 'Total UNDP grant, Pat. That they thinking.' He covers his mouth again. 'For Keshamoni.'

'Half a mil,' says Pat thoughtfully, as though discussing a feasibility study for a Punakaiki Rocks disabled track. The penny's dropped. The buggers who've kidnapped Biswas's sister think they can extort the total UNDP grant. When his performance measure means he can expect next to nothing and at best a little saucerful of condiment after all the skims have cleared the table. 'Hell's teeth,' says Pat, and regrets it. Biswas doesn't have a clue what that means. 'Never mind,' she tells the man with barely trembling lips across the table from her. To all appearances they might be a normal business couple having a discussion about venture options on the Coast. About kebab franchises.

'Eat more,' suggests Biswas, nudging the remaining biryani towards her. When the restaurant owner shows signs of approaching, the hard Biswas look drives him away to the cash register. '"Never mind", Pat?'

'I mean, never mind "hell's teeth", Biswas.' The look he's giving her is patient. 'Okay,' she says. 'Let's keep it simple. First, what's your deal? Then we'll think about what to do. Not that we can. From here.'

'Okay,' agrees Biswas. It's a word he's getting used to repeating. 'Simple, Pat.'

Another silence. Biswas drinks deeply with his little finger elevated from the water glass, and waves commandingly for more plates to be cleared. Then he looks at Pat across the table. On the other side of the room, the Americans Babs and Frank have entered and are noticing Pat and Biswas – Pat keeps her head down, avoiding their hesitant waves. There's a party of German cyclists with shaved, tanned legs. Some dark young women are speaking Spanish interspersed with words relating to the Routeburn Track further up the coast. Argentinian, thinks Pat. The professional, warhorse part of her brain is doing its work. But another part, the part that made her patient while Biswas shifted himself through the gears of his story, the part that is watching for the snare in the track of his narrative, that is preparing her to step back from it when she detects it – this part of warhorse Pat's attention is simple, now, its vision narrowed to the signals of the man across the table from her. Not taking in the semaphores of Frank and Babs from Fort Lauderdale, the lamentations of the Germans who have not found a wilderness along the backpacker bike trail. Not even the inventive curses of the Argentinians, which Pat's adequate Spanish translates as 'D-cup full of liquid shit'.

'Yes, please, Mr Biswas.' She also ignores the kheer pudding that has been delivered to their table. 'Really, really simple, please. The deal. The problem. The solution. How you see it, Mr Biswas? From here. Where we are, right now.' There are proudly glossy photos of river boats and paddy fields on the walls of the restaurant, as well as samples of rickshaw art painted on bits of tin. The phrase 'where we are, right now' sounds pedantic to Pat, but she keeps her expression simple as well. Please, no Secret Birds, no moonlight on rivers, no absolution of sins.

'Please to listen,' says Mohammed Baul Biswas. He counts the simple facts off on his fingers. 'Number one: Dacoit got Keshamoni. Number two: asking twenty lakh UNDP cash. Number three: Keshamoni . . .' Biswas hesitates, as if deciding what to put at number three. Pat sees him shift an item down the list. 'Number three: UNDP cash, already sixty per cent gone. Number four: only expenses on receipts, like airfare, before report.' Biswas holds his fourth finger, thinking. He sighs, as if admitting something and then holds up a thumb. 'Number five: get my fee after finishing report.' He smiles. 'After UNDP approving report. After Parjatan approving.' A head shake. 'Number six: KPI bonus for action plan. Economic impacts. Projected benefits over five years, Pat.' Biswas makes the 'projected benefits' sound like a quote. The smile again, the head shake. 'Parjatan paying.' Biswas picks up his spoon. 'Paying *bonus*,' he says, shaping the word elaborately with his neat lips and trim moustache, finishing it off with a deft smile. 'Is simple, no?'

Pat's thinking, why would you be silly enough to sign a contract like that? Might as well shoot yourself in both feet. The Biswas smile and head shake say he knows she will think this. They also say, had no choice. Biswas spoons the rice pudding into his mouth. He seems to be collecting his thoughts.

Pat's also waiting for the bit that explains why the kidnappers are silly enough to think they can get their hands on the UNDP total. And for the bit that explains what the risk to little sister is. Nasty 'road trip' feeling about that one. Can't quite get it in the frame with the Swanndris, gumboots and drench.

'Number seven, Mr Biswas?' Pat doesn't feel like her kheer.

'"Purity and Beauty",' says Biswas. He's carefully wiped his moustache. He's not holding a seventh finger and Pat guesses this isn't number seven. He gives the words the same quoted sound as 'projected benefits' and 'bonus'. 'In *Assessing Cultural Tourism Initiatives: a Comparative Model*, isn't it, Pat?' He's making it very simple for her. He passes the words of the CTI mission to her across the table of the Bangladeshi restaurant in the place with the shop window and its display of working clothes and boots, the black-and-white cows, the green grass, the snowy mountains. Where they are, right now. There's a restaurant with the same name in Chittagong, where Keshamoni is, perhaps. Or is she in Khulna? The phantom of another map's beginning to show through the tracery of the one Pat knows from a lifetime of looking. The Shoganda in Chittagong is where he meets friends in the tourism business. In the businesses that operate under the cover of tourism. The businesses that are getting there before the tourists do.

Pat wants to reach across the table and touch his brown hand where he's placed it, palm up, as if showing off the ridiculous words. But she doesn't.

Biswas raises his hand and grips a seventh finger. 'Number seven: dacoit thinking they can get twenty lakh.' Now he's looking at Pat as if expecting her to ask a question. His eyebrows raised, waiting.

'And why is that?' asks Pat, feeling the solution part of all this getting closer.

'Why is that? Number eight: because tourist operatives telling them, isn't it, Pat? Maybe even my business associates. Maybe Parjatan. And why is that? Number nine: because not wanting UNDP, or World Bank, or International Monetary Fund, looking at their business.' Biswas makes a fence with his fingers. 'Looking past emerald-green-rice-paddy, Sundarban Bengal tigers, river boat trip, isn't it. Looking at smuggling, pirates.' Biswas is watching her, waiting again.

'And road trips,' suggests Pat. Biswas waits. 'Someone's leaked the information about the total grant because they don't want you to finish the job. They want the kidnappers to get greedy and ruin the project after they've had a decent skim of it. They want a diversion. They want to hide their business. Their real business. Because there isn't really any tourism. Except.'

'Yes,' says Biswas. 'Is simple, Pat.'

'Call that simple?' Simple where he comes from. Pat feels like a clod.

And then Biswas gathers the fingers of both hands into a cluster, as if making the simplest summary possible. 'Have to understand, Pat.' His hands are pleading with her.

Here we go again, she thinks. Simple, simpler and simplest.

'Bangladesh is a house where the rain comes in though the roof. Barsa – this is wet season. Rest of the world talking about floods-disasters. Everybody remembers 1991, 2002, big flood years, but every year village ponds get clean water, paddies get rice, villages get fish, ducks, every year tea grows, every year jute grows, every year new char islands in the delta.

'Every day, Pat, washing clothes, every day family washing at ghat. Every year basanto cool, dry, grisma hot and leaves falling, and the water getting bad and dirty, only little left, sometimes getting spoiled with salt from shrimp gher. But then barsa, with floods, maybe, sometimes, people living on platforms, not cooking food.' For Mohammed Baul Biswas, this is what's simple. 'The rains, Pat, the water, the rivers! The rivers, Pat – life, isn't it. Bhaga, Pat. Bhaga.'

'Bhaga?'

With his left hand, Biswas makes the shape of a platform raised above the water – bracing the platform shape with his straight forearm, turning his elegant hand at ninety degrees. He dips his right hand in the thick kheer and passes a morsel to his mouth with the tips of his fingers. These fingers are pursed, their tips petalled out. He holds the pursed fingers, sticky with sweet rice, below his bent, platform hand. Pat can read the simple architecture of the left, platform hand. But the eating hand, with its cupped palm and pursed fingers, is also a something, part of a composite sign – this 'bhaga'.

The Bangladeshi's voice is patient and polite. 'Living with village family, 2002, came down from Dhaka,' says Biswas. 'Got a baby coming.' He makes a sweeping movement with his platform hand – the other remains pursed in its pod shape. 'River flooding, isn't it. All gone – but not Keshamoni. My sister.' Again, the platform and the other, right-handed pod or purse shape, poised above his rice. 'Bhaga – life, Pat, is life, is river, is barsa.'

'I'm sorry, Mr Biswas,' Pat says.

'Yes, Pat – wife, baby gone. Mother, father.'

'Yes, sorry about that, very sorry, Biswas. But what I mean – I'm sorry, I don't understand. I know it's simple. But I don't understand you. Bhaga, Biswas? Barsa?' Pat copies the pursed fingers shape, the bowl of her palm, the fingers gathered in a funnel. Biswas is nodding – he draws the purse shape down against his lap.

'Barsa is flood season, is raining,' he says. 'Is the river. And bhaga is the part of a woman.' His face is very still, but a single tear has run from each eye into his moustache. 'Bhaga, Pat – woman's part.' He swipes the tear tracks away, concealing them from the restaurant owner. He leans across the table. 'Sorry, Pat. Please to understand.'

And then Pat sees it – the bamboo platform inside the flooded house from which the Biswas family was swept when the river changed its course and sent a muddy giant through the bamboo walls, and the female shape of his right hand, the uterus, down there in the flood water under the platform. The hand that you also eat with, the hand you use to show the river swelling under the platform, the hand that is Keshamoni *in* the river. The hand that modestly makes the simple shape of his sister's private part. The hand that can utter the part of his sister with minimal shame.

'Is difficult to speak, Pat.'

Biswas drops his left, platform hand out of sight to his lap. Pat remembers it as the hand that caught Keshamoni by the hair. He assembles a taste of kheer with the other hand, leaving the spoon aside. On the back of this hand is the scar welt where the bamboo dagger went through his palm and pinned him to the platform. He lifts the kheer neatly to his mouth, drinks water and wipes his lips. He has that hot, dry look that Pat dreads – but calm now. Pat's trained ear is hearing the confident, spitty German of the cyclists. She hears them in a shocked chamber in her head.

Barsa. Bhaga.

If she was doing her job properly, Pat would be chatting to the diners. How they found the Shoganda Restaurant this far from the life-giving catastrophes of Bangladesh's barsa floods. From rain-through-the-roof and brand-new chars of mud. From little Keshamoni, whose dark head rose above the rushing water.

'Getting very worried, Pat,' says Biswas, after sipping water. 'Sorry about the mirrors.'

Pat's old trouper instincts have shied at the edge of the word 'we' in 'What are we going to do, then?' Biswas takes his cellphone from the inner pocket of his nice, plain suit jacket. 'Excuse me, Pat,' he says. 'Got to wash hands.' He selects a function of the phone whose screen flickers with a greenish light against his shielding hand. Its light spills between his fingers. He passes the phone upside-down across the table to her. 'Please to look, Pat. Please. Excuse me.'

Biswas rises from his chair and walks firmly to the restaurant toilets at the back of the room. The sound of his vigorous throat clearing and mouth washing briefly stuns the conversation in the Shoganda. When he returns, with clean hands and thrice-rinsed mouth, Patricia is sitting as he left her. The cellphone, switched off, is on the table beside her untouched dessert of sweet kheer rice. So is the paper napkin with which she has wiped her eyes. The restaurant owner is discreetly not looking their way, but Frank and Babs are.

'Christ Almighty, Mr Biswas.' She pushes the cellphone across the table to him. 'What are we going to do?' She has no trouble with the 'we', now. Pat: Decision Making, Power and Authority and Working Under Pressure. Biswas is waiting for Pat to say she can fix it. 'Don't worry,' she says. 'We can fix this thing.' It's true – she can feel the solution, the possibility of it. That's the main thing. She can feel her determination to solve the problem pushing back the image of the kid with her hands over her poor little bhaga.

'Please,' says Mohammed Baul Biswas, simply.

'First,' says Pat, pushing words after her certainty, 'you have to keep writing the report. Because then no one can see that anything else is happening. And you get a bit of money, at least. And you're still a threat to the guys who set you up. Second, you never know, might be able to find a bit here.'

'Yes, please,' says Biswas. 'Is very rich country.'

'But don't count on it. So what we need is something to trade with your little sister. Something worth cash.' Pat feels her solution converging on the junction of Mr Biswas's problem, the place where no tourists come to Bangladesh, the place of Keshamoni's danger, the road trips. Pat leans across the table. 'A business your associates understand. What the gangsters are into. The smugglers. Where your sister's headed unless we get her. What the road trip tourists want. What the rest of the bloody world wants, Biswas.'

The Biswas eyes have widened.

Then the same wide, dark eyes drop to Pat's own substantial breasts inside the zippered, outdoorsy shirt – what Biswas calls TPU. Tourist Pilgrim Uniform. His joke. The heat rushes up from them, from her chest, and across her shoulders and neck. She feels it mottling her face and rising all the way up through her hair. Moisture springs from the skin under her eyes and across the top of her lips. The blush blazes and Biswas smiles – radiantly.

Pat is shying from the amazing Biswas smile the way she shied from the 'we' in 'What are we going to do?' You must be joking. But this time the solution rushes her forward into what Biswas is saying about the milkmaids. About Krishna's companions. Making them appear voluptuously before her. Rocking his arms and swaying his neck.

You must be joking. But he's not and nor is she. Basic warhorse wisdom: trust your intuition. Solutions that feel right often are.

'We can fix this.' Pat feels her blush fading. 'That's all I'm saying.' The immense stook of Connie lupins, shedding dew on the bar-room table. The Bangladeshi's quavering song. Keshamoni's knock knees. 'Miracles can happen,' says Pat, firmly. She was going to say, 'You just have to make them.' Instead, she says, 'We just have to love her enough. Your little sister.'

'My Keshamoni,' says Biswas. 'Yes. We love her, Pat.'

'That was delicious food,' she tells the proprietor, giving him a project card. 'We'll have to spread the word.'

'Nice to see you again,' she says to Babs and Frank. 'Hope you're still enjoying your trip.'

'The Routeburn – brilliant,' she assures the Argentinians.

'You want the wild stuff, you have to get off and walk,' she tells the sullen Germans.

Outside, Biswas is bending towards Stan, politely shielding

his mouth as he plies a toothpick. His manners have returned. The mini-bus is parked theatrically at the curb with its driver door open. There's no sign of the team. Biswas shrugs. 'Stan saying, Nancy's gone? *Gone?*'

'Rest of them are looking all over the place,' fills in Stan. 'Then they reckon you should meet them near the police station. Couple of blocks over that way. Give it an hour.' Stan coughs, as though excusing himself from the report he has to give. 'She just disappeared,' he says. 'Left her crutches behind. Mind you, it was dark.'

Pat no longer has an echoey, shocked sensation in her head. Instead, a sense of strongly converging crises. Not a bad feeling, despite the circumstances, which are in a class of their own. Something about knowing that everything could quite easily turn to shit, go pear-shaped, become custard. Has probably started to.

'Okay, Stan, thanks,' she says. She's watching the expression on the Bangladeshi's face. Biswas is delicately picking his teeth and looking at a middle distance of economically challenged greenstone craft outlets. At the citizens of the town assessing Manchester and garden tools.

Stan looks a bit odd too – gazing off into space and whistling in that way he has. Pat stands still and breathes through her nose. An old instinct, one that has served her very well, causes her – the old warhorse, the old trouper, the safe pair of hands, the solid foundation, the hugely experienced Pat who can be depended on to get to the bottom of things – to say, firmly, 'Meanwhile, under the circumstances, we should all keep our traps shut until we find out what's happening here.'

Mr Biswas gives her a look of austere incomprehension. *Traps?*

'Of course,' says Stan ominously, lighting up another smoke. 'Under the circumstances.'

thirteen

Loneliness

There was something a bit comical – tragic but funny – about the stiff set of his shoulders as Mr Biswas marched off to his own quarters after installing his flash little laptop video cam in Pat's unit. Right here was surely one of the most tawdry locations on God's earth. But hardly for God's sake in the same league as the slums that Biswas had described around Kamlapur railway station in Dhaka – the 'scenic attractions' negotiated by getting-there-first tourists catching a train to Chittagong or Sylhet. But Biswas walked away from Pat with a kind of horror in the not-looking-left-or-right speed with which he zeroed in on his own unit's dark door. No beggars around here except the scruffy keas further up country and the only obvious cripples were the clapped-out utes parked behind the pub. Biswas was avoiding eye-contact with the almost empty pub car park and its tacky row of motel units, dimly lit by a few surviving outdoor spots. Departing drinkers captured the thin, scampering foreigner in their headlights as they tore off into the deserted streets.

It was pretty obvious that the Bangladeshi's body language had something to do with Pat's fatwa on him looking at anything he wasn't supposed to. He scurried to his unit without glancing back at her. The world of the pub car park was a frightening place of secret codes for Biswas. She had to smile. Travel Alert for infections shooting from the dark eye of the video cam in her unit. Biswas slunk stiffly along the side of the chilly car park and disappeared with a slam into his overnight accommodation.

From the back window of Pat's own deadshit concrete block unit at the edge of the deadshit emergency stop-over pub car park that night after Nancy disappeared, there'd been a view of a farm-and-industrial pumping and drainage company forecourt. Its bluff signage ('Get Totally Pumped') had a lot in common with the laconic affection of television ads for cattle drench, four-wheel-drive utes and manly beer that made a bloke's Adam's apple surge up and down. Pat was fond of their fantasy world and she enjoyed them without turning the sound off in the cosy comfort of her flat above Oriental Bay in Wellington. There, she had a decent view of the tidily glittering city lights and of a yacht marina whose restaurant patio was loud with boastful conversation and laughter during the summer regattas. And she would often think, watching the deadpan Speight's Beer musterers or the gumbooted chap with the drench gun, that a damn good squirt of something very toxic near the arses of some of her colleagues at the Department might rid them of the toadying, risk-averse parasite that leached them of enterprise while causing them to beef up their career capital and sand-bag their mortgages.

In the deadshit view outside her unit, the pumping signage was overlaid on that of a local tourism venture. Not feeling too flash, Pat, 'under the circumstances'. But the view cheered her up heaps after poor old Biswas departed stiffly without a backward glance. She spent some time looking at the 'totally pumped' view in the bleak illumination of the sodium streetlights. Before getting down to the major job at hand.

The video cam would capture Pat's 'immersion in sportive dalliance'. The Bangladeshi tourism operator's UNDP-funded laptop would store the video clip. Biswas would transmit the clip to his Parjatan IT consultant cousin in Chittagong. This cousin was a moonlighting webmaster and video editor. He'd backdrop the clip of an ample Kiwi milkmaid with one of the many spectacular landscapes that Pat had herself captured on her own video camera. He'd post the product on the net where the dacoit in Khulna could assess its value.

'Your cousin,' began Pat.

The Bangladeshi's silent look suggested he'd rather not talk about the skill set and off-track business of his cousin in Chittagong.

'Don't say "sportive dalliance" again, Biswas, or I'll probably clock you.'

'Okay,' said Biswas, not understanding 'clock' but getting the look in Pat's eye.

'This is a trial, okay? No promises.'

'Trial?'

'Maybe this works. Maybe not.'

'Not promising, Pat.'

The tourism venture out there in the 'totally pumped' view behind Pat's 'sportive dalliance' film set consisted of a suite of themed wilderness experiences. They were in a corrugated iron warehouse whose façade had been mocked up as a mossy rock face in a muddy, plaster-like substance leaking fibrous matting at its edges and painted with snow, tussock, keas, pongas and flax bushes. Above the shed, a giant sculpted eel had reared up on a rickety gantry. Inside, visitors were promised live exhibits including eels that could be fed and kiwis that couldn't be seen. The front of the building, including its street-front window, was devoted to merchandise such as the usual chunky knitwear, various things like ug-boots and car-seat covers made out of fluffy sheepskins, and homogenous, vaguely indigenous greenstone artefacts. There were also soft toys in the shapes of kiwis, lambs, wekas and seals, a bit lumpy, probably made in the local Sheltered Workshop. There was a quantity of local landscape art whose views obeyed a rule of being depopulated. Excellent examples of the 'lonely beauty' benchmark with which Pat grimly measured the genre's adherence to a rigorous standard. A fifteen-second walk-by had sufficed to grade that lot. Tragic.

In the overnight unit, Pat pushed down and pretty much drowned out the responsible, droning, reliable sound of the professional part of her consciousness. The part that was meant to show leadership and management skill. To notice, with professional chagrin, the piss-poor quality of the tourist attraction with its tacky façade and third-rate merchandise. It was *Making Cultural Tourism Futures: a Comparative Model* report material, but largely ignored by Pat 'under the circumstances'. Pat enjoyed saying it aloud, trying for Stan's extra-sinister vibration outside the Shoganda Restaurant after lunch.

She also shut down the grin that was interfering with the simply purposeful part of her going full bore at the front of her mind. The grin was for the dejected humour of the hearty pump signage on top of the tired eel thing. Cowpat firmly closed the grimy curtains of her unit, outside which cars were gunning from the pub's car park. She briskly secured the curtain join with handy traveller's clothes pegs.

The unit's stale smell of cigarette smoke and spilled liquor advertised it as a fuck-and-crash post-pub solution for local drinkers. Its interior, brightly lit by fluorescent tubes at the end where the grubby stainless steel sink unit was, or hardly lit at all if you went by the single pinkish bulb above the bed, looked like the kind of place she'd seen in road movies. Barely secure from the pursuit car that would zoom in towards the sputtering roadside motel neon and the rifle butt that would crash past the flimsy lock on the door. Unlike the luxury accommodation where Mr Mohammed Baul Biswas had smashed all the mirrors in which he'd seen the modest body of his family desecrated. It made what Cowpat was about to try and do seem unbelievable.

This wasn't the Pat who could top up her solo glass of wine while hearing the skitey babble of the summer yachting crowd across the road from her Wellington flat. Who could take her leery Minister firmly by the arm and frogmarch him out of the reception lounge where he'd just crossed the indiscretion border yet again with one of the catering staff. The Patricia who could get away with doing this because it never occurred to Hands-On that good old Pat had a sexual nerve in her body. Who could meet and greet foreign tourists in the Shoganda Restaurant right here in the same town where wee Antsy had gone through a crack somewhere. Where Pat had just had her heart broken by the little image of Keshamoni Biswas begging not to be seen.

Maybe the elated expression on her face in the fluorescent-lit mirror above the sink had a bit to do with the cold water she'd thrown over her head and neck in preparation for a good pore-closing towelling prior to applying a spot of make-up. But how come, in the weirdly tacky setting of her unit, she'd visualised the complex unzippings of her TPU with a kind of thrill? How come the little unseeing eye of the video cam brought on the flush of confident power and amusement she enjoyed when going into meetings she knew she was going to dominate?

The rest of the team had been docile when Pat took control in the aftermath of Nancy's disappearance.

'How far can she have *gone?*' grieved Bill, sitting with his long arms hanging off his knees.

'Only as far as she had time to,' was Pat's businesslike answer. They returned to the search one more time before going to the cops. They drew a one-kilometre circumference around the Erewhon – about twice as far as Ants could have gone in thirty minutes. They walked it again, as the light faded. A half-dozen streets, spoked out from the pub's dining room. Barking dogs that would have barked at Nancy. Kids who would have noticed a thin little stranger cripple hobbling along. Shopkeepers with too little trade and too much time to look out the window. No distinctive footprints in the damp sand by the two or three access roads to the beach. No wee Antsy on the park benches by the river.

Pat filed the missing person report. Gloria went to the

hospital. William booked the shitty overnight units. Joris skived off to check an outlet.

'But she can't have just *disappeared*.' It was Bill who said it first – the team's most rigorous sceptic. 'She just disappeared. I think she said something like, "I have to go." I was telling her about Erewhon being Nowhere spelled backwards.' No one had ever seen him look this miserable. 'She knew about it,' he added. 'She was really interested.'

'It was dark in there,' said Stan. 'She was really sick,' said Gloria. 'I should have kept a closer eye on her. Too busy stuffing my face.' 'She was really small,' added Joris – as though darkness, sickness and smallness could explain Ants's disappearance.

Her crutches had remained propped by the lunch table of the pub, like the cast-off evidence of a miracle. Though Antsy, brave wee soul, had sometimes gimped around on her stork legs without them, grabbing hold of the backs of bar chairs, symposium lecterns and hotel lounge furniture, it seemed unlikely she would have done so as far as the toilets, say, at the back of the Erewhon bar. Or that she could have done this without Bill noticing her effort. Even Bill holding forth about Erewhon. Even in the dark. Even if she was small.

The crutches, together with Ants's cash and document bag with her passport and a wee medical kit in it, and what had looked sadly like a last wishes letter in an envelope, were now with the local police. Her next of kin was her dad, in retirement from the Rydges Sydney Cronulla Hotel, keeping up his regime of exercise on the beach after a morning swim, for the benefit of his tanned, busty Hell.

'A little birdie,' sobbed Gloria. A smell of coal smoke infused the chilly, salt air that poured through the town from the sea. 'It's too cold for her out there.'

'Police are saying, leave it to them. They'll have sniffer dogs here in the morning. They don't want us mucking up the scent. Because we've probably got her smell on us. If she's nowhere obvious, she'll be somewhere sheltered.' Pat opened boxes of pizza in the mini-bus. Misty spray blew past the street lights on the embankment above the dunes and the bus windows fogged up.

'Cops find her for sure.' Joris paused with a thought, lifting a string of mozzarella on one dainty finger. 'Pity she don't have a good jacket like one of mine.'

And even though Pat was now embarking on a trial whose outcome might save the naked kid with the imploring look on the Bangladeshi's cellphone, it was the ordinariness that was weirdest. The occasional car accelerated aggressively nowhere in particular and then seemed to return just as pointlessly to the place it started from. The night's almost pure, starlit silence was only faintly clouded by the dull, stony whisper of surf on the nearby beach. The CTI team's overnight surroundings in the neighborhood of nowhere spelled backwards were every bit as down-to-earth as Pat's. As ludicrously tacky as the sounds of Pat's zippers purring as she toyed with the removal of her clothing's multiple components before the small, looking-but-not-seeing circular eye of the flash United Nations Development Programme laptop-cam. Part of the worse-than-useless Biswas contract. If only the UNDP knew.

What Pat noticed: it was the purr of the multiple zips that made this weird thing begin to work for her. And, second, it was the way the little eye for which she'd begun to perform looked at her. That worked, too. Yes, it was looking. Attempting at first to overcome her sense of utter bloody absurdity, she gave the eye a silly little wave. But she soon had no sense of being seen. She was looking straight back at the little eye, which had an uncanny, black, infinite darkness within it, kind of bottomless or endless. What are my Cognitive Communication Objectives? she asked it. My Affectives? She was looking back at it the way she stared down her counterparts across the conference table. She had that 'they haven't got a fucking clue' feeling. That 'what they're looking at is one thing but what they're seeing is another' feeling.

The video cam's clueless stare gave her a surge of heated confidence. She felt on her warm face that smile of power and confident authority. The winner-already smile, the 'one-jump-ahead' smile, the 'we've-done-the-due-diligence' smile, the 'but-in-the-end-we-all-know-what-this-comes-down-to' smile.

The Pat smile, also known in some quarters as 'Pat's Great White', came on full bore in the stinky enclave of the fuck-and-crash hotel car park unit where she'd decided to go for the total available lighting. The neons down the back by the sink were sending a pallid industrial illumination along the space to where she stood near the pinkish glimmer of the forty-watt light bulb dangling above the ghastly brown candlewick bedspread.

The zip on one of the removable sleeves of her padded parka purred through half a cycle and back again, and back again – and then all the way round, until the sleeve came away at the shoulder of the puffy parka and Pat drew it down along her arm, imagining a cheesy dance-routine rhythm, revealing a nice, long-sleeved white cotton skivvy from Untouched World.

See, that was another thing. As well as not being seen as such, as the Pat behind the Great White, it was as though what was being looked at by the little what-would-you-know black eye of the video was the woman in the singlet-and-shorts togs from the Wonder Country railways brochure of 1924. The one where she's looking at a coastal view with a sailboat out there and a smoke-puffing train going into a tunnel while some seagulls observe her. As the second sleeve's zip purred teasingly to and fro and the sleeve eventually dropped to join the other one on the brown candlewick bedspread, Pat was visualising the woman in the beret and cable-knit sweater in LC Mitchell's Sport in New Zealand trout and salmon fishing poster from 1930 – where she's holding up a big rainbow trout whose mouth gapes above a staring, circular eye.

The 1933 Hermitage Mount Cook (low combined rail and motor fares) one with the stylish woman in leather knee-boots, jodhpurs and with a cigarette in her right hand and a straw hat dangling in her left was a beauty. Pat drew the growlingly purry, hefty zipper at the front of her now sleeveless padded parka to the end of its run while thinking about this poster, one of her favourites – the premier holiday resort in New Zealand. The poster-woman's side-pocketed hacking jacket is buttoned across her fashionably flat chest and it was this jacket that Pat imagined the cam-eye looking at as the woman shrugs it casually from her shoulders, while changing hands with the cigarette and dropping the straw hat carelessly on the patch of white Mount Cook daisies at her feet. The slewing thud of the soundtrack was slightly comical 'under the circumstances'. Behind the woman, who is now clad only in a thin, long-sleeved cotton skivvy in the fresh alpine air – air that has caused the woman's nipples to stiffen visibly – a man with a smart camera bag around his neck, and another man who seems to be earnestly botanising with two interested children have not noticed what the woman's doing. Had they looked, they'd have seen that the slender woman now owns a pair of handsome breasts which Pat has hefted for the video cam inside their snug, expensively plain Untouched fabric.

But in another Mitchell silk-screen print from the 1930s there's no way they couldn't have noticed, because the group of two men and two women picnicking beneath a ponga fern on a grassy bank above the shores of Lake Waikaremoana (sea of rippling waters) with the Panekiri Bluff silhouetted in the background have already stripped to their swimming togs and are athletically bare-legged on the grass.

Pat sat on the edge of the tacky unit's bed to unzip the lower halves of her trouser legs and felt the heat of her confidence reach a crisis threshold. This was familiar to her from many crisis moments, though none like this. Would this negotiation now go forward or not? Would she retain her composure? Would she stay inside the armature of her conviction? Would her role-playing survive her own informed derision – the titter of power behind her implacable Great White? And what quota of her power would she have to draw down in order to get her across this threshold?

But she needn't have worried. The heat then increased its authority. She felt it carry her forward across the crisis moment with a surge of pleasure. She saw the inevitability of her approaching triumph. There was no need, then, for the Great White to show itself – her expression became slightly taunting, perhaps, but discreetly so. Something like modesty, or at least something like a modesty of effort – nothing ostentatious, nothing try-hard – characterised the firm, decisive unzipping actions with which her trousers became shorts. The bottom halves of the trouser legs flew extravagantly across the room out of camera range.

It was the smoothly tanned legs of the blonde woman on the mountain bike in the foreground of the second-generation Absolutely Pure campaign posters, the ones that added activities and people and the warm shades of sunny, yellow summer grass to William's intellectual originals, that Pat imagined the little black eye of the video cam looking at as she felt her running-hot confidence override William's disdainful sneer. Just like she'd overridden (as if on a mountain bike) his sneering objections to this dilution of his creepy vision of a place that really was nowhere and home to no one. The woman's bicycling down a hot, grassy hill after a man on another mountain bike and the hills in the distance are folded with dark creases of shadow where bush grows and where tawny saddles and ridges are upraised into the light.

Naked then, sumptuously fleshed and bushed, pale-mounded against the brown bedspread, her yoghurt skin-tones warmed slightly by the unit's grudging low-wattage bedroom bulb, Pat spoke for the first time to the gormless eye of the video camera. She imagined what she couldn't visualise because, unlike the posters whose images were the daily stock-in-trade resource database of her professional beliefs, she had no useful mental pictures, no poster images, of the Krishna milkmaid proposed to her by Biswas. He'd managed, with an incongruously decorous and unsmiling mimed rotation of his thin wrists, neck and hips, to convey an allure at once sophisticated and voluptuous. But not much to work with.

'How's this?' she said, feeling how the warmth of her triumph made her gestures and movements supple, even unjointed. 'How am I doing? Do you like this? Is this what you like? This is what I like.'

Looking but not seeing.

'This is what Cowgirl likes.'

fourteen

Purity

'Do I know you?' Gloria can smell what Uncle Mat calls stinkers a mile off, even here in smelly old Rotorua – home of Ngati Stinkbomb as studly cuz from Rawene said, way back at Milford. Now that was a long time ago. There's another handy Uncle Mat expression: 'Don't give me that princess look, girl!' Hinemoana knows how to fit her face into it when she has to. Right now, Uncle Mat. For this stinker. Here he comes. Seen this little prick before. Oh yes.

'My friends call me Rick,' says the slight, beaky man whose youthfulness fades under a weary cross-hatching of lines on his pale face as he leans closer, offering thin, cigarette-stained fingers. He's placed his almost empty coffee cup next to Gloria's wine. 'It's great to see you again, Hine.'

'Richard,' says Princess Hinemoana, ignoring the stinky fingers. 'What can I do for you.'

'Manaakitanga conference, 1985. Maori Tourism Task Force, 1987. We were both a lot younger.' The man withdraws his fingers and is even amused by Gloria's princess reserve. Got that naughty boy look. Better at shit-stirring than good manners.

'But, and correct me if I'm wrong, Richard, you were still Pakeha, back then?'

'You mean, what was I doing there then?' Ageing naughty boy Rick looks delighted. 'Which is really another way of asking what I'm doing here now?' He winks. 'Not what I was doing then, never worry.'

Gloria looks around – the team's scattered tonight. But

this grinning mongrel's dreaming if he thinks he can isolate her. 'If you want to get bitten, watch the dog's teeth not its bum,' said koro Mat. Stinker Richard's not wagging anything. In for the kill. Trying to read the upside-down text of her report. She's had a not-too-bad glass of Chard Farm or two in the past and God knows she's already written the same report at least six times in her life and koreroed it at least sixty, always to the nodding heads, especially the nodding Pakeha heads. Not getting a lot of fun out of the wine, either. Not really reading one, not really drinking the other. Listening to batsqueaky koro getting in her ear, telling her off for doing both of them. Now, she turns the report over with its title page down and takes a stone-faced sip of the wine.

Biz and Pat are, as usual these days, in a huddle over in the lounge area. Putting out the big signal that they always meet in public spaces, not in each other's rooms – as though the rest of the team gives a shit. As usual they're shuffling their joint Purity and Beauty chapter around. Bet your life stinker Richard would have paid good money to see the effect their draft presentation had on the Minister's peer review panel this morning at DoT. Seriously spooked them out. Hands-On went as red as a beetroot and the others puckered up. Sex tourism, undeclared GNP and black-market supplies of Viagra and anti-STD Zithromax – and that was just Purity! Hard act to follow.

Poor old Biswas is still in his plain suit, all wrinkled up with travel. No sign of a smile for four or five days – not since the smashed mirrors. Wouldn't news-hound Richard love that one, too. No one's talking about it. Maybe Biz doesn't want to look himself in the eye. More spooks. And then there's warrior woman Pat, she's practically radioactive these days, what's more she's given up on the ghastly outdoor zip-ups for a while, ever since Antsy had to go. Since she went. Tonight, Pat's in the baggy cotton pants from Untouched World, as though that's more formal, like her mate's slept-in suit. Someone should tell the girl, but it won't be me, thinks Gloria.

And if stinker Richard wants a who-can-last-longest silence competition, that's fine. His sour cigarette smell's overlaid with a too-sweet cologne or aftershave – cologne that would have to be, because his shave isn't too recent and the stubble on his pointy chin is silvery. Are we all getting past it? I'm tired, koro, says Gloria to Uncle Batsqueaker – need some of what that little Aussie had, that don't-ever-give-up spirit. But then Ants did. Called it a day.

Gloria sees Richard mapping the room with her own silent survey. Bill has stuck to bits and pieces of the Boris outfit and it still makes him look dressed-up as someone else. He misses you too, Antsy – you played with funny old Absolutely Pure William. Made him laugh, made me look hard and see things again. Made me listen to Uncle Mat again.

Bill's watching the replay of a cricket match on the bar's television and drinking a moody succession of gins. Joris hasn't returned from a survey of adventure marketing in the town.

Yeah, right.

'So – this is the team,' says Richard brightly. His shit-stirrer instinct stops it sounding like a question. 'Minus one, of course.'

'The nature of a country's dependence on tourism and on the way that dependence brands the country will together determine the kind of tourist experience the country produces.' Gloria's read as well as heard the Bangladeshi tourism operator's draft, after Pat's edit. Pat's work is deadly, but it barely conceals the document it's slapped a coat of departmental-type language over the top of. 'Bangladesh conforms to the IMF and World Bank profiles of a Developing Nation or even of an LDC (Least Developed Country) – its economy is international aid dependent. As such, Bangladesh does not need tourism, is certainly not dependent on it and has not developed the infrastructure to support it.' Gloria ranks the Pat-assisted Biswas Purity report chapter as one of the weirdest documents she's ever encountered. Quite fabulous, a work of genius. She wishes she had the guts and optimism to write her own version of it. 'Because Bangladesh does not need, or have, tourism to contribute to its national brand, the kinds of tourist experiences it produces lie beneath the brand – are effectively concealed by it. They are secret experiences that benefit from their concealment beneath Bangladesh's reputation for underdevelopment, natural catastrophes and civil disorder.'

In the DoT seminar room that morning, Biswas hid his usual fabulous smile as well and it was about then that the silence in the room began to go septic. Hands-On went red. Squeaky noises of bums shifting in seats. The first part of the 'Purity and Beauty' thing was interrupted now and again by quotes from someone Biswas said was the Baul poet Lalon Shah. Everyone was meant to know this? Biswas plodded through a long catalogue of the Western media's obsession with natural catastrophes in Bangladesh – floods, tidal bores, famines and epidemics. Next was a one-paragraph summary of Bengal's history as the most fertile country in the world. You could see where Biswas was going with this. He did a snappy summary of the colonial destruction of Bengal's wealth, British textile protectionism and slave-subsidised American cotton. Then, a one-paragraph description of Bangladesh's place among the Least Developed Countries (LDCs) in the world.

And then the summary of what Biswas and Pat have called 'Undeclared Gross National Product'.

Gloria watched the Minister's tame peer-reviewers' lips secretly tasting the shape of UGNP. But the shit began to hit the fan in earnest when Biswas droned his way into a catalogue of what UGNP consisted of. Revenues associated with smuggling, drug trafficking and sex tourism.

'Known as "road trips",' enunciated Biswas woodenly. 'RTs.'

Several panel members, including the Minister of feeling-up-the-hospitality-staff, made throat-clearing noises at this point. Water glasses got topped up. Hands-On was looking at Pat, who was looking back at him with her best 'Yes, and?' expression. You could feel the lightning bolts ripping across the table between them. In Gloria's ear, Uncle Mat was pissing himself. Then the Bangladeshi suggested that the environmental and social impacts of progress, including eco-tourism, should be included as negative effects in calculations of GNP. A lot more chair-shifting and the Minister of manaakitanga-in-my-suite had done a really obvious 'Now, now,' throat-clear.

Like a story you know being told in a foreign accent, Gloria thought. Especially the bit where seven hundred Mro families were resisting plans to open an 'eco-park' on tribal land in the Chittagong Hill Tracts.

Richard lights a cigarette – the little prick's daring her to break her silence and tell him to put the filthy thing out. Instead, a barman does so. Richard stubs it in the saucer of his cup after a long drag.

'Sorry,' he says, cheerfully. 'It's just so easy to forget some things.' He keeps his ferrety eyes on her. 'Others, you never forget.'

Back at DoT in Wellington that morning, Biswas chose to be oblivious to the distress signals coming from across the conference table. His report summarised the dire travel alerts (TAs) for Bangladesh of the major international tourist client providers. The Americans, British, Japanese and assorted Europeans were told that if they didn't get sick they'd probably be mugged or would die in gruesome transport accidents by land, sea or air.

'The question is,' read Biswas, raising his eyes to look at the DoT panel members and leaving his neat moustache and lips in a little snarl around the word 'is' – 'The question is,' he repeated, more slowly, 'who is coming?' This question he also repeated, twice, giving the words an oddly elided emphasis.

'Who-is-coming?' Holding the looks of the discomforted panel. 'Who-is-coming?'

The other bit where Biswas got animated was whenever he used a phrase, 'shonar Bangla'. Kept saying it. Like everyone should know. Next, his team-mate Pat tramped reliably across the familiar terrain of viewable natural beauty and even chucked a few of her video examples up on the screen. 'Shonar Bangla' kept echoing among the spectacular mountains, coastlines, recreational and cultural facilities and viewing infrastructures of 'Beauty'. But the video clips had a soothing effect on the panel – some of them made mooing sounds of pleasure as the national museum slid out of the panoramic frame and a glittering harbour came in, as more ocean wobbled under lurexy sunshine beyond the Moeraki Boulders, as jet boats unzipped rivers, the Cleddau pistoned into its Chasm, Mitre Peak thrust up from its own reflection and pissed punters poled under city bridges. How could the girl keep doing this?

But when Biswas crooned 'Shonar Bangla' over and over during his Purity chapter, it was like a taunt – like a wero. Nobody was going to pick it up. Each time he said it, he flashed his teeth and adjusted the sheets of paper he was reading from.

'Is meaning, golden Bangla.' Biswas kept the teeth showing long enough to finish a flourish of his hands and a sway of his head. The last part of Purity was full of 'shonar Banglas' and menacing shows of the Biswas teeth. He flashed them at festivals and descriptions of ordinary Bangladeshi life breaking the surfaces of catastrophe reports and travel alerts.

'Is life-and-death,' said Mohammed Baul Biswas, pushing his Purity paper aside. He might as well have handed the panel hammers and invited them to nail down his report's coffin. 'Is living, not looking. Life, isn't it. Not lovely view.' At the last moment, Biswas tore loose with his best smile – as though he'd been saving maximum wattage. The smile wasn't charming and when it flashed across the conference table it scared the living daylights out of the peer review panel, including Hands-On. 'What is Travel Alert (TA) for beauty?' Biswas passed the discussion to Pat using a courteous, open-palmed gesture. 'Is maybe Pat to tell.'

'Thank you, Mr Biswas,' said Pat, staunchly. 'You're a very hard act to follow.'

'So, how's it going – the cultural tourism initiative?' Richard's enjoying pricking at Gloria's silence. 'I must ask one of you some time, one of the team, those that remain, Hine, exactly what it is you mean by "cultural tourism".' He manages to say 'cultural tourism' with just the right amount of shit-stir, and Gloria loses her cool.

'As I remember it, Richard, the last time we had dealings was a bit more recent than 1985 or even 1987, when we were, as you say, younger. And greener. The last time was when you wrote a story in which you implied, way too safely to get done for libel, that what you called nepotism was rife in the Maori tourism sector and that I was one of the pipes – "conduits" was your word – to it for government funding. Especially in the north – Tai Tokerau. Seem to remember you mentioned Ruapekapeka and . . .' Gloria feels Uncle Mat's hackles go up, so she doesn't mention Waiomio, his marae. 'Would that be about right?'

Richard snaps his fingers – his expression is delighted as well as surprised. 'Of course – how could I have forgotten? Sorry about that. But you probably know how it is. How detail wipes itself out as you go along. There's always that other story waiting.' He is looking at Gloria's upside-down report. 'Or that other non-disclosure to take care of.'

On-screen above the bar, an Australian batsman has just made his century with a show-off six into the top of the stand at Eden Park. Bill cheers mockingly – Gloria sees him raise his empty gin glass and then look into it. His own interim report on Identity, twinned with Joris's on Adventure, is an impeccable, deadpan, not-one-word-too-many, almost robotic mini-masterpiece of dutiful bureaucratic formatting and citation, with succinct digital images and a judicious use of flow-charts and pie-diagrams. The fact that it summarises the state of Identity, and especially National Identity initiatives and impacts at regional, site-specific and Adventure-related levels seems pretty much totally bloody irrelevant. What it does is, it gives you a sense of orderly intelligence, of problem-solving that will now be well within the grasp of (now) better-informed Ministry officials. Just the kind of report, Gloria knows, that will probably produce no action because, like the perfect shopping list, it seems to have done the job already.

The DoT review team loved it to bits and the Minister of bad-sauna-jokes congratulated the team as a whole as though William's bare-faced cynicism had made up for the Bangladeshi tourism operative's bizarre flights of fancy about TAs for Purity and roadshow sex tourism, Pat's dependably thorough stocktake of natural Beauty, Joris's energetic diatribe about the absence of venture capital and her own how-many-times-do-I-have-to-do-this, shut-up-please-Uncle-Mat, polite, patient, soft-spoken interrogation of the borders of commercial positivity and manaakitanga.

And then, last, there was dear wee Nancy's unfinished analysis of road signs. It was how she did her Authenticity thing. How could a paper about something like that be so simple and so angry? Richard is still looking at her upside-down manaakitanga pages as though he can X-ray through them to Ants's ones, which Gloria has tucked inside her own as if that way they'll keep warm.

'"... the highways of cultourism are littered with the burned-out wrecks of enterprises that failed because they lost heart, or never had one,"' read William in an unemphatic, professional-sounding voice. He did it because Gloria couldn't have trusted herself to get through Antsy's paper without breaking down all over the big DoT conference table. '"It would be appropriate to begin with a grand sweep rather as Marco Polo did in the thirteenth century when collaborating with Rustichello of Pisa in writing an account of his travels: *Let me begin with Armenia*,"' read Bill without smiling, though Gloria did and she imagined Bill, too, was hearing the quiver of amusement in the little Aussie's quick, birdy voice. Bill didn't lift his eyes from her pages. '"There are, in some cultures, places that seem to be nowhere because they only exist when brought back into being and back into time by ritual, narrative or seasonal events."' Gloria held the sob at the base of her throat, but Bill continued to push Nancy's clear voice out into the DoT seminar room using his own dry, unemphatic, factual tone. '"We need to consider that it may be better, sometimes, to get lost, to not understand, to not know where you are, than to never escape the comfort zone of official direction."' Bill was turning the pages neatly and adjusting their margins as he read. '"We see the colour drain from these exploited places,"' read Bill, '"we watch them becoming exhausted, we see their souls fade and the souls of their exhausted viewers fade, too, like the old snapshots of their past outings down roads whose rich narratives have been reduced to the impoverished captions of directional signage."' Probably, it was only because William was reading Nancy's paper and because the DoT peer review team and their Minister were besotted with him that they didn't rebel at the audacious Aussie's full-on challenge. It went on for several more pages, 'signage, burned out wrecks, ghosts and all'.

Bill didn't lift his eyes from these pages even once and remained seated through all of them. But he looked up finally when the last page had been added to the neat, margin-adjusted pile of those he'd read and everyone saw that he was moist-eyed. And then he said directly to the Minister, almost as a challenge of his own, but in the same dry William voice, 'I consider this to be an especially fine piece of work and I'm sure I speak for the team when I say we miss our dear Australian colleague greatly.'

'I'd offer you a drink, *Rick*,' says Gloria with overt malice, finishing hers. 'But I know you don't. Any more.'

'Clearly you still do,' says Richard. 'It's been nice seeing you again, Hinemoana. Hine. Looking good on it, too.' His conspiratorial wink is a micro-measure away from insulting, but he picks up his cup and saucer and is gone before Gloria can reassemble her princess look. Little shit – she'll have to give him that round.

The cricket has finished – the last show-off six was the fucking coup-de-grâce. Bill looks up from a meditation on the backs of his hands. The greenish veins that faintly distend the papery skin there are like subterranean lodes of solid, possibly frozen, turquoise water and their tranquil solidity and motionlessness have their equivalents in a silence that is mineral, a formulation of impervious stasis that can only be reactivated by the introduction of a molecule-shifting chemical agent. Is that molecule-shifting agent of change Boris? Corrupt, mendacious, egregious – agonisingly, viciously, irresistibly charming Boris? Is it this horrible charm that has caused the perfect, hard, mineral, turquoise ice of William's blood to begin to move and flow inside Bill, that has made the backs of Bill's hands look like maps of new, unknown places, that has made him want to step out into huge spaces where huge flows occur under huge skies, that has made him astonished at his affectionate grief for the bright, brave intelligence of Antsy, that has stopped him at the moment when an automatic, wry, disclaiming habit of satire might have changed the lump of grief in his throat to a derisive laugh?

But it is the sound of a fresh glass with ice being placed on the table next to him that makes him look up from his meditation and that announces the arrival of Richard. Not Boris. Boris is still out there, somewhere – in his mercantile adventure territory, his game park of little, tanned, sinewy, blonde sluts, his moist-fingered, Good-2-Go geishas.

'Barman said it was Bombay with bitters, hope you don't mind,' says Richard who has himself come prepared with a glass of aerated mineral water and a twist of lime. He takes a long sip while Bill looks at him and he looks back at William. Bill sees someone he does not know but recognises immediately. The freshly flowing blood in his hands, his sense of wide open spaces filled with hope, despair and sadness – these shut down, they contract suddenly like the defensive apparatus of a sea anemone, like a turtle shrugging itself under its shell, like William stepping back behind the glassy screen of his disdain. Bill does not want to be William, not right now, not when he has begun to feel something new happening to him and to the pure chemistry of his fear – but how can Bill even begin to measure the distance between his immediate dislike and fear of this thin, peering man, whom he does not know and whom he has no reason to dislike or fear, and his love of Boris, whom he has, increasingly and incrementally, many reasons to hate, mistrust and avoid?

This is not a measurement Bill is prepared to investigate tonight, given also that Boris had promised to be back an hour ago, but is not. But never is. Never fucking is. And certainly, Bill is not prepared to start such an investigation at the margin where he knows it is Boris's blatant attempts to manipulate him, Bill, and Boris's almost-taunting, barely concealed disdain for Bill's infatuation for him, Boris, that only increase Boris's tormenting appeal to him, Bill – Boris, Boris the stupid fucking joke nickname, Boris whose light cuffs to the side of Bill's head (which he now no longer ducks) have become slightly vicious with impatience.

On the other hand – Bill's face does not show this, but a sudden rush of something like agoraphobic terror makes his testicles rush up into his stomach, which clenches above them – on the other hand, at the other margin of the measurement, where this unknown man of slight build and uncertain age is managing to sustain unruffled, patient eye-contact over the rim of his frosty glass, Bill's first startled, chilling thought is that he, Bill, must now . . . For the first time in his, Bill's, William's, life, he must now look as though he could be worthwhile picking up. That the ferrety-faced man who has brought, *bought*, him, Bill, a drink! – is 'hitting on' him?

Has William changed that much? How does it show on Bill? How does he, Bill, look?

How finely, earlier in the day, at the DoT debrief in Wellington, he had calibrated his anticipation of the expectations of the peer review team and how calmly he had seen his own sensation of egregious fraudulence barely concealed in the blank expressions of his project teammates, who all, with the exception of the bizarre Mr Biswas, knew precisely what he was up to and despised him for his callousness, the review panel for its suggestibility and themselves for their cowardice and disingenuousness. But how unexpected to also recognise, with unfamiliar distaste and self-loathing instead of self-satisfaction, his, Bill's, sense of superiority at the trivial gratification of the peer reviewers with his cynically apposite report.

He, Bill, had discovered, looking at the familiar, gloating relief on the Minister's face which seemed, even more than usual, to have become thickened with a masturbatory relish of self-vindication during Bill's presentation, and looking at the barely concealed rage and impatience ('Why you don't do this for me?') in Boris's lightly head-cocked attention – Bill had discovered himself looking back, or in, at William as though from a slight, double-vision distance, and realising that he, William, had indeed changed. That the hard, reliable blood in the backs of William's hands was moving in new maps. That these maps were Bill's adventures, his wide open spaces, his risks, forfeits and rewards, his show-off sixes over the stand.

How do I look?

The stranger across the table is still looking patiently at him and Bill has a moment left in which he remembers, that morning at DoT, reading aloud in an officious, self-protective monotone, Antsy's lovely, sometimes angry, almost forensic description of the roads they had been travelling all these days while Boris's hard thigh's warmth reached him in their cosy two-by-two seat in the mini-bus, and while the sound of Antsy's quick, careful words and long, quivering silences came indirectly and indistinctly to him from the seat next to Gloria's. What an effort it cost to say what he said at the end, looking straight at the Minister's fleshy, onanist's face – to say that this, Dr Nancy Shapiro's, was a good piece of work, a great piece of work! In order to say that he had to heave the words over an immense lump in his throat that was there not just out of grief for whatever had happened to wee Nancy, but out of a sudden flood, a surge of unlocked or unfrozen feeling for the new person he seemed to have begun to become – a great flood of feeling, like frozen water flowing, for this Bill who could see exactly what Absolutely Pure William was up to and could despise it every bit as much as he could see his team-mates despising it. But who, equally, could see that Bill's ongoing humiliation at Boris's hands was both degrading and the engine of poor, pure William's liberation.

Bill stands up. He feels rigid – as though he might break apart and fall to the floor with a tinkling sound like broken glass or ice. See? – both Gloria and Pat are watching to see what is going to happen with this encounter, this 'pick up'. He feels light, angry, amused, even a bit flattered – flattered less by this unattractive man's attention than by his own attention to his new self. Yes, he has had a few gins, but that is not all there is to it.

'Sorry,' says Bill. 'Dance card's full.'

The strange man manages an instantly constructed look of astonished disbelief. 'Surely you don't think that I . . .?'

But Bill walks quickly, leaving the fresh drink behind, trusting to his forward momentum, towards the lobby lifts and his room near the top of the building with its balcony, its view of the lake, and the mephitic atmosphere that gusts from the thermal wonderland below. He knows, because he has already done it, that he can now stand at the rail of the balcony and look out and down for short periods of time without reeling in horror and vertigo at the vastnesses of day and night under the big sky, the immense depth of space and the terrible width of horizons. Just to get there, to the balcony, and practise being unafraid – that is the thing to do right now.

There'd been a moment back at Wellington DoT Central that morning, when Pat had caught the Minister out with a look on his sensual face that had come as a bit of a shock. Known the man professionally and on a great many palsy-walsy social occasions for years and years. Heard the usual hot gossip about him and remained unsurprised and, bet your life, unoffended by his obvious lack of sexual interest in her. Knew better than most in the industry that he humoured a vigorous appetite for young things in hospitality. Always counted herself lucky to be armed, apparently, with natural disincentives. Of which age was only one. What didn't get talked about at the water-cooler was the number of occasions when the fleshy Minister, known in some quarters as 'Hands-On', had had to get baled out of pretty seriously compromising and on one or two occasions career-threatening dipstick bloody fuck-ups. Good old Pat's own premonitory, problem-solving skills had got the silly bugger out of his own squalid mess more than once.

He was on very thin ice right now on several counts. How did Pat know this only too well? Not just because the Minister told her so himself. Because the whole bloody tourism environment did. Tell her. The sector was asking for some leadership and vision. His Prime Minister was asking for some media-rich policy outputs. The NGOs including Maori were lobbying him day and night. The Borises of this world were whingeing on about investment and venture capital. The air was filled with the thin, plaintive cries of the disappointed and the clotting of email traffic was life-threatening to the Minister's political prospects.

Whence the Cultural Tourism Initiative (CTI) career-buttressing move. And with it, Hands-On looking as though he might pop his foofoo valve this morning when Biswas launched into his Baul poet rant with sexual tourism and 'roadshows' thrown in for good measure. No amount of Pat's bureau stucco was going to cover the bulges and cracks in that lot, pardon the expression. The Minister had been directing an especially questioning look at her as the team manager and a senior member of his ministry's staff long trusted to wrangle his pet schemes for him. Knew it well, the look that said pretty directly, 'What the fucking fuck is this, Pat? What did I tell you? Keep this one together? Didn't I tell you that?'

Managed quite well earlier, in her Ministerial one-to-one, to fudge the broken mirrors debacle back at the glacier by implying that Mr Biswas, unused to Western amenities, had lost his balance while . . . ('All right, Pat, thanks, I get the picture.') The disappearance of that bloody Australian brainy hotshot could hardly be held against her as team manager, but, warned the Minister, his office had received some fairly interested media enquiries. 'Need to keep this one tidy, Pat.'

See, and now there goes old Bill, pissed as a fart, heading in a straight line with the destination-focused precision of a drunk man towards the lifts. How do you expect me to keep that 'tidy'? Ground him? What's more, Pat sees the joker she knows by reputation as a shit-stirring investigative look after Bill with an expression of greedy, triumphant delight on his weasly face. And there's Gloria over there watching the action too with a very Gloria look on *her* face. It's happening to Pat again, that sensation of disaster-convergence.

Just imagine. Wouldn't it be great if bloody William decided to come out of his Absolutely Pure closet and start trying to root another member of Hands-On's CTI team? Just after one of its international members has gone mysteriously AWOL? And after another UNDP-sponsored international appears to have gone totally psycho, smashed flash hotel mirrors and written a report on sexual tourism? And if, at that very moment, requiring experienced hold-this-together team-leader management skills, a shit-stirring investigative decided to show up and ply the newly vulnerable team links with tongue-loosening drink? At least William had the nous to clear out, thank the gods of small mercies.

But what to make of the unusual event on the Minister's face from earlier on, this morning, across the big table down at DoT? This is what now returns sharply into focus at the very moment Pat's premonitory, disaster-convergence instinct lines up Bill appearing to rebuff an advance from a journo, Gloria's molten lava expression and the journo's 'on-to-something' look swinging her and the Bangladeshi's way.

The project team, bless them, got their best, blank, see-no-evil, hear-no-evil, speak-no-evil expressions on their faces and the motley assortment of Hands-On's tame peer reviewers rather more fishy looks accompanied by buttock-shifting and paper fiddling, as Biswas, with polite formality, took them through his completely off-the-wall shonar Bangla presentation. And then, swear on something or other holy, in the midst of Hands-On's 'what-the-fuck' look straight at her during this, no doubt about it – something else entirely happened in the Minister's brain. This event rushed directly, hotly, a tidal wave of uncontrollable blood, into the thickly layered tissue of his face.

Now the beaky-faced investigative's approaching with neat, mincing steps, across the rather swirly patterns of the bar's carpet. Behind him, Gloria's making a slicing gesture across her throat. Pat's curt nod is for Gloria, but the journo takes it as his.

'It's the CTI team, isn't it,' Richard says, with that provocative non-questioning inflection. 'Unwinding a bit, as you do. Mind if I sit down?' He lowers himself into the seat opposite Pat and Biswas without waiting for an answer.

He extends his smoker's fingers to Biswas. 'Name's Richard,' he says. 'Richard Brawn, *National Inquirer*.' He knows better than to pause here. 'I'm interested in your project. Cultural tourism. How would you define that, exactly? Cultural tourism?'

Biswas shakes his hand, but his attention has suddenly shifted to the three dapper, swarthy men who have entered the lounge. They are the same men who have shadowed the progress of the CTI team since the turquoise southern lakes. 'Excuse me Mr Richard, excuse me, Pat,' says Biswas. He stands up, carefully, methodically, calmly zipping the contents of his report into his attaché case. He leaves without fuss, but one wing of his shirt collar's come loose above his rumpled suit jacket and it had been clear, while he was still sitting, that he is not wearing socks with his black leather slip-ons.

'Okay, Mr Biswas, see you later,' says Pat. 'We'll polish it off in the morning, probably. Have a quiet night.'

'Biswas, was it?' Richard leans forward. 'Let me guess – Bangladesh.' It's clear he's done his preliminaries. 'Too bad, everybody's leaving. Including your Australian, I hear.'

Pat knows about this guy. She has no trouble marshalling her best media manner and Richard spots it a mile off. Third stonewall in a row. He won't have much trouble figuring out that this story's going to be well worth the effort. Pat leans back, smiling, and waits for the moment when she'll have to respond to him. But meanwhile, what about that moment? Back at DoT? The one when Hands-On's hot blush and facial whacko got the better of his familiar 'what-the-fuck' piercing look? – the glare he'd probably copied from the Prime Minister and practised in front of the bathroom mirror in the ministerial flat?

But the whacko blush had been completely unrehearsed and totally out of control. If only for a nanosecond. And – it had been all about her. About good old, solid as, safe pair of hands, warhorse, Great White Pat. An image of her had whacked Hands-On right smack in the action gland bit of his brain. She might as well have reached all the way across the conference table and grabbed him by the nuts. In all the years she'd known the man, sidled carefully around the edges of his sleazy ways, turned a blind eye to his escapades, counted herself lucky not to be anywhere near his dodgy radar, she'd never seen or imagined she ever would see him look at her.

Look at her like that.

He'd tucked the jolt back inside his piercing look so fast she hadn't been sure, then, that she'd seen what she thought she'd seen. But she had. Oh yes. Bet your life on it.

Richard's prepping up to do professional journalist-type jousting. Few wee signs of strain starting to show. Here's another lead, Mr *National Inquirer*.

Cowgirl. Add that to your list of research topics. After the berserk Bangladeshi, the missing Aussie and the deviant National Identity brander. Because, it now dawns on Pat, as Richard 'sharpens his pencil' and takes a preparatory swallow of his fizzy water, she'd never imagined she'd ever see her Minister, see Hands-On, look at Cowgirl like that. Look at broad-based Pat, see Cowgirl.

The bugger's been to Cowgirl.com! The sensation of this thought's not unlike the triumphant power-surges of Pat's nightly Krishna milkmaid performances in front of the little black eye of the UNDP-sponsored Cowgirl-cam.

'Yes, Richard,' says Pat with a pleasant smile. 'That's right. I imagine Mr Biswas, who is indeed from Bangladesh, has gone to pray. He does so five times a day. He's a devout Muslim, you know.' She gives Richard the benefit of her best artificial pause. 'And, clearly, you do know.'

The lift is lined with mirrors. Mohammed Baul Biswas ascends calmly – but he closes his eyes. Peaceful, isn't it – like dreaming. The elevator hums and vibrates gently, rising through many floors, rivers of electricity, floods of hot water, heat and light and aircon, telephone, room service, cable, internet – like a busy street other side of the smooth walls, voices of cable video, of hundreds of radios and wake-up calls, the air thick, muddy and dreamy with them.

But the music is always there too and he can't rest.

Can't sleep at night because not wanting to dream of Keshamoni and getting so tired and then going up and down through the dreamy bodies of hotels and offices in elevators like jute divers in thick water, hearing the world noise far off through sarat harvest water. It is then that Biswas drifts towards other places where he begins to see Keshamoni and has to wake himself up quickly – not-seeing Keshamoni, not looking and not seeing. Not even sure of the time, the clocks and watches saying one thing but body-mind not sure. Praying more than five times a day, doesn't matter any more. The comforting sensation of water rinsing his mouth, of its cleansing, blessing coolness on his face, the relief of his feet free of shoes, mind free of the strange words and the strange not-understanding silences like this morning at the Presentation (DoT). Better, thoughts and words bathing him in the simple, familiar routines of prayer. Making these words fill his mind to keep out the music in the elevators, in the hotel lounges and restaurants, even in the mini-bus.

The elevator stops with a bump that almost wakes him – his eyes open under water at first and he walks out into the corridor feeling the sound of elevator music dragged away from his forehead, its weight and pressure falling away from his temples and brow. He is waking from the sounds of his dreams, the cheap, writhing, repeated, taunting sound of a music track for a video in which a girl might-be Keshamoni can't-be Keshamoni sidles around a small room looking for a way to turn the music off, because while it plays she can't stop, she has to keep taking off her clothes. And then Biswas wakes and she is dressed again and then he sleeps or almost sleeps, in the elevators, in the lounges and lobbies of the hotels where the music always plays, in the elevator of the DoT office and Keshamoni was there, too, when he did the

Presentation. Keshamoni still prowling in the room looking for the music that will not stop to let her sleep, will not let her stop taking off her clothes.

In his room the mirrors are covered by towels. Biswas sets up for the night's Cowgirl transmission. Khulna not happy with missing whales, like Cowgirl promised: 'Whale-of-a-Time'. Tonight, is mud and geysers: 'Geyserland'. Not, never looking. Not thinking about sportive dalliance streaming into his laptop and on to Parjatan IT consultant webmaster cousin in Chittagong and dacoit in Khulna. He sets up the wireless connection for Cowgirl-cam in Pat's room, all ready.

The dacoit in Khulna like Cowgirl very much and so do webmasters – already on 3000 pay sites and getting 20,000 hits every 24 and growing. Biswas sees the comfortingly factual data in his cousin's emails stretching across the surface of a wide river or lake like a trail of moonlight towards the other side where Keshamoni waits for the revenue target to be reached.

He changes to a lunghi and steps out on the balcony. The light rain has stopped and no longer dampens the strong, comforting smell of geyserland. Down there, stinking steam rises across a landscape encrusted with the town's buildings like the giant silica deposits and encrustations below the hotel. The buildings cover a giant rubbish dump, like bushti shelters along railway near Moahkali, on road to Narayanganj, in garbage heaps on road to Comilla – only this is the earth's rubbish not the city's and these tourists with expensive video cameras and hotels with never-stopping music are bushti on the surface of Prakriti nature.

There are hot pools connected with the hotel and Biswas can hear the languid sounds of people bathing there, but further off a path of moonlight has appeared on the lake as the clouds and rain blow away. How calm – how pure, to walk out into the bright lake and be blessed by moonlight on water, to join hands in full moon chait prayer and be forgiven.

Here, is not Absolutely Pure – the air is thick and smelly, world skin dangerous and thin, like a prawn gher, like a stopbank, like jute floods, like islands of char silt.

Behind Biswas the dream hotel is humming with light, heat, electricity, television, food, and the taunting music that will not let him sleep. In Pat's room, the eye of Cowgirl-cam. Out there is moonlight, the lake, smelly, purifying steam, the thin skin of Prakriti. 'I have become filthy,' says Biswas, at a loss for the appropriate song words of Lalon. 'I am sinful. What has happened to my heart? How can I forgive what took away my wife, my child, my mother and father? Why must I still pay for saving Keshamoni? Why is my heart a machine to save Keshamoni, a screen, a video, a wireless, not a man's heart? How to be simple again, to sleep and dream and wake up, to pray, to live, to feel, to look, to see – to look-see again? Not this machine-heart that will begin to glow inside music hotel when Cowgirl talks to Chittagong, to Khulna, tonight.'

There is no music in the back stairs of the hotel and Biswas descends nimbly through its body close to its humming flank and emerges in a service area to one side of the coach park. No one there – he spies the CTI project team's mini-bus which Stan drove up to meet them after the team flew to Wellington, missing Kaikoura 'Whale-of-a-Time'.

The air is cool around his bare legs in the lunghi and Biswas eagerly skirts the fenced-off, steaming, spot-lit places in the parkway leading to the lake. It might be a smile that begins to comfort the ache of calmness in his face. He does not mind when a car flicks its headlights at him crossing one of the hotel's lakeside approaches and a man's voice shouts angrily as the car passes and as he steps through the thickly planted berm of flax and hebe. There is a place with picnic tables where cars can park at the lake's edge and Biswas smells ganja smoke coming from a group of young men and women at one of the tables, but he does not mind, either, when they laugh at him walking fully clad into the icy water across a patch of sand that seems to be heated. The moon trail that was visible from his hotel balcony is concealed by mist on the surface of the water, or it might be steam – tendrils of warmth wrap his legs as he wades further in, bringing his hands up before his face, shuddering at the icy chill yet feeling warmth in it.

Joining his hands he stands within the watery body of Prakriti who destroys and saves, who comforts and frightens, who chills and warms, who drowns and gives life, from whose brown, stinking, swirling surface the dark crown of Keshamoni's head had risen, in which her long hair had streamed out, black enough to see against the yellow water, so he could seize a handful while he clung, was pinned, to the listing bamboo poles of his family's platform, while the bamboo dagger drove through his palm.

Also remembering the warmth of Keshamoni's thin little body against him in the chilly brown water of the torrent that had pushed aside the flood-bank with one hand and taken his family with the other – the same water that had always seemed cool and friendly when you bathed in it, when you walked out on the bottom step of the ghat and felt it bear you up as you swam little-way out. And then one brown hand of the river had lifted Keshamoni up to him, had handed her to him, had placed her within the grasp of his own hand.

Where Keshamoni still was, where he held her above the chilly water, where he kept her little body warm, where he would one day soon be able to look at her again, where one day soon she would let him look at her again and see Keshamoni herself again.

O my God! Allah! Shelter of the world! Emperor of all! It is in Your power to keep us afloat or to sink us! After sinking us, You bring us safely to shore. Hold back Your hand, Your wrath; that is why I call on You. There was a prophet named Noah. You set him adrift on vast flood waters, then You mercifully set him ashore. All this is known by all in the three worlds.

Biswas cups water to his face and fills his mouth, he does this three times, rinsing and spitting, weeping, tasting water that has flowed from the body of Prakriti, that is thick and pungent, that smells, that is pure because it is alive. He lets the water drench his shirt, he fills his ears with it and drains it away again, hearing the echoing roar of water pouring from the hollow places of his skull and peace returning to those hollows – the endless misery and wheedling moan of the elevator music has gone, Keshamoni is resting, and Biswas hears his own quivering mouth, moistened with the thick, sulphurous water, managing to sing again.

Someone on the bank turns on a car's headlights and points them at him, and an empty beer can lands on the water beside him.

Singing: Everything happens by a stroke of luck, of fortune; the name of luck is Gopal Chandra, the name of luck is dung.

The headlights veer away and the car squirts gravel from beneath its tyres as it accelerates out of the picnic spot.

Back at DoT Presentation earlier in the day, after flying from Christchurch the day before wearing headphones but not switched on, a long white-lipped coastline with Absolutely Pure mountains beside it, a zone of complex inlets and waterways, the plane bumping and slewing across a space of grey, stormy water, no sleep only thinking of saving Keshamoni, thinking Cowgirl's *White Bait*, *Arthur's Pass*, *Garden Party*, missing *Whale of a Time*, then *Seat of Power*, next *Geyserland*, and DoT bosses not understanding Presentation, no-body talking to him at lunch time, only 'Are-you-comfortable-no-I-am-come-for-tea' politeness with jokes. What, did these men and women think no Kiwis went on sex road trips, bulk-buying azithromycin in black-market pharmacist? What about Travel Alert (TA) for sexual sickness, what about TA for abduction, for bastard men like the kebabers – dacoit, mafia, gangsters, Zithromax for tourists, nothing for Keshamoni?

Yes, he had done his Presentation with Pat helping but he had been looking at the faces of the men across the seminar-room table. These were rich men who travelled, these men stayed in hotels, these men had Zithromax and Viagra and these men looked like dacoit wearing smart Western clothes at Kermitolah Golf Club, drinking alcohols. Mohammed Baul Biswas had told these men how it was, truthfully, politely – how to think about purity and tourism. About shonar Bangla. But he had wanted to leap across the table and smash them with his fists, snatch the breath from those thick necks that might one day gasp above Keshamoni, dig out those alcohol eyes looking at Keshamoni.

But now his teeth begin to chatter with the cold of the air and the water whose mysterious, pungent, holy tendrils of warmth have faded and Biswas is cleansed of this anger. He feels real stones under the aching soles of his feet and it is real anger that clenches the shivering palms of his hands into fists. Not those fools of the morning who thought purity lived in unholy emptiness not in Prakriti.

Insh'Allah, Keshamoni will be saved and pure, Cowgirl will pay her price and that filth who took her will pay theirs. Insh'Allah they will pay and they will pay again and again in torments and shames, in agonies, in deaths died in pain of being born to die in agony again and again.

Shivering, Biswas pushes his numb feet into the slip-on shoes and hobbles without any feeling in his legs, with chattering teeth, clutching his jacket around himself, his chilly lunghi and shirt plastered to his skin, across the spot-lit obstacle course of the hotel parkland, through the barriers of rattling flax and sharp-edged toitoi, towards the steam rising from its hot water pools. With his hotel-room swipe card he gets a towel from a grinning attendant ('She'd be a tad chilly, the lake, tonight?') and enters a small booth in whose mirror he confronts what he has become: this wildly dishevelled man, whose teeth may be bared equally with pain or ecstasy, whose hair stands on end and whose face is patchy with unguided shaving. Biswas divests himself of everything but his tucked-up lunghi and hastens crouching to the steaming pool.

A dozen heads float above the steaming water in the murmurous, sloshing space, barely visible, some seeming to sleep. The water is shockingly hot after the lake – like his real anger, like feeling actual stones on the bed of the lake, the Biswas grin of pleasure and relief is renewed after his time of numb sleeplessness. He slips almost immediately into a doze but it is as though he is waking up. He submerges until only his nose is above the water and inhales steam. Under the water, his tense grin relaxes to a smile. A little of the warm water trickles into his mouth and steam condenses in his nose. The warmth is delicious and so is the silence of the pool, where no music plays, where the sound of water is gently lapping and pouring, where no one is talking, where he is alone, unknown, unwatched.

Almost sleeping – maybe sleeping tonight. Maybe not dreaming about Keshamoni. And maybe Keshamoni herself will be sleeping and not dreaming tonight, or dreaming about when she can be looked at again.

And then Biswas, who is almost dozing and yet is awake again, his loose smile dipping in and out of the warm water, his eyelids heavy with forgiveness, steam and peace – then Biswas hears the sound of filth spoken in Urdu. He hears it and knows he is not dreaming it – a loud, gratified, guttural, disgusting expression of pleasure likened to a child's forbidden parts. The shock of it makes him swallow water and choke. Coughing, Biswas hears another one laughing and repeating the disgusting expression in the language of power and oppression. The real, hard, stony anger flies into Keshamoni's brother's hands and into his eyes which spring open and see nearby the floating moustaches, grins and matted hair of the three kebaber men.

These men whom Biswas has hated and feared on sight have never yet spoken to him except with their scornful and questioning looks, which he easily recognises and understands. But they have looked at him now many times with expressions that say, 'We will speak to you soon enough, but that will be when we decide, not you, peasant, Bengali turd.' Biswas has recognised the three kebabers as the kinds of men he knows well. These men he knows have now entered the pure water near him and have turned it into filth. They have poisoned its comforting, holy warmth into something forbidden. With their grinning, filthy, forbidden pleasure.

The rage in his hands and eyes flies out towards them.

Biswas follows his rage, as he did not on the morning of the DoT Presentation – he flies with it out of the water and across its surface, his hot body icy again but with rage not absolution. His rage to kill closes around the thick neck of the large man who first uttered the filth in a voice of horrible satisfaction and the fingers of Mohammed Baul Biswas sink into the man's thick, imperious flesh, Keshamoni's brother's thumbs gouge into the gross gristle of the filth's Adam's apple. The raging spit of Mr Biswas flies through steam into the devil's horrified face from which his eyes suddenly bulge. Biswas hears the man's breath whistle in his throat before the fat pervert head goes under the surface of the water with frantic bubbles.

And he may have been too late, because the Urdu filth the monster spoke has already transformed the warmth of the water into the childish warmth of Keshamoni's body. Her slight warmth Biswas always remembered from the swirling flood, the warmth he had felt in the lake's tendrils of forgiving water. But Biswas has to do it anyway. He has no choice. And maybe he is not too late as the other filth devils and perverts grab his hair and ears, as they tear at his arms, as the pool attendant leaps into the water and yanks the Bangladeshi's head back with one arm while lifting the bubbling fat man above the surface with the other.

Maybe he has not been too late, because as Biswas is dragged bellowing off the filth and towards the side of the pool, he sees a look in the pervert's eyes when they open that says, 'Yes, you heard me and you understood me, scum, and now we will see what will happen, you Bangla shit-scum, laying your miserable hands on me. And you will see what happens personally you mother- and sister-fucking Bengali peasant!'

But Biswas sees a look, as well, of fear and shock and shame in the gross devil's purple face, because what does this prove? That nowhere is safe, that wherever you are, someone will see and hear and know you for who and what you are.

fifteen

Home

'I promise, Pat. By Allah.'

'Promise by Keshamoni.'

'Promising by Keshamoni, Pat.'

'Because if I ever thought you were looking, I wouldn't do it, I couldn't do it, Biswas.'

'By Allah and by Keshamoni. By my drownded family, Pat.'

'Drowned.'

'By my drowned family, Pat. Is not to worry.'

'"Not to worry"? I've never done anything like this in my entire life.'

'I believe you, Pat. By my drowned family I believe you.'

'You have to believe me, Biswas.'

'By my drowned family, by my mother, by Kesh–'

'Okay, Biswas. So long as you promise.' Pat paused, then, at an edge of intimacy and trust that her pride hesitated to cross. 'I don't even have a man, Biswas. In my life.'

'I promise I believe you, Pat. Promising not to look, okay? Never. Believing you are pure, Pat. Absolutely Pure, isn't it.'

Perhaps that was the Bangladeshi's idea of a joke – in any case, they both managed to laugh. Seems an age ago now – the awkward laughter of people who've entered into 'unexamined risk' together. Who are now at the mercy of each other's 'inadequate due diligence'. Who have, each separately, to trust their own 'professional judgement'. The language of the management manuals is a kind of tinnitus in Pat's ears. She'd prefer to say, they have to trust that the laughter they're hearing is the matey laughter of allies and code sharers, not the dodgy laughter of cheats.

But it's been with the serenity and confidence of absolute trust that Cowgirl's emerged. Has unzipped, you might say, from the Pat who now, dressed in the secret zippy identity of Keshamoni's only hope, presides over the CTI project team's crestfallen breakfast.

Have to lift the blinking mood, thinks Pat. Have to keep the show on the road. Just for as long as it takes. Keep the old differential gear meshed. Keep the main cogs lined up. 'Keep this one together.'

She's looked carefully and simply, indeed strategically, as her experience has taught her to, at the three key components of her current happiness. Which seems to be in stark bloody contrast to the dour mood of the team. Pat knows she's happy. She feels it strongly, the happiness. But also her complete, thoroughly examined, diligent confidence in it, the happiness. Here, in the generic breakfast room of the international brand-name chain hotel with its generic room-package breakfast buffet of fruit juice concentrates, sugary pastries and covered warmers of hot cooked eggs, bacon, hash browns and fatty sausages. Her happiness has also emerged like Cowgirl from a fussy pretence of being careful with food, a blustery pretence of not giving a damn about her steady progress towards spinsterhood and a hearty social pretence of not being lonely.

Pack of lies.

And she knows, professionally, confidently, diligently, that this happiness is built securely on three completely ridiculous planks. One: on the absolute confidence she has in the promise of Mohammed Baul Biswas, in his faithfulness really. Two: on her knowledge that she's going to make a life-and-death difference to somebody. And three: on the fact that she's found a way to be looked at. A way that she thought would be a piece of cake because it was silly and trivial. Now it's not silly any more. A kind of truthfulness has entered her life. A way of being in control of exposing herself to others as she's chosen to be laid bare to herself.

A couple of tour parties were welcomed the night before with a generic traditional powhiri. They feasted on a substantial traditional hangi meal of fatty steamed meat and vegetables. Now they're lining up at the buffet to heap their plates with the package-deal cooked breakfast foods. It's a sight that Pat's loathed for years and never more so than when she's seen herself reflected in the false hesitancy of guests pretending to themselves and to the bored buffet attendants that they'll be declining to pincer up yet another rasher of bacon with the gleaming bacon tongs. That they won't be helping themselves to an extra spreading of wrapped butter in case they run out because they have, after all, already lifted that extra slice of healthy fibrous toast to the side of their plate.

Pat's not even remotely in love with the sweet, sad man who's emerged from behind the fixed, glamorous, all-purpose smile, from behind the hot, dangerous stare, the terrible ranting grief and fear, the incomprehensible quavery songs and poems in Bengali, the awful, dishevelled calm. But now she looks with affection at his plate of porridge, pot of tea with much sugar added directly to it and at his slender, dark fingers carefully peeling a mandarin and lifting the fragrant skin to his nostrils to sniff. She's not in love with him and no longer even thinks lustfully about his thin, wiry body inside his neatly pressed clothes, within the slightly spicy ambience of his carefully groomed odours.

But she knows that she is in love. She is in love the way you can be deep inside a situation, like a home. A place constituted by faithfulness, unselfconsciousness and the power of life and death. She's at home in love and at home with its intimate codes. Being at home inside love makes her happy in the nowhere-in-particular chain hotel breakfast buffet. Happier than she would have been back in her terrific little flat across from the jolly yacht club in Wellington. Fed, fucked and financial, maybe, on a good day there – but nobody home, really. Nobody home there, when she thought about it, now. Nobody home there inside the Patricia, the Great White, the hugely reliable. In the terrific prime location apartment with its view of the bay and the national museum – nobody home there inside Pat for bloody years.

Grafting away up the career path, tidy little empire in the DoT Beauty portfolio, indispensable special consultant to the Minister, plenty of disposable, certainly enough for the occasional semi-professional resort naughty with the obliging room-service or dive-instructor talent or the occasional escort treat. Prime-site investment apartment, all mod-cons, upgrade the car every couple of years, investments and mortgage going nicely in opposite directions. And the thought of losing the whole bloody lot makes no difference to her happiness. Her happiness based on being inside love. Which is based, she reminds herself, on a scarcely known Bangladeshi man's promise not to look at her, her spectacular success as a fat porn star with a zipper fetish and the fate of a kid she's never going to see.

Is it possible to be happy without laughter? Probably not. Not this time, anyway.

Biswas sees Pat smile at him. It is a smile he knows has a secret meaning, but no one else knowing this. No one else can see or know their secret and even he can only see a part of it, not another part. He drinks his sweet tea with noisy appreciation, quells the agitation in his thigh and, wiping his moustache, prepares his best not-secret smile, the smile he will present to the CTI team when Pat tells them he is going home. But first, he gives Pat a little nod. Because he is not going home. He and Pat know this but nobody else will know this.

'My God,' says Pat. 'What an incredible critical mass of talent.' Everybody in the team pauses in their breakfasting because they recognise this as the opener to one of Pat's tribal communiqués. 'What a loss to civilisation as we know it,' she continues heartily, 'were some bloody great geyser to suddenly wipe out the lot of us.'

Now the project team's waiting. Pat's about to make an important announcement and they have a hunch about its content. No one's looking at Biswas, whose all-purpose smile, radiant and inclusive, has anticipated Pat's bulletin. Richard Brawn, the *National Inquirer* investigative, is sitting at a table nearby. He's making no effort to conceal his interest. Pat gives him a little wave. 'Now listen,' she says – she might as well be talking to him.

Bill and Boris are not sitting together this morning. Bill may be sulking – at any rate, he's eating a large, eccentric breakfast of cinnamon and raisin Danishes, Rudolf Steineresque bircher muesli and successive cups of strong espresso coffee. Boris is snacking lightly, as usual, on fruit and toast, while his attention snacks lightly on inputs. He keeps his back turned to the tour party gorging from the buffet and wearing Good-2-Go franchise clothing more suited to alpine rescue than to thermal spa bathing. He's also keeping his back turned to his mutinous tour guide Seiko. Gloria's eating heartily of a cooked breakfast and talking to Stan. Stan has an instant breakfast drink in a carton. He holds its straw in the corner of his mouth like a cigarette.

'"Ahi" and "para", probably burning fern, fire in the fern, maybe cooking ferns,' says Gloria into the silence following Pat's critical mass of talent announcement. 'What? Whoops, sorry, pep-talk is it?'

'I have sad news,' Pat announces to the team. She's speaking with obvious, even show-off unconcern for confidentiality. 'As you know, Mr Biswas was involved in an unfortunate incident in the hotel's hot pool last night. The details aren't important, though I can tell you Mr Biswas can hardly be blamed for what happened. Some other guests grossly insulted him and he . . .' Pat pauses, looking at Biswas as if to suggest he could think about delaying the smile for a while yet. 'He took to one of them. Rather effectively, I might add,' says Pat. She does, after all, have a reputation for being droll as well as tough. 'Unfortunately, the gentleman our esteemed team-mate took to is the head of a significant trade mission from Pakistan. Who has the substantial support of the Ministry of Foreign Affairs and Trade. And this gentleman at once contacted his consulate – as soon as he could speak, that is. And his consulate at once contacted Hands-On, begging your pardon, at once contacted the Minister. Our Minister. The Minister for Tourism. Who rang me,' says Pat with good cheer, stopping to sip her orange juice, 'at two in the morning. He was quite unhappy, which I've explained to Mr Biswas. Mr Biswas has agreed that, under the circumstances, it might be best if he left the project a bit earlier than expected. And went home,' Pat adds, as if to emphasise there's no alternative.

Biswas resumes his smile. Now everybody is looking at him, including also the thin man, Richard, who shook his hand last night. Richard is sitting alone nearby and behaving in a way no-problem in Bangladesh but here is known as 'staring', very impolite.

Friends and colleagues also staring at him, Biswas. Including also Pat who is soktishali, very strong and not stupid the way he first thought when she used to make the joke about his name. Pat is good – good to do what she is doing, Cowgirl, how to explain that in mosjid?

'Mr Biswas? Anything you'd like to say?'

Behind his smile, the Bangladeshi's dark crow, the invisible Biswas bird, his kak, is cackling away.

'Mr Biswas?'

My fate, says the Biswas bird, is in your hands, baba, but you are in the hands of this rice pudding beshya and she is in the hands of your sister's oppressors, how does this feel? What kind of power and dignity is this, baba, my broken cage, my perch fallen down into shit?

'O Boatman, take me to the other shore,' recites Mohammed Baul Biswas softly in the golden Bengali of Lalon Shah, in the language that pours out of his heart like a river refreshed with snow and mud, like a tube-well fountain jetting out into the emerald paddy, like an earthenware pot of doba water tipped down a hot farmer's back. 'Here I am, O Merciful One, sitting stranded on this side. I have been left alone at the landing place; the sun has gone down already.'

Because he has seen it happen before, Biswas knows that the shine in his friend and ally Pat's eyes is close-to-tears weeping, he has recited carefully and quietly so as to rebuke and quieten his secret bird, but he is surprised to see a shine also in Gloria's eyes and even more surprised to see it in Bill's. Boris looks interested, the way he does when Biswas can see he is really thinking about something else, and Stan is doing a staring-back rudeness at the Richard man.

'Remembering,' says Pat, as if to regain the composure she has not quite lost, 'that we are bound to be confidential. About the team's work.'

'My friends,' says Biswas formally, 'it is a sadness and shame to me to be leaving the Cultural Tourism Initiative (CTI) team under distressing circumstances. I am indeed very sorry that, as Patricia is saying, there is trouble last night. I make apology,' Biswas goes on, assembling the joke he has been practising in his mind, 'for losing my cool in the hot pool.'

Pat is still shining, Gloria blows her nose into her paper table napkin, Boris tilts his head in an interested way and only Bill laughs. He does so around a mouthful of raisin Danish and next coughs and chokes. Biswas waits until Bill is better again and grinning in teary, mute applause at the joke.

'And so,' continues Biswas, sticking to his rehearsed idea, 'I am bidding farewell to my Cultural Tourism Initiative (CTI) friends and returning to my home.' But now he departs from his script – there is sadness on the faces of the CTI team and Biswas surprises himself with the thought he next speaks. Surprises himself enough to have to clear his throat at an emotion he has not expected – an emotion that slides through the bars of his bird's cage and silences the mocking crow there and that makes the brilliant Biswas smile quiver while he dabs at his eyes, like Gloria and Pat are, with his paper table napkin. 'Is like leaving my other family,' quavers Biswas across the shine of his smile, 'whom God to bless, please, insh'Allah.'

'Light duties, I think, today.' Pat gets a grip. 'I'm back from the bloody seat of power later this arvo. After explaining all this to you-know-who. May need the usual therapies.'

'Danger,' realises Joris, 'that's what you got there, everything, got it made, man, why stay here anyway, you got floods, snakebites, any tigers left?' He pauses, sensing a familiar silence. 'What, I say something wrong again?'

sixteen

Fear

The moment she walks into the Minister's office Pat can tell he's onto it. She knows him well enough to see that he's making a special effort to keep his best hard look in place. Behind it she has, more than once, detected the guilty defiance of a naughty boy. Or the truculent defiance of a powerful man caught with his pants around his ankles.

This time, as she does her best who-gives-a-flying thing and walks breezily across the office in her freshly laundered zippies, direct from the front, straight off the site, from the middle of the fray, she knows damn well that fear and triumph are very close to the surface of that hard look. The Minister's eyes are deliberately widened but he's not letting his brows ask questions, his lips are jammed together and there's that sour thing happening at the corners, and in his solid jowls he's keeping his jaw muscles flexing slightly.

This is a man she thinks of as a silly bugger rather than as bad or a prick, not unpleasant to work for, not without professional gifts and personal charm, gives her room to do her stuff. But you have to push 'silly bugger' up a couple of clicks when you see his not-bad impersonation of his own boss. Pat is pretty sure he'd have spent a while getting the expression right after his secretary announced her. She'd been expecting a version of it.

But also that the zipper outfit might make the hard-man expression crack a bit. Wilt a bit, more like.

Pat fears one thing only. The failure of Cowgirl to see this thing through, to rescue Keshamoni. Failure to make love flower again in the lonely place where poor old Biswas wanders, unable to rest until he finds Keshamoni safe. Unable to go home, unable to be at home when he does go there again, until his little flower is safe and sound again.

Pat doesn't wear the zippies any more these days – only Cowgirl does, in the nightly sportive dalliances of *The Chasm*, *White Bait*, *Arthur's Pass* and the others. Cowgirl's zippies have been wildly successful. Zips have become cataracts lazily descending the flanks of mountains. They've been jet boats rearing up from their own foaming wakes. They've been highways whose dashing white dividers have gone tearing into sunsets and sunrises. They've been the tremendous contrails of jets parting the blue bulge of the sky and they've been slatted boardwalks dangerously skirting the eruptions of tidal blowholes. Even so, it had been a strategic no-brainer, the decision to climb back into the zippy gear again by day for good old Pat's meeting with Hands-On himself.

And, there you go – she does see it, again. The mini-tsunami across the Minister's face, just like the other day. And she sees it in Hands-On's extra control. She sees it the moment she steps into his office in the full professional clobber of Cowgirl.com. She sees his fear.

What's the Minister afraid of? Anyone, but especially Pat, finding out that he's been 'zipping'. This is what Cowgirl chats and blogs call it. And why does this fear paralyse his triumph? Because his negotiating hold over Pat can only be activated if he blows the whistle on himself.

This is a situation that negotiator Pat calls the 'Choker'. The harder you try to take advantage of what you know, the more it chokes you. The Choker's exceedingly common in leaky power environments. Of which Hands-On's ministry's an excellent example. Pat's been in the Choker many times. She knows it well. She can see when it has its fingers around someone else's neck.

To avoid choking, the Minister has to imply very delicately that he knows what's going on. He has to imply this knowledge without any hint of how he's come by it. He has to sustain the power of his knowledge to leverage Pat's compliance. He has to suggest it will be in her best professional interests to look after number one. To not imagine that what she knows about him will do as much damage as what he knows about her.

But what he doesn't know is that Pat no longer gives a flying fuck. Or rather, Cowgirl doesn't. She only cares about the flowering of hope, the sweet smell of victory, the radiant Biswas smile and its sister on the face of the knock-kneed kid she'd glimpsed on the Bangladeshi's call-to-prayer cellphone. The kid whose look of not-being-there had pierced Pat in the Shoganda Restaurant out on the Coast. Had pierced straight through her to the very place the Minister himself has learned to value the most. The place where nothing, but nothing, ever, stops the Great White from getting the job done.

If he knew this, the Minister's triumph would be useless. It would be all about his fear. That's why Pat has to keep his triumph alive. The Minister with nothing to lose, driven only by fear with no Choker triumph to check it, will destroy whatever it takes to keep his fat arse in his chair in the office Pat has breezed into overfamiliarly as Cowgirl. He'll sweep Biswas and Keshamoni aside along with Pat, he'll see to it that Cowgirl is destroyed to warm the padding in his chair and the hospitality in his portfolio.

And so Pat has to make the Minister aware, but very delicately, that she knows he knows. But that he has nothing to fear so long as he doesn't go too deeply into why Pat has chosen to come charging into his nice sunny office wearing the zippies.

And so the first sign that all is going well so far is that the Minister, well choked, offers no comment on Pat's outfit.

'Boy oh boy, let me tell you,' begins Pat, pushing her familiarity a couple of clicks past the no-go bar of professional deference – just to let him see a hint of her power.

But the Minister interrupts her – as he has to. 'Sit down, Pat.'

'Yes, sir.' The only seat is lower than his, an easy chair.

'I'm hearing some very disturbing reports and rumours,' says the Minister, ostentatiously drawing out a pause while he swivels to give Pat the full benefit of his glare. She repays him by relaxing into the chair with her zip-trousered legs apart and one hand dangling over its arm. 'About the CTI project,' he continues, making sure she's registered his pause and his decision not to go there. But Cowgirl's got this one in the bag now. If the silly bugger had had any brains he'd have sat her pretty much out of sight across the desk from him. As it is, he has to address what he can't show he's seeing. Which is Cowgirl on full display in his Ministerial office. In the zippies.

'I'm sure you are,' begins Pat again, and this time it's her pause that the Minister has to measure with antennae made hesitant by Cowgirl's unprofessional sprawl in pleasant sunshine. 'It's been quite a trip,' continues Pat, nudging the margin of deference. 'Bit more than we bargained for.'

'I thought, when we met the other day, that I made myself clear,' says the Minister. 'There's a lot at stake here. The government's investment. The sector's expectations. Professional careers.' The Minister doesn't specify which ones. 'Major sponsors. International agencies.' He tightens up the look. 'There's a lot of people watching, Pat.'

'I know that, sir,' says Cowgirl. 'Quite a few more than we bargained on.'

The Minister's gaze drifts thoughtfully to his window and the view of sky and clouds in it, as though there, rather than in the leisure-wear sprawl of the woman he knows has unzipped against digitally enhanced vistas of cataracts, geysers, jet-boat wakes, poling on the Avon river and the Punakaiki blowholes – there, in the vacant blue of an uneventful sky will be found the appropriate measure of their accord. Their dignified, unspoken agreement about a way to loosen the Choker. That neither of them has anything to fear so long as.

So long as. 'He's been under a lot of pressure,' says Pat,

keeping her card with its ambiguous third person face down for the time being. 'It might be best if he went home.' The Minister's gaze returns from the window and waits. 'If he retired,' says Pat, watching the fear begin to shine in the Minister's cheeks, waiting just a second longer while he says nothing, 'from the project. From the CTI,' she says, and sees him wait. She turns her card over. 'Mr Biswas.'

'Mr Biswas,' says the Minister, grasping her card, the 'he' on it, the crazy bastard who'd come within a hair's breadth of buggering up the review.

'He's been under a lot of pressure,' says Pat. 'Trouble at home. Troubled country, as you heard the other day. And we think we have trouble coming up with an image. With a brand. With something that will grab them. Grab the punters, sir.' Oh no we don't, says Cowgirl's comfort in the easy chair.

'That business at Rotorua,' says the Minister – but it's over. They both know it. The Choker is off. 'The mirrors at the glacier. All that stuff the other day about,' and he pauses for effect one last time, to seal their complicity, 'sex. Sex tourism.'

'Like I said, Minister,' says Pat, 'domestic issues. Culturally complex. Yes, he lost his rag at the glacier. Managed to sweep that one up. Excellent staff there. And the night before last.' The night of Geyserland, thinks Cowgirl. First-class episode. Talk about steamy pressure building up. 'Some Pakistani businessmen said something he took exception to, probably with reason. In the hot pool.'

'Yes, I heard,' says the Minister, who can now afford to be irritated. 'Why else would I have asked you to come down?'

Why indeed, thinks Cowgirl. But we know why. Don't we, Hands-On?

'Of course, sir,' says Pat. 'Goes without saying. Then you'll know there's no love lost between the Pakistanis and the Bangladeshis – on quite a few counts. Apparently one of the

Pakistani gentlemen made a filthy remark. Which Mr Biswas took personally. Took to be about his young sister, sir.'

Hands-On's fear slides away, like a shadow nudged aside by warm light. The Minister basks slightly in his relief as his fear comes to rest at a margin where they can both manage it. Of course, Pat will write a note for him anticipating a Question in the House. She'll draft an undefensive press release in case one might be needed. She'll get a bit of advice from the Ministry of Foreign Affairs and Trade and draft a letter to the Bangladesh High Commission in Canberra, just in case. Unlikely to be needed, but she'll get another one ready for the Pakistanis. The Bangladeshi's contribution to the report will be – will be tidied up. His visit will be cut short but his valuable contribution praised. A letter for the Minister's signature will be prepared, by Pat, to go to the funding agencies of the CTI project, and another to the specific supporters of Mr Biswas. The specific letters will go to the United Nations Development Programme, the Parjatan Corporation, to the appropriate skimmer at the Bangladesh National Party in Dhaka. These letters will establish excellent value-for-money in the contribution made by Mr Biswas to CTI. Couple of tame peer reviewers can chuck in their ten cents' worth. Glowing testimonials from other team members.

'All that crazy stuff, Pat.' The Minister gets a bit of glare back. 'That "road trip" nonsense.'

'Gone,' says Pat. 'Nothing to it. Can't imagine what it had to do with us, sir. Bit of a rewrite. William can give us a hand.'

'William, excellent. And the Australian woman?'

They are going through the motions.

'No word,' says Pat, as though she hasn't said anything like this before. 'Poor wee thing. Complete mystery. Got the cops out on the Coast more occupied than they've been since Stan Graham took to the bush.'

They are getting to the point of cracking a joke or two.

The Minister addresses his intercom. 'Some coffee please, Margie.' His use of a nickname signals his relief. He's not going to notice Pat's outfit. He's retained his threat, his triumph, in reserve. He still has it over her. So he believes.

'I thought they were going to shit themselves,' says the Minister with a small guffaw. 'Bunch of lemon-faced bastards.' He's talking about the review team. The one he appointed himself. He's relaxing unwarily, as is his wont. Usually it would be Pat's job to take him carefully by the elbow at this point. This time, it's Cowgirl's job to let him dig his own big hole and jump in all by himself.

When the coffee arrives, his receptionist pays more attention to Pat's unusually casual daywear than the Minister does. He's just not seeing it. It fills his entire field of vision, but he is not seeing it. Looking, maybe, but not seeing.

'Good girl,' he says to Margie. She gets his best sweetie smile – in years gone by he might have patted her bottom. Pat sips her coffee as the Minister continues to not see Cowgirl.

It's got to come soon – his sign-off, his declaration of complicity, his offer of protection. Pat begins to count him down as he drifts towards small talk. Apparently his oldest daughter is thinking of opening a resort-cum-meditation centre in the Marlborough Sounds. She stayed in one in Mexico. You got smeared with cactus jelly.

The Minister makes a decisive gesture with his cup – he empties it and clanks it firmly down on its saucer. Here it comes.

'Just be careful, Pat,' says the Minister, giving her a roguish look. She feels like saying, 'What, sir, with the way funding will one day go to the cactus juice place in the Marlborough Sounds?' – but restrains herself. Because there it is – his trump card, the card he believes is his trump card, on top of that one of hers, on Pat's 'he' who might be better advised to retire. And it's now that the Minister allows himself to be seen to look at and actually notice her zippy outfit. He exposes his gaze, he opens it right up, he makes his gaze linger on her down there in the easy chair, he savours his viewing experience from the viewing platform of his desk. 'Love the safari gear, Pat.' It's the first time Cowgirl has been directly looked at, in the flesh. Because, obviously, you have to know it's Cowgirl before you can look at her. And see her. 'All part of the brand, I suppose,' jokes the Minister. His unwary face is swelling up the way it does. 'The project brand, eh, Pat?' His chuckle is way too complicit.

'You know me,' says Pat, thinking, Oh no you don't, you smug bastard, on both counts. 'Careful is my middle name.' And now, Cowgirl draws his gaze towards her, she visibly relaxes before him in her low chair, she makes herself porous so his unwary look will soak right into her. 'As for the brand,' she says, standing to be excused and preparing her handshake, 'the project brand, that is – we all know it could do with a bit of venture money. At the portfolio level. We talked about this once before.' The Minister's hand is soft and humid. 'Perhaps we should talk about it again?'

As the Choker goes back on, Pat sees the Minister's fear return. It edges back into his voice when he says, casually, 'Venture money? I don't recall that. When was that, Pat?'

'Milford Sound,' says Pat. 'The Chasm.' He drops her hand as though it might be infectious. 'You'd remember that one.' The episode featured Cowgirl with an especially good video clip of Pat's, the tireless piston of the Cleddau lathering the rim of the mossy chute. 'You made a speech, sir. You told some excellent jokes.' You got pissed, thinks Pat, wondering if she's pushed her game too far. You committed an indiscretion with a talkative member of the caterer's bar staff. 'You admired the tumuaki's suit, sir.'

'Right, right,' says the Minister. 'Of course I remember.'

Over his shoulder, Pat can see his chair and his desk. The chair is empty because he's not in it. She needs him there, in it, just afraid enough, with just enough of the Choker on, for just a while longer. For long enough to finish the job.

'Anyway,' she says, 'don't worry. There's nothing to worry about. Nothing to be afraid of. I'll get it sorted.'

'I know you will, Pat,' says the Minister. He's got a lot to be grateful for. 'That's what you do.' He recaptures her hand for a final squeeze. Is the hand hers or Cowgirl's? 'We'll talk again later,' he says, 'about the venture fund idea. Very good idea. Another time.'

Cowgirl allows her bum a bit of extra roll as she crosses the anteroom of the Minister's office. She hears the door to the room with the desk and the empty chair close at the very last minute. She needs a word with Margie.

The note slides under his door as Biswas is packing in his room. When he reads it he knows he now has more to fear. Or, that he should have more to fear. But he does not feel more afraid. The note says that the Pakistanis from the hot pool will look for him. They will see him. They have obtained his details. This disgraceful matter will not be going anywhere near the police in New Zealand. He will not be charged with his disgusting crime. He is theirs alone. He belongs to their justice which is not the justice of the New Zealand police. Nor is it the justice of the flea-swarming pi-dog Bangladeshi shit police and their poxy, disease-cunted sisters and mothers. He is theirs – he, and his unfortunately bred relatives. Soon, he will be reunited with those cripples and half-wits in that backward slum of a shit-hole country he calls home. May it drown in its own floods of stinking shit. That will be the moment when he should prepare himself, because at that moment or soon after it he and his subhuman family will present a tidy target to his coming punishment under their justice.

Biswas puts the note, carefully folded, with his other papers. What they do not know, the pool filth, two things: he is not going home yet, he is staying in the land of Absolute Purity until Keshamoni is safe, until Cowgirl has finished her work. And he has only one close family left, this they don't know, only Keshamoni. And Keshamoni is safe from them because dacoit abductors have her in a secret place.

So, thinks Biswas, folding the sleeves of crisply ironed shirts across their chests in his suitcase and tucking paired socks down the sides, no need to be fearing pool filth. Now, got to be afraid of dacoit not protecting Keshamoni! Also, got to be afraid that Pat's bosses find out he is not going home, not yet. Because then they will send him quick smart and then the filth will find out about Keshamoni and pay dacoit to harm her.

Biswas has uncovered the mirrors in his room because he feels better about looking at himself and the body of his family now and he sees himself reflected in the one on his wardrobe door as he lowers his folded jackets and trousers into his suitcase. The Biswas he sees looking back at him is smiling and he realises that this man even thinks the situation is funny.

Should be afraid, Mohammed Biswas, but he is trusting mishti doy beshya Cowgirl to protect him and trusting dacoit to protect Keshamoni. The smiling man in the mirror does not look like the one who passed through Kuala Lumpur another life ago. Biswas wonders how that could have been him. And he wonders how the man in the mirror can be him, now.

William steps to the edge of his balcony and Bill stands there looking down at the hotel parkland until he begins to get dizzy. Then he steps back and rests a moment. Then he does it again. Each time he does it William's breath gets short and his chest tightens up, he feels sick and his stomach churns. Each time, though, Bill stands a bit longer at the edge of the balcony and each time he lets go of the rail a bit longer. Each time he lets go, Bill makes an effort to look down at the parkland for longer, to look at things in it – not at the unfocused blur with which he makes the distance soft and easier to manage. He makes his eyes focus on the details in the big space, in its distances, in the spaces made by the horizon and those made by the depth of the downward distance from the ninth floor of the hotel. Each time William steps forward and Bill looks down and out, the distance between William and Bill also gets focused. Each time he does it and focuses, he tries to see something clearly, such as Gloria sitting on a bench over towards the lake a bit, with her shoes kicked off, talking on her cellphone. He watches her talking while she is sitting down and the next time he looks into that distance after approaching the edge of the balcony again, he loses her for a while and then sees her walking around a little way off, still talking on her cellphone and waving one arm in the air.

And while he is looking for and then at Gloria in the distance there, talking and talking on her cellphone, he is also looking into the space between William and Bill where he sees himself, a skinny white leek of a kid who forgot to 'lash' his specs with a 'lanyard', punching up from under the sail of the capsized Moth after tipping out. He sees himself not being able to see his mother and father not seeing him do this from the picture window of their bach above the beach. He sees himself not seeing them but knowing they are not. He sees himself walking close to the inward side of the path around steep bluffs on the Abel Tasman track and his father laughing when he grabs William by the little backpack that is cutting his shoulders and play-shoves him towards the edge where the track overlooks a gully. Another time, he looks at and focuses on a moment when he freezes on a branch of the walnut tree in the backyard, freezes with his arms around the trunk and can't move. His father has to get up a ladder and prise his fingers loose and then, laughing, drops him into the soft pile of grass cuttings on top of the compost heap. He breaks through their crust and sinks over his ankles in the stinky muck underneath. When he jerks his feet out of the compost they are covered in pink worms. Another memory he focuses on, before stepping away from the edge again and standing with his back against the wall of his narrow balcony with the sliding doors that, every time, William wants to open so he can step back inside – another memory is the one where his mother is watching him jump off the riverbank into the cold pool which is, however, too shallow, which he knows but deliberately is not focused on, and when he cuts his foot on the sharp rock and looks up, he sees an expression of impatience and it could be dislike on his mother's face when he yells that he has hurt himself. 'Of course you have, you dope,' she says in his memory of the event. 'It was way too shallow, what were you trying to do?' And the same question he wants to ask then and has always wanted to ask whenever he thinks about the event: 'So why didn't you stop me?'

Joris watches the neuken idiot Bill walking back and forth on his narrow balcony: like he's training, for what? From between the painted iron balusters of Joris's balcony it looks like Bill's walking through the frames of a little movie – over and over. Boring film, thinks Joris, even worse than the Adventure promotion with that shit falling sequence: all meant to make people looking at it afraid but also meant to make them want to feel fear, want to buy fear but also want to buy protection. That's the thing: sell the opportunity twice. Sell the fear and sell the safety, sell the desire and sell the protection, control the demand-side and the supply-side.

Looks like Bill's thinking about jumping off: don't do it, Bill, thinks Joris. First, write my campaign, write the fear, design the fuk fear you idiot. Absolute Fear. Maybe I have to let you suck my dick. Or whatever you want. Like Seiko.

Back and forth, back and forth. Is like a zoo animal: someone need to let you out. Joris watches from his balcony recliner, out of sight of William. He lights another Drum cigarette and sips the drink he's made from the little vodka bottles in the minibar and the fresh orange juice. Last night supposed to meet Bill in the hotel bar, got there late, Bill's gone – then the big fuss about the Bangladeshi going mad in the hot pool. You want to know what failure smell like? Smell like this neuken CTI project.

'Smell like shit!' says Joris aloud. Failure shit!

Back and forth. Failure shit, loony shit. What's he doing, the loony shit?

And then Joris sits up on his recliner with a scary thought: the loony shit's trying to not. Joris knocks his vodka drink over and the glass rolls to the edge of the balcony and stops against the kick-board base of the railing: see? It's falling off, but it stops. Fear and safety. Demand supply. That works always good so far, only now.

Only now the loony shit's trying not to feel fear. Is what he's doing: fear management. This maybe works? But to sell fear management, first you need fear supply-side. Or, maybe he changes too far, Bill does, to be any use? Sure: maybe he learns to manage fear, we can supply the management. But can he supply the fear? If he's not any more afraid? So frightened people demand the fear management?

Joris has watched Bill emerge from the Italian greatcoat, he's watched Bill's feet trudging in the Joris boots and Bill's head sink down gratefully between the wings of the Good-2-Go parka. But now, maybe: he loses the fear, he won't make it happen for Add Venture. Just like the shit fuken multimedia: nobody in it's afraid so no one watching gets the fear.

And now Seiko's gone. Taking a big piece of his easily frightened Japanese market. Easily frightened, great supply-side. 'Sorry, Joris, should have listened to weather forecast, too late now, boss,' little cunt.

The smell of failure? This shit project, Seiko's cunt. And the smell of fear: same as the smell of failure.

Now, loony shit yelling something: sounds like 'Gorilla'.

'Gloria, hello!' Bill's standing at the edge of his balcony, with his arms flung out. Why don't you jump, then, idiot, thinks Joris, retrieving his glass. 'Gloria, hi!' Since when did Bill ever shout happy like that? He's waving but Gloria's not paying any attention, what did he expect, idiot? Professor Absolutely Pure, Doctor Fear.

There's no more neuken vodka in the minibar. It's all going to shit. Failure shit, fear shit, failure fear shit.

The grass feels pretty good under Gloria's bare feet, real, spongy and tickly on top of solid and it has a real smell, too, in fact several real smells, there's the real smell of where it's just been cut, the real smell where it's dried out as a mulch around the cultivated bases of the ornamental plants by the car park and the real smell where Gloria's appreciative bare feet are squashing it. The blades poke up between her toes, too, which is also pretty real.

Sound of koro Mat bashing away in her ear about getting her feet on the ground – that's real enough. 'What you afraid of, girl? Losing your fancy job? Remembering where you come from?' William yelling at her from way up there's getting a bit unreal, because when did he ever do stuff like that?

But what's unreal is the cellphone thing. Nancy's, Antsy's voice on the cellphone.

'Okay, so you're nowhere,' says Gloria. 'This can mean several things, but let's not go there.'

. . .

'Yes, that does sound like "one of my jokes", sorry, girl.'

. . .

'No, you're right, I'm not sorry, but I miss you.'

. . .

'Of course I miss you.'

. . .

'Why? Because you woke me up. I was half-asleep, girl. Not looking at anything any more. Not listening to bloody old Uncle Mat, either, thanks very much.'

. . .

'No, I'm not really scared, not surprised either. Not scared to hear you, not surprised. Hell, I've been going on about it enough years, should have heard me at DoT the other day.

Blah blah blah. Their eyes glazed over as usual. That's when you should have called up. But then they'd just have thought you were somewhere, right?'

Across at the hotel, Joris seems to be throwing things at William from his adjacent balcony. William's ducking and then he goes inside and sunlight flashes on his ranchslider door's glass as he shuts it behind him. Then Gloria sees Biswas on his balcony a couple of floors up – he's looking over at the lake and then he, too, goes inside and closes the flashing glass screen that separates him from the world outside.

'Tell you the gospel truth, Ants, darling,' says Gloria. 'The whole blooming project's gone weird. Completely bloody hoha. Good old Pat's gone tearing back down to Wellington this morning to explain why manaakitanga-in-the-back-of-my-limo's pet project's turned pear-shaped. You disappeared without trace, apparently. Poor old Biswas got a bad dose of the Banglas or something and broke stuff in his room a few days ago back at the glacier and then last night he got stuck into some guys in the hot pools and nearly killed one of them. He's been sent home. If you know what I mean – back to good old shonar Bangla. William's finally decided to come out in a William kind of way and hotshot Joris's business has just gone phut. And now, here I am talking to you on a cellphone.'

In the distance, a high-powered speedboat lets rip on the lake. Back at the hotel, a coach tour is being greeted by a Maori concert party. The faint, melodious sound of 'Pokarekare Ana' reaches Gloria at the edge of the car park, behind the thick plantings of flax around the parkland. 'Look at this,' says Gloria into her cellphone. 'Ornamental flax. What's real about that? And it should be "Nga wai o Waiapu", not "Nga wai o Rotorua", typical bloody Te Arawa. And look at me, Ants!' Gloria snaps her cellphone shut. She begins to laugh because it's the only way to stop herself bawling her eyes out. She wants to stuff her mouth with the sweet, mown grass. 'Talk about mad,' says Gloria, laying herself down, waiting for her laughter to change gears into blubbing. 'Tell me about it.'

Stan helps Mr Biswas load his bags in the mini-bus. Through the flax and hebe border at the edge of the car park they can hear Gloria laughing loudly even for her, Miss High and Mighty Maori Princess. The hotel's Maori concert party is singing a waiata to a coachload of Japanese tourists – the tourists all stand to attention and then, all together, raise their cameras and videos. Next, they take turns posing with the concert party. A bossy Seiko-type young woman's organising the photo opportunity. Behind Biswas, Stan sees the journo bloke furtively giving him the thumbs-up before stepping on his cigarette and going back inside the hotel. They'd both, Stan and the journo, watched the dark men leaving in their van. One of them had his neck in a brace. Richard offered Stan a smoke. Not that he knew much. But, yes, he was taking Mr Biswas to the airport. Yes, he'd been there when the Australian sheila disappeared 'without trace'. Yes, they'd been staying in all the best places, but that's what it was all about, wasn't it?

'"That's what it's all about",' Richard said, making it clear he was repeating Stan's comment. Tricky bastard.

Stan's twinge of fear and guilt is soothed by his feeling of defiance as he drives the silent Mr Biswas past the resort city's motels and second-hand car marts festooned with gaily coloured plastic bunting, the malls, service stations and scenic flight billboards, the images of giant trout leaping, of pallisaded Maori villages and immense grimacing tekoteko with curved, protruding tongues and claw-like hands. Must look pretty strange to Mr Biswas?

The Bangladeshi tourism operative's answer surprises Stan. 'I like this place, Stan,' says Biswas, smiling around at the clutter of human enterprise. 'Is people busy here, living, isn't it?' He pinches his nostrils above the smile. 'Is smelling good, also.'

Gloria's laughter turns, inevitably, to tears. 'Sorry, Ants,' she cries to the closed cellphone, talking also into the thick, sweet nap of mown grass where she lies face down, looking at the intricate weave of leaves and roots, the teeming tiny life of ants and things down there, the sense of a pelt or skin on a soft, accommodating body that she wants to dig her fingers into like a wee marsupial might, clinging to its mother – like her wee nowhere friend might, only she can't, any more.

'Sorry, Antsy, it's not you, sweetie, it's what you did for me. You woke me up, girl. Know what I'm most afraid of? Getting used to it. Not looking any more. Saying the words. Not caring any more. Not caring enough. Not believing. Going to sleep on the job, Ants. Doing it by numbers. Being safe, in the end. Knowing where to find the whitebait fritters, Ants. Knowing a good pinot. Knowing who owes who what. Knowing everyone. Cruising along with the team, Ants, with my eyes shut.'

Gloria buries her face and mouth in the fresh, gritty grass. The dampness from its recent watering soaks through her blouse. The cellphone rests face down, too, next to her head on the grass.

'You were great, darling. The way you looked so hard. The way you saw everything. The way you got close to it. The way you got inside it. All that stuff we stop seeing, Ants.'

Gloria tastes the fresh, earthy, herbaceous lawn. 'Herbaceous' is how she might describe the bouquet of a good sauvignon blanc, only they're getting too fancy these days, too namby-pamby, too damn grassy by half, thinks Hinemoana, and feels someone's hand pressing her quaking shoulder. Too late to pretend it's laughter that's shaking her, now – she lifts her face wet with tears and grass and there's funny old William, or Bill, probably, more likely, these days.

'You okay, Gloria?'

See, when did he ever call me anything but Hinemoana?

Bill gives her his nice handkerchief and she mops up. Second time today.

'Just having a wee chat to our Nancy, to Ants,' says Gloria. She retrieves the cellphone but Bill notices it.

'Let me guess,' says Bill. 'She says she's happy, she's at peace, not to worry about her, and she and Sir Apirana Ngata are getting on like a house on fire.'

'Absolutely,' laughs Gloria. 'And she says to tell you, Bill, you're huge over there. Mr Nowhere.'

'Of course I'm flattered,' says Bill. 'But did she say why?'

'She said it's because no one else has managed to get so many of them in the picture,' says Gloria, slipping gratefully into the routine Bill's offered. 'Like, the more you can't see them, the more you know they're there, right?'

'"I see dead people",' mimics Bill.

Gloria blows her nose – Bill waves his handkerchief back to her. 'Christ almighty, look at me, what a wreck, demolition derby.'

Bill's new kind of laughter is untried and sounds surprised at itself – not like William's confident, hyena-like barking. He is also surprised to find himself being hugged by Gloria.

'Never you mind,' says Bill to the thick damp hair on the crown of Gloria's head. It smells of lavenderish shampoo and grassy mulch. 'No one's looking, and anyway, even if he is, Joris is totally pissed at three in the afternoon, he's been throwing his empties at me.'

'What else can the poor man do?' says Gloria, holding the stiff, hesitant William a moment longer until she feels Bill accept her embrace and until she feels herself accept the comfort of his skinny arms when they do, finally, go around her, as though he's never done anything like this in his life before. 'The whole damn country's got a load-bearing restriction on it. No one falls off anything any more, Bill. You just have to jump, I reckon. Like Antsy did.'

'You just have to go for it,' says Bill, sounding like no one he knows.

'Listen to your heart.'

'Don't know about that,' says Bill. 'Reckon mine's lost the plot.'

'The plot thickens.'

'Scary.' Bill turns towards the hotel, steering Gloria through the flax bushes. The concert party has lit cigarettes and is retreating in the direction of the service entry. 'We could all use a drink.'

'That we all could,' agrees Gloria, speaking for Antsy too and noticing that Uncle Mat isn't complaining either.

seventeen

Identity

Boris has warned him that it is a long, steep climb and that when they get to the top Bill will shit himself.

'Even normal people do,' said Boris at breakfast in the camping ground cookhouse. He turned the cheerful cruelty of his grin into little puffs at the hot surface of his coffee.

Below the cookhouse terrace some little water birds were ducking and diving in unison, as if to endorse the wacky morphic resonance theories of Rupert Sheldrake, whose name sounded like some kind of duck to William, and as if to rebuke William's long held and defended and championed preference for solitude, autonomy and solipsism – anything but morphic resonance! The solitude he has, all his adult life, paraded in public triumphs. The autonomy he dreads now when Boris does not return when he said he would.

Once, the spectacle of the little birds' slavish flocking would have filled William with a gloating distaste for the communities of nature, the signs of collective efficiency and evolutionary time-and-motion, and distaste especially for the counter-evidence of sociability in such depressing mob behaviour. What could be more social, William has argued, than the tensioned encounters of individuals differing from each other, of individuals who disagree with each other, even of individuals who dislike each other? Where is the sociability in synchronised head-nodding, in the choreographies of organised worship, in the brutal unanimity of the sports crowd, the goose-stepping ranks of cultural commissars imposing their identity programmes on the compliant masses? Why turn sociability into a matter of product placement or of the involuntary, peer-pressured capitulations of memetics, according to which half the fucking planet starts to wear its cap brim-backwards?

What is so good about brand-slavery, William would have demanded, as he sought out the exclusive and expensive brands most likely to distinguish him from his peers – the fine Italian greatcoats, Florsheim wing-tip brogue shoes, sumptuous velvet neckties by Armani and Rolex wristwatches whose expandable bracelets he toyed with obsessively, as if counting the amber on a string of prayer beads? Why, he was heard to ask sardonically as early as the first week of the team's expedition, would anyone want to zip themselves into the composite and collective identity of that disgusting backpacker tourist uniform of weak-shit-coloured, sweatshop mass-produced, ill-fitting, excessively zippered and pocketed safari gear, when what you were mostly planning to do was mingle with people who looked and smelled the same and carried the same backpacks as far as the same tour coach parked only as distant as the kerb outside the same budget accommodation?

'Why,' Pat responded, though God knows why, because this was an old game with which they were both bored, 'do men wear Y-fronts?'

'Because they're dicks, Patricia.' William pre-empted her punch-line, adding one of his own. 'I suppose, then,' he finessed, 'you have all those pockets for the snake serum?'

Why, William argued passionately in the days of his greatest professional triumph, would you want to compromise the enormous potential of an utterly empty, totally unsocialised in any conventional sense, Absolutely Pure landscape – why would you want to compromise its ability to become the site of astonishing, original, undreamed-of, unscripted encounters? Even including the excellent category of encounters with yourself? In the mirror lakes, so to speak? The viewing platform that invited you to indulge in the tourism-sanctioned, the view-blessed, the William Wordsworth (William loved this bit) sanctified activity of infantile narcissism? Why would you want to dull the edges of such potential encounters out there in the void spaces (your zippered pockets full of truth serums) of infinite possibility – why would you want to dull those dazzling edges with pre-scripted activities, the boring drone of insincere bunk-room small-talk, the pretences of tolerance and of human brother- and sisterhood? Why not confront the noble fear of your actual aloneness in an implacable place, where no one was going to coddle you with the nattering drivel that usually passes for socialising?

Why would you want to say a fucking word when you had the chance, for once, to say nothing and hear nothing in response? Why would you want to make that terrifying emptiness into just another identity emporium stocked with junk like mountain bikes? With shop-worn concepts like 'grandeur', which is relative to the size of people dropped into the immensity like scale-establishing models? Or 'adventure', which requires other people to be doing what you never will have the guts for? Or even the concept 'unspoiled' whose corollary is, of course, 'spoiled', which is what sociability, also known as stampeding, mobbing, group-booking and tour-partying, causes places to become? Why, most of all, would you want to imagine the chilling austerity and absence of effort in the Absolutely Pure campaign could be improved, somehow, by the sight of sweating mountain bikers – even by the erotic cliché of the lycra'd buttocks of sweating mountain bikers plunging downhill?

But that morning, before moving on to the steep ascent of the much vaunted Panekiri Bluff, Bill viewed the little, slickly ducking-and-bobbing-up-again birds with amusement and affection and did not look for an audience for one of his arch, sarcastic diatribes – an audience that usually, as if to prove his point, shrank to himself. What is more, Bill is now completely clad in the branded accoutrements of the flock he has most despised, those who pretend they are going to enter the vast spaces of rock, snow and kea-patrolled air, when in fact the closest they will ever get will be a viewing platform convenient for their bus or a seat in the multimedia experience that made William suck his thumb. Bill is dressed from head to foot in the Quixotic clothes of the wilderness tramper; what is more he is heading out into it guided by the country's leading Adventure impresario.

The irony is not lost on Bill as he toils upwards, gasping, along a seam between the dark forest interior and the increasing altitude of the sheer, sunlit drop.

What is more, the day before, on the way in, he felt sad about the depleted little flock in the CTI mini-bus – felt a disproportionate sense of absence and loss and loneliness. Why disproportionate? Not enough 'morphic resonance'? His sadness was caused by the disappearance of Nancy and the enforced retirement of Mr Biswas. But something more than two people had left the project. Something more than their combined biomass, their displacement of space in the bus, their gross of team effort. What had also left was their unpredictable spirit. They were two crazy people. Nancy playing, Biswas praying. They had given William the confidence, within the manageable confines of the team and its twin-seater, to become Bill.

Bill knows that he is no longer William, but also that his identity remains incongruous, effortful, anxious, eager to please. The man he is most eager to please, in whom he would most like to see reflected the image of his own resolved self-confidence, Boris, seems content to dawdle on the horribly steep track. Boris has to dawdle, anyway, if he is not to outstrip the gasping Bill in a matter of minutes and disappear into the beech forest ahead where the track ascends spectacularly along the edge of the Panekiri Bluff above the intricately spread-out waterways of the shining lake. The lake's surface is already too distant and in any case too wind-ruffled to see anything reflected in, but Bill is edging his field of vision across in the direction of its mirror, as if to see there an image of his growing, if under-branded, confidence.

Bill nurses his aching chest up the path and before long has to take off his jacket and next his polyprene jumper as the sweat begins to trickle from his armpits into the waistband of his Good-2-Go lightweight pants. He stuffs them into the pack which also contains his sleeping-bag and which reminds him of the one his father had often, with ambiguous playfulness and impatience, in the years of William's childhood, hoisted from behind, taking the weight from William's toiling legs as he plodded along the inner edges of tracks skirting deep, scary gullies. It only takes the initial lengthy incline to make Bill's knees begin to ache, too, and he knows, because Boris has told him so, that it is a good five hours' walking to the high point of the Bluff at Bald Knob.

'Will be snow there, probably,' said Boris at breakfast, being provocatively offhand. 'Freeze your arse as well as shit your pants.'

Bill knew what Boris wanted – for him, Bill, to begin to be afraid in preparation for real fear at Bald Knob, to begin to really understand the demand-side of Joris's failing Adventure enterprise whose declining, or more appropriately perhaps falling, terror thresholds were fucking up his demographic. And what was making Boris impatient and vindictive and making his deliberate scare tactics sound silly and ineffectual, and therefore making him even more vindictive and taunting, was that fact that Bill, this half-creature that Joris has coaxed out of William the way he has coaxed Bill out of William's Italian greatcoat, is now only afraid of one thing, and that is that Boris will cease to have any use for him and therefore will cease to torment him with slaps to the side of the head and with verbal slaps, and with taunting displays of his loose-slung genitals, his narrow, sinewed wrists and his spitty, insulting, mint-scented breath on Bill's ear. Because while all these degradations continue, Bill knows that Boris, too, is locked in to his own kind of desperation, his own desperate need for Bill.

But what, Bill wonders, will happen if he becomes unafraid? Will he see joy and admiration in Joris's eyes, a reflection of his own, of Bill's joy? Or will he see rejection and hatred because the source of Joris's power – Bill's terror – has gone?

And besides, now they are alone.

There was an unseasonal dump of snow on the pass as they drove through last night. The mini-bus seemed empty, as though the combined absences of Nancy and Biswas had depleted the CTI team's critical mass, as Pat liked to call it. Passing the Tamaki Brothers Model Maori Village, Stan soon turned the mini-bus towards the distant, ominous, black and purple loom of the remote mountains. They passed through the vast cultivated pine plantation of the Kaingaroa forest which, in the writer Katherine Mansfield's day in 1907 had been a pumice-and-tussock wilderness. Bill reminded the team of this as their bus sped in a straight line across the serried ranks and defiles of the man-made forest. There had been a woman at a store out here, Bill said, who had gone crazy and probably shot her husband. Katherine Mansfield wrote a story about her. Christ knows what she would have written if she had seen the Tamaki Brothers Model Maori Village and the artificial, headachy flicker of the unnatural pine forest going by at speed.

'"A mean, undersized brat, with whitish hair and weak eyes,"' quoted Bill with relish. 'That's the murderer's daughter as seen by the celebrated writer.' He turned himself into a hunchback and made claws of his hands. 'A goblin child. You are now entering the New Zealand gothic.'

And then the bus zig-zagged into the dense primeval chaos of the native forest along a narrow dirt road that commenced soon after the sign that said it was closed because of landslides.

'Always says that,' Stan informed them. His jeer insinuated that the CTI team did not include experts on danger, mountains and the indigenous estate. 'No bugger ever gets around to changing it.'

There was a smell of dinners cooking in late afternoon in Te Waititi, a haze of mutton-roasty woodsmoke drifting across the scattered houses and weedy paddocks below the dark forest and a wet, cold mist was sinking into the purple valley from the mountains. A young man in a red-and-black Swanndri and a knitted hat with long dreadlocks hanging out below turned his tattooed face towards the mini-bus when it slowed behind his pack of dogs. He had a rifle over one shoulder.

'What, fellas can't train your pig dogs up here?' Gloria yelled at him out of the bus window. He grinned and jerked his head at a couple of muddy steers grazing in the patchy scrub above the road.

'You never know what's going to turn up, eh sis?'

Boris has disappeared into the forest where the track begins to wind through thicker bush and more complex terrain after the initial climb, and Bill struggles upwards with a memory of the last kilometres of the night before's drive in seeming to wait for him at the darker edge of the forest ahead. The winding road was making him feel sick, then, and so were the sheer drops, unfenced, which the mini-bus sometimes had to edge past where slips had narrowed the road. And then Stan pulled the bus over as darkness was falling across a broad vista of the lake. The bus's windows framed a hulking, lumpy skyline and the black, foreshortened and flattened flank of a mountain range.

'What's up, Stan?' asked Pat. She had kept her seat next to her Bangladeshi counterpart's empty one in the back – as Gloria had kept the one next to Nancy's. 'Be good to get there while the store's open.'

Stan levered himself out and lit a smoke. He waved the

cigarette at the dark mountain horizon. 'Colin McCahon painted that,' he said as if to imply that Pat should not have asked. 'Guess you all know that. It's in the Visitor Centre at Aniwaniwa.'

The top edge of the range retained a faint, acetylene glow. As Bill stepped from the mini-bus the glow began to fade. The folds of the gullies descending in abrupt diagonals down the flanks of the mountains were black on almost-black, with here and there the darkened ochre of slips. In the sky above were a few bright, early stars. Stan stood with his back to the team and the glow of his cigarette as he lifted it to his mouth was like the pointer of a lecturer indicating sites of significance.

'Got a bit of a thing about Colin McCahon, come to think of it, has Stan,' whispered Pat.

'So do Tuhoe,' said Gloria, not whispering.

And then the snow came, with a preliminary crash of hail on the roof of the mini-bus. And what Bill is carrying in his mind now, as he places one booted foot after the other along a seam between the bright vista of the sunlit lake and the dark interior of the forest, is a memory of a moment last night with the mini-bus pulled over brooking no argument before the sombre view that had required Stan's homage – a moment that Bill is now suddenly thinking about with a sense of exultation, but also with fear as he wonders where Boris has gone – a moment when the seam between the dark, barely gleaming lake and the matt black flank of the mountain disappeared, an instant Bill noticed with, at first, an awful squirm of nausea in the pit of his stomach as the harsh, level planes and abrupt verticals of the world suddenly folded themselves together and he felt himself sliding across the vast side of the world as it tilted out and away from him.

And then he felt himself tip up again. He righted, just like the mast and wet sail of the little Moth yacht when it capsized as his mother and father watched (but did not see) from the picture window of the bach. And then he saw the same folding-together happen at the dimming acetylene skyline as the sudden hail and snow-cloud wiped out its demarcation. But this time he did not feel the awful slither of space and distance rushing away around him and he even wanted to ask Stan to stop a while longer so he could stand out in the freezing hail and the black darkness and know that he was upright. That he was not sliding uncontrollably down the vast incline of the world into a black pit.

There is still no sign of Boris and Bill guesses he must have got impatient and gone on ahead, even though he is carrying both their supplies for the hut at Panekiri. Bill has removed his cap and stuck it in his pack also and sweat is running into his eyes. His chest is burning and his legs have begun to tremble when he pauses to catch his breath, but even so he continues to feel triumphant, his memory of righting and standing upright in the dark, immense space of last night, where he really could not see anything, could not 'see his hand in front of his face' – this memory stays with him as he skirts the edge of a bright, visible precipice to his right. The drop is sometimes closer, with only some thin scrub and skinny tree trunks between him and it, and sometimes there is a thicker barrier of bush with big trees.

He wants Boris to see him – he wants to see in Boris's cool, blue, mocking eyes the reflection of his own nerve. He wants Boris to smack him across the side of the head and call him Bill-the-Bugger, as he has begun to, because then he feels safe within the perimeter of Joris's, of Boris's, scorn. He wants to see Joris waiting for him at the dark edge of the trees with a mocking smile on his face and he wants Joris to playfully snatch away the water bottle as Bill reaches for it. He wants to hear Joris say, with grudging admiration, 'Bill-the-Bugger not going too bad today, but you wait, you're going to shit.'

Bill does not find himself hoping for the thick bush to come back when the safety margin thins out. In fact, he is triumphing when the track veers close to the edge and, gasping, he has to clutch at bushes and exposed roots to haul himself up the steep rises.

To his left, now, the forest is dense with occasional glimpses of the distant ocean across a rolling vista of treetops. The depths of the forest are cool and green with a softly dappled floor of leaves and humus and a comforting smell of soaked leaf mould and in places it plunges away into rich shadow and a mushroomy odour rises out of the gullies. But Bill does not want to edge closer to this. As a kid he always wanted to walk on the inside of the track and he liked the leafy hiding places and hut-building possies better than the cliffs with pohutukawa roots hanging down that were supposed to be good for climbing. When he looked out from the shade of these places into the brightness beyond them he liked to let his eyes go out of focus until the distance collapsed into a soft blur close to where he was. He liked to burrow, to build bivvies and to crouch in the smelly recesses of caves while the others hauled sarking timber up trees to make lookouts.

But now, shucked free also of his padded coat and the high skivvy neck of his jumper, Bill navigates the edge of his old terror, he sidles towards its terrible space and light and height across the seam that has traversed and divided his mind all his life that he can remember. The seam whose absolute division of the universe into back here and out there, into William closing his eyes to sleep in his apartment where the light to the toilet comes under the bedroom door and the Bill who now stops on the edge of an immense precipice to suck air into his burning lungs and sees, through a sting of sweat in his eyes, the slim figure of Boris grinning at him from the dark shade of the ridge's crest ahead – this division which is the source of his worst nightmares and his best visions.

A thin shaft of sunlight transects Boris who is standing beside the pack he has propped against a tree. As Bill pauses to look up at him he lifts his water bottle and tilts his head to drink. The bottle replaces the grin and now Bill can't remember what kind of grin it was. The shaft of sunlight flashes on Boris's dark glasses as he tilts his head and it also lights a streak of his pale hair and shines on one side of his smooth, tanned forehead. Bill would like to pause for long enough to get back the breath with which to call out to Boris, but the longer he waits, gasping, with one hand bracing his trembling body against an exposed tree root, the more he feels his exultant confidence waning, the more he sees himself as pitiful in Boris's flashing, UV-mirrored eyes. His anticipation at meeting up with Boris again is anxious, because he does not know how long Boris has been watching him from the rim of trees and he does not know how Boris will have interpreted his slow but steady progress up the steep hill. Will he have felt scorn or admiration?

In the time it takes to cover the final distance between them, Bill has prepared his greeting. But as he opens his mouth to say, 'A mean, undersized brat, with whitish hair and weak eyes,' Boris's strong fingers grip his arm, he feels himself lifted the last step and turned around and pressed down to sit on Boris's pack, and with his mouth still open to say the sentence about the feeble goblin child from Katherine Mansfield's story 'The Woman at the Store', whose gluey ears and traumatised defiance had always made him feel a kind of secret affection, as if this child of loneliness and of the violence of loneliness could be recruited to the goblin army of William's gothic stormtroopers and sent to terrorise the scenic wonderlands of picnic spots and views – with his mouth still open to say his prepared wise-guy quip, he also feels Boris's strong fingers nudging at his back as he unclips the straps of his pack and lifts it from his shoulders.

'Long way to go yet, Bill,' says Boris in his noncommittal tone of voice, handing Bill down the water bottle whose self-sealing cap he has already, thoughtfully, opened. 'But that's the real long steep bit, okay? You did good, considering.'

Bill swallows from the bottle, and if he feels close to tears it has got more to do with the sensation of Boris's competent fingers unbuckling his pack than with having arrived where

Boris has been watching him struggle up the hill, or than with a feeling between gratitude and relief that Boris has not jeered at him.

The water in his throat is delightful and lightly flavoured with the sachet of gastrolytes that Boris had tipped in back at the camping ground and when he passes the bottle back up to Boris and prepares, again, to make his joke about the undersized brat, now that he is getting his breath back, he feels Boris's fingers again, this time at the neck of his T-shirt, and then Boris squirts a jet of the cool drinking water down Bill's naked back and then another onto the crown of his head. And then the strong fingers grip at Bill's shoulders and give a few firm squeezes to the neck and shoulder muscles aching with even the minimal load in his pack. It is almost a loud sob that comes up out of Bill's burning chest as he turns and finds Boris's slender hips next to his face, and he has almost reached out to clasp Boris around the hips and bury his face in the front of his thin tramping pants when Boris smacks him across the side of the head. The smack may be a bit harder than usual, Bill can't tell, because all his senses are bruised and tender and he does not know if there is more violence in the cuff or less resistance in him.

'Okay, so let's go,' says Boris. 'Otherwise you stiffen up.' And then he laughs, that infuriating all-purpose laugh, which could mean something or nothing at all, and Bill is icy inside as though he has been squirted there also, because he does not know if Boris has just made a flirtatious joke or not and he does not know whether to connect the sexy joke (if it was one) with Boris's fingers toying with the fastener on his pack and he does not know, now, what the line about the weak-eyed child might sound like or what it might be better to say to Boris instead.

Now Boris roughly yanks his own pack from under Bill and before Bill has managed to get his own one back on, Boris has marched off again and Bill hears him singing in an exaggerated comic German accent, 'I loff to go a van-der-ink!'

It is true, the track is never so long and steep again, but it ascends and descends the sides of gullies and in places where the sunlight has not reached there are still drifts of snow among the trees. Here and there, as they get higher still, the track is icy in the shade and Bill has to cling to clumps of tussock and to spiny bushes that scratch his hands.

'We have lunch at the Knob,' says Boris at another of their brief rests. 'It's the highest.'

'That's where I'm going to shit myself, right?' Bill is now moving forward like an automaton and when he speaks it is as though someone else is talking – someone he is instructing or willing to speak on his behalf. The Bill who is still walking and the one who is directing Bill to keep walking seem also to be different. Boris has taken Bill's entire pack and slung it across the top of his own and he seems more concerned that Bill will make it to the top than with his actual state of exhaustion. He feeds Bill chocolate and nuts and adds another glucose and salt sachet to his water.

'That's right,' answers Boris, who is now no longer smiling and who has not massaged Bill's neck again. 'Because you think you've seen awesome but this you haven't seen yet.'

And then the track clears from stunted goblin beeches shaggy with moss and lichen and thick drifts of snow along the melt-line of the sunshine and a chilly gust of air flies up over the edge of a sandy-surfaced rock bluff whose edge, Bill sees, is completely bare where it meets the blue glare of the sunlit lake. Even exhausted as he is, Bill's stomach heaves at the sight of this escarpment, but Boris pushes him up a short stair cut in the rock with a wire cable to hold on to and he comes out on a bare rock place with nothing but wind and light between him and the sheer thousand-metre drop to the water.

He has never been this high before except in an aeroplane and he has never been this high standing up without any protection or without anything to hold on to. His body is shaking with exhaustion and his legs are weak and unsteady.

Even the moderate breeze of the heat convections rising over the bluff pushes at him and makes him stagger on the small, bare space of the Knob. For a moment the world begins to reel and sway the way he is familiar with and he wonders how he can lower himself to be flat on the surface of the sandy rock without falling over or flying off-balance from the edge. For a while he does not dare to make any move at all, while he waits for his usual giddiness and nausea to overwhelm him. Boris has appeared above the cut with the steps in it, pushing the two packs ahead of himself. He is immediately looking expectantly at Bill standing frozen in his place on the absurd platform of the bluff, arms held out slightly from his sides, eyes wanting to clamp shut but prised open by the knowledge that he has not, yet, fallen down in utter terror and clasped the bare rock.

Boris is watching him as he emerges fully from the cut and then crouches to sit with his back against the packs at the far side of the stone platform furthest from its edge. He is watching Bill to see his utter terror. He is watching Bill with a small smile on his lips, which are barely puffing with the effort of the last climb. He sits, smiling and at ease and observes Bill frozen where he stands and can't move to retreat from the edge or to sit down or to step three times, steadily, to where Boris reclines at a comfortable distance from the void. He is still smiling as Bill begins very slowly to relax, he is smiling when Bill's arms drop to his sides, he goes on smiling when Bill turns in a full circle, carefully but surely moving his feet, but the smile has begun to change from one of vindication and pleasure to something else.

When Bill completes his full circle and now stands at ease with his back to the appalling void only a couple of metres from where his feet are steady on the rock, he says, with disbelief that he can even speak, 'So when do I shit myself, Boris?'

A triumph he has never imagined fills Bill's burning, aching body – he knows the huge precipice is at his back and should be filling him with terror, but instead it is as though his whole life of fear, his whole life of ineptly leaping and capsizing and making his eyes go out of focus in order to persuade others he is not afraid, has ended.

Bill knows he is grinning like a complete idiot and that standing here for as long as he has is showing off, but he wants to see Boris's smile, which has gone cold like a snarl, break open and admit that yes, Bill has done it, he has overcome his fear and now he, Boris, can see that he is not going to shit himself after all, not even after the longest climb Bill has ever attempted in his whole life.

'When, Boris?' asks Bill. Surely, now, he will see himself reflected in Boris's smile of love and admiration. But the glaring look on Boris's face does not change while he reaches down and unzips the fly of his tramping pants and takes out his long penis and his testicles loose with the heat of climbing.

The chill floods through Bill's body, as though the wind over the Bluff, clear and cold like the distant water, has poured into his blood. He freezes all over as Boris lightly fondles his penis and it begins to stiffen with a couple of little jerks.

'What do you want, you fucking fairy?' asks the snarling smile in Boris's face. 'Is this what you want? What I have to do, fuck you, what, you neuken fuk?' Boris's smile puckers inward suddenly and he hauls up a gob of phlegm and spits it at Bill. Bill has imagined something like this, not the spit but Boris naked or the moment when he will feel the Dutchman's smooth body against his own. But the smile is back on Boris's face, only now it is full of pleasure, as though he has passed a moment of rage and now enjoys the possibility of another, more spectacular result. 'Come on, then,' says the gloating Boris, the Boris reflecting defeat and hatred, the Boris who will not, will not, will not fail.

Bill has taken a step back in his shock and now knows that the brink of the precipice is at his heel as Boris lifts the flange of his penis over its head and spits again but this time downwards, onto himself. The edge of the drop is at Bill's heels but he is not afraid yet, not even when he feels himself begin to fall, so that he has time and presence of mind to turn his gaze and his body away from smiling Boris and face the great shining lake and push himself out from the edge as he begins to fall – to push off and out with the sunlit water beyond and below him, diving, like a water bird, below the blue surface of the air.

eighteen

Home

'It's like he's in there.' Pat heaves out an immense sob. 'Christ almighty, I never even thought I could ever like the bloke.' She blows her nose and adds the tissue to a pile on the bunk.

'In where?' asks Gloria. She's sitting on the edge of the bunk with her arm around Pat's hefty shoulders. 'In where, what do you mean, "in there", sweetie?'

'In that fucking landscape,' rages Pat. 'That Absolutely Pure fucking place he was always scared witless of. Jesus, how could this happen? What was Joris thinking?'

'Maybe it's what he wanted,' suggests Gloria.

'What? To literally scare him to death?'

'Doubt it, and why? Because, in case you hadn't thought of it, not very likely, that's goodnight, that's haere ra Good-2-Go Enterprises. He's gone, girl. Phut.'

'Then what?' trumpets Pat, shaking. 'What the fuck was going on?'

'Whoa, steady girl,' says Gloria. 'What I mean is, maybe it's what Bill wanted.'

'You mean William,' says Pat, sobbing afresh. 'You mean poor old William. Too scared to even look out the window, seemed like. Remember how he threw up at Aorangi, up the Hooker track? Why did we push the poor sod, Glor?'

'No, girl, I mean Bill. Maybe it's what *Bill* wanted. See how he got into all that gear of Joris's?'

'Oh, for Christ's sake, Glor,' says Pat, exasperated and beginning to get a grip. 'You must have seen it. The poor old bugger was completely besotted with Joris, Boris, whatever the fuck we call the prick. Mr Smartarse. Poor old bloody William, half-blind, built like a stack of pick-up sticks, did you hear the cough? What kind of chance do you think he had? Joris had half the glamour on the circuit after him and not just the glam sheilas like that little Seiko with the Add Venture Jap parties.'

'Of course I saw,' says Gloria. 'I saw Joris playing him like a bloody hooked fish.'

'So what – you think Bill, if you must, jumped? A lover's leap? You think he wanted to go?'

'We don't know that,' says Gloria. She gets up and opens the window of the cabin. Cool lake air blows into the room and there are pleasant sounds of cheepy lake birds and of kids splashing each other. 'There's no way we can know that. Maybe he did. Jump. But maybe, too, Bill wanted to beat the fear. Maybe he got sick of it. Maybe he wanted Joris to take him up there for that?' Gloria sucks in a big breath of fresh air. 'I watched him practising. On his balcony at Rotorua. Joris was biffing stuff at him.'

Below the cabin, around the weedy shallows, the little grebes are ducking and diving in choreographed flocks. Stan and Joris are in Wairoa where Joris is filing an accident report with the local police. The search-and-rescue team has already returned from Panekiri with Bill's remains in a blue plastic bag – they were out most of the night. The grebes have the piles of the jetty, the bobbing moorings, the placid weed-banks drifting in the wind-driven currents, all to themselves.

'And yes,' says Gloria, sticking her head out the window into the chilly breeze and looking at the little birds. 'I know what you mean.'

'About what?' Pat's got a grip – she's bundling her snotty tissues in a plastic bread bag and consigning them to the cabin's rubbish bin. She's doing this with the efficient bluster of someone wanting to restore their own confidence.

'About "being in there",' says Gloria. 'And don't look at me like that, girl, like, what's this spooky Maori shit? You said it first.'

'Come off it, Glor, that's not what I meant,' begins Pat, but stops.

'What, then?'

'Maybe it is what I meant, Glor,' Pat begins again. 'Spooky Maori shit. But I'll tell you something. William and me worked together on and off for years. We never liked each other but we got on with the job. We were professionals, like they say. But he was the weirdest creative I ever met. More like an accounts clerk with a secret hobby or a lower echelon policy advisor good at drafting speeches, you know the ones, give nothing away but sound informative. Or maybe a minor NGO strategic planner who knows how to keep his eye on the government's statement of intent objectives even though he knows they're shit, because staying sweet with Ministry incentivisers means he gets to fluff up his performance bonus. But he had a brilliant knack for the brand. Looked like an overdressed fucking HR manager in some corporation but had a head full of vision. He always got it right – that feeling of something new and exclusive. He used big concepts – what about his New Zealand Gothic campaign, you remember that one? All blues and greys, everyone in half-profile with the shadow across their faces and one eye shining yellow, like a wolf's, and the moonlight just catching the pure white merino knit where their black leather coats are open. Magic. How did it go? "When it gets dark, get into something light – pure New Zealand wool." Sold more Woolmark product than anything before or since. But I'll tell you what.' Pat joins Gloria at the windowsill and heaves her big chest full of chilly air. 'He never seemed to care. Always took the piss out of them, his campaigns, even when the accounts were making him stacks of dough, which they were. He was rolling in it but he didn't care about that, either. Bought flash clothes, went for holidays flying first class, never looked like he was having any fun. Didn't care about anything. Not until Absolutely Pure, that is. That one was different. He got a real thing about it, Glor. We had a big fight when the pundits all said he'd gone too far this time. Some academic even wrote a paper suggesting it was fascist. *Lebensraum.* But he wouldn't leave it alone. Got real obsessive. We had some real yelling matches. Had to overrule him. He went completely nuts.' Pat pushes her forehead against the window frame. 'That's when he started serious drinking.'

The CTI mini-bus pulls up outside – they hear Stan's hard-as-he-can door-slam and the screech of his cough as he lights up. But no sound of a second door.

'Hello,' says Gloria. 'Sounds like Stan's on his own.'

'Point is,' Pat continues, 'he so cared about that one, about Absolutely Pure. It was nuts. We used to call it the One Peepee at DoT. He didn't just care about it as a brand identity guru. He cared about it really, really personally. And what I mean is, I think that's where he wanted to go. Fuck's sake, tell me to shut up. I don't know. I'm just guessing, Glor. Because he was sick of being afraid, which he was. Was afraid, was sick of it. Because he wanted to impress Joris, you saw that. Because he wanted to go there, really, into that Absolutely Pure place, only he didn't know that's what he wanted until he saw what Joris was up to.'

'And what was that?' asks Gloria. Stan's knock, urgent and officious, rattles the door.

'Selling fear,' says Pat. 'You heard him – supply and demand. People want a thrill and then they want protection. You supply the fear and then you supply the safety as well. Joris sells fear the way William sold quality merino knits. The way he sold bottled mountain water, the best sauvignon blanc and that famous swivel chair thing. The way he sold that ultra flash dishwasher. Only Joris is going bust. "Demand-side problem".'

Gloria lets the urgent Stan in.

'Tell me I'm wrong,' says Pat. 'Tell me I've lost it. But I

reckon that's what Joris wanted Bill to do. Sell fear. I used to listen to him egging Bill on, in the bus. Had to read him the riot act about his contract a couple of times. And he couldn't do it, Bill couldn't. Not just because of his contract with CTI. He just couldn't. Couldn't bring himself to. So he went there. He went home.'

'He went home?' repeats Stan, astonished.

'He went where he'd always wanted to go. But never could. For whatever reasons. For God's sake, stop me now, Glor,' says Pat, 'before this gets any worse. God help me. If Hands-On could only hear me now.'

'It's okay,' says Gloria.

'Shut the door, Stan,' says Pat, zipping up her jumper. 'It's bloody freezing in here. And no, it's not okay. Let's get real. Tell us what happened, Stan. With Joris, down at the cop shop.'

'Colin McCahon painted it, you know,' suggests Stan.

Pat is getting the project log book and a note-pad out of her briefcase. 'Come off it, Stan,' she admonishes him, briskly making a fresh page ready. 'Bad enough having the team manager losing the plot without having the bloody driver going haywire too, Stan.'

'He did, though,' persists Stan, stubbornly. He takes Pat's biro from her fingers and draws a blocky rectangular shape with a dotted line descending next to it on the fresh note-pad. 'Jump.'

'Is this your idea of a joke, Stan?' warns Pat, taking the biro back. 'Because if so, knock it off. There's been more than enough jumping already, in case you hadn't noticed.'

'"Jump" series,' says Stan. 'At the gannet colony at Muriwai. That's where McCahon painted them. We're supposed to be going there. Though at this rate.'

'Though at this rate what, Stan?' asks Gloria, who is looking at his little sketch. 'I've seen these paintings. Scary. About the young bird's first flight, right? When they just have to jump off?'

'Maybe,' says Stan. 'But he was scared, McCahon was. He painted that, too. Being scared. Maybe he thought about it.'

'In case you hadn't noticed,' says Pat, 'we have a missing Australian, a repatriated Bangladeshi and a jumped-but-anyway-dead brand identity specialist. We have a journalist hot on our trail. We have an underperforming Minister who will turn off your ignition, Stan, even quicker than he decides to shit of a morning. We have an incomplete and frankly bizarre report that has cost a number of dollars, not ours, but those of influential agencies. I have the feeling I've said this, or most of this, before. We have smashed mirrors and an important Pakistani man with a brand-new speech impediment. There are now only three of us, or four, counting you, Stan, our resident art historian. But what we should be pondering now, team-mates, is the place of art history in the fucking scheme of things, Stan, right now?'

'Take it easy, Pat,' says Gloria. 'I think he's right.'

'You what?' yells Pat.

'I think he's right,' says Gloria, calmly. 'He's not saying anything stranger than we were. Than you were. "It's like he's in there"?'

'"Gone home",' Stan reminds them.

'That's right, Stan,' says Gloria.

'"Ahipara here I come back home where I started from",' quotes Stan.

'Seen that one too,' agrees Gloria. 'That painting. In Te Papa, the museum, when we did that team-building.'

'The point is,' tries Pat very calmly, 'we don't know he jumped. Tell us what we do know, Stan. Since Joris is not here. For example, tell us where Joris is, Stan. Has he, perhaps, decided to jump himself?'

'He's back at the station,' says Stan, who is beginning to get fed up. 'And he did.'

'And who did what, Stan?' Pat is right into Great White mode.

'Jump. He did jump.'

'Who did, Stan – Colin fucking McCahon, Joris or William?'

'There's no need to talk to me like that, Pat,' says Stan, who is getting really angry now. 'Maybe if you'd all shown some respect none of this would have happened.'

'Respect for what, Stan? Let's get this straight. Respect for the Minister who wants to sandbag his portfolio? For the department who won't read the report or if they do won't understand it? For the crooked entrepreneurs flogging whistle-stop photo-opportunities to people who don't speak English? For you, Stan? For what, Stan, respect for what?'

Gloria is making wide eyes at Stan, at the same time as holding Pat by the shoulder.

'Respect for the views,' says Stan with the dignity of a martyr. 'None of you have any respect for the bloody views.'

'I'm speechless, Stan,' Pat informs him.

'Wind it back a bit, Stan,' suggests Gloria. 'You said two things. You said, "Though at this rate." And then you said, "He did jump." What say you finish off both of them?'

'Thank you very much, Hinemoana,' says Pat with extreme calmness. 'Thank you for reminding me that Stan has more significant intelligence to transmit than the latest gossip about Colin McCahon or the CTI team's attitude to views.'

Gloria lets go of Pat's shoulder. 'Tell you what,' she says. 'I'm going to make a cup of tea. And after that, I reckon it would be a good idea if Stan told us why he thinks the project isn't going to make it, which I guess is what "Though at this rate" is all about, and why he believes William jumped.' She gives Pat a shove. 'And stop jumping on poor old Stan.'

'The problem is,' the inspector says to Joris, 'the deceased landed a full eight to ten metres out from the drop line consistent with the edge of the cliff. He either flew, you don't mind if I call you Joris, sir, or he was propelled.'

'Yes, that is so, I can see that,' agrees Joris. The polite blankness of his expression is clearly irritating the inspector.

'That being so,' continues the inspector, who himself has the weathered tan of an outdoors enthusiast, the stringy look of someone who exercises a lot and the rough hands of a farmer or bushwhacker, 'we haven't yet agreed, Joris, on the most likely scenario, flight or propulsion. What is your professional view, Joris, as an, what was it? An Outdoor Adventure Specialist?'

'No, sir, he didn't fly,' says Joris with a deadpan expression. 'At least, not as far as I could see.'

'You'll have to excuse me, Joris,' interrupts the inspector with a polite, interrupting gesture of his calloused hand. 'But I'm afraid you're not taking me seriously. If you weren't looking, the deceased might well have flown, for all you know. Since you wouldn't have seen. But you say he didn't fly "as far as I could see". And how far was that?'

'How far was what, sir?'

'How far could you see, Joris? Since you have agreed that the deceased did not fly and that you know this because you could see him.'

'I didn't say I could see him,' says Joris. 'I only said I didn't see him fly.'

'You and I both know,' says the inspector, making his weathered face wrinkle at the corners of his eyes and with a significant change in his tone, 'that your business is down the fucking gurgler, Joris. You don't – outdoor adventure specialists don't get to have fatalities on their excursions more than once. Now you've had yours. Your one fatality. We both know that the deceased was not an experienced tramper and may have suffered from asthma. We both know, because we've both done it a few times, that the walk in to the Panekiri hut and the elevation achieved, while a bit of a doddle for men like us, are both substantial. We know there are minimum standards of safety required for guided tramps and that harsh penalties attend the failure to observe them. I get all sorts of dickheads in here, Joris,' continues the inspector without taking his eyes from Joris's serene look, 'including amateurs who've gone in there in their fucking pyjamas, Joris, and old bushwhackers who've shot each other because they thought they were deer, not to mention the odd rope-head growing dope, but I have never yet had a leading "outdoor adventure experience specialist" professional end up in this office with a fatality consisting of a frail, inexperienced and possibly exhausted tramper insufficiently safeguarded on one of the most hazardous places in the country, who has nevertheless managed, not to fly, we have established that much, but to get himself a full ten metres out from the edge of the cliff, Joris. This is a first for me. I need your help, your professional help, to understand not just how you, the seasoned outdoor specialist in question, but more especially the physically weak deceased, could have managed to do this.'

The inspector pauses.

'I imagine,' he continues, as if with an afterthought, 'that your team's driver, Stan isn't it, will by now be close to informing the rest of your party including your team leader that you have been detained while you offer every assistance in our inquiries, Joris, but also that their late colleague landed a good ten metres out from the edge of the cliff.' The inspector watches Joris. 'Don't shrug,' he says. 'It gives a bad impression. Take me, one more time, Joris, through the sequence, and then let us focus on the moment when, as you have testified in the presence of a witness, the constable here, and on the video tape-recorder, Joris – the moment when you did not see the deceased fly.' The inspector waits a moment. 'Would you like me to start?'

'As you wish,' says Joris, politely.

'Okay then. Very well. You made the ascent slowly, taking care the deceased had plenty of liquid and you also carried his pack most of the way.'

'That's right,' says Joris. 'But nothing much in it.'

'You reached the Knob.'

'We reached the Knob, yes.'

'You went up the cut steps to the lookout first.'

'I went up first, yes.'

'You pushed the packs, both of them, up ahead of you.'

'Yes, I pushed both the packs in front.'

'Then you assisted the deceased to come up the cut.'

'Yes, I helped him to come up.'

'Where were the packs?'

'At the back of the lookout. I put them there first. Is safer. Out of the way.'

'And then you returned to the cut and assisted the deceased.'

'I pulled him up, yes.'

'He had the strength to climb up that far.'

'He did, yes, by himself.'

'And then you reached down and hauled him up the last bit.'

'That's the hard bit. That's where.'

'That's where you can lose your balance, right?'

'You can.'

'But you didn't see the deceased lose his balance.'

'No, I did not.'

'You had turned around again to go to the packs and sit down.'

'Yes, William was up safely.'

'But this is also the moment where, as you have testified, you did not see the deceased fly.'

'No, I did not see William fly.'

'You did not see him fly because you were facing the packs, or you did not see him fly because he didn't fly?'

'Inspector, people don't fly,' says Joris politely.

'Then how did he end up ten metres out from the cliff?'

'I don't know,' says Joris. 'I didn't see.'

'You weren't looking.'

'Was a split second,' says Joris. 'I turn my back.'

'You weren't looking at your physically weakened client,'

continues the inspector, holding his finger over the video remote, 'at the very moment he was first standing unprotected on a rock ledge one-thousand-and-something metres above Lake Waikaremoana, knowing he suffered from weak lungs and possibly from a fear of heights. You turned your back.'

Joris does not speak.

'Yes or no?'

'Yes,' says Joris. 'I turn my back.'

The inspector switches off the video. 'Ten metres,' he says. 'Must have been flight. But we'll never know, will we, constable? Because our "outdoor specialist" wasn't watching. Didn't see the deceased fly.'

'May I go now?' asks Joris. He smiles politely at the inspector. 'Last night I didn't sleep. After we were looking.'

'I imagine you were, looking,' answers the inspector, also politely. 'Looking but not seeing, I imagine. Until later.'

'I'd like to go home,' says Joris. 'I mean, back to the camp.'

'How about the River View Motel?' suggests the inspector. 'Since your driver's already gone to tell your team leader about the ten metres. About the miracle of flight,' says the inspector with a smile, 'off the Panekiri Bluff.'

'That will be okay, thank you,' says Joris.

'They say it's very comfortable,' says the inspector. 'A home away from home. I hope you won't be lonely.'

'I'll be fine,' says Joris. He smiles agreeably at the inspector. 'Being alone, out in the wilderness, I'm used to that.'

'I'm sure you are,' concludes the inspector, looking at the constable. 'But please, Joris, do stay there, at the River View Motel. Which, I probably don't have to tell you, doesn't have a view of the river. Thing we all have about views and lookouts. Please stay there, with or without the view. That would be best for us. You can meet up with your mates in the morning. When,' he says pleasantly, 'and look after the videotape please, constable, I guess you'll have a lot to talk about. With them. The rest of your mates.'

Pat's gone out of the cabin with her video camera to get some footage of moonlight on the lake. Why for, who knows? thinks Gloria. Probably wants to be by herself for a while. Trying so hard to be the tough one. Like Uncle Mat used to tease, all prickly on the outside like a kina but full of goo when she cracks. Gloria lies in her sleeping-bag on the upper bunk with her eyes closed, but not sleeping. The window of the cabin's ajar and she can hear the rustle of reeds and flax at the edge of the lake and the sloshing of water stirred up by the same wind. There's a ruru up in the bush calling 'Morepork!' and 'Koukou!' but then there would be, wouldn't there? It's going on and on about William, but then it would. But then Gloria realises it's also her cellphone, down in her bag. No use climbing all the way down there because the camp is out of cellphone range, so it can't really be ringing.

'How do you do that?' she asks.

'It's a funny thing,' says Antsy, in that after-a-long-silence rush of words.

'Strange choice of words, Ants, under the circumstances?'

'No, what I mean – it was poor old Bill who didn't see me go. He was the only one who was in a position to not see me go, when I went. None of the others were. He was giving me one of his Bill-type lectures about Erewhon and Nowhere. I found him an immensely interesting man,' adds Antsy with formal respect.

'I was listening too, Ants.'

'Sure you were, Gloria, but all the same?'

'All the same what, Antsy?' Gloria begins to cry quietly into her miserable, flat, bunkhouse pillow. 'Look, Ants, I'm crying into their skinny pillow, look what you're making me do. Just like last time. Crying all the time, these days. What's the matter with me? Just as well Uncle can't see.'

'All the same, Gloria, don't cry, you weren't in a position.'

'You mean I wasn't looking, Ants? Because I feel so bad about that.'

'No, because what you can do is see when you look. That's what's great about you. You see life. But Bill.'

'You think that's what made him hoha all the time, made him act so mad and sarcastic, made him so sad? Made him so lonely?'

'It was a big empty space, for Bill, the world was. He knew what most people are afraid of because he was afraid of it all the time. You heard him talking. All those words, all that knowledge, it was how he kept safe. How he filled the empty space up.'

'But Stan says the police reckon he landed a good ten metres out from the cliff, Ants. How could he have been afraid? And done that?'

Gloria's tissues are down in her bag after all. Her pillow's getting too wet and she has to blow her nose. She climbs down. See, that's the thing. He can't have been afraid. Ants can't have been afraid. Otherwise neither of them could have done it. That's the good thing about it. They both went because they could. Went home. Toi whenua. Sunk to the bottom. Where you can't be seen any more. Not even by people who can't see.

Oh, shut up! she tells herself, climbing back up the little ladder in the dark. What a load of rubbish. Leave the tough stuff to Antsy. You know what's happened, girl. Just don't try to talk about it, make a blooming fool of yourself, tie yourself in knots. Leave that to the old buggers, the Uncle Mats, half-blind in actual fact, reckon that's how they can see. Or not-see, whatever. Leave it alone, Hinemoana, keep your eye on the life stuff. That's what you're good at.

And then, because she feels a bit better, she begins to go to sleep. Turns the useless skinny pillow damp-side down. The ruru are still moreporking away up in the bush where the old Lake Hostel used to be, at least two of the blighters – koukouing away to each other like Ngai Tuhoe, asking where everybody's gone.

It was true, what the inspector said, there's no view of the river, what's a view of: is failure, the whole fuk place and including the squad car outside. What: they think he's going to run away? From what? Run away from this room maybe with the pictures of native bush on the walls and a panorama of the lake again?

Joris leaves the curtains at the front of the unit open so the constable in the squad car can see him making a cup of instant coffee and turning the television on. He watches *Game of Two Halves* and is careful to laugh loudly, throwing his head back. But then the squad car drives away and Joris feels sick, from the instant coffee, probably. He watches *Game of Two Halves* and sees Bill go up onto the rock ledge by himself, he sees Bill turn and push himself off, like he nearly did fly, he went way out. And then he was gone and Joris was sitting there with his hard cock out.

'I went up first,' says Joris, as Marc Ellis smashes his hand down on the team's bell and answers a question wrong. 'I pushed the packs up in front. Only a split second, I didn't look. He was gone. I climbed up ahead of him to get the packs up out of the way so I could help him. He was up fine. Then: I turn around: he's already gone. It was best I get up first and be able to help Bill, after getting the packs up, he couldn't do that. He did real good: was a long walk for him. I helped him by pulling him up, he was fine. I didn't see what happened to him.

'I let him go up first.'

The really bad *Game of Two Halves* band is playing crap. The guest is a swimmer, she's got that triangular upper body and just smiles. In the next unit a man and a woman begin to argue. 'Who's had the most drinks, you have you fuckin' pig don't bullshit me, fuck off! Don't you fuckin' dare lift your hand!'

'I made him go up first, Poppa: make him shit himself, the faggot. "Up you go, Bill, be fine." He went up first, up there all by himself. I let him stay by himself for a while. Poppa,

Poppa, I'm sorry.' Joris imagines his little smiling dad lifting the lid off the rabbit goulash and telling a lie about it being chicken.

'I went up first,' Joris starts again. The *Game of Two Halves* stops for a commercial break. A man speeds a four-wheel-drive ute truck out of sight over the green crest of a hill. He goes up, and over. The ute seems to fly – it stalls against the sky and then is gone.

'Give me that fuckin' bottle you cunt!'

'Take me home you bastard. I want to go home. Just take me home.'

On screen, Marc Ellis romps around the *Game of Two Halves* studio in a funny hat doing a charade.

'Just take me home,' mimics Joris savagely to the screen, to the wall behind which the woman has yelled, shrieked, screamed, to the window from which there isn't a view of the river, nor of the squad car. And then, as if pushing itself off from the sound of her motel unit's door slamming, there is a view of the yelling woman running across the forecourt of the River View Motel, hopping to take off her one shoe, like a charade of something: going home perhaps, Joris thinks. That's what she looks like she's doing: Going Home.

Pat reckons she's probably got about ten video minutes' worth of pitch darkness with moonlight on the lake and the bulk of the bluff in the distance on the far side of the southern arm. The spotty reproduction of an 1880s watercolour in the visitor centre at Aniwaniwa shows all the coves around this arm of the lake chocker with people. Canoes out on the lake and beached up next to the settlements. But now it's empty – unless you count the odd fizz boat with someone fishing. Or the trampers doing the Great Walk. Feels as if what's gone almost silently into her video camera is the emptiness that Percy Smith, not the 1880s watercolourist, saw a bit over a hundred years ago. Not because the people were all gone, though some of them probably were, after the wars, but just because there was no place for them in the view any more. The view didn't see them because Percy didn't want them there.

There's a couple of watercolours by Percy in the national library. 'Branding With Beauty', the conference paper she wrote a lifetime ago, had them in its PowerPoint slide show. Ooh-aah piccies. Views from where the Lake Hostel and later the Lake View Hotel would be built. The surface of the lake is 'wind-ruffled' and the dense, majestic forest leans over it. Make that 'majestic'. All the words of Pat's trade are getting harder and harder to use. Soon she might have to toss the whole lot out. The 'wind-ruffled' and of course 'rippling' lake, the 'majestic' forest. The paintings by Percy Smith are empty except for these elements of beautiful landscape views. Empty of people and of smoke rising from cooking fires. No one out on the water or busy around the shore. No dogs, kids, old people.

From the Lake Hostel, once it was built, you didn't see any signs of life. Pat listens to emptiness purring into her video camera. That's because Percy Smith didn't see it when he imagined the hostel being built. The scenery being 'preserved'. His looking removed it. When he viewed the preserved scenery in his mind's eye he imagined a holidaying couple in outdoor chairs with a backdrop of the looming, the 'looming' Panekiri Bluff. They're on the Lake Hostel lawn on the promontory above the 'rippling' lake. They're being served refreshing drinks by a waiter in a white dickey. After their strenuous ramble. When Percy looked at this scenery that the future couple would admire the view of, he stripped the life from the place. He emptied it.

Maybe bloody old Stan's right. What do we care? Maybe he went back into it, poor scared, lonely, clever William. He got that separation all right, that way-out-there-ness, that emptiness, that loneliness. He got it Absolutely Pure and that's why Pat hated it.

'Is that what you did?' she says aloud to William, meaning

both things. Getting the emptiness right and then going into it. 'I'm sorry, William. I'm really, really sorry, Bill.' It feels right to be actually talking to a dead man. The way she hardly ever did when he was alive. 'I'm not sure what I'm sorry about, Bill. But I'm really sorry about what happened to you. Not just what happened to you yesterday, but what happened to you in general. In your life.'

Just the kind of waffly statement he would've loved to massacre her for.

Pat lowers her hand into the cold water of the lake. She feels a simple need for some kind of ritual. The water moves against and around her hand, driven by forces within its own mass and nature.

'Hope you're okay now, Bill,' Pat says to the lake. She'd watched the squashed William being carted off that morning in a blue plastic bag. She wipes her wet hand over her face. Wipes her wet tears away with the water.

A couple of moreporks are pooh-poohing away up in the bush on the promontory where the old hotel used to be. Glor's probably had enough time for her own wee nightly weep, and for the funny little mumbled talks she has with herself just as she's going to sleep. Like a little kid saying its prayers, or talking to Mum through telepathy from stink holiday camp. 'The food's yuck. I don't like my bed. I want to come home. Do you read me, Mum. Come in, Mum. Over.'

Stan has the cabin to himself because Joris is helping the cops with their inquiries back in Wairoa. He closes the notebook in which he writes down his thoughts about art.

(1) People who don't respect views don't respect themselves.
(2) They're in the views they're looking at.
(3) They'll never feel at home anywhere because they'll always be away from it.
(4) They'll never get there (home).

Stan has underlined,
(5) <u>Colin McCahon understood this which is why he was shit-scared</u>.
Then he opens the notebook again and adds,
(6) See esp. the Beach Walks.

Then he opens the cabin window and lights a smoke, blowing it out into the cold air. His breath steams up and mixes with the smoke. Pat's trudging back along the dark foreshore from the jetty, but he doesn't put his smoke out and he doesn't bother to greet the high and mighty bossy cow either when she goes past, not seeing him or pretending not to, bloody typical.

Biswas is in a Sea View Motel somewhere near Kohimarama in Auckland, but he does not have a view of the sea because his unit is at the back facing the car park. In any case, the motel with the sea view is a couple of blocks back from the waterfront and Biswas doubts that you could see the sea even from the top floor of the motel facing the right direction, in the way he could actually see it when he ate a good dopiaza with dhal and bhaji at a footpath table outside a restaurant called Sayeman. Same name as height-of-luxury restaurant in Chittagong where celebrating success with friends by eating mughal food and some of them drinking illegal beer and whisky. Smuggling success, usually, from Burma or up from coast at Cox's Bazaar and Teknaf.

Alone among the diners, Biswas was also the only one eating with his fingers and the only one not drinking many beer. He drank Coca-Cola noisily with his little finger extended from the glass and asked for water and a napkin for his hand. In the motel bathroom he washes again and checks his moustache and teeth for food remains. There is more whiteness now in the clipped hair above his ears, which a barber cut for him at the airport, and trimmed his moustache, while Biswas almost drowsed with satisfaction and after not-sleeping at hot pool hotel. There are dark bags under his eyes and Biswas stretches one out, delicately, between finger and thumb, and lets it go again. It stays a little baggier at first and then returns to normal. His deep sigh mists the mirror – Biswas turns the light out in the bathroom and goes to sit in a plastic chair on the narrow deck of his unit. He sits with his back to the sea on the other side of the building somewhere and looks at the large height-of-luxury houses on the far side of the motel car park. Many have their lights on and he can see families passing back and forth across the windows, with here and there the chilly flicker of television.

Is feeling homesickness, barii mukhi, not surprising, and waiting for Pat, also hard, the waiting. In this land, in this place, Mohammed Baul Biswas sings to himself, listening to the voices from the houses and from the owners of cars at the Sea View Motel. In this land, in this place I have had this pleasure, this happiness. Where do I go next? I do not know.

He sings out loud, 'I got this broken down boat, my life has been spent baling out water.' Some people in the car park look up at him. Biswas goes inside and switches on the television. Is a programme call *Game of Two Halves*.

Biswas watches *Game of Two Halves* without laughing, while his thigh jigs. Everyone on *Game of Two Halves* is mad. Is five hours before email from Khulna.

nineteen

Pride

'Okay, Stan, let me run this back past you.' Richard flips to the start of his notes. He and Stan have been drinking tea and smoking steadily during the interview, but now Stan lights up another. His hands are trembling when he goes to fire up his Bic lighter. Colin McCahon was a chain smoker but his hands shook because he was an alkie. Stan doesn't drink that often because he gets wound up.

'Like I said,' he warns Richard. 'This could get me fired. Or worse. I've signed.'

'Of course you have, Stan,' says Richard with amusement. At Stan's insistence he'd made a little drama out of drawing the curtains of his motel room, though, as he'd pointed out, there wasn't much chance of anyone else on the CTI team spotting them way out at Kohimarama. 'And so have all the excellent whistle-blowers up and down the whole blessed country.' He grins at Stan. 'You keep us in work and we keep the people who spend the taxpayer's money honest.' Richard finds his place among the scribbled pages. Stan has agreed to the notes but not the tape-recorder. 'Anyway, Stan,' he says, shaking his notebook, 'bit of leg-work to do yet. And I can't see myself getting much out of the rest of your crew. Certainly not out of three of them, anyway.' Stan doesn't find this funny. 'Especially not the poor bugger who fell or jumped.' That's not funny either. Richard gets ready to review his notes with Stan. 'Or was pushed,' he adds as an afterthought, licking his yellowish thumb.

Stan's pride's been wounded more than once on this

bloody trip and now he feels pretty irritated with this journo as well. He's told him what he knows, which is a bloody sight more than he's going to get out of any of the team and a whole lot more than he'll be extracting from the DoT mob, the Minister's office, or any of the others who usually chatter away like bloody canaries in the backs of limos and mini-buses Stan's driven over the years.

'Listen, mate,' Stan warns the ratty-looking bloke who under other circumstances he wouldn't trust any further than he could kick him. 'I'm not doing this for money and I'm not doing it . . .'

'For fame and celebrity?' suggests Richard, pouring himself more tea. 'Not likely, my friend. While this story is piling up some sensational elements, it's not the stuff of headlines yet. One more cup for the road?'

'But I won't be named in any case,' Stan reminds him. 'And that's not what I was going to say.'

Richard seems to be considering calling it a day. He takes a patient sip of tea and closes his notebook. 'Let's get real, Stan, old man,' he says with genial impatience. 'I've promised not to name you or identify you in any way and I'm a man of my word, so I won't. But I will be trying to talk to a couple of people. You've kindly provided me with the leads, Stan, for which I'm in your debt. I will find the caterer whose staff member complained about the Minister's improper advances at Milford. A visit to the glacier hotel may be fruitful, there's bound to be a tittle-tattle there somewhere. As will a couple of phone calls to members of the review panel, second-rate academics will do anything for an audience. And so forth – a bit of good old-fashioned leg-work.' He opens the notebook again, with renewed determination. 'But you, Stan, you're the prime source. That's the main reason I won't name you. You've been there all along, pretty much. And that,' says Richard, leaning forward across the motel unit's coffee table, 'is why you have to be ready.' He puts his hand on Stan's arm but Stan pulls away.

'Ready for what?' he wants to know. He's still thinking about Richard's term 'tittle-tattle'.

'Ready, Stan, for the obvious fact that there are only four of you who could have supplied me with a consistent, beginning-to-end storyline,' explains Richard. 'You're a "reliable source" because you've got the whole yarn. So your three mates are going to be looking at each other and at you and wondering who the "reliable source" could be, aren't they, Stan? You must have figured that out for yourself by now.'

Stan doesn't say anything.

'And when this general looking at each other is going on, probably fairly soon, Stan, one of you will actually know who blew the hooter, and that's you. That leaves three who are wondering. One of them is the team manager, crafty old cow, not very likely. Another, my old pal Hinemoana, wouldn't talk to me if I was covered from head to foot in Belgian chocolate, which she likes. That leaves the Dutch fellow who, however, is under investigation himself and hardly likely to go opening up at the seams.'

Stan stubs out his cigarette and stands up.

'Hang on a minute, mate,' says Richard, flapping his notebook. 'You need to help me with a quick expert check of these excellent notes you've given me.' Richard smiles up at Stan with his head tipped on one side like a little parrot and with his eyes widened in mock innocence. 'Let me make you another nice cup of tea, Stan, my friend.'

'You can stick your notes up your arse,' says Stan.

'Think I might stick them up the arse of cultural tourism,' says Richard, happily. 'Kind of like an enema.'

'You can stick them up your arse,' repeats Stan. 'I didn't do this for money,' he goes on, finishing what he'd started. 'I didn't do it because I like you, which I don't. I did it,' Stan tells the grinning journalist, 'before you interrupted me last time, because . . .'

'Let me guess,' Richard interrupts him again, holding up

a nicotine-stained forefinger. 'You spilled to me because you care.'

'Because I care?' yells Stan. 'Listen, you little twerp. I feel proud. When I stand in front of those views. I feel proud to live here. To call this place home. It's a responsibility.'

'Wow,' says Richard. 'Now there's a quote.'

Outside the motel, the Auckland air's muggy and the harbour's giving off an extra salty smell, as if it's got thick and concentrated, or as if the wind that smells of it is just going round and round and getting saltier. It's how Stan's head feels – muggy and trapped. He needs to go for a bit of a walk after that session with Richard. Doesn't regret it, not for a moment, but the bastard managed to get up his nose all right.

It's as he's going a few yards along the waterfront, sniffing the thick, salty air and calming down, that he could swear he sees Mr Biswas and Pat. There's an Indian restaurant on the other side of the road, its sign says it does Mughul Cooking and their backs are just disappearing inside. Stan keeps walking quickly – he's not meant to be out here at Kohimarama either, he's meant to be servicing the bloody wagon over on Great North Road.

But then he thinks – bugger it, if he's not meant to be here at Kohimarama then the Bangladeshi certainly isn't, let alone the project manager who's supposed to have sent him home.

Stan crosses the road and walks back past the Sayeman Restaurant. He looks in through the front window as he passes. Can't see them, but he could swear he did. He could bet his life on it.

'You all right, Stan?' asks Pat. 'Go on, have a sandwich. You look a bit clapped out.'

'Thanks,' says Stan. 'Didn't manage lunch.'

'There are several reasons,' says Pat in the safe confines

of her hotel room, 'why we all need to be very clear about what's going on.' The rest of the CTI team are there and so are a room-service tray of club sandwiches and a pot of coffee. 'Some of the reasons are obvious, but some are not.' Pat takes a hearty bite out of a sandwich and turns it sideways to examine its contents. 'What do they put in these things?'

The team has experimented with calling itself the Survivors, but no one has a taste for it.

'Leftovers, I reckon,' suggests Gloria. 'I reckon they make the meal scraps into these things.'

'Now there's a thought,' tries Pat. 'We can call ourselves the Leftovers.' Stan is tucking in, now, but Joris hasn't touched the food. 'Talk about the cone of silence,' complains Pat. 'Joris? Stan?'

'Mine's salmon,' Stan informs the team. 'With yellow muck.'

'Okay,' says Pat. 'Enough trying to be jolly. Nobody feels like it, including me. The question is, should we go on? With the project? Of course,' she adds, 'we may not have a choice.'

'And why's that?' Stan wants to know. He's rejected the salmon and is sampling another one with lettuce on the bottom deck. 'Why would you want to stop now?' He takes an aggressive bite. 'Give me one good reason,' he challenges around his mouthful – 'reason' comes out as 'reshin'.

Pat's look of astonishment is carefully guarded. 'I know you're keen, Stan. Good on you. Wish I could say the same for the rest of us. But it mightn't be up to us. And as for one good reason, what about not less than three?'

'But why's that?' Stan persists. Anyone would think he was conducting an aggressive interview.

'Because.' Pat makes big, encouraging, up-stirring gestures with her hands and arms. 'Because, troopers, old Hands-On in Wellington might get the heebie-jeebies and pull our plug. He might take the ignition keys off you, Stan. He might stop our credit. He might give me a poisonous drink. Because the sponsors might no longer find us an attractive brand association. Because there are now only the Leftovers to write the document required by our contract. Unless, Stan,' Pat tries for a joke again, 'you'd like to make an art historical contribution. Know anything about the visual culture of Bangladesh?'

Feels like a very long time ago, but Hinemoana can still remember her koro's prickly shirt-front on her cheek and the two or three things he said to her the day she took off to start her new job. Remembers the whistling, creaky sounds of the 'pipes' in his chest and the tinny vibration of his pretending-to-be-mad voice. The whole pack of them standing around the car before she got in, bawling their eyes out, big drama. Aunty Rewa's little 1930s silver mesh evening bag with the fifty-dollar note and the addresses of whanau in Wellington in it. The photo album they'd all made with funny messages. 'Don't get too big for your boots,' with a photo of her, aged about four, in koro's gumboots up to her waist almost.

'Hang on a minute, Pat,' says Gloria, smelling a rat. 'Why would Hands-On pull the plug? Hasn't he got more to lose if the thing crashes? That's pretty much his Ministerial warrant down the toilet. Won't he do whatever it takes? It's not as if he hasn't survived a few in the past, anyway. Crises.' *Make us proud, girlie.* The words vibrating on her cheekbone. In other words, don't make us ashamed.

'To be frank,' says Pat, who is ignoring Stan's sullen lapse back into silence, 'it's because we now have the ripe aroma of scandal about us. About us Leftovers, appropriately enough, and now I've gone right off my tucker.'

'But hang on a minute,' Gloria objects. It's the memory of saying goodbye all those years ago that is shoving her into the present. Not to mention the farewell cups of tea and sandwiches all over the district. 'Where's the scandal? Misadventure and bad luck, maybe, but scandal?' *Don't blooming well forget where you come from.* In other words, don't forget who supported you to get where you are. Uncle Mat's skinny back marching back up the driveway while the rest of them stood in a bunch waving hankies. *Don't you forget, girl, in the end it's not you that matters.* His couple of old arthritic huntaways close to his boots, one on each side. Looked impressive, all right, but it was probably time for the classic movie reruns on TV.

'Yeah,' says Stan. 'Where is it? Where's the scandal?'

'I need to say something, now,' announces Joris suddenly, in that way he has, as if blithely unaware of what is going on.

'That would be appreciated very much, Joris,' says Pat. 'I can feel our discussion heading in an unproductive direction. And you've been right in the firing line.'

'You say is a scandal. Is already a scandal.'

'No, Joris, I did not say that. Believe me, my friend, our major supporters will be well and truly gone by the eve of any real scandal bursting into song. I said there is now the aroma, let's say the possibility, of scandal associated with us. So far we have a string of misadventures. Thank you, Gloria, you're right. Quite a long one, but as yet no blame no shame. Nothing we can't manage. However.'

'Because,' continues Joris, ignoring Pat, 'is my reputation, my business, my credibility, that is destroyed. After all: this is the scandal.'

Looking out the back window of the car before it went over the hill, she saw Uncle Mat turn on the porch of the homestead. The two dogs settled symmetrically on either side of him. He'd pretend to kick them as he went inside to the classic movie reruns on TV, just to make the point that, officially, they weren't allowed in the house. Later on, he'd let them in by the back door. They had sacks to sleep on by the range. Koro turned and watched her go and at the very last minute he lifted his arm and waved, a big, slow arc of waving. He looked all alone. Down at the gate, the rest of the family and assorted hangers-on were all having the big drama of hugging and crying all over each other. Getting the most out of it.

Make us proud, girlie.

Don't blooming well forget where you come from.

Don't you forget, girl, in the end it's not you that matters.

And that was the last time she saw old Uncle Mat.

'Not sure I follow you,' announces Gloria loudly, standing up so fast she topples forward and tips over the sandwich plate. 'What are we saying here, Joris? That the worst thing that's happened so far? Forget about Bill getting killed, Antsy going missing, poor old Mr Biswas? That the worst thing? Are you suggesting the worst thing that's happened so far is the damage to your fucking business?'

Pat stands up – she begins to make herself into a big, soft barrier between Gloria and Joris. Joris is a funny waxy colour, like someone feeling seasick. Gloria is manoeuvring herself around the table towards him.

'You think I pushed him? Is this what you're saying?'

'Now why would I think that, Joris?' Gloria is standing over him, shouting. Even her shoulders seem to be inflating with the heat of her breath.

'Because if you do, say it, then. Go on. As if something make you so pure. When everybody knows.'

'Knows what, Joris?'

'That funding: you don't remember?'

'Now, now,' Pat intervenes. Joris has stood up and is trembling, face to face with Gloria's heat. 'Hell's teeth, Gloria. Settle down, children. No one believes for a minute that you pushed William. For Christ's sake, Joris, what reason would you have to do that? And besides, we've heard your account of what happened and what you told the cops in Wairoa, so let's not go there. But this brings me back to what I was going to say.'

Still, Joris does not sit down. He moves away from Gloria and stands over by the window. Outside, the city's artificial glow backlights his sallow, trembling outline. The street is a dozen or so floors down, but the evening's entertainment traffic has begun to rev up and a deep, subwoofy bass thuds against the hotel's body from a nearby bar.

'We all need to be clear about what's going on,' continues Pat, 'with the damage control and the interest being shown by the media who, trust me, will not be far off having a crack at us once they get the sequence of events stitched up.' Pat shepherds Gloria back in the direction of her chair. 'I know I don't need to, but I will anyway remind you that we are contractually bound to confidentiality agreements and if anyone is going to talk to media it will be me. Sorry, had to say that, no offence.' Pat presses Gloria down into her chair. 'Gloria has personal reasons to know that the *National Inquirer* chap who's been sniffing around is pure poison, so just don't go swallowing anything he might have to offer. Sorry again, just doing my job.'

'So, what did he do to you, Gloria?' Stan's question comes out a bit offhand.

'He pretty much buggered up my reputation for a few years, back home,' says Gloria. 'Our mate Joris remembers, apparently. If I had my time again, I'd rip his heart out. Richard Brawn's, that is.' Don't cry unless it's when you're coming home or leaving, said koro. Kia kaha, girl. Stick up for yourself.

'Yes, everybody knows this.' Joris is keeping his distance, over by the window.

'Moving along,' Pat continues. 'We have also to bear in mind the Minister's great need for a successful outcome to the project, and our depleted capacity. These are the obvious things that are going on,' says Pat, looking at Joris, who is still visibly trembling where he stands over by the window. 'You all right, Joris?'

'I'll say something in a minute,' says Joris. 'I'm fine.'

'The less obvious things we need to be clear about are, frankly, the kinds of things we do need to keep the lid on.'

'What kind of things?' asks Stan, still offhand.

'I'm coming to that,' says Pat. 'Could you stop prompting me, Stan? And I wish you'd sit down, Joris, you're making me nervous, backlit like that, like a PowerPoint.'

'I'm fine,' insists Joris, trembling.

'I doubt it, and I think I'd be worried if you were. However,' says Pat steadily, 'in my list, the one that keeps me from my beauty sleep at night, we have a best-kept-quiet situation behind the obvious distress of our friend and colleague Mr Biswas. It's not as though we haven't noticed that something was wrong there. Mr Biswas has obviously been under a lot of strain. A bit more strain than riding around in a bus with you lot.' Pat's droll armour is impervious. 'Listen guys, I'm really sorry about this, but it may be possible to disclose something of the situation with Mr Biswas at a later date. Can't just yet. Then,' continues Pat, looking hard at Joris now, 'there are some culpability issues, most of which land on me, on yours truly, for example, the fact that none of us actually saw what happened to Nancy Shapiro. Try explaining that to a hostile media, let alone the detective inspector at Westport. This is a man who eats three-and-a-half Weet-Bix for breakfast, not four and not three. He told me why, too. In order to make the point that everything has an explanation.'

'Including what happened to Bill.' Gloria is pumping rage carefully through her body – her long, slow breaths seem calm, almost sleepy.

'Indeed,' Pat agrees. Her calm matches Gloria's. 'Out of this arises the issue of team culture which, despite the excellent bonding session at Te Papa which we all remember with gratitude and affection, may be seen to have something to do with our collective behaviour. Which, viewed from a distance, for example, the distance of sensational journalism, has included vandalism, unexplained team-member disappearance, violent physical assault and now,' Pat makes her calm point directly to Joris, 'a charge of manslaughter at worst and not all that likely, but certainly one of negligence. Under circumstances that suggest all was not well with relationships within the team. With the team culture,' finishes Pat, who, while calm, is perspiring freely. 'Which, and not wanting to whinge about it, is also my responsibility. My neck on the block.' Pat takes a bite of a nondescript sandwich. 'Christ, they are so awful. So that's my big speech, folks, fellow Leftovers.' She's looking at the trembling Joris. 'Was there something you wanted to say, Joris? About the "real scandal"?'

'My father always say,' begins Joris, but then he suddenly takes a stride across the room and sits down again. 'Is maybe not the best time.'

'Joris, no one would blame you if you wanted to quit the project now. After what you've been through,' says Pat. She pushes the sandwich plate away. Most of them have fallen off. 'Remove these, someone, there's nothing worse than worry food.'

'No, I don't need therapy,' Joris suddenly goes on. 'What, you think I don't have difficult situations before? No: I don't want to leave the project, make another failure to add. Don't want to deny responsibility for what happened with Bill at the lake. That was very bad: worst thing ever happen to me. I take my responsibility and I swallow my medicine. But I don't fail. I keep my pride,' asserts Joris. He wears again the adept expression of someone moving ahead, his clear blue eyes on a destination. He might be involved in an interesting conversation.

Gloria is pushing herself up with both hands on the arms of her chair.

'My Poppa always say,' resumes Joris, genially, 'you only fail if you give up. He never gave up. He never. He came here speaking only very little English and he made a business that works good,' says Joris with precision. 'Worked hard all his life. He looked after us. He got us what we needed, always. What made him keep going, this little short man? Was his pride: he had a tall pride. So he couldn't fail. I have my own pride,' Joris finishes his speech. 'So: I won't fail. In spite of what happens. Good-2-Go is maybe finished now, but so is danger. But not so is Joris. Never.' Joris taps himself on the chest as if to identify who he's talking about. 'Never Joris!' He sits back and crosses his long legs.

Gloria makes a noise halfway between choking and spitting. 'Should have thought of that before you dragged poor old William up the bloody Panekiri Bluff,' she shouts.

'Could you pass me the interesting sandwiches, please?' he asks her, politely. 'All this discussion, makes you hungry.'

'Makes me sick,' spits Gloria. 'You make me sick, you horrible little man.' She bunches her fists and shakes them at Joris across the mess of spilled club sandwiches on the table between them. 'Supply-side! Demand-side! Fuck you!'

Then it's Pat who stands up. 'I'm really tired of this,' she says. 'Tired of the team leader thing, tired of you bickering, tired of silly bugger Hands-On, tired of wondering when all of this is going to appear in the six o'clock news. Tired of being the one who keeps the team spirits up, the Leftovers. So you can all go now.' Joris and Stan stand up – the team shifts uncertainly towards Pat's hotel room door.

'Pat, sorry,' tries Gloria.

'Shut up, Gloria,' says Pat. She's still calm, but she holds her hands up in front of herself, palms out, fending off Gloria's hug. 'The very last thing I needed right now was a Hinemoana Oliver hissy fit. Just get out of my room.' The bass thudding of music that agitates the building from the street below might be Pat's steady, pounding heart. 'Tomorrow morning Stan and me will be waiting outside with the door of the bus open at nine in the morning, okay Stan? And then we will close the door of the bus at ten past nine and drive up the over-developed east coast towards our final few target destinations. If any of you are inside the bus when we do this, well and good. Otherwise, too bad.' She holds the door of her room open. 'I'm having breakfast here, by myself, too.' She waves the team through – they don't protest. 'Don't say anything,' Pat warns them. No one says anything.

'See, I have my pride, too,' says Pat. 'Whatever that really means. Gloria, Joris, Stan. Good night, Leftovers. Sweet dreams.'

Her phone rings.

twenty

Authenticity

Dr Hinemoana Oliver steps out of the shower in her hotel room and the woman she sees in the bathroom mirror, even blurred with steam and the angry tears she swears she won't be crying any more, doesn't look much like the slip of a girl who groped her way out of Richard Brawn's motel unit shower stall twenty years ago in 1985 and threw up lots of drinks called Harvey Wallbangers into his hand basin.

Blood's thudding in Gloria's ears – like the bass beats reverberating dully from the bar below in the hotel. Down there, shouting above the noise and going drink for drink with the table, she'd feel different. Too late now. Uncle Mat's gone quiet again. Pat's face in her hotel room doorway had that waxy shine on it that Gloria knows from many occasions, but what they all have in common is sickness. The sickness of being at the end of your tether. And what does she do? What does Hinemoana do? Does she make them proud? Does she remember where she comes from? Does she forget that it's not her that matters?

Gloria wraps up in the big white hotel bathrobe and piles most of her hair in a towel. She makes wet footprints across the carpet and gets Dr Nancy Shapiro's report chapter out of its folder. Koro didn't speak to her all those years, can't blame him. Now he's shut up again. What's she done this time?

Have a read of this, Uncle.

AUTHENTICITY AND CULTURAL TOURISM
1. Executive Summary: A Challenge

'My research aims to test a simple theoretical proposition,' begins the Challenge heading the Executive Summary of the incomplete draft interim Report by Dr Nancy Shapiro (PhD), Professor of Diaspora Studies at the University of New South Wales, Sydney. 'The proposition is that contemporary, globally situated culture needs to be dialectically tolerant in order to generate rich and satisfying effects and sustain enriched and satisfied communities. National cultures, which typically now contain diverse communities which do not agree with each other, must encourage conversation and exchange across borders of marked difference. They must accept that tolerance grows from difference not sameness.

'It follows,' continues Antsy in a tone of voice that Gloria can hear transcribed eagerly to the report, 'that the institutions that manage culture and that are not separate from it, should also be engaged in discussion around problematic difference. Tourism is such an institution and cultural tourism especially so.'

> We need, then, to be asking of the effects of 'cultourism' that the New Zealand Ministry of Tourism's Cultural Tourism Initiative team is observing: are these effects supported by a consolidated industry that is dialectical in its professional practice, tolerant in its social and cultural behaviour and intellectually engaged with problematic difference?

Water's dripping from Gloria's head onto Antsy's paper. Probably it will look as if she's been blubbering again. But she hasn't, won't be, either. Gloria gets up and fetches the bottle of Mount Difficulty pinot noir. When she twists the cork out, a life-giving breath rises from the bottle into the room. It's amazing how good wine can smell and taste like ash sometimes and other times like the life-blood of the earth itself, warm with stored-up sunshine, infused with unrelenting minerals. But Gloria doesn't fill a glass just yet. Though far from the dry, stony terraces where Mount Difficulty makes wine happen in the south, the bumpy hilltop of Ruapekapeka in the north is what she's smelling. Even on a clear day, the blue mist sits down along the bushy ridges and folds of the country below the old pa site with its soft remains of bunkers and trenches. What all that must have looked like when it was still big forest! The sea is so far off you can't see it but the wind that blows across the hilltop from the coast out east always has that fresh tang. Uncle Mat used to sit at the back of the fenced-in site, where an ordinary five-strand number eight wire fence separated the old battlefield from a paddock, and sniff a handful of grass and dirt he squeezed in his fist.

'Smell that, girlie. Sweet.'

There was a spring of water there, too. Kawiti knew about that, it was why he built his bat cave there back in 1846. Batsqueaker Mat used to fill an empty plastic Raro bottle there to have with him when he was working.

'Best drink in the whole world.' When it was going down his throat he used to tilt his head back and you could see the stringy old sinews in his neck, the strength there that wasn't about size, it was about not giving up.

> There is another, more ideological way of pushing the issue of fruitful tolerance to the front of this investigation. I am a careful scholar who loves science and admires thinking that solves problems. But I do not hesitate, here, to suggest, on the evidence of the research I have done over many years and in many different countries, that an aspirational challenge like the following is appropriate for our work as the CTI team.

The seat of uncle's baggy woollen shearer's pants used to get wet from the grass on the mound where he sat at the back of Ruapekapeka and sometimes he'd spill Kawiti's spring water down his front. He'd wipe the moisture away carelessly with that not-giving-up kind of gesture. That's why Gloria couldn't be sure if he'd been crying or not the time she found him there after she got the scholarship to go to Wellington.

Make us proud, girlie.
Don't blooming well forget where you come from.
Don't you forget, girl, in the end it's not you that matters.

Old bugger – what a way to make you feel good about getting out of that dead-end place. Gloria pours a glass of the Mount Difficulty pinot, smelling the fruity dirt in koro's fist, the ocean too far away to see through a blue haze, something tangy in the spring water.

> This is my challenge: cultural infrastructure that supports the healthy diversity of cultural production in a nation's communities can become cultural superstructure that directs the hegemonic requirements of a national identity and brand; and *this should not happen*.
>
> The Minister of Tourism in New Zealand is to be congratulated for his initiative in assembling this CTI team and launching its research project. He and his review panel might like to consider this challenge in another form. Scholars of the sociology of culture are fond of a distinction – a dialectical one, again – between two German terms: Gemeinschaft and Gesellschaft. As the daughter of Holocaust survivors lucky to have been settled in Australia after World War Two, these words have special resonance for me. Gemeinschaft describes social relations between people based on intimacy and community. Gesellschaft, on the other hand, describes the social relations formed by impersonal duties to society or to its organisations and institutions. The two may mutate into each other and they are always in tension. The careful and scrupulous observer of social and cultural behaviour

will detect moments where emotional commitment might become civic duty, intimacy become dissociation, participation become roster; and authenticity – the key word for my participation within the Gemeinschaft of the CTI team – become Production.

Gloria lifts her glass. The pages on the table in front of her are splattered with water but it's not tears. Not likely. Good on you, Ants. Cheers, Uncle. Leaning forward over the paper, Gloria feels her soft belly folded on top of her thighs. Not what the little squirt pup journalist Richard saw all those years ago. Maybe Gloria's drinking to Uncle Mat and to wee Antsy because now's the time to let the little white squirt and the scared, pissed-as-a-fart, green-as-grass, no-tummy country girl back into her thoughts. Back in – then, haere ra, cheerio, good riddance, no hard feelings. Get over it.

In the smeary mirror above the tap she had on full bore to get her sick down the plug hole, she saw wax candle Richard get out of the motel shower as well. Trying to stick his tongue in her mouth back in there, but she just wanted to make her sick feeling go away. His pinkish dick was sticking up and next she felt it poking between her thighs from behind. She turned around and pushed the skinny little guy away – his face was all screwed up and he grabbed his dick and gave it a few tugs. It looked like one of the white-and-pink blind salamanders her little brother used to keep in a slimy fish tank. Its little mouth gasped and then it shot a mucousy glob onto her tummy. Then Richard dropped to his knees on the flooded bathroom floor in front of her. One thin hand gripped her ankle.

'Fuck,' he said.

A last heave of sickness flew up through Hinemoana's throat – the watery vomit landed on Richard's wet hair. His white shoulders began to shake. He was laughing!

'Fair enough,' he said. She tried to get her ankle away

from his grip, but he wouldn't let go. 'Fair enough, girl. Tit for tat.'

'Statist demands for the Gemeinschaft-type commitment of citizens to programmes for national identity and even national unity, with the compelling incentives of massive tourist dollar windfalls, must be scrutinised with sceptical rigour.' Antsy's voice could get quite nippy sometimes. 'The Minister's review panel may or may not be pleased to hear this challenge, but in any case they will already know that the highways of cultourism are littered with the burned-out wrecks of enterprises that failed because they lost heart, or never had one.'

By the time the little prick turned up again at the Taskforce hui in 1987 Gloria had no trouble telling him to piss off. You can learn a lot in two years, or you think you can. *Fair enough. Tit for tat.* In return he had no trouble dobbing her in for nepotism.

'Looks like you and me are finished with the customary concept of manaakitanga, on a personal level,' he said, grinning. He was already a chain smoker but still didn't look a day older – this weedy, cigarette-smelly, funny guy like a white wax candle. 'So let's talk about the customary concept of whanaungatanga instead, and how it differs or not from nepotism,' was what he said before she told him to get lost.

'You need to come up and talk to Uncle,' was what the aunties' letter said. 'He's upset with you carrying on with that Pakeha fellow.'

'But I'm not – tell him.'

'Now he's upset about you getting mixed up with some whanaungatanga nonsense or other.'

'But I'm not.'

Two years later, same thing again, little prick Richard, making strife. 'Now koro doesn't want to hear your name mentioned in the house. Says you've brought shame.'

'Fine.' What – Uncle can't be proud that his girlie's going to Washington to do her PhD? 'Tell him I don't care.' What kind of aroha was that? 'I don't need the miserable old bugger telling me what to do.'

But I do, koro. After all these years. What have I done wrong this time?

2. 'Let me begin with Armenia.'

'The coherence of any system of signs intended to transmit authenticity,' continues Nancy quickly, after her challenge, 'depends above all on two factors.'

Gloria's read this before. She's drunk Mount Difficulty before. Both comfort her.

> I will leave aside for now, a discussion of how our expectations of the term 'authenticity' and its meanings have been produced. It would be appropriate to begin with a grand sweep rather as Marco Polo did in the thirteenth century when collaborating with Rustichello of Pisa in writing an account of his travels: 'Let me begin with Armenia.' However, both the historiography and the contemporary agency of 'authenticity' have been treated in substantial literatures, which I summarise later in a suggested and probably optimistic list of readings.

Gloria pours another large glass. Maybe she drank the last one a bit too fast – too bad. One reason she finds this stuff funny is because she can hear Ants's intense, trembly little mouth saying it and can see her sparkly eyes and her busy nose in the action as well – the whole of her excitement and humour. Another reason is because she can imagine the gripe Antsy's language is giving her uncle whose silence is just a big act, really. Bet on it. Bet he knows she's headed for the sweet-smelling hilltop with the spring of pure water on it. The place that now has the flash heritage signage pointing to it from the main road, the signs that say where Ruapekapeka is but that hide where Uncle is.

The reason she finds it sad is because she can't see how far she's moved on from the day she caught him out probably having a bit of a cry at the back of the old mounds and trenches on top of the hill, with the loose seat of his pants all wet from the grassy mound. Only one way to find that out. Have to go back. Then measure the distance from there. See what it looks like.

> A paragraph like the one I have just written, which has summarised what it had promised not to say until later, will serve as a warning. It is a warning about the actual substance and extent of the discussion required. But before readers of this report feel too relieved about being let off this large hook, I recommend they – we – pay some minimal attention to the following simple suggestions.

Gloria can hear Ants's silence as she gathers strength for an under-the-radar expedition to Armenia. What she hears first is Richard Brawn.

> The Ministry of Maori Development Te Puni Kokiri has cleared Dr Hinemoana Oliver of any conflict of interest or other impropriety in her application of Maori customary concepts to taxpayer-funded tourism and cultural initiatives in her tribal area Te Tai Tokerau, especially in the Pekapeka-rau and Waiomio caves region where hapu of Ngapuhi and Ngati Hine predominate. Dr Oliver was however cautioned to be more prudent in her interpretations and applications of customary concepts such as manaakitanga (hospitality) and whanaungatanga (family business).

'Don't bother coming up,' said the aunties on the phone. 'He's really mad at you. Especially that bit about family business. Let him cool off first.'

Cool off? Gloria takes another swallow. Sad – happy – sad – happy. Let's get it over and done with, Uncle, because this is driving me crazy. Driving me to drink, more like.

Turn the pages.

> Issues of authenticity within cultourism are, then, it hardly needs to be said (although I have) complex and capable of causing damage if not well understood and theorised and treated with sympathy, tolerance and humility.

'Sympathy, tolerance and humility,' says Gloria aloud. It's not often that a bottle of wine's enough to make her drunk these days. Must be all the other stuff that's going on. Must be . . . 'Tell you what,' she says, looking for another one. 'You two would get on like a house on fire.' There are a couple of silly little bottles of cheap champers in the minibar – Gloria slams the door on them. She gets the good Aussie shiraz out of her bag. 'One of you doesn't deserve this,' she says, yanking the cork. 'Sympathy, tolerance and humility, you old bastard.'

'I leave much of the extended discussion of authenticity within the social contexts of hospitality to my colleague in this chapter of the Cultural Tourism Initiative Report, Dr Hinemoana Oliver,' continues Ants with a wink. Gloria acknowledges her with a sip.

> I now return to the two simple factors with which I promised to preface these case studies. These two factors are recognition and repetition. And obviously, they reinforce each other: recognition may be the result, in part, of repeated encounters, of familiarity; while repetition is only possible when we recognise the sameness that is being repeated.
>
> A common example of this is the ordinary signage of the tourist route. In New Zealand, all ordinary public directional signage is black on white. It has a standard point size and font and it obeys a style manual that, for example, is consistent about whether to abbreviate 'Road' to 'Rd' or 'Mount' to 'Mt'. When local consumers see this, they recognise it as part of a national infrastructure of roading. When foreign tourists see it repeated, they recognise that there *is* a national infrastructure of roading.

'Tell you what – stand Uncle up on the marae and let him get on his high horse, he'd be a match for you, Antsywantsy.' The Australian wine tastes and smells foreign. It doesn't have the hilly, bushy, shady, blueish look. The sea isn't over there. It doesn't have old holes and tunnels to fall down. It doesn't have a plastic Raro bottle of spring water. It's not squeaky, like koro's 'pipes'. 'You're getting pissed, girl,' Gloria tells herself. She pushes her glass away with the careful determination of a Gloria who is, really and truly, getting quite pissed. 'Looking good on it, too,' was what fuckface Richard said. What he was remembering, the smooth little honey in his shower, the one who threw up on his head after making his horrible salamander spit on her.

> Signage that has to do with the conservation estate and with the tourism assets of scenery and wilderness is produced within the Department of Conservation's brand identity and is invariably yellow on green. To the local, this affirms that there is a national conservation infrastructure and that the conservation ethic is sustained at an official level – it further reinforces a sense of national responsibility, or of national intervention, depending on your point of view. To the foreign campervaner, the yellow on green signage indicates a scenic or natural environment opportunity. In a sense, such foreign tourists do not need to *read* the sign once they have understood its generic significance after a few repetitions: it is the sign's brand that designs their responses.

Here comes the good bit, Gloria reminds herself. Listen up, koro.

> The Heritage Department in New Zealand has a wide national presence which is signalled by its repeated and consistent palette of white on brown signage. To the local who has come to recognise this brand as having to

do with the nation's history, the signs say, first of all, that the country has a history and secondly, that they will find here a monument to one of its moments. To the foreigner whose experience of repetition in the heritage signage has made them aware that there is a national heritage infrastructure, the signs point to opportunities that can be aligned with historically oriented itineraries.

Thought you'd like having that sign down on the main road, Uncle. The interpretation up on the hill. Where the British had their big guns in 1846, that they dragged all the way up there through the bush. The history trail. The parking space, the tracks, the weatherproof labels. 'Waste of time, girl. He won't talk to you.'

The importance of this fundamental system of signs in the visual landscape of cultural tourism at its most basic cannot be overstated. There are two reasons why its obviousness matters and can easily be overlooked.

'Won't talk to you on the phone. Won't talk to you if you come up, either. He's mad as.'

One reason is that local cultural confidence is built on a kind of forgetting. It is the very reliability of such things as a national infrastructure of road signage that allows these signs pointing *to* a culture, to become subliminal in the citizens of that culture. Because the signs are reliable, they no longer require conscious attention. We can forget them even as we rely on them to affirm our cultural sense of direction and our sense that our culture – that is, the national culture of which the signs are the evidence – our sense that our national culture has direction.

Said everybody knew the money for the signs and all that didn't come from round there – didn't belong to the iwi, the families, wasn't whanaungatanga. Didn't want a bunch of ignoramuses coming up the hill. Said he'd put his old dogs on them – as if! Gloria goes for a pee and splashes her hot face with water at the hand basin. Looking good on it, too. Well, I'm coming, koro, ready or not.

The words on the pages are sliding around. The booming bass down below gets a lot louder when she opens the silly, complicated window for some fresh air. It's wet outside and the breeze that comes into the room is like moist car exhaust fumes. She rinses it away with the kick-in-the-guts Aussie shiraz.

> It is important, when looking at the ways signage inculcates the kind of cultural confidence that can result in forgetting, to note how that signage itself may forget and endorse the forgetting of alternative and suppressed cultures and their histories, names, natural orders and sites of significance. It may, then, be the responsibility of an alert and ethical critique of cultourism initiatives to demand the subversion or supplementation of such coherent systems of signs as directional roading signage. For every sign that promotes a feeling of confidence and of cultural direction in both local and visiting consumers, the critique might want to add another – not another more authentic one, but rather one that suggests cultural authenticity may not be the single thing official infrastructural signage makes it, but rather something complicated, contradictory and unforgettable.
>
> The second reason why the obviousness of official signage matters and can easily be overlooked is that its civic authority and evidencing of governance may in themselves be utterly foreign to many visitors and indeed to alienated or dispossessed minority cultures within the national body. There are places that seem to be nowhere because they only exist when brought into being and back into time by ritual, narrative or seasonal

events. There are places, such as the intersections of camel caravans across the deserts of Arabia, which only exist when people re-encounter them and each other on their caravanserai travels and when they sit down in those places to rediscover their names and their stories.

At this point, Gloria usually asks, again, '*Camels*, Ants?' – but wee Antsy had known where her caravan was going and this time Gloria just fills up her glass again and doesn't even imagine Ants in a burnoose or something.

I am not, of course, suggesting that tourism in New Zealand should be catering for camel-drivers from the Arabian deserts – if such people even still exist outside of Discovery Channel. I am, however, suggesting that this report has to face the possibility that its industry's confidence about coherence and accessibility, about visitor comfort and support, about the basic hospitality of giving good directions, about national identity and cultural authenticity, may be based on trivial assumptions. As a result of these trivial assumptions, the experiences of visitors and of locals alike may be culturally degraded. People may lose heart.

'People may.' Gloria salutes the thought. She's not going to get to the end of Nancy's paper tonight, but she is going to get to the end of the plodding camel-train Australian wine and so she's going to keep reading until that's accomplished. In addition, there's a creaky, batsqueaky sound that the petrol-moist bass thumping of the club bar can't drown out – it's Uncle Mat coming back in range. Uncle Mat, this is my wee mate Nancy, she's a clever girl, just like you said I was. Have a listen to this.

We need to consider that it may be better, sometimes, to get lost, to not understand, to not know where you are, than to never escape the comfort zone of official direction. It may be better, sometimes, to ask for directions and receive the hospitable response of local knowledge, than to be sent off down the road with a comprehensive set of signs ahead of you.

'See? What did I tell you?' asks Gloria. 'Pretty much what you told me off for, Uncle. Now you're both ganging up on me.'

In a nation renowned for its beautiful scenery, the viewing platform may be the simplest example of such conceptual weakness. It may, indeed, be an excellent example of supportive infrastructure becoming authoritarian superstructure. While the viewing platform offers comfort, safety, amenities such as toilets and litter bins, and while it easily calibrates journeys into rests and allows for the visitor's experience to be organised coherently within an infrastructural system of views and ecologies, the viewing platform, recognised and repeated as the single most potent sign of a culture hugely invested in viewing and the scenic, may in itself also be the most obvious but most easily overlooked sign of a danger.

What is this danger? Leaving aside the danger of infrastructure mutating into superstructure, of Gesellschaft taking Gemeinschaft hostage, the danger at the heart of my inquiry is the *inauthentic* in its most simple form, a form for which deep reading can prepare us but which common sense will also allow us to recognise. It is looking but not seeing. It is the authentic as Production. It involves a slippage between Gemeinschaft and Gesellschaft, between intimate, internalised knowledge and dissociated, didactic or ideological presentation.

And then you had to go and die, koro.

I am not preaching a kind of essentialism or purity here, but suggesting all the evidence of my research shows that the authentic as Production makes the spectator weary, dissatisfied and culturally dissociated. This visitor becomes unable to see past the banal surface of the view to any social or historical depth of reality. The view increases the space between the person and the place, where that space could and perhaps should become intimate. Because the relationship is not intimate, it risks becoming exploitative and unethical. We see the colour drain from these exploited places, we watch them becoming exhausted, we see their souls fade and the souls of their exhausted viewers fade, too, like the old snapshots of their past outings down roads whose rich narratives have been reduced to the impoverished captions of directional signage. These places and the lives in them will fade and disappear, they will become ghosts haunting the borders of cultural memory and they will haunt the crisp, helpful, definitive signage of national roading systems.

Now Gloria's given in to weeping again. 'Look what you're making me do. You, Uncle, not Antsy. Okay, you too.' Her hair's dry, so now it's tears that are dripping on the blurry, wobbly pages in front of her.

Members of the review panel will, I hope, forgive my unscientific and subjective excursion in this Introduction . . .

'Unforgivable!' The shiraz is good at staining white towelling bathrobes.

. . . and in particular, perhaps, my use of words like 'ghosts' and 'haunting'. I intend my excursion and my challenge to provide emotional but also contextual terms of reference for what follows – which are case studies developed along the road: signage, burned-out wrecks, ghosts and all.

'Ghosts and all!' Come on, Uncle – if you're going to join the party, make up your mind!

> Following the case studies, I will look at the etymological and discourse histories of some key words which are frequently used in the popular contexts of scenery-based cultural tourism. These words include 'spectacular', 'sublime', 'picturesque' and 'beautiful'. Here, I will intersect with the section of the report authored jointly by Dr Patricia Smart and Mr Mohammed Biswas. These words are familiar in the vernacular – for example, in the New Zealand expression 'Beauty!' They are also in the tool-kits of discipline specialists, especially art historians, who may have to learn to relinquish their professional sequestering of them and to ratify their common usage.

But never got to tangi you, miserable old koro, had to go and die when I was too far away.

> It is at this point that I will review the discussion of the historiography and contemporary agency of the concept of authenticity, and will point to the key readings mentioned earlier.
>
> Finally, I will introduce the notion of hospitality as a key indicator of social authenticity, judged both by professionalism and by the domestic cultural benchmarks of threshold, hearth and sustenance. This will be when Dr Oliver takes over the baton of our collaboration.

'"Takes over the baton of our collaboration,"' repeats Gloria aloud. She swallows the last of the shiraz. Nancy's paper's a mess – hair water, wine, tears again. When are they going to run out? The tears? 'How do you like the sound of that, Uncle?' The creaky wheezing might be that silent laughing thing he used to do – usually when he wanted someone to hear him but didn't want to own up to it.

Only one place to deal with this. I'm coming, Uncle, just start talking to me again. I can't stand you squeaking away like that. I'm ashamed, she tells herself, putting the pages aside. Poor old Pat – tired and angry. Poor old Bill – reading Antsy's words in that schoolteacherish voice he used. Poor old Biz – whatever's gone wrong there. Poor Joris, maybe – so far from home.

Poor little Richard. Little shit.

Gloria turns out the lights and climbs into the big, luxurious bed. The room spins around for a while and, because she's done it before, she'll wait until it stops before she closes her eyes. That booming bass – good to go to sleep on. Rainy air through the window. Soon, instead, there'll be the smell of the ocean you can never see from the lumpy old hilltop, the smell of the dirt and the grass by the old mounds, 'sweet'. Nice drink of water. Then Gloria closes her eyes and all the 'ghosts' and the 'hauntings' that Ants has slipped between the neatly footnoted, bibliographed and double-spaced pages of her chapter arrive at her bedside. The ghosts rebuke her, gently, and she's not wounded by this. She understands what she has to finish. She has to go to places she's become too used to talking about. Then something else will have to happen.

She'll be on that damn bus tomorrow, Gloria will, because there's a job to finish. It's maybe not the one Hands-On has in mind and Gloria's not even sure she knows what it is any more. But there's only one way to find out and that's to keep going where you have to ask directions when you thought you knew the way and where you have to rely on the hospitality of strangers you thought you'd recognised. Thought you'd known all your life.

twenty-one

Home

NATIONAL INQUIRER

HOME TRUTHS
Richard Brawn investigates

GOVERNMENT TOURISM PROJECT CRASHES
Is this what it's all about?

'This is what it's all about,' said a member of the Cultural Tourism Initiative team who preferred to remain anonymous, when quizzed about the trail of destruction in the wake of the project's 'research-driven' journey through New Zealand's prime luxury tourist facilities.

Our informant was disgusted by the wasteful and cynical behaviour of team-members. The informant described nightly scenes of excessive drinking in the bars of New Zealand's luxury tourist hotels and a cynical, 'once-over-lightly' express tour through the most obvious scenic and cultural attractions including Milford Sound, the Hermitage at Aoraki Mount Cook and the thermal region of Rotorua.

'Cultourism'

The CTI project is the brainchild of the Minister of Tourism, Hon. Brian Fellwill and is administered by the Department of Tourism. It has the support of international agencies including the United Nations Development Programme (UNDP) and, curiously, the official tourist bureau of Bangladesh, Parjatan, whose website reveals that it operates under the strikingly optimistic trading slogan, 'Get here before the tourists do.'

Known officially as the Cultural Tourism Initiative (CTI)

and nicknamed 'cultourism' by its members, the project's brief is to 'assess and analyse the cultural tourism sector's capacity and capability, identifying strengths and weaknesses and to make recommendations for policy development'.

But what is 'cultourism'?

'Cultourism' seems to involve spending a lot of money.

A spokesman at Te Papa, New Zealand's showcase national museum, confirmed that the national institution, funded by the taxpayer through government vote, had hosted an initial reception for the CTI team in its swanky Icon restaurant, where 200 invited guests from the 'tourism sector' had been treated to a selection of fine New Zealand food and wine. Their numbers were swelled by guests from government and associated ministries, diplomatic and corporate regulars, the bejewelled 'friends' of the museum's less popular functions, some well-known food writers, most of the museum's board members and several of its senior staff.

The *Inquirer* has been able to establish that the wine list at this function whose purpose was to launch the CTI probe into the nation's hinterland culture included a range of products 'above the $40 a bottle' threshold at which fine wines were deemed to commence by the restaurant's sommelier.

The 'hinterland' foods included Bluff oysters, whitebait, New Zealand lamb, salmon and mutton-bird (the latter cooked in a bath of high-quality New Zealand olive oil and wrapped in seaweed) and a range of award-winning New Zealand cheeses and fresh fruits.

Live entertainment was provided by a string quartet. The menus were a high production value, three-colour print job and guests received 'souvenirs' in the form of whimsical shapes cut from paua, including jetboats, surfboards and kiwis.

When approached by the *Inquirer*, the restaurant's management declined to comment on the unit cost of a plate of its food. A restaurant staff member, however, who requested anonymity, suggested that a retail menu price of $70 to $100 per guest was a good estimate when the little things on sticks and semi-liquid muck in pastry cases were added along with incidentals such as individual menus and 'souvenirs', and that the beverage cost would have been in the region of $50 per guest, 'allowing for the welcoming glass or two of champagne' and, the *Inquirer* was informed, the 42-Below vodka sorbets.

Add in the cost of invitations and marketing, additional hospitality service and entertainment, board member travel costs, loss of revenue from retail trade, security, potted palm nutrients, cleaning, snapped viola strings and the rest of it, and the *Inquirer* reckons this launch-pad junket into hinterland culture probably cost the nation in the region of $80,000 to $90,000.

Sliced-bread sandwiches, hard-boiled eggs and a thermos of tea were not on the menu here.

The *Inquirer* was not among those media organisations lucky enough to get an invite to this event, but more fortunate colleagues in the trade report that the insurable value of clothing and costume jewellery (including the increasingly popular greenstone pendant) could have met the venture capital needs of a medium-to-small tourist start-up in Middlemarch.

Not a nylon tracksuit in sight let alone the increasingly popular zip-up pants with useless pockets.

Team-building

The taxpayer-funded museum had also sponsored a 'problem-solving and team-building' workshop day for CTI team members at the museum.

Run by Up-Keep, a 'corporate team- and culture-building consultancy' active in the capital city, the day included activities such as the allocation of nicknames to team-members, 'duo-bonding' exercises, character and personality profiling, leadership and team-building challenges and, not least, massage of and by the 'duo-bonded' members of the international CTI team.

The Wellington CBD-located office of Up-Keep Consultants Inc., on the sore-neck-and-shoulder maximum stress Pinstripe-Mile of the Terrace, would not disclose the cost to the taxpayer of this duo-bonding day. However, the *Inquirer* had no trouble getting a quote for a similar session and can reliably report that the per-person cost of the day would have been in the region of $1000 not including morning and afternoon tea and lunch, which were generously thrown in by the people's museum.

Given this sort of preparation and the level of investment by the state and other agencies, the citizens of New Zealand should expect to hear some substantially researched news from this 'research-driven' national and indeed international project when it presents its report to the Minister responsible for it, the Hon. Brian Fellwill.

The Minister is widely reported to prefer a hands-on approach to traditional Kiwi hospitality.

Junket rampage

The Hon. Fellwill may not be feeling well just now. To date, the CTI team, which delivered its interim report to a review panel in Wellington last week, has racked up a list of damages and incidents worthy of a provincial rugby team on a victory rampage.

Staff at the Milford Sound Lodge have revealed that team-members spent the evening of 14 November drinking in the bar on an uncapped project tab. 'They ordered the most expensive wines on our list,' reported a member of the bar staff, who said a CTI member claimed they were 'product testing'.

Team-members are also alleged to have complained when the most expensive items on the bar's blackboard menu were no longer available for 'product testing'. They are said to have thrown French fries and mayonnaise at each other.

At the Hermitage, one of New Zealand's most luxurious resort hotels, where an official reception for the international CTI team was jointly hosted on 16 November by the Department of Tourism and the Iwi Development Corporation, the Minister of Tourism himself is alleged to have been intoxicated and to have made improper advances to a member of the catering staff.

Wall of silence

The luxury hotel's management was tight-lipped about the incident, saying it did not involve their in-house staff and that they had received no complaints.

A similar wall of silence was met with by the *Inquirer* when we probed reports of major vandalism at the Glacier Hotel at Franz Josef on the wild West Coast on 19 November.

Senior management at the

hotel declined to comment on rumours that mirrors had been smashed in one of the hotel's luxury suites. However, a staff member was able to confirm that the mirror damage had taken place in the luxurious suite of Mr Mohammed Biswas, an international member of the CTI team whose visit to New Zealand is jointly sponsored by the United Nations Development Project and Bangladesh's national tourism organisation, Parjatan.

Telephone calls and emails to Parjatan have not been responded to. However, we understand from the profile retained by Up-Keep, the corporate team-building consultancy contracted by the Museum of New Zealand Te Papa Tongarewa to pull the CTI project team together prior to its 'research-driven' safari, that Mr Biswas belongs to a tourism cartel in Bangladesh.

This gentleman's Dhaka office told the *Inquirer* that the cartel's members promote river cruises, hill-country trekking and Bengal tiger spotting in the Sundarban jungle. When asked how often tourists saw the nearly extinct Bengal tiger in its native habitat, the Dhaka informant would not comment.

The Biswas company, known as The Guide, operates under the Parjatan brand-slogan, 'Get here before the tourists do'.

Sex tourism

Mr Biswas recently left New Zealand before completing his assignment with the CTI project and has returned to Bangladesh, but not before adding to the CTI team's record of sensational incidents.

Officials at the Ministry of Foreign Affairs and Trade (MFAT) confirm that on 25 November the Bangladeshi tourism operative physically assaulted a senior member of a Pakistan trade mission who was sharing a hot thermal pool with him at Rotorua's plush Geyserland hotel.

No charges were laid and the incident was reported to have involved a personal issue between the two men. However, the morning after the incident, Mr Biswas was driven to Rotorua's airport in the CTI team's air-conditioned mini-bus.

Quizzed about the content of the CTI team's interim report presented to the Minister's review panel the morning before the hot-pool incident, a panel member,

Dr Ian Wade, Professor of Leisure Studies at the Albany Campus of Massey University outside Auckland, admitted to being 'puzzled' by the presentation by the Bangladesh Parjatan Corporation's favourite son.

'It seemed to be mostly about sex tourism,' said Professor Wade, adding, 'I don't know what that's got to do with us here in New Zealand.'

Gone missing

Mr Biswas is not the only member of the CTI team to have left the project under mysterious circumstances.

Police in Westport on the West Coast confirm that Dr Nancy Shapiro, an internationally respected expert on diasporas (communities living away from their homelands) and the team member assigned the Authenticity section of the CTI report, went missing on 20 November from the Erewhon Hotel in Westport, where team members were enjoying a lavish whitebait fritter lunch.

Dr Shapiro, who suffers from Charcot-Marie-Tooth disease, a muscle- and nerve-wasting condition and who walks with the assistance of crutches, was not seen leaving the lunch by other team-members, who were at the time enjoying 'product testing' the local boutique brewery's 'Miner's Special' beer.

Police had no comment to make about the frail Dr Shapiro's unobserved disappearance, saying the matter was still under investigation. The hotel's proprietor, Mr Mitch 'Smoky' Malloy, refused to talk to the *Inquirer*.

Tragic fatality

The CTI project and its substantial official and industry support appear to have struck fear into the hearts of hospitality professionals the length of the country.

Not only were hotel managers unwilling to comment at Milford, Franz Josef, Westport and Rotorua, but the manager of the Department of Conservation administered camping ground at Lake Waikaremoana was also tight-lipped about the CTI project's most spectacular catastrophe to date.

On the afternoon of 28 November, Mr Joris Vanbloen, the Director of 'Good-2-Go: We Add Venture' promotions and tours, returned unexpectedly and in distress from a tramp up the area's famous Panekiri Bluff, a natural feature that rises to a height of more than one thousand metres at the south-western end of the lake.

Another team-member, whom Mr Vanbloen, an experienced outdoor adventure specialist, had been escorting on a tramp up the Bluff, had apparently fallen to his death from the tramp's highest point at Bald Knob.

The pair had undertaken the tramp, which involves a steep climb through rugged bush, following an unseasonal but not unusual fall of snow.

Mr Vanbloen is also a member of the CTI team. The dead man, Mr William Honey, was his 'duo-bonded' counterpart on the team and was responsible for the Identity section of the team's report. Mr Vanbloen was responsible for the section dealing with Adventure.

An adventure was what the duo-bonded pair seems to have had, although with tragic results.

A celebrated brand identity advertising specialist and Creative Director of the advertising agency Honey Corp, Mr Honey was best known for his Absolutely Pure campaign for the Department of Tourism.

Police at Wairoa would not comment on the tragic fatality, saying there were aspects of the misadventure that were still being investigated.

Mr Vanbloen could not be contacted for his comment on the disaster but a former colleague and staff member of his company Good-2-Go Promotions, Miss Seiko Matsu, confirmed that at the Hermitage ten days previously on 18 November, while guiding an Add Venture party of Japanese tourists up the Hooker Valley, she had observed Mr Honey in a distressed state.

'He fell off the path,' said Miss Matsu. 'He was sick.'

Financial failure

The *Inquirer* can confirm that Mr Vanbloen's Good-2-Go company, which runs an extensive circuit of 'adventures' and scenic tours in New Zealand for the Japanese and European markets, is facing insolvency.

The company's retail product arm, which licenses the manufacture of outdoor 'survival' clothing, is also reported to be in financial difficulty.

Miss Matsu, formerly a guide with Mr Vanbloen's enterprise, confirmed that a number of employees and short-term contract workers with Good-2-Go's Add Venture operation had been made redundant or had left the organisation.

Many were now seeking restitution through the labour courts.

She added that she herself had left 'before it was too late' and had set up an independent operation in partnership with a Japanese package tour company, Global View.

Team spirit

The *Inquirer* wonders why such a high-profile project as the CTI would want to involve a Bangladeshi operator whose company's slogan ('Get here before the tourists do') admits there are no tourists in his country, a seriously ill Australian academic specialising in displaced communities, and a financial basket-case outdoor 'adventure' professional who failed to prevent the fatal accident of the CTI team's celebrity but 'sick' advertising executive.

In addition, the team includes Dr Hinemoana Oliver, a well-known professional in the hospitality and tourism business and one of the star graduates of initiatives begun at the Manaakitanga conference in 1985 and the Maori Tourism Task Force in 1987.

During a twenty-year career in the industry, Dr Oliver has survived a number of accountability crises, some of which have impacted on her sector. In 1998 and 2000, for example, Dr Oliver was on the receiving end of probes into nepotism in respect of government investment in the sector.

Cleared by a Ministry of Maori Affairs appointed commission of inquiry, Dr Oliver was nonetheless warned to be more prudent in her application of 'customary concepts' such as whanaungatanga or family business and manaakitanga or hospitality, to government-funded initiatives.

Official view

A large part of the CTI project team's work appears to involve views and scenery. They have often been sighted looking at the landscape, sometimes from the terraces of strategically sited tourist establishments.

Is there an official view of the team itself?

A spokeswoman at the Department of Tourism agreed

that a number of misfortunes had dogged the CTI team, but added, 'We have every faith in the team's professionalism and do not believe the unfortunate incidents are in any way connected or that they detract in any way from the team's innovative and ground-breaking work.'

Leaving aside the sensitivity of the term 'ground-breaking' in the context of the CTI team's tragic fatality, the *Inquirer* can only say, 'Good luck.' Although an audit of the CTI project's expenditure of the taxpayer's dollar would perhaps be appropriate.

Team management

The Minister of Tourism, Hon. Brian Fellwill, could not be contacted for comment because he was 'in the field' and out of cellphone range. Not walking the Lake Waikaremoana Track, which includes the Panekiri Bluff, we hope.

A spokesman for the Minister confirmed that the project would continue even though its team had been depleted by half.

'The team is in the very capable hands of Dr Patricia Smart, a Department of Tourism veteran and an experienced project manager. We have every faith in her ability to bring the project to a successful conclusion despite its unfortunate setbacks,' said the spokesman.

Staff at the Department of Tourism confirmed that Dr Smart is an able administrator with a 'firm' management style. They were able to add that Dr Smart's nickname in the Department is 'Great White' in recognition of her ability 'to scare people out of the water'.

Asked about the CTI project's budget and rumours of excessive spending on its expense account, the Minister's spokesman told the *Inquirer* he did not believe the CTI team had done anything excessive by the standards of the sector and that the project had been reported on schedule and within budget.

If a fifty per cent attrition of team capacity, vandalism, violent assault and fatal misadventure are the best the Great White's 'firm' management can do, the *Inquirer* wonders what kind of pressure had been building up in the team, and why.

Where does the buck stop?

Contacted in her Auckland hotel room last night for her views on the state of health of the 'research-driven' cultourism project, the team and project leader, Dr Patricia Smart, suggested that 'joining up the dots' did not amount to the 'full story'.

Asked what the 'full story' was, Dr Smart suggested the *Inquirer* obtain a copy of the full report when it was published.

Asked if the report would include records of 'product testing' and of hazardous adventure tourism dangers, Dr Smart said it was too early to speculate about the report's final form.

Asked if the report would explain what the term 'cultural tourism' meant, Dr Smart hung up and 'Home Truths' had to go to press with that vital question unanswered.

In a final comment, the *Inquirer's* reliable source said, 'I feel proud to live here. To call this place home. It's a responsibility.'

They should have told the rest of the CTI team that before winding them up and sending them off.

Next week

Load 'em up, drive 'em out and drop 'em off –: the scandal of photo-op tourism. Plus more on the sensational Cultural Tourism Initiative – can it get any worse? More to the point – can it get better?

twenty-two

Loyalty

The door to the CTI van is open but no one is getting in.

'Never you mind what I said or didn't say to that bloke.' Stan pauses to think about what he is saying now. 'Or even if I did say anything,' he adds, preparing to follow up.

'So which is it, Stan?' Pat is in best Great White mode. Her fresh copy of the *National Inquirer* is rolled up like a riot baton. 'You did, you didn't, or you might have? No, sorry,' she says. '"Might have" isn't any good to me. To us,' she adds, waving the *National Inquirer* at the team. 'To any of us.'

'Before you get stroppy with me,' warns Stan, 'tell this "us" you're so keen on why Mr Biswas is still in the country? Why you were meeting up with him in Auckland? Out at Kohimarama?'

This is the watershed moment that everyone has felt coming. It has been coming for days. Never mind the disappearance of Ants, the sacking of Biswas, the death of Bill. Never mind that Boris is under investigation for manslaughter or at very least gross negligence or that Gloria has started talking to herself and never mind that good old reliable Pat has finally lost her rag – this is where everything stops.

Joris stops failing, Hinemoana stops grieving and Patricia stops managing. All around them, people keep on checking out of the hotel as the morning advances and taxis, limos and shuttles continue to arrive and take them all somewhere else. But the CTI team just stands there by the open door of its air-conditioned mini-bus and does not move. It is past the 9.10 a.m. when Pat said she would be leaving regardless. Around them, the city is roaring dully with unseen activity, but the tour members of the Cultural Tourism Initiative project deemed to have crashed by the *National Inquirer*'s 'Home Truths' columnist Richard Brawn do not get into their van and move on out to advance and complete their mission of national and international importance. In the sky, the self-important contrails of aircraft going somewhere vital zip shut a heaven that might otherwise seem ready to rain down judgement, but no one moves to take shelter in the safety of the project.

'I saw you,' says Stan, almost contritely, 'going into that curry place on the beach at Kohimarama. Yesterday lunch time.' No one says anything. It is as if they are stunned not so much by the revelation as by their own intuitive, complicit prior knowledge of it. 'I got the van serviced later,' says Stan, as if to exonerate his treachery.

'Thanks very much, Stan,' Pat begins menacingly, preparing a routinely cutting comment about how a well-serviced van will help them to get away faster. But everything has stopped. 'Oh hell,' she says. 'Take us to the beach, Stan. Get us over that fucking bridge.' She chucks the *Inquirer* into the minibus and follows it there. 'I'm off radio,' she says. 'Nobody talk to me. Not until there's a view of Rangitoto and I know Mr Richard-bloody-Brawn isn't watching us with his cheap duty-free binoculars. Take us to Cheltenham Beach, please, Stanley.'

Gloria is appraising Joris. 'Really, Boris? Dinkum? Down the gurgler? Good-2-Go's kaput?'

Joris shrugs – this offhand gesture has begun to replace his offhand smile. Last night this crazy woman was going to hit him: throw him out the window, maybe. And since Bill's death, nobody is calling him Boris any more. See: this you can't hide. But Joris's face, which has always appeared smoothly impervious to weather as well as to emotion, seems paler. There are red rims around his light blue eyes and his smile does not reveal his nice teeth, instead stretching itself straight across his face so that his lips thin and whiten and deep creases appear beside his nose.

'Move on,' he replies. 'That's what my poppa always say. What's next? That's what he said when no chances at home post-war so we come here.'

'Is he still alive, your dad? Your poppa?' Gloria is ignoring the mini-bus's open door. Joris looks at her with weary curiosity. 'Sorry about last night,' adds Gloria. 'Hit a rough patch. No hard feelings?' Joris jerks his chin at the door – the gesture may mean get in or yes: Poppa's still alive. Gloria stoops to enter the bus.

'Maybe this finish him,' says Joris. 'I think I just lost all his money.'

Stan drives cautiously past Victoria Park towards the harbour bridge on-ramp. The life of the city flows past and around the CTI team. A couple of boy-racer cars with thudding sub-woofers snarl past on the inside lane and for once Stan does not curse the day kids got to customise cheap Japanese hatchbacks. A large billboard promotes holidays in the Cook Islands and has a border of frangipani flowers and hibiscus. Another billboard urges the motorway traffic to go for a holiday in Australia where there is 'a world of opportunity'. A trashed-looking four-wheel-drive station wagon with surfboards strapped to the roof-rack overlimits past in the outside lane and Stan does not have a comment to make about driving too fast and getting there just as quick if you go steady.

Below the on-ramp, the Westhaven marina is full of parked-up yachts. Their idleness emphasises the aura of humdrum luxury they convey to frazzled commuters tailgating down the bridge's cityward inclines. A few other yachts are out on the harbour, just mucking about. Thick, sluggish traffic lanes of work commuters are crawling towards the city. The drivers have cellphones pressed to their ears. The heat and exhaust rising from their vehicles seems to be shimmering with urgent data. The traffic in the other direction, the direction of the CTI project mini-bus, has a truant air. Happily sparse, speeding away from the city with CDs and radios going full bore, this traffic consists of irresponsible leisure seekers, people heading for the beach, buggering off, clearing out, getting away. Some have surfboards, chillybins and kids with towels. Others have smoked-glass windows and sunroofs through which the CTI team glimpses the tanned faces of habitual long-weekenders. The mini-bus joins this flow as if to smuggle itself away from its responsibilities — as if to pretend that it, like the surfer wagons and the flash beach-house BMWs, lives in a world of perpetual, carefree leisure. As if it has become the billboard for what it hopes, itself, to represent: destinations without responsibility, journeys without anxiety, experiences without consequences, relationships that are all pleasure — worlds of possibility within fragrant borders, life without work, not a care in the world and views whose beauty defies death. Prospects to die for, but not really.

At Cheltenham, Pat leads the silent team across closely mown buffalo grass to the beach. Stan morosely lights a cigarette, as if expecting to be executed.

Pat has kept her vow of silence all the way over. 'The thing is,' she next says, parking her bum on the edge of the grass by the sandy beach and considering the soothing outline of Rangitoto's volcano shape across the teal-blue water, 'there's nothing to tell.'

'What, you saying Mr Biswas isn't here?' Stan is still prepared to be outraged.

'No, Stan, I mean there wasn't really anything you could tell Mr Brawn, was there? Except fibs? But I don't think so,' Pat finishes quickly, before Stan can react. 'That's not you, Stan. I know you. Whatever you did, you did . . .'

'Because I "cared"?' mocks Stan.

Pat is astonished. 'Whoa, take it easy, friend,' she says. 'You know what I mean.' She pauses, as if listening for a cue. 'And don't forget – I could sack you for talking to that bloke.'

'So: here's what I think, then,' interrupts Joris blithely. Stan's mouth is open – he has heard his opportunity for outrage. But Joris keeps going. 'You know I didn't push Bill but is true: we have some trouble, maybe I frighten him. Many accidents happen like that, but still accidents. Sure, Stan talks to the journalist, is obvious. But so what? Going to happen anyway: no big deal. Maybe Stan was angry: maybe there's a reason? Okay. And now,' Joris turns a look at once exhausted and dispassionate on Pat, 'looks like Pat's doing something she shouldn't meant to, okay: we all know she is, is obvious, only nobody's talking last few days.'

It is still that watershed moment. 'I don't know,' says Pat. 'What are we going to do? Have a great big team confession?'

'What about me, then?' asks Gloria. 'I feel left out. What have I done wrong?'

'Oh, you,' says Joris with affable scorn. 'You drink too much. And anybody can see you're going to quit.'

'Don't you two bloody start up again,' warns Pat. 'I've had a total gutsful of that nonsense.' The island of Rangitoto is dependably present on the near horizon and the stretch of water across to it looks swimmable. When Stan begins a shrieking cough and fires his cigarette butt at the sea, Pat offers him her bottle of spring water. 'You first, Stan,' she says. 'Away you go. Spill your beans.'

'Thanks,' he says, swallowing. 'I did, yes, you're right. Talk to him. That journo.' He takes another swallow, grinning around the neck of the plastic bottle like a man reprieved. 'How did you know?'

Joris shrugs, but everyone is looking at Pat.

'Moment of truth.' Pat takes her water back and swallows large gulps. 'How come smokers make everything taste of themselves? No offence, Stan.' Pat looks at Rangitoto. It's both ordinary and spectacular, familiar and bizarre. Why would there be a volcano floating within swimming distance in the harbour where desultory yachts are mucking about? Pat swam the channel once, with a university marathon team, when she was completing her Masters in sports administration and thought that was where she was headed. The island never got any closer until she was almost there. Then she woke up in the middle of the night weeks later with an image of the cone-on-a-plate shape, at the moment it seemed close at last, vividly, almost materially, in her mind's eye in the darkness of her bedroom. One of those totally satisfying changes of direction, thanks to Rangitoto. She pursued that night-vision image of the thing into the marathon of the rest of her life.

All those doctoral thesis images of Rangitoto – yachts, swimmers, fishermen, pohutukawa flowers framing the cone, sand castles, the nineteenth century watercolours again – Pat still needs to come and look at the real thing once in a while when visiting Auckland. Its dependability reassures her – its basic credibility. The way it just does look completely like a volcanic island, nothing too flash. Like a diagram of a volcano shape coming out of what can only be sea, because of the way the horizon extends behind the plain cone. Not madly dramatic like Mitre Peak or silly and pointy like Mount Taranaki.

Is Rangitoto beautiful? If it is, its beauty's got something to do with a mundane moment of proximity. It was all at once comfortingly closer to her eyes almost blind with the salt inside her goggles and her body leaden with exhaustion and burning with jellyfish stings. And its beauty has to do with the other moment when the island volcano visited her in the middle of the night with a question about the connection between her tired, sore body and its own unforgettable appearance.

'Short version or long version?' she asks, still looking at the island not at her team-mates. She might as well be asking for their view preference, the simple scene before them whose foreground is slowly filling with other early summer truants, or another, more elaborate and compromised one.

'Short,' says Gloria. 'I'm brain damaged.' She is keeping her eye on Joris as he glares without interest at a Pacific Island family whose numbers are increasing on the shady grass below some pohutukawa trees. 'But then long, if it's interesting. Or funny,' she adds.

'Oh well,' says Pat, still measuring the distance between herself and the island. But then, as if swimming, she swings her handsome, well-balanced head with its thick, healthy wings of pale hair to one side, she takes a deep swimmer's breath and surveys the activity on the beach. Plain, strong, substantial, well taken care of, in control of herself as far as all appearances go, dressed comfortably and even stylishly in practical cotton, not burdened this morning with her video camera or Palm Pilot, scrubbed, fresh, nails trimmed short and buffed, breathing evenly, lightly perfumed with a decent squirt, as she likes to call it, of androgynous CK1 – Pat might be out here on the first morning of a long weekend during which, later, she'll drop her standards a bit, relax, get into an old lavalava and bare feet, have an early glass of wine and leave the salt of a midday swim in her hair until night.

That's how she does it. That's Pat. Only her crew, who have travelled with her now for the many long days of the CTI journey, can see the details that say there is something else going on. The Pat who always seems to be at home in her simply well-managed self is not really there at all.

'Well,' says Pat again, heaving in a big breath of sea air. 'The truth is that it's hard doing four jobs at once. Probably about six. Don't think I'm complaining, Glor, but you know what I mean. You talk about it yourself from time to time. In your case, doing a job, being Maori, being a woman and coping with rednecks. Doubt if you'll be laughing about this one, though, long or short. Sorry.' She is not looking at Gloria. 'Not that funny. Even if I try extra hard.'

'Don't get me wrong,' says Gloria, taking Pat's hand. 'Just trying to, you know.'

Pat removes her hand. 'See, I'm the head of Beauty, of natural beauty no less, at DoT and consultant to the office of Hands-On. Taking care of Hands-On is a task, let me assure you. Getting him to whack it on the head. Then I'm a big woman and if you don't think that's a job you need to get re-educated. Then I'm the poor bugger who has to manage you lot, what was it "Home Truths" said? With a "firm" style. And apparently my esteemed colleagues back at DoT Central are quite happy to prattle on about me, the "Great White", apparently, to that piece of excrement Richard Brawn. That's three. Or is it four. And then, Glor,' Pat pushes Gloria's hand away again, 'I have to be funny. That's five, or maybe six, by my count.' Pat appears to be breathing steadily through her nose.

The Pacific Island family under the pohutukawa trees has brought a portable gas barbecue and several chillybins down into the shade by the beach. Two young men and one older one take a net down to the sea. The two younger ones begin a sweep along the beach while the older man shouts instructions. The women setting up the barbecue yell good-humoured insults at him. Their kids run into the water ahead of the net and splash to drive fish into it. A toddler in a bright orange flannel sunhat staggers bow-legged towards the sea and is scooped up with efficient indifference by an older girl. At the near end of the beach where the cliffs come down into the sluggish waves, some Asian men are fishing off the rocks with immensely long rods. Two teenage mothers wheel their pushchairs to the edge of the buffalo grass and take their babies down to the sand. They light cigarettes while the babies stare at each other on a blanket. An elderly man in a yellowed Panama hat and white bowling trousers has walked the length of the beach barefoot on the firm, damp sand below the high tide mark, with an ancient cocker spaniel trudging beside him. Now he is returning. He is talking to someone vividly present to him. From time to time the dog also seems to notice the phantom. From nearby in the beach suburb comes the sound of a lawnmower, a chainsaw, talkback radio. A windsurfer scoots around the point, executes a neat gybe and tears back out of sight on a thin, speeding wake of white foam. Behind the CTI team, back at the road, a rubbish truck pulls up and metal bins crash against the sides of the truck's tray. The truck's radio is playing opera, it is *Turandot* and the rubbish guy is singing along, 'Te che tremi se ti sfioro!' in a loud untutored tenor voice. Then the truck drives off at speed, trailing ice, death and sacrifice.

'You who tremble at my touch,' translates Pat. 'Add translator to the list. Make it seven.' No one else says anything. 'Christ almighty,' says Pat. 'Look at all this. Isn't it just bloody lovely? That should be our report: "It's just bloody lovely." End of it. Says it all.'

The Pacific Island women have fired up the barbecue and are cooking sausages. They are laughing loudly and shouting lewd comments at the elderly man directing the netting.

'Okay,' says Pat. 'Enough self-pity. Enough beating about the bush, too. Is Mr Biswas still here? Yes, he is. Did Mr Biswas and I conspire to keep him here without the rest of you knowing? Yes again, I'm afraid. I'm afraid, so to speak, but I'm not sorry, and this is where the long version starts, Glor, if you still want it. If you don't want to drown me right here, right now. End it all.' Pat studies her team. 'Are we having fun yet?' she looks at Gloria. 'Funny enough?'

'Getting the message,' growls Gloria. 'And you know what? You owe it to us. All this cloak-and-dagger.'

'Do I, Dr Oliver?' Pat is calm. 'I did warn you all a couple of days ago during one of my attempts to manage "with a firm hand" that there were aspects of the situation I wasn't at liberty, as we quaintly say, to discuss.' She pauses, hearing herself what she sounds like – a warhorse, Great White. 'Fuck it,' she says. 'Brace yourselves. Here it comes.'

Down on the beach, the elderly netting expert is maintaining his dignity by keeping his back turned to the lewd women cooking sausages at the barbecue under the trees. But everyone can see his shoulders shaking with mirth. A sausage lands beside him in the sand. He turns, finally, and gestures at it derisively, rocking his hips.

'But first,' says Pat, 'and don't say I didn't warn you, it's a bit complicated, you have to get your heads around a couple of things.'

'Is always simple really,' says Joris. 'But: okay. At least you come clean now.'

Pat keeps her steady look on him and seems to be considering a response. But then she just goes on. 'We have to stop calling Mr Biswas "Mr Biswas" for a while, let alone "Biz". And not "Balls". We have to call him Baul, which is the familiar name he's chosen for himself. It explains some things about him that you need to know. He tried, sometimes, but pretty much gave up. Tried to talk to us about stuff.' The CTI team remains silent and a mottled blush begins to rise up Pat's chest and neck and across her face. 'But first,' she says, 'I'm sensing that you need to know something else. No, Mr Mohammed Biswas, let's call him by his formal name again at this point, Mr Biswas and I never did get jiggy or anything like that, whatever you want to call it. Just in case there's any lingering doubts on that subject. Not that it would have been any of your business. Not bloody likely and don't expect me to say "More's the pity", in case your grubby minds are still having the thought, it was just never on, okay?' Pat, whose neck is a mosaic of blushing, notices Gloria. 'What's so funny?'

Gloria's loud laughter, merry and contralto, has shut the barbecueing women up. 'You are,' says Gloria, wiping tears. 'I knew you could do it.'

'If you say so.' Pat's blush drains away, leaving her pale, perhaps with rage. 'So yes, Stan, you were quite in command of your senses. You did see us. I guess that makes us quits. Lucky for you.'

'So: why?' asks Joris, neatly. 'Not sex: must be money.'

'Such a clear thinker.' Pat begins to go back on the attack. The evening before, Joris stood trembling against the dim back-lighting of the hotel window at night. Now, he seems backlit by an approaching summer with nothing in it for him. His smoothly, innocuously handsome face, unmarked by any signs of stress or effort, has begun to appear drawn and papery and almost old. 'Well, yes,' she says. 'In a sense. That's right, Joris. Money. We'll come to that. And by the way, you look like shit. You need to take it easy.'

'I'm never better,' says Joris. The smile that turns his mouth down at the corners is like a ghost of Bill's.

'But first,' Pat ploughs on, 'this Baul thing. My ignorance is profound but as I understand it Baul's religious faith is Muslim, but he relates strongly to a version of it that mixes up all kinds of stuff. He calls it the soul of Bangla. It's where all that singing of his comes from that no one can understand a word of – lovely singing voice, though.' Pat may be lightening up a bit but she continues doggedly as though from an autocue, one she has known she will have to use sooner or later. 'It seems to have a whole lot of Hindu and Buddhist stuff in it as well, and we thought they were all intent on killing each other.' Pat pauses. 'Here's the hard bit. Baul's Baul belief system, if you're following me, says we're all female unless we're, you know.'

'No we don't.' Gloria sounds a bit hostile. 'This is our first lesson, Pat.'

'Don't be sarcastic,' says Pat. 'God knows I'm trying. Unless we're making love,' she continues. The blush does not return to her neck and chest. A chalky whiteness has begun to invade the complexion around her mouth. 'Then the male emerges.'

'He went on to me about it once,' exclaims Stan. 'Back at Lake Pukaki. "Sok-something".'

'Prakriti,' says Pat. 'Got a lot to do with rivers, water, life forces, floods, washing, praying, you name it. It's why he loved washing. Quite apart from the prayer thing.'

'Hot pools,' suggests Gloria. 'He's got a thing about them, too?'

'We're getting to that,' says Pat. 'But first. Baul believes that the water is sacred. Even when it knocks off all his family in a flood, which it did. All except his little sister who's called Keshamoni. Remember that name, Keshamoni. Training to be a primary school teacher. She's about fifteen or sixteen, I think. He says that although the floods take life sometimes, they give it back abundantly. They give water, fertility, food, cleanliness. He says that Prakriti gave Keshamoni back to him. That's more important than what was taken.' The whiteness has crept across Pat's cheeks and perspiration beads her upper lip. 'This is the hard bit,' she says. 'I'll give it a crack.' She swallows water. 'Bear with me.'

The fishermen return with a couple of flounder and a bucket of small mullet. The noise of the picnic around the gas barbecue increases. The young mothers pack up their babies and wheel off across the grass – one of the infants begins to cry like a seagull. A fisherman on the headland yells loudly as a wave washes up close.

'Tide's coming in,' says Pat. 'Christ, what do any of us know, really? Anyway – Prakriti gave Keshamoni back to Baul. Back to her brother. Got that much straight. He also believes that she lives in his own body. He has to respect his body in order to respect hers. He has this man-soul that he calls his secret bird. It lives in the cage of his body and, from what I can tell, gives him a hard time.'

'Is all quite interesting, all right,' says Joris wearily. 'But: what really happens?'

'Closing in, Joris,' says Pat. 'Just bear with me.'

'The mirrors,' complains Joris. 'What's in the newspaper. The pool thing?'

'Exactly.' Pat is patient, but tired also, like Joris. 'Because Baul has his sister's body in his own, because he's responsible for it there as well as where it actually is, anything happens to her he can't bear to look at himself. That's that one. The mirrors. Back at the glacier. Am I clear?'

'But: what happens?' insists Joris. 'To the sister? Exactly: what?'

Pat ignores him. 'And then, because water, especially warm water, is sacred and is also the Prakriti body of his sister, he can't be in it if someone defiles it. So that's that one. The hot pool. Back at Rotorua.'

'What's happened to her, Pat, to Biswas's sister? Kesh-what'shername?' This time it's Gloria. 'Something awful happen to her?'

'He broke the mirrors because he couldn't bear to look at himself. He tried to kill that Pakistani fellow because he'd defiled his sister by saying something filthy in the hot pool.' Pat takes a deep breath. 'It's so simple when you know it but so hard to talk about. Short version again. On the scam market in Bangladesh, some less informed people think Baul is worth the gross value of the total project grant to put him on the team, which is about half a mill our money. Sadly, Baul's worth nothing until he gets the report done and then bugger-all anyway once his costs and about sixty per cent skim of the balance is taken out. So he's in the shit.'

'Why?' asks Joris. 'Got all his costs covered: no risk? Lucky man.'

'Unfortunately, and this is the bit where little sister Keshamoni comes back into the story, the people who have overestimated Baul's value want him to give them all the money he doesn't have and won't get. At least not from the CTI, bless its bleeding heart. Despite what Richard-bloody-Brawn thinks.'

'Ransom,' says Stan, standing up. He shakes a cigarette from his packet and inserts it between his lips. He continues with a smoker's squint above the first exhalation of smoke. The squint gives him a shrewd expression, like someone who has understood a negotiating point or a secret code. 'It's got to be. You read about it all the time in the paper.

Abductions. Some bugger's got her, I'll bet. Am I right?' Everybody looks at him. 'I read about it in *Newsweek*,' he explains. His face shows there's more. 'Organs,' he whispers. 'Kids' organs. Child sex.'

''fraid so,' says Pat. 'You've nailed it, Stan.' Her face is now ashy and the gleam of perspiration has spread across it. She wipes her sleeve carelessly across her mouth. And then her big white face drops into her hands like a dead weight. The big, strong body of the boss of Beauty is suddenly soft with exhaustion and the voice that comes out from between her fingers is not the voice of the Great White. The Safe Pair of Hands' voice has gone up an octave as though Pat is talking through a mouth no larger than a child's and with only the breath of a child's lungs to inflate the huge words.

'Poor little thing. You should see her. Like a little dark broom handle. Got these eyes that don't want you to see her. So pretty. What could happen to her?'

'What could, darling?' This time Pat doesn't push Gloria away.

'They'd put her in a brothel,' finishes Pat, sobbing. The tears run through her fingers. 'They'd put her in porn videos. Rape videos. She'd get AIDS.'

'So, Christ, why didn't you tell us? What are you doing, Pat?' Gloria holds the big swimmer's shoulders.

'He's got to stay here,' says Pat, and even now she begins to get the grip everyone is used to. 'He can't go back until we've sorted it. Until she's safe. Keshamoni.'

'You mean,' says Joris, 'until you get the money: to buy her back, this kid?'

'Yes, Joris, that would be one pretty simple way of putting it, yes,' agrees Pat. She blows her nose and mops up. The smell of grilling fish blows across from the Rarotongan barbecue picnic – its participants are watching the CTI drama with close interest. They may be arguing amongst themselves about what's going on.

'Hey, palangi!' calls out one of the women. 'Want some

fish? Nice and fresh, good for you! Fun you up!'

'Kaiorana, kare umukai, kia orana,' Pat replies, waving cheerfully. 'And no,' she adds under her breath for the benefit of her team. 'My husband hasn't just left me for a young woman.' Her laugh is short and businesslike. 'And we aren't planning to beat him up, are we?'

'You speak Raro?' asks Gloria.

'I take holidays,' says Pat. 'Believe it or not.' She looks at Rangitoto. It's within swimming distance.

A kid arrives with four sausages between slices of white bread. 'Mum says have a sausages instead,' he says.

Pat holds her sausage sandwich up between thumb and forefinger and grins at the kid. 'Tell your mum thanks a lot,' she says. 'Meitaki ma'ata.' She takes a bite. 'Secret vice,' she says, chewing. 'Resort holidays.' There are still small tears squeezing from her eyes. They are not big enough to track down her cheeks. 'So here we all are, then,' she finishes, as if to the whole beach full of miscellaneous strangers and friends. As if to include everyone in the horrible plight of their little sister way over there – but swimmable, in the place they have to get to before the tourists do.

twenty-three

Beauty

Yes, Mohammed Baul Biswas remembers very well the scene in the first video.

A slippery sheen across the view which shivers the yacht putting up sail just outside the breakwater of the marina. And then the video surging forward and the huge picture windows of the national museum's top-of-market restaurant revealed as causing the oily shiver, as the camera exits the restaurant past the dark, blurred shapes of people. They are drinking alcohols and eating little snacks and Biswas remembers the loudness of their shouting. Biswas could only smile at this noise because he could not penetrate it with his understanding.

Knows-where-it's-going, the video camera, and it glides past the shiny glass on to a terrace through a revolving door that flashes light into the scene. An almost-empty harbour of water blue-black like paddy mud glitters away to dark mountains long-way to distance, a horizon furry with mist. From the edge of the terrace, the video zooms to the yacht which is lifting sails and going faster with its mast standing up against a view of houses and apartments on a hillside. Pink colour light flashing from far-away windows. The video makes the sun-setting yacht come closer: its sail is shaking against the tall mast, white water behind. The quivering yacht getting smaller as it sails away from the camera.

Biswas is not seeing Cowgirl in the video because she is not in it. He is keeping his promise, not looking. He is looking only at Pat's video background views before Cowgirl is edited on top. This, his IT-webmaster cousin does in Chittagong. Chittagong is six hours by train from Dhaka but sometimes takes twelve. To Khulna from Chittagong is further than to Khulna from Dhaka and very difficult except by air but first he will go to Chittagong from Dhaka. There he will wait to see what might happen, before going to Khulna for Keshamoni or before Keshamoni coming to Chittagong.

Pat's home is somewhere beyond the yacht's creaming wake, she has showed him where, near the boat harbour, but he can't see that either. He can't see Pat's home because it is too far away to see even though it is there, in the video, but he can't see Cowgirl because she is not there yet in this room even though she is there now, everywhere else, on Cowgirl.com, 10,000 webmastered pay sites and 60,000 hits every 24.

Biswas watches the semi-erect yacht sailing ahead of its unzippering wake towards his revenue target. Towards the time when he will take the difficult route from Chittagong to Khulna.

'*Hello Sailor*,' says Biswas aloud. This is the name of the Cowgirl episode with Pat's video of the yacht. The unit at the back of the Leigh Hotel is the worst he has ever stayed in. A huge, noisy crowd is watching a game of rugby in the hotel bar and he has long ago closed the unit's only windows that look out at the car park and he has pulled the curtains neatly across them. Earlier, his cellphone called him to prayer as darkness was falling – when he opened the curtains to see where was sunset, he looked straight into the face of a man standing close to the window outside. The man's expression did not change or show that he was seeing Baul Biswas staring at him in amazement from his side of the window and Biswas only realised the man was urinating against the front of his hotel accommodation unit when he turned away and walked off between the cars, zipping up his fly. Sun setting behind the hills beyond the car park. Biswas closed the curtains again, washed and did namaz on the floor space between the bed and his bathroom.

'*Garden Party*,' he says as the punt parts the trailing fringes of willow and the young, smiling man in a funny hat leans his weight down on the pole that is like the ones Biswas has seen thrusting rafts of bamboo down the Karnifuli River below the Kaptai dam or where the mill is at Chandraghona. Only, the punt has two young women in it, they are lying indecorously across the seats of the punt, one has splashed water on her blouse so that her breasts are showing and the other has pulled her dress up so Biswas can see her underpants. They are drinking out of a bottle and one of them is smoking a cigarette. Then the punt moves in close but below the video camera so that Biswas is looking down into it before it disappears smoothly into the arch of a bridge as the young woman with her dress pulled up lifts the bottle in a greeting to the video. This is where Cowgirl will be unzipping, Biswas thinks, because his cousin has told him about the immense success of the zips. The punt re-emerges from under the bridge on the other side where the video has gone to find it and Biswas watches it disappear into fringes of green willow.

The day the candle goes out the city of love will become dark. The Happy Bird will fly away, leaving off the dawning of happiness. Biswas is humming songs as he selects another video-clip on his laptop. He watches the videos to immerse himself, to bathe, to be forgiven, in the medium of Keshamoni's redemption. He watches as if his looking-with-hope will stream into the videos in his laptop, in the motels with no views and the units where men who behave as if they were blind piss on his front door. His looking-with-hope will stream out again at Cowgirl.com. He is joining his looking to the views that will have Cowgirl on top of them but not, ever, never Keshamoni. As though his looking at and Cowgirl's appearance in the videos he looks at without her in them are what, together, are keeping Keshamoni out.

Out of the views. It is like another prayer, watching the videos that Pat has taken – the lakes, mountains, boulders, geysers and cataracts.

In the distance, a cluster of large, glistening, smoothly rounded boulders lie on a beach. The world-famous Moeraki Boulders, G1A. The video zooms in – the rocks are pockmarked and wrinkled and Biswas remembers *Got Balls*, as a young woman with astonishing red hair, a red, lipsticked mouth and retro-1950s sunglasses embraces one of the balls and grins at the camera. When the sea washes over her feet, the silent video records her mime of a shriek and as the water recedes, leaving shining sand streaked with scum, her red-painted toenails are revealed.

Biswas does not try to imagine Cowgirl in *Got Balls* at Moeraki. He does not try to imagine Pat, either. He will not let his cousin tell him what happens after the zips and he has instructed him to email only the figures. Five per cent of cash target reached, thirty per cent growth and increasing steadily, webmaster licence value growth at fifteen per cent, residuals including DVD gone 'through the roof'. Nearly one million viewers total, estimate only, can't really count any more.

What happens, asked the last text-message from dacoit in Khulna, if you don't reach target before returning to Bangladesh, pi-dog? Let us tell you what we think will happen.

The water-skier tears open the surface of the lake, at once savage and graceful. He creates sinuous curves across the wake of the speedboat.

Biswas is rocking to and fro on his chair in front of the laptop. His movements might be a kind of devotion, or he might be urging the water-skier to go faster, faster, towards the revenue target. A great, shining, muscular tube of water plunges foaming into its dark, accepting chasm. Even the air around it is wet. '*The Chasm*,' prays Mohammed Baul Biswas, rocking and urging, '*Bridal Veil*,' he hopes, as the cataract's white, gauzy mass drifts down the black precipice of rock,

'*Get it Up*,' he implores the contrail opening the blue dome of heaven.

From the pub's sports bar comes the roaring of a crowd, the one on the widescreen TV and the one drinking in the bar. They merge into one voice yearning for victory and revenge – yelling like the single, enormous, rehearsed voice of an Awami League hartal demonstration: 'Zindabad!' In his unit out the back of the pub, which stinks of crayfish remains from the pub's rubbish bins and of urine against the wall beneath its window, Biswas joins his voice and the caw of his black Dhaka crow and the sound of the imam's call to prayer echoing over the thick-aired city at dusk, to the one million voices of Cowgirl's devotees. He hears the sound of a great congregation of people shouting '*Broad Walk*!' as the wetland track writhes across the flower-decked floor of the Hooker Valley, chanting '*White Bait*!' as a net rises, dripping, from the surging water of a mighty river and '*Arthur's Pass*!' as the video camera, beginning to be schooled now in its secret purpose, watches drenching falls of mountain mist collect in the tight, hairy coils of tree ferns.

Where once Biswas had found the affronting purity and waste of these spectacular views impious and dreadful, had been sickened and enraged by the malevolence of Mitre Peak's black fang, by the insult of Lake Pukaki's aquamarine and turquoise water against which he could only imagine the Pankhali woman skirting salt ghers where her children had drowned, and by the meaningless emptiness of the old glacier's track, now he implores and rocks his prayerful body before the shining waterfall and the lake shore rich with Connie lupins, the strange 'beach' forests and the gleaming calligraphies of volcanic silica, the sudden outburst of the geyser, the strange shape of the floating volcano across the water from the Sea View-with-no-view motel at Kohimarama, the sound of the mod-drinking horde in the bar – he implores and beseeches them to free his Keshamoni, his beautiful sister. To redeem her and her beauty with their own beauties, to sacrifice their beauties to Cowgirl.com so that Keshamoni can come home. He implores them and he thanks them for their sacrifices, knocking his forehead against the Formica rim of a table scorched by cigarettes, lit by the flicker of a CrystalBrite LCD screen.

Another great shout goes up from the hotel bar and reaches Biswas through the muffling defences of his windows and curtains: 'Blue! Blue!' Baul Biswas, rocking and moaning in the trance of a Baul dervish, implores the blue, so-blue water and the blue sky of this so-beautiful land to uplift Cowgirl into the parched minds of her devotees starved for love of Krishna's sportive milkmaid – her millions of helpless Purusha arid with the lack of her seasons, her life-giving and life-taking floods of Saraswati snow and mud, her rains that will drench her followers in a shonar golden country with a broken roof where the cleansing rains come in.

He does not hear the knock at first because the sound of the crowd chanting 'Blue! Blue!' and the sound of his own imploring prayerful thoughts spill from the LCD screen in front of him where an immense, crimson-flowered tree has been occupied by sunbathing bodies stretched out in sunlight along its elephantine limbs with a view of blue sea and sky beyond.

'*Bushed*,' murmurs Biswas, coming to his senses and going to open the door for Pat. This is the newest of her videos. But it is the journalist Richard Brawn who is standing there, grinning, with a takeaway pizza in a box and a large bottle of Coke.

'What, still working? Not watching the footie? No rest for the wicked, eh, Mr Biswas?' Brawn puts one foot across the threshold. 'Thought you might be hungry,' he says, 'so I got one without ham.' He puts his other foot across. 'And it was Coke, wasn't it, if I remember rightly?'

twenty-four

Home and Adventure

'Hello, Pat.' Hands-On's put the call through all by himself – there's no Margie to begin with, not bloody likely, not this time.

'I've seen it, sir, front page,' says Pat. 'Little shit.' She's listening to the Minister's silence and knows that he's listening to hers. She has no doubt she can hold out the longest. Asset value of Cowgirl.com, including the banked profit, about $80,000 shy of target. It's the liquidity that's the worry. It's foreign exchange cash that these buggers in Khulna understand.

'We just have to pull the plug,' says the Minister, losing his nerve first. 'You can imagine why.'

'Got told to by?' imagines Pat, obligingly.

'I did warn you, Pat,' suggests Hands-On, succumbing to self-pity. If he'd like to increase the level of threat in his voice he's careful to conceal that wish. Pat has no doubt as to the depths of his resentment at her staunch history of baling him out of gaffes. She can measure, without opening her eyes or even being fully awake, the extent of his shame at her subaltern power. She won't be surprised when he calls time on the critical mass of the secret armature she's assembled for his support and maintenance over the years. He knows that now is when the last bid goes in. This is when, one way or another, he'll cast off from the life-support he's come to hate and resent. The safe pair of hands he's come to hate and resent – the hugely reliable, the broad-based, the firm, the foundation, the warhorse, the Great White Patricia. His tone's almost resigned – a voice Pat's familiar with when a dressing-down has been administered to him from a great height and the Minister is, for a brief time, contained by his chagrin.

There's no need for Pat to remind herself to breathe through her nose – she's at peace.

Pat looks out the window of the bach. The varnish has long since peeled off its cedar frame which is pushed out across the top of an old hibiscus bush. The hill slopes down to the sea, of which a thin slice can be seen at the mouth of the bushy gully. A creek runs down the gully and into the tidal inlet below. When the tide's out, the wet, corrugated, shell-roughened sand extends as far as water glistening in the channel, where an old yacht's moored, swinging on its hawser as if its only function's to indicate the directions of tide and wind. Sometimes, seagulls take up helpful wind-direction positions on its topmast spreader. An equally ancient dinghy with flaking blue paint lies on its side in the inlet when the tide's out, and when the tide's in floats grudgingly, a wash of rainwater and leaves in its bottom, on a rope tied to a mangrove.

It's a view that Pat's retained deep in a part of herself that needs to be able to answer a question she doesn't know how to ask. Though she doesn't know how to ask it, it's what makes her peaceful. The question's taking shape – is getting framed, somehow, at the intersection of the blue dinghy on its side on the mangrove bank, the profile of Rangitoto suddenly massive as a destination for her exhausted body and the absurd parable of Connie Lupins as a remedy for the awful loneliness of Beauty.

Her friends have gone down the shell-and-clay track for a late-morning swim in the inlet while the tide's in, but also to leave her with the red-hot copy of the *National Inquirer* and her cellphone. Home Truths' second instalment of the Cultural Tourism Initiative story has made the front page for the first time in Brawn's byline career. There's a photograph of Pat and Biswas next to the taxi in the Leigh Hotel car park – Biswas has turned back to face the camera as he appears to be ducking for cover into the back seat of the cab. He has an inappropriately brilliant smile on his face – the Biswas smile Pat adores. There's a large crowd of football supporters in the background, many wearing blue scarves, some of whom are punching the air as if celebrating a victory of which Biswas is the obscure, oblivious celebrity, focus. She should probably congratulate Richard Brawn, the little prick. If she was his editor she'd be offering him one of the three-day resort packages that travel agents toss the leisure section from time to time. She wonders if Joris, Gloria and Stan have read the paper yet. Probably the phone will ring again soon or she'll hear a text message arrive.

What's the matter? Who cares? What's up? The question is all and none of these. What's next? It's that, too. It's a question about what does matter, who does care, what is happening, what to do about it? It's a question whose answer's already shaped by the peace Pat feels. What is beautiful? She can answer that by telling herself it's a place that's simple when you finally arrive at it after a lonely struggle, where your loneliness makes sense. That's how you know what to do next. Knowing what to do next is what makes you peaceful.

What's different about staying with friends is that you are what they, themselves, know you to be. You're the sum of the years they've known you to be what you are. When they say, 'Make yourself at home, Pat,' you know that they mean you can bring everything they know about you into the present – you can walk in unannounced with a Bangladeshi man in a lunghi and with a frozen smile of guilty politeness on his face, and they'll do a very slight eyebrow thing to ask if you two want a room together and when your own eyebrow thing says no, they'll make up a kid's bunk in the old sleep-out, no questions asked.

She can see Biswas in the shade of the pohutukawa by his

sleep-out. He's facing inland, gazing up the slope of mature kanuka at the blue sky beyond the ridge. In late morning, big humid grey and white clouds begin to assemble above the hills. He's told her that the rains in Bangladesh are late this year – that basanto and grisma are long, the ponds dirty and almost empty of water and fish and the trees dropping dry leaves which have to be swept up every morning and burned. Their ash goes along the bean trellises and around the okra, but these are not growing well because the rain is not coming. This, his webmaster cousin is telling him.

'What to do, Pat? What to do?' He was holding her hand, his thin, almost limp fingers familiar to her by now. 'Is finished, Pat.' He was talking about the plan to redeem Keshamoni, not the rain. But he himself had begun to dry and shrivel, as if expecting an inevitable disaster, another one, but a drought this time, not a catastrophic, life-giving flood like the one that had both taken and saved Keshamoni. But Pat sensed their plan had reached a moment of critical alertness and possibility. This was when Keshamoni would be redeemed, when her loving brother would go home and release her from the terrified guardianship of his own body, and when Pat would 'open her parachute' – the phrase her long career of staying aloft has taught her to save till last.

Rule of thumb: you can't break the Choker because it's only useful when it's on. But then, it's only useful when you need it – when you need it to keep the status quo in a holding pattern. Therefore, says a logic that Pat's tested many times behind the impervious demeanour of Great White – therefore, when the Choker's no longer strategic, when you need to gain the advantage of a forward-moving, tie-breaker decision, you can't break the Choker yourself. You have to spot the moment and the person who will break the Choker for you. The tie-breaker has to be seen to be externally inevitable. Sometimes, you have to arrange for someone to do it. Sometimes fate organises it. Fate's best. No one can blame fate for anything, but everyone can, nonetheless, shift all the blame to fate.

Ushering the distraught Biswas from the shocking piss-hovel at the back of the Leigh Hotel and into the taxi in which she'd arrived for her secret rendezvous, Pat felt the fateful moment arrive. She felt it like a surge of old pleasure and anticipation and she recognised its gift of power. She'd last felt this when shocked into horror and pity by the image of Keshamoni, knock-kneed and gangly on the little screen of the call-to-prayer cellphone in the Shoganda Bengali restaurant on the West Coast. The power surge had an electric charge of inevitability and her spirits lifted as if shocked back into action once more. She felt her own exhaustion and despair depart from her very body, from its large, tired, awkward mass, so that she felt light and graceful and muscled – like Cowgirl. Like a swimmer buoyed up by salt water. The sadness and loneliness of her mission left her, as if leaving a weary, close-to-cramp, jellyfish-welted swimmer's body at the moment the destination shape of Rangitoto became inevitable and safe. She was looking across the car park at the journalist Richard Brawn.

'Don't you worry, Biswas,' she said. 'This will work out just fine.' The rugby crowd was spilling jubilantly from the pub yelling 'Blue! Blue!' and she saw Richard Brawn smoking a cigarette by a rental car on the far side of the car park. He'd opened the pizza box on the roof of the car and was eating heartily from it with his non-cigarette hand. He waved a slice at her cheerfully as she pushed Biswas towards the back of the cab. And then he put the slice back in the box, dropped the cigarette and photographed Pat and Biswas. The thrice-repeated flash of his camera made Biswas hesitate – he turned towards Brawn as the journalist took a fourth picture and gave them the thumbs-up. Good on him: he'd nailed them both, red-handed. Pat expected to read the term 'red-handed' on at least page two come Sunday. Excellent work, Brawn. Here, why don't you accept this three-dayer at

Surfers as a small reward for a great story. I'm sure there are unmentionable things you can find to do in a tourist squeeze joint on the Gold Coast. Just don't try to write about it. It's a family destination. She gave him the fingers – he wasn't to know he'd broken the Choker for her.

'So,' begins Pat, using the peculiar sight of Biswas facing inland away from the sea view to focus her end-game with Hands-On. 'Are you resigning or what?'

Sometimes, it can be so easy, as though there exists what her Scots grandmother used to call 'Providence' or what she's heard Biswas call 'Murshid' – the guide within. She feels her confident, unassailable, mellow voice guided from her and into the Minister's ear. She can see her destination. The Biswas eyes are closed but his lips are moving. Sunlight, dappled by the pohutukawa, flickers across his face. Probably, he's singing, which is sometimes like praying. Praying for rain. Making rain happen.

Joris looks with indifference at the jetty beside which dinghies are neatly stacked and padlocked to chains in storage racks, at the clearly signposted rubbish disposal unit and at the sign prohibiting fishing from the jetty which is being ignored by kids with rods catching live bait in the tidal channel. The smell of their work and the flies attracted by it hang about the scale-encrusted planks. The possibility suggested by the live bait, that there might be much bigger game available, does not seem to occur to Joris. He does not approach the kids with his usual light, flattering interest, to find out what kinds of big game might be waiting offshore in the deep, blue waters made famous in 1925 by the celebrity American big-game fisherman and writer of cowboy novels, Zane Grey; nor what kinds of inshore sport might be exploitable by the alert entrepreneur. He is not interested in the well-appointed, recently renovated public toilets, which will add value to the location's allure for the organised tour party (for example the fishing tour party), nor is he interested in the picnic table under the big old pohutukawas where Stan and Gloria are sitting with a breakfast thermos flask of coffee and a paper bag of Sally Lunn iced buns from Leigh. He does not want one of Gloria's early-season apricots and he has not joined in the speculation about Pat's absence and the note telling them to carry on without her until tomorrow. He is unworried by the fact that the critical mass of the Leftovers has now fallen below what is required to sustain a professional conversation or even the pretence of one. He is not even interested in professional conversation and has stopped taking notes or photographing the evidence of adventure either as it exists or as it might be developed and exploited.

He has not accepted the cigarette Stan offered him, although he had asked for it only moments before. He is not looking at the sign pointing trampers along the coastal track to Ti Point and he has walked off, rudely, halfway through Gloria's desultory explanation of the shell middens along the coast, even though their presence ties in nicely with an undemanding but picturesque ramble around the headland under old pohutukawas and with fine views and outlooks to the ocean and across the broad inlet and estuary to the distant sand bar of the Omaha peninsula.

It is the kind of location where a number of possibilities might converge, allowing economies of means across organised adventure, interpreted archaeo-historical rambles and scenic picnics, but Joris's entrepreneurial spirit does not revive in these surroundings. He is not seeing here a way to trade out of his present catastrophic situation. He does not see that the same shell midden with its associated narratives of Polynesian landfall, inhabitation, warfare and European colonisation might be viewed equally from a double sea-kayak or on a sun-hatted stroll in the company of an expert tangata whenua interpreter, nor that the same inlet might equally attract eco-tourists interested in the rich biodiversity of the mangrove estuaries or thrill-seekers wanting to reel in something big that the same estuary has nurtured. He is, somehow, looking past all this physical evidence and past the ventures it might imply, as if at a miraculous mirage on the complex horizon that lifts in bands above the Omaha sandspit.

The yachts moored out in the channel towards the Omaha peninsula do not command his attention, nor does the evidence that kayakers make use of the channel both to get around the coast at Ti Point and to venture inland up the mangrove channels of the complex tidal inlets. It is clear that there already exists a viable amateur infrastructure that could be rationalised, professionalised and marketed internationally to the Adventure client base as well as to eco-tourists, ethno-archaeo-authenticists and those who would like, simply, to sit down to a catered lunch in a picnic spot under the magnificent pohutukawas and with clean ablution facilities close by. But Joris is, perversely, rudely and with an expression of dazed incredulity, looking across the trickily sparkling surface of the estuarine bay at the distant white line of the Omaha sandspit and its surf beach – not at a foreground rich with cultourism possibilities.

He is looking at a distantly structured view, a kind of multiple horizon. It rises in stages from the prevaricacious shimmer of the wind-chopped estuary and its flurries of white-capped waves. It ascends through the line of distant breakers between the teal-blue sea and the brilliant white sand of the spit and up through the khaki and olive-green line of sandspit flora. Above the white beach and its obscurely smudged, greenish dune plants, is another strange, pink-and-grey band which flashes and glitters. Above this unexpected layer in the view are the further-back hills, covered in scruffy scrub with ochre and yellow clay gashes where holiday houses are being built. The hills rise into a blue sky in which humid white and grey clouds are beginning to assemble. It is a complex but familiar view and its strata are easy to identify: the bottom layer of sea, the breakers, the sandspit, the greenish coastal plants, the hills and the sky. But now, there is the flashy pink-and-grey band between the dowdy sandspit vegetation and the hills with their colonising gashes of clay.

Joris's gaze drifts repeatedly upwards through these strata as if buoyed by a mental flotation device and then sinks back again to the newly inserted mystery band of flashing pink and grey. His gaze and his thoughts settle, finally, on this band – Gloria, miffed by his arrogant walking away from her little lecture, watches him tilt his elegant head to one side in the gesture of droll opportunism that had been his familiar trademark before the disaster of the Panekiri Bluff.

'Go on, Pat.' In other words, you must be joking.

'Of course *you* don't resign, sir. I do. Just kidding.'

'I'm afraid you have to, Pat.'

'I take all the blame.'

'It was your watch, Pat.'

'I lied to you about Mohammed Biswas.' Pat urges the Minister forward.

'And you disobeyed an instruction to sort it out. After assuring me you would.'

Biswas is experimenting with the deckchair. He reclines it and lowers himself back into it, modestly gathering his lunghi between his skinny, dark legs.

Right, then.

'But no one's told Richard Brawn at the *National Inquirer* about Cowgirl.com yet,' continues Pat smoothly, making sure all the words are clear and distinct, as if discussing something mundane, like the catering for a product launch at the national museum, for example, the launch of the Cultural Tourism Initiative project about a century ago.

'About *what?*'

'Cowgirl.com, sir. The fat woman porn site. With the zips in it. There was an episode about the Chasm.'

'I'm not following you, Pat.'

'The one you've watched, Minister. The *Chasm* episode. With me in it.'

'I don't know what you're talking about. Are you mad? With you in it?'

'Margie's logged you.'

Now, the Minister's silence is different. Though he won't have figured it out completely yet, the applause of amazed blood in his ears is the sound of Keshamoni's freedom, the body-heat that makes his eyes bulge out into the office from which Margie's been temporarily barred is Biswas embracing his sister, and what makes his hair stand on end is the sight of Pat's parachute opening, out there, in the sky beyond his window, where he's often looked for the comfort of emptiness, for evidence that good old Pat's done her thing as usual, that there are no portents sky-written for all to see above the capital city and its seat of power.

He, too, is going to be free, but alone, and on notice. His silence in the cellphone that Pat has, momentarily, placed in her lap, is no longer measuring her silence and her ability to sustain it. Now, the Minister's silence is waiting to be told what to do. As it has so often in the past waited to be told what to do, but never for the last time.

'So, here's how it can go. Sir.'

The Cultural Tourism Initiative team's mini-bus follows a Kea campervan across the causeway to the Omaha sandspit real estate leisure development.

'Aha,' says Joris. 'See? This is interesting. What I tell you? This is: a lot of money.'

'Offshore investors,' says Gloria sourly. 'Only people making money round here are the banks and the builders.'

'What about people installing satellite TV dishes? Saunas?'

'Waste disposal,' adds Gloria. 'Lawn sprinklers.' She makes the terms sound like communicable diseases.

'Money is money,' enthuses Joris. He is right in the band of the view that had signalled to him from the Ti Point jetty across the bay. He seems to have woken from a torpor or depression. It is as though the air of the realty venture on the sandspit has revived him.

'Foreshore is foreshore,' says Gloria, contrapuntally.

'Is Frank and Babs!' yells Joris, suddenly. 'Toot, Stan. Toot!'

Stan toots the mini-bus horn once, minimally, without comment. The Kea campervan wobbles on its course but recovers. Gloria's silence is making a point of not picking a fight. And indeed, it is possible to see where money has been spent on one side of the causeway and not on the other. On their right, a mangrove swamp at the limit of the estuarine arm survives between neglected farmland and the fast-growing leisure real estate of the spit. On their left, the other hemisphere of the tidal swamp has been in-filled and now supports a golf course where water sprinklers make rainbows above groomed fairways. Elderly men and women in check-patterned shorts and peaked caps are trundling their golf clubs towards the links. Some are riding on motorised karts. Money has also been spent on paving the sandspit settlement's roads with interlocking red bricks and on decoratively branded street signage. Perhaps the bricks are designed to have a less industrial appearance than black asphalt and the signage is intended to mark the location as distinct from everyday suburbia. The place has been branded as native and natural. The berms are extensively planted with flax which is flourishing and with hibiscus, which is not. Many of the crescents and side streets are named after native plants: there is a 'Tawa Grove', for example, though tawa would not have grown on the sandspit, nor would the hibiscus favoured by the landscape gardeners of the berms. The golf course has largely closed out half of the mangrove estuary protected behind the sandspit; the remaining half is fed by a culverted channel across which the causeway suggests access to a safely moated zone of privilege and security.

'Follow them!' cries Joris, as the campervan doggedly seeks the end of the spit still under development – the glittering, miraculous mirage spotted by Joris from across the water. An austerely rectilinear, grey, two-storey house with feature corrugated aluminium panels and immense smoked-glass picture windows is under construction next to a pink, shipping-container-shaped box on stilts above its triple carport and a silver-roofed, UV-screened barn based on the hemispherical, steel-frame structure of an appliance shed. What they have in common is their immense expanse of viewing glass and the fact that none of them has a view of the sea. They have views of each other. The street-side lamps are curved structures from which the globes stoop down attentively. They imply a need for illumination to pay sympathetic attention to the reddish concrete skin of the earth, as though there are hidden meanings beneath it whose glimmerings require super-sensitive perception. There are above-ground junction boxes from which unresolved cables are still sprouting. Few of the builders are present – it is Sunday. Nor are there any other people to be seen. A sinuous boardwalk leaves the red-bricked footpath in the direction of the beach and the sea on the far side of the low dunes. There is a large billboard near the boardwalk with a picture of a tern on it: this is also a bird sanctuary.

The campervan of the American videoists seems to hesitate at this unresolved or simply unfinished terminus in the real estate project that is the Omaha sandspit. It has a purpose, though – after hesitating at the turning bay by the bird sanctuary billboard as if to check out progress on the housing initiatives, it seeks another street, an older, more finished one, with no-exit groves and crescents coming off it. The corrugated-iron builder's sheds, concrete mixers and piles of timber give way to footpaths that are almost suburban. The grass of the berms has withered to yellow with here and there an anomalous green strip where a house is occupied and sprinklers are at work. Though it is a Sunday, the picture windows of the holiday houses are mostly blinded or curtained and the roller doors of their garages are shut.

Following the Kea campervan, the CTI team mini-bus drives slowly through these streets of the blind.

'We are here why, Joris?' demands Gloria – she has slumped down in her seat and is staring out the window with sullen horror. 'This is plain fucking creepy, any way you look at it.' Ahead, the campervan wobbles to a halt by a turn-off and a street sign. 'Zombies,' says Gloria. 'Any minute now. Foreshore zombies.'

'Pull over!' orders Joris. Stan parks abruptly behind the campervan and gets out, slamming his door. He walks across the road and sits on a concrete block wall with a half-pipe terracotta border on top. His cigarette smoke rises through shimmering heat-haze in front of the TexMex villa behind the wall. A street sign finger-post is almost obscured by the substantial kowhai tree that shades the berm on the street corner. The tile-roofed villa has a complicated nest of television aerials and satellite dishes sprouting from it and there are rows of pollarded dwarf yuccas in pots along its first-floor patio. A bougainvillea has almost expired down a trellis on one half of the street-front wall and this provides a fading, pastel backdrop for Stan.

Joris has begun to approach the campervan of his acquaintances Frank and Babs, but his attention seems suddenly to be jerked back towards Stan on the other side of the road. Stan's expression, at once truculent and indifferent, does not react to Joris's stare at first. But then Joris begins to laugh, pointing in Stan's direction. He doubles up. He makes funny falsetto hooting noises that are nothing like his normal, unamused, serve-all mirth. He is really laughing at something funny and Stan stands up and prepares to take action. But when he throws his cigarette away belligerently and takes a step in Joris's direction, he sees that Joris is actually pointing and looking past him.

Joris is looking at the finger-post street sign under the kowhai tree. It is clearly the sign that Frank and Babs have been seeking, because they have now descended from their

Kea and are unlocking the chain-link fence to the TexMex villa's garage.

The sign on the corner next to Frank and Babs's place reads, 'Success Court. No Exit,' in soothing white lettering on a green background.

Pat watches Mohammed Baul Biswas stand up again out of his deckchair. He's looking up at the sky as his cellphone rings. It's calling him to prayer. He makes a cross shape with his arms extended and rotates like a dervish. Pat guesses he's reminding himself of the direction of Mecca. It's hard to imagine Mecca in the New Zealand bush although, on the East Coast, you'd have to say that the direction of the sea was pretty reliably the direction of east. Biswas goes into his bunkhouse sleep-out under the old pohutukawa tree and emerges with his prayer mat and his little hat. He washes himself with the garden hose which is running on a lemon tree next to a feijoa hedge. She watches him investigate a feijoa and take an experimental bite. He spits out the first attempt and tries again, squeezing some of its contents free of their rind. He savours the fruit carefully, collecting the rinds in his extended fingers. These he places fussily behind the trellis at the back of the feijoas. Then he has to wash and rinse his mouth out three times all over again. He hawks and spits heartily and puts his hat on. Then he does that thing with his ears and begins to pray.

Pat guesses he must be facing in the direction of Mecca. She's never thought about distance looking that way in New Zealand.

Her right telephone ear's burning hot but the silence around it, since she finally put the cellphone down, is utterly cool and tranquil – not quite completely silent, because her inner ear's still humming a bit from the long phone call, but peaceful. The silence of the phone, extending on from the Minister's silence, seems to have reached inside her large head which feels quiet and empty, like an argument-filled meeting room that everyone's left but you. The noise of words sinks into a peaceful sediment of resolution and closure. Then the sounds of the scruffy bush-section garden, the cicadas and the distant ocean and its birds begin to fill her head up again. It seems like a long time since she's heard these sounds.

Mohammed Baul Biswas is looking at a typical New Zealand scene from a look-out on the coast, but she imagines he's seeing his sister. She can see his lips moving and she knows that he's saying verses from the Koran, but she imagines he's talking to Keshamoni, telling her not-to-worry. Now, everything is okay. Is okay Biz, isn't it?

The inside of the TexMex smells of household cleaners and heat trapped in overstuffed sofa cushions. From the patio with its rows of stunted yuccas, there is a view along Success Court, which is deserted. A trailer-sailer is parked in the dead-end turning bay. When Frank switches on the mains power, a default air-conditioning unit hums into life and he knows to deactivate the independent security alarm in the pre-programmed grace-time of three minutes. Punching in the new security code on the alarm, he steps back with a cry of triumph: '28-12-05!'

'28-12-05, Babs!'

'28-12-05, Frank!'

'That's our growth,' explains Frank to his guests, the Leftovers. 'Franchising out at twenty-eight per cent expansion per annum as at December 2005! My friends! Doesn't get any more secure than that! That's our code, Babs!'

'The code, Frank!'

'So: this?' asks Joris, miming slipping and falling over in the shower, miming showering himself sitting down, miming himself in a domestic hammam unit fanning heat from his face. 'This is here? You got this here? Like we talked?'

'Allow me,' proposes Frank to the Cultural Tourism team.

'See, here's what we got here. Safe beach and next best thing to private on the coast. Only one way in, lessen you come by sea. You like to come in by sea, got one of those blue water boats, we got safe moorings round back of the spit in the estuary. Deep water in the channel never going to silt up, golf course holds back the run-off off of them hills.'

'Run-off off of,' tries Babs admiringly. She opens the door to the expansively tiled facility out back. Sunlight enters it through UV-screened glass panels in the roof. The tiles are white with an imprinted shell motif – a nautilus. This textures the surface, improving grip. There are also roughened tile tracks between the major facilities. The tracks are two tiles wide, one for each foot. The roughened, non-slip tiles have the surface appearance of a white, shell-sand beach.

'She's real flat, like you folks have noticed I dare say. Every unit got drive-on secure parking. Shut down right behind you afore you have to step out of your car or wagon. In the nature of the sandspit.'

'Nature of the sandspit.' Babs, too, emphasises the two-part specificity and completeness of the term for the land they have built on.

'Anybody say not to build on sand like in the Bible, well, they're wrong. She beds down real firm and works real easy. Throw up a unit in just one month yo to go.'

'Yo to go.'

'Then, we're out of our car or wagon in the secure drive-on, we got elevators in the units and we got wheelchair elevators lift you right up into the living area come that's necessary. We got dumb waiters go straight up to the food preparation areas and the coolers you want to get your foodstuffs, beverages and domestic supplies up there the easy way. In the garages, we make allowances for mobile golf carts you want to trundle right to the course like that. Dignified.'

'Just drive straight on down like that,' agrees Babs. 'Me, I like to do that.'

'Temperature control. Atmospherics. Humidity. Want a little breeze in off the sea? Tell you about it. See, this unit is the first one we built out here, but you just point and click.

This is how we like our homes. This is how we fixed it in Fort Lauderdale where it gets real hot let me tell you. Real hot. Some old folks.'

'Real hot.' Babs is preparing the first of the appliances for inspection. She does not complete Frank's musing about 'some old folks' – they both let the obscure threat of the heat to some old folks hang unspoken in the shining, hygienic, safe, facilities room.

'Same when you want to fix the temperature of these units. No taps, see? Too many accidents with taps. Touch pads we prefer. Just rest your hand right there. No sudden twisting movements. Don't hardly need to move. This is our home away from home.'

'Home away from home.'

'See, people like to come here. It's safe. It's natural. It's pure. You got cute birds, beautiful mountains. We took this promotional video material, it's just gorgeous!'

'Gorgeous, Frank. He's so good with that thing.'

'See, this here's the Hydromass doored sit-down bath. Slide you in there, right off your wheelchair if that's the requirement, otherwise just take a seat real comfortable and easy. Close the door here. Got the finger-touch control pad fill her up any temperature you want. This door never leaks, why? Because the water-pressure inside presses out against the seal. That's the beauty of it.'

'The beauty of it. Never spills.'

'Then we got this one here. The superior model. Same as before only you got the hydromassage. You got the massage on top of the mass. These jets right here, you're in, slid in, door shut, water temperature just how you like it real comfortable, then a little bitty pressure on the control pads and hey!'

'Hey!'

'We got hydromassage. Feels real good, don't it, Babs?'

'Real good, Frank. Real soothing after a day on the golf course.'

'But that's not all. Here we got the vertical unit. Got the cascade, the lateral jets, the jets for the soles of the feet, the infrared spot, the lumbar jets and the, um, cervical jets. Not to mention, of course, you can fill 'er up, just like the Hydromass sit-down. And then!'

'And then!'

'Not to forget our piece of resistance, is what we call it, don't we, Babs?'

'Our piece of resistance, Frank.'

'The Hydromass Hammam. She's got that essence diffuser as well.'

'The essence diffuser,' chorus Joris and Babs, in unison.

'That's right. So there you have it. The bath, the shower, the massage, the hammam . . . and the essence diffuser!'

Joris seats himself in the sliding-in bench of the combination hammam and Hydromass superior sit-down bath. He slots himself, fully clad, into the shining interior of the device and suspends his finger above the touchpad. Gloria and Stan look at his elegantly greyed head above the steam-seal collar of the hammam. He is shining with hope. His sinking adventure threshold and his rising demographic meet and greet right here at Frank and Babs. Good-2-Go meets Hydromassage.

'Waste,' begins Frank, delicately.

But the CTI Leftovers know it is time to move on.

'I stay a while,' says Joris's head on top of the sit-down hydromassage hammam. 'Catch you up,' he lies.

'Okay, Joris, suit yourself,' says Gloria, not wanting this to sound like a farewell. 'You want your stuff out of the bus?'

'Boris,' says the professional outdoor experience expert, his voice resonating slightly within the chamber of the appliance. 'Call me Boris. I like that better.'

twenty-five

Hospitality and Triumph

Stan pulls over in the shade of a small stand of bush with Historic Places signage in white and brown. A tractor goes past with a trailer full of hay bales, followed by a dog. The dog diverts to piss on the team mini-bus before streaking off after the hay. A rooster is crowing and crowing on the other side of the hill.

'Sounds like bloody old Uncle Mat,' says Gloria.

The place is high and once Gloria, Stan and Pat have passed through the waharoa at the entrance to the old battleground of Ruapekapeka, a blue-misted vista opens out below the hilltop.

'How the hell did they get all that gear up here back then?' Pat wonders.

'You mean the Brits?' Gloria is walking steadily, almost formally towards the back of the old battlefield, past the remains of dugouts and earth walls. In one hand she has a folder with her CTI report on manaakitanga and in the other a sprig of kawakawa from the bushes by the car park.

'Well, your lot knew what was here, didn't they?' Pat is keeping pace with Gloria, but Stan is dawdling, peering into the remains of trenches. 'In the middle of the old forest?'

'Kawiti did, no road signs in 1846, nothing to tell you there was water up here, either, but they'd been walking all over the place for generations. Knew where to fortify the summit. Knew where to cut big timber to open a field of fire and build a stockade and they knew how to dig and cover bunkers and tunnels. Hone Heke knew the way, too, when he turned up to reinforce Kawiti's garrison. The Brits didn't see him arrive. Uncle Mat used to say, "We know all this, girl, what do you want a whole lot of signs for?"' Gloria stops near the back of the fenced-off pa site. 'I'm back, Uncle,' she says, 'grumpy old beggar.'

The signposted Historic Places track wends back downhill to the positions occupied by British troops who hauled their heavy artillery all the way up here from the coast. Stan is taking a photo of it.

Gloria lays her kawakawa sprig on a grassy stockade mound by the back fence. 'Here I am, Uncle. I've brought you something.' She opens her folder with the report chapter in it. 'No need to hang around, Pat. Won't take a minute.'

'I'd like to, if it's okay with you,' says Pat. She sits down on the damp grass. Stan has inserted himself into the remains of a dugout and is peering over the top. The rooster goes on yelling on the other side of the hill.

Gloria puts her spectacles on and begins to read her report to the kawakawa leaves on the mound.

'E kore taua tangata e manaakitia e Ngapuhi.'

The new *Challenge* section of Dr Hinemoana Oliver's Manaakitanga chapter has been refashioned as a counterpart to Dr Nancy Shapiro's. 'The advantage,' suggests Dr Oliver, 'did not, in the end, lie with outright military victory. It lay within the mana-sustaining contexts of manaakitanga – of hospitality. The outcome of the war in the North was not decided at Ruapekapeka, which the British declared to be a victory but which the Maori knew was not, nor even the year before at Ohaeawai, which the British knew to be a defeat and which the Maori knew to be their victory. The Ngapuhi of Kawiti and Hone Heke also knew better than to claim either Ohaeawai or Ruapekapeka as final victories of their own, though they could have, since the British had failed to subdue Ruapekapeka through heavy bombardment and had in fact then been lured into an ambush.'

> The Ngapuhi confederation of Hone Heke and Kawiti knew that victory lay not just in the military conquest of your enemy, but in the diplomatic skill with which you were hospitable to the futures that your victory had opened.

You should be proud of me, Uncle. You should all be proud of me. This is the best thing I've ever done.

> Hone Heke, whose understanding of the power of rhetoric and symbolism had already been demonstrated by his repeatedly felling the British flagpole at Kororareka, with its rangitiratanga- and mana-offending customs excise signalling balls, now claimed a derisive rhetorical victory by presenting Governor George Grey with a pig as a token of peace. This mocking act of manaakitanga referenced Heke's previous dismissal of Governor FitzRoy's bounty on his head of £100, which Heke had likened to the base transaction of purchasing a pig rather than winning a victory.

You'd be proud of me too, Ants.

> But this was an easy jibe whose levity was a measure of its unimportance. It was a gesture whose wit increased Heke's mana and diminished Grey's by its throwaway irony. The serious event by means of which a significant agreement was reached did not occur until 1849 and it had almost nothing to do with Governor Grey, although he was present and although the great hakiri or feast of reconciliation organised by Tamati Waka Nene was understood by the British to be the moment when peace was declared in the North. The importance of Waka Nene's immense and sumptuous hakiri, whose ostentation was deliberate and hyperbolic, can be measured against the derisive insignificance of the single pig presented to Grey

by Heke two years previously, and this comparison would not have been lost on the many hundreds attending the feast of reconciliation. Also important would have been the fact that it was the enemy of Hone Heke and Kawiti, their relative Tamati Waka Nene who had aligned himself with the British, who was providing for this sumptuous diplomatic hospitality. The peace that was being declared was principally between the factions of Ngapuhi and incidentally with the British. It reconciled or established a balance between the mana of Hone Wiremu Heke Pokai of Ngapuhi extending from Kaikohe through Pakaraka, Waitangi, Paihia, and Rawhiti, and the mana of Tamati Waka Nene's Ngapuhi and Ngati Hao iwi and hapu in the Hokianga.

I never forgot where I came from, Uncle. Who supported me. Even when you wouldn't talk to me. Even when you didn't want me to come home. Even when I convinced myself I didn't want to come home.

You will not find this landscape of mana, let us call it, in the public signage with which most New Zealanders and visitors to New Zealand navigate the official infrastructure of the country. Does this matter?

'I am responding, now,' continues Gloria's wero or challenge, 'to the challenge presented by my highly esteemed colleague, Dr Nancy Shapiro, in the first part of this Authenticity and Hospitality section of the Cultural Tourism Initiative report. In doing so, I am offering a wero of my own. What happens when the Minister picks it up, if indeed he decides to do so, is for others to determine and for time to judge.'

Pat laughs and applauds Gloria's operatic presentation of the manaakitanga report. The rooster has shut up. 'See?' says Pat. 'That's shut him up.'

And I don't think I'm more important any more, koro. Maybe I did, for a while.

'Wouldn't count on it,' says Gloria. 'Just getting his breath back.'

Stan is mooching about just within earshot. 'You jokers nearly finished?' he yells. 'It's going to piss down in a minute.' Dark purple clouds sail across the hilltop and the patches of long grass shiver in a sudden wind.

'Just ignore him,' says Pat. 'He's dying to get across to his favourite Colin McCahon moment, over at Ninety Mile Beach.'

'Nearly finished, anyway,' says Gloria. 'Couple more pages. You go, Pat.'

'Not on your life,' says Pat. 'But I think I'll stand for the rest. Getting a wet arse, here.'

The Cultural Tourism Initiative team was privileged to be welcomed by the Museum of New Zealand Te Papa Tongarewa at the outset of its journey, and to be shown some of the great store of taonga of which the museum is kaitiaki. It was hoped that, by viewing these taonga, the team-members would be inspired to measure and appreciate the dimensions of their responsibility. Among the treasures we were shown, and about which the museum's experts spoke to us, were two that were not apparently connected by any system of signs like those described by Dr Shapiro as constituting a public infrastructure. These two great treasures seemed, indeed, to be total strangers to each other: to be out of sight of each other within their shared home in the nation's treasure house.

One of these treasures is a painting by a naval officer, Captain Richard Aldworth Oliver, called *Feast in the Bay of Islands*. It was painted in 1849 on the occasion of Tamati Waka Nene's great manaakitanga in the North. The other is a taiaha kura or spear decorated with scarlet kaka feathers of Ngati Hao that belonged to Tamati Waka Nene and which he had, once, gifted to the Wesleyan missionary Gideon Smales as a mark of protection and spiritual sponsorship.

The rain arrives – the purple clouds unleash a sudden, big-dropped squall. Stan runs yelling for the mini-bus. The long grass on the hilltop flattens under the weight of water and steamy mist blots out the wide, blue vista across forest and distant pasture. The pages of Gloria's report are getting wet but she reads on.
Just you listen to me, Uncle – you too, Antsy.

The careful reader of the painting by Captain Oliver, having gasped at the scale and grandeur of the feast platform, will notice the scarlet pennants fluttering from its masts. The observer of the remnants of kaka kura or scarlet parrot feathers attached to the awe or decorated collar below the tongue of the taiaha may wonder if there is a connection between the signage, let us call it, of the scarlet pennants and that of the scarlet feathers. And indeed, an important narrative attaches to the significance of the kura (red) and of the kaka kura, the red parrot, and the rich discourse that surrounds the red feathers of this esteemed parrot. The narrative linking kaka kura, Waka Nene, the taiaha, and Reverend Smales, would extend to the customary association between kaka kura as leaders of flocks and important ariki or hereditary leaders such as Waka Nene as rangatira or chiefs of iwi. The rarity and significance of kakahu kura or kaka feather cloaks would also be relevant.

Back at the mini-bus, Stan is tooting the horn. 'I'll wring his neck,' Pat promises. She is sheltering Gloria's pages with her jacket. But then the rain squall stops as abruptly as it began and the sun comes out. Both Gloria and Pat are standing there, drenched, while steam begins to rise around them. The usual after-rain birdsong starts up.

'Nancy would have loved this,' says Pat. 'That was one weird little Aussie.'

'Especially this bit,' says Gloria. 'Thanks, Ants.'

Was this 'signage' read by Governor Grey? By the Reverend Smales? Can it be read today? Is it possible for us to redeem the magnificent and chiefly parrot, whose mountain-dwelling relative, the kea, has become the performing beggar-clown and hostage of the tourist viewing platforms of the scenic south? Can we recover the dignity and mana inherent in the strategic and professional hospitality of the 1849 hakiri of Tamati Waka Nene as a benchmark against which to measure our commercially driven industry? Can we recover a sense of the phantom narratives – the spooks, as Dr Shapiro has called them – that haunt our cultural landscape?

There, koro.

'This is my challenge to the Minister's review. Kaore e kume roatia te korero, heoi ano, noho pai mai I roto I nga manaakitanga katoa.'

Gloria bends and rakes up a handful of grass and muddy soil. She lifts it to her face. 'Sweet,' she says. 'So that's that, koro.' She drops the grass and dirt next to the kawakawa leaves – her hand is wet and muddy and so, now, is her report. 'And that,' says Gloria, closing her file and handing it to Pat, 'is why I dragged the Leftovers up here. Also,' she now adds, 'because Joris was right, the bugger, good riddance. I'm calling it a day. That's some of my whanau over there making all that racket. Think I'll go to ground for a bit.'

Pat holds the wet, muddy report carefully away from her sodden clothes. '"The diplomatic skill with which you were hospitable to the futures that your victory had opened,"' quotes Pat. 'Hell's teeth, Gloria, do you expect anyone a hundred metres either side of Hands-On to understand what you're talking about?'

'Not really,' says Gloria. 'But you do, I reckon. So does Nancy and so does my bloody old uncle.' Gloria is washing the mud off her hands at the spring. She lifts a handful to her mouth as well. 'That's what matters.'

The rooster is crowing again on the other side of the hill from the bunker- and dugout-cratered battlefield and the hay-trailer dog has sought these strangers out and begins to bark importantly at them from the edge of the historic site. The driver of the tractor appears and whistles the dog. Gloria waves at him – she and Pat are walking in his direction through the soaking grass. 'My nephew,' she says. 'He took over koro's farm.'

Here's how it will go. Pat will take all the blame. This is her plan. She's explained it to the Leftovers. The Minister will act decisively and sack her. He's agreed to all this. What's orchestrated to look like a modest media campaign to explain what's been going on will be boosted to blow out as a major scandal. The Minister will act even more decisively and will have substantial material prepared for Question Time in the House. Pat will have prepared the substantial material, as she always has in the past. It'll be officially disclosed that Pat's developed an improper, conflict-of-interest relationship with an international member of the CTI team and, contrary to orders, has secretly kept him in the country at the project's expense and, as the *National Inquirer* has revealed, has been visiting him in his accommodation separate from the CTI team.

Mr Mohammed Baul Biswas, however, will have been sent home this time and won't be available for comment.

The project will be shut down ahead of schedule but the contractual requirements of its members will be met. A report (the *Assessing Cultural Tourism Initiatives: A Comparative Model* report) will be provided to the Department of Tourism, as agreed. The report will be widely praised as innovative and challenging. It'll be endorsed by members of the Minister's peer review panel. It'll become part of the case-study resource in the Department of Leisure Studies at the Albany Campus of Massey University.

The Minister will approve the balance of the CTI budget to complete the report and achieve contractual sign-off. The delegation of the sign-off will revert to him from the former project manager, Dr Patricia Smart. As Minister responsible, he'll want to take the closure in hand personally. It's not for nothing that the Minister's known as Hands-On.

The decisiveness of his actions and the quality of the report (all the more commendable considering its circumstances) will be to the Minister's credit. He'll be praised by the Prime Minister as an example of answerability and open government. The positive deluge will swamp any attempts at further scuttlebutt. The story's done its dash, anyway. The only good news is bad news. There's not a lot to be wrung out of the rag of 'cultourism' once the inter-racial sexual scandal is over.

The Minister, whose vision and leadership have been endorsed, will confidently continue to park his arse in the chair of the office whose door once opened to admit Cowgirl. He'll know, also, that the balance available in the CTI budget's roughly what's required to take up the slack in the ransom demand on Keshamoni Biswas. It's enough liquid stuff to bolster the argument for the asset value of Cowgirl.com as collateral for Miss Keshamoni. At the present rate of profit and asset value growth combined, it's enough to buy Miss Keshamoni back and bring her home. This isn't information the Minister's likely to talk about, even in his uneasy sleep.

The Minister will approve the expenditure and the CTI team will complete their contractual obligations on time and within budget.

No one will talk to Richard Brawn about Cowgirl.com and, once it's all over, Pat will destroy the back-up CD of the Minister's on-line log. The Ministry's agreed to sponsor Margie's degree course in the Department of Leisure Studies at Massey University – the Minister's said he'll miss Margie.

This suits the Minister and it also suits Pat who, in addition, won't be around to remind him that he did once speak to her about his daughter's scheme to open a retreat in the Marlborough Sounds where people get smeared with cactus juice.

'I still can't believe you did that,' says Gloria, wiping away farewell tears. 'Cowgirl. Bloody hell.' She waves again at her waiting nephew. 'No,' she says, 'I won't tell him. Or Stan. Or anyone. Promise.'

'It could still all go pear-shaped,' says Pat. 'This we know how?'

'We're experienced?' suggests Gloria.

'Sieves leak,' says Pat. 'It's their nature. We know this. But what the hell.'

'What the hell,' agrees Gloria.

'No regrets,' suggests Pat.

'Only two,' says Gloria. 'I wanted Antsy to come here with me. And I wanted her to meet Uncle Mat.'

'That's only one.' Pat grasps the wet, chilly hand with which Gloria has scooped up spring water. 'Bet your life they're getting on like a house on fire.'

'True.' Gloria retains Pat's hand.

Stan has already walked off in the direction of the team mini-bus. When he meets Gloria's nephew on the far side of the old pa site, the two of them light up cigarettes.

'I told Stan to finish the itinerary on his own,' says Pat. 'There's only one more stop, anyway, after Waitangi, and I'll go that far with him – Ahipara at Ninety Mile Beach. Stan can commune with the ghost of Colin McCahon all by himself before he heads back to Wellington. He told me it's a special McCahon spot.' Pat waits for Gloria to ask her where she's going next, but Gloria drops her hand and heads off towards the smoking men along the mown path across the grassed-over fortifications. Her nephew and his dog both run towards her. There are piping larks high in the sky and a single jet contrail heading out into the Pacific towards Los Angeles. It doesn't matter, anyway. Pat thinks Gloria will soon get sick of the noisy rooster and even sooner will start to miss her pinot noir.

Then Gloria turns around and walks back. She has the 'Where next?' question written all over her face.

Pat points up at the contrail unzipping the blue sky.

twenty-six

Doubt

The guy who fixes bicycles next to the food stalls at the back of the bazaar off Kemal Ataturk Avenue near DIT Circle 2 in Gulshan, Dhaka, has made a papier maché scale model of the Shaheed Minar monument to the Language Martyrs. The papier maché is made out of newspaper pages featuring poems in honour of the martyrs of 1952 and in addition the bike-repair guy has pasted a copy of the Amar Ekushey poem by Mahbub-Ul-Alam on the side of his stall above the platform where he keeps the recycled spare tyres tied in bundles according to quality. The tilted-forward shape of the Shaheed Minar with two rectangles flanking it on both sides is perfectly in scale and clearly in view from the road and the busy footpath beside the bazaar. The bicycle wallah has not painted over the papier maché as you might have expected, Biswas thinks, because he wants the cut-up fragments of the Ekushey poems to be seen. He is paying his respects to the martyrs, but he is also taking out a little insurance against the Awami League vigilantes who might decide to punish him for working during hartal.

This is the place where Mr Mohammed Baul Biswas always alights from his rickshaw in the mornings although, occasionally, he treats himself to a stroll in the park up Gulshan Avenue where the rich amma and didi make their haughty circuits of the green lake.

On this morning of Ekushey he notices the miniature Shaheed Minar monument and the rickshaw wallah sees him notice it and makes a quick, clever joke about what might happen if the law-makers in the Jatiya Sangsad cared as much as the bike-repair guy and bothered to turn up for work as well as pay their respects. The joke is clearly also an oblique reference to the fact that the rickshaw wallah himself is working on a day when he might expect to be pulled from his bike and beaten by Awami League hartal vigilantes. Biswas has the money for the rickshaw wallah ready in his hand as he alights and looks admiringly at the miniature Shaheed Minar, but because of the joke he gets his wallet out to find an extra five thaka note for the rickshaw and a two thaka for the bike repair guy. Then they all stand around for a minute or two commenting on how many people are working, the dryness of grisma and the number of rapid action battalion crossfire killings.

He knows he is now running late, but partly because of that and because he feels resentful anyway, Biswas decides to have a cup of tea and a dhupi in the stalls behind the bazaar. Some men are erecting a canopy over the stalls and there will be some special festival food available at lunch time with extra tables set out in the roadway. The flower stalls across the road are full of white gladioli and Biswas drinks his tea with little nibbles of the sweet dhupi while watching the four-wheel-drive Pajeros of the Aid consultants and diplomats pull in to buy bunches of the long-stemmed, dripping Ekushey blooms. It is not that the foreigners emerging from these vehicles and getting their drivers to bargain for them are strange to him, but he feels a great distance has opened up between the man who will shortly unlock the door to his little Gulshan bureau on the second floor of the bazaar complex behind the Philips Lighting and the man who felt the big white woman, Pat, push his head down and into the taxi in the car park noisy with mod-drunk men and women shouting 'Blue! Blue! Blue!'

When he thinks of that woman it is with a complex emotion of great love and gratitude and awe at her strength and wisdom. But also feeling disgust that returned to his body few days after seeing Keshamoni walk out of the Air Parabat arrivals in Chittagong airport with a synthetic rice-sack bag in her hand and a smile of great happiness on her face. When he looks at Keshamoni he is also, every time, not looking at Cowgirl and this not-looking turns his stomach. He eats dhupi and andosha and swallows sweet tea to soothe his disgust and he is becoming a little plump around the middle and under his chin.

'This is how you will live, Kaka,' says the crow of Mohammed Biswas. 'You will sleep when you wake and you will wake when you sleep, and your life cannot be sweet because you have poisoned your eyes.'

'But I didn't look, ever,' says Biswas in his crow-dreams and when he sees the foreign women buying the gladioli on the other side of the road. 'Didn't look, didn't see. I promised.' But when his crow laughs at him he knows that it is right, he has poisoned his eyes and there are ghosts and phantoms that he does see now at the edges of his vision, so that he has to flick his head away from them in order to not-see and as well as becoming little-bit plump he has begun to twitch his head so that Keshamoni thinks he is getting old too soon.

And he is sad much of the time, because whenever he looks at Keshamoni and is happy, this happiness makes him sad that he will now, forever, feel sondehu doubt for the great soktishali woman who helped him and saved his sister. He knows that his doubt and sometimes his disgust is the sacrifice she made and he knows he should fight this feeling and overcome it. But he knows he cannot and he also knows that Patricia knows he will not. He is sad that he has to be sad and that nothing can change it. He is sad when he and Keshamoni are happy looking at the DVD videos of beautiful New Zealand views on the wide-screen plasma. He is sad when Keshamoni is happy going to the training college and when he is happy watching her go.

Next, having finished his tea and drunk a glass of water, Biswas listens to the Baul singer with the accordion and gives him some money for food. The singer is on his way to the Banani train station where he will jump a train and sing to captive travellers. Finally, knowing he is now very late but not caring because he would not have come all the way up here from Bakshi on Ekushey day without a special appointment, he walks to the front of the bazaar on Circle 2 and ascends the stairs to the light fixtures shop in front of his office.

The bomb explodes as he enters the corridor past the lighting shop. It was expecting him to be in the office by now. It blows the front out of his office and on its way to Biswas its blast collects the contents of a storage rack full of fluorescent tubes. It shatters the tubes and blows them into his eyes and hurls him out and down a storey into the road where the sparse, hartal-nervous traffic is not-seeing the traffic lights.

twenty-seven

Viewing

Stan's smoking inside the mini-bus which is empty although, being empty of them, he finds it a bloody sight easier to talk to the members of the Cultural Tourism Initiative project team. None of the buggers did much listening that he ever noticed and half of them did precious little looking either where views were concerned. So he might as well talk to them now as then, what's more they're missing what might be the best bit of the whole itinerary though you wouldn't know it at first sight.

That's because when Ahipara enters the windscreen of the bus on the road from Kerikeri the hill's shape's nothing to write home about. It's a big feature, agreed, but it looks more like a lot of hills and headlands you've seen already, than like something unusual, such as Mitre Peak. It looks like something you know. There's the gradual slope up and to the west and then the steeper slope down towards the sea with a kind of skirt at the bottom. That forehead sort of shape. It's always dark, for some reason, though there's a kind of on-its-back L-shape of cleared pasture on the flank facing the road. That scribbly, scruffy kind of scrub everywhere else. Probably because it got burned off all the time to grow fern, like Hinemoana said. Some pines planted on it, probably by the farmers who own the red shed at the bottom, the one whose roof slopes the other way to the hill. It's got one white-framed window, like a little eye, and it's in a paddock of yellow buttercups. For some reason, there's always yellow in the view that fills the windscreen, every time, the buttercups or some gorse on Ahipara. McCahon saw that yellow and he always put it in, he scrubbed and scruffed a bit of yellow into the greens in the paintings. The yellow might have been something in particular like buttercups or gorse or clay landslips or even something unusual, can't think what, but he made it stand for something you just saw everywhere, he made yellow stand for yellow.

Then the sea appears just above the skirt of the hill. It looks just like the sea.

This bit always makes Stan cry and he's glad the CTI team he's talking to isn't in the bus. It's got something to do with the fact that the sea looks just like the sea, the way Ahipara looks exactly like the kind of dark hill that slopes up slowly and then goes down steeply, like a forehead, to the beach. It's got something to do with the fact that this hill that looks so much like what it is always looks brand-new when it fills the windscreen. Every time.

It's also got to do with the fact that McCahon saw that and painted it. 'Ahipara here I come back home where I started from.' He didn't just paint the thing, although he did that and got it just right – he painted the thing being looked at. He painted what happens when you recognise the thing you're looking at, even though it looks new every time.

Stan gets out of the mini-bus by the public toilets above the beach in the elbow of the bay below Ahipara. There's a smell of marijuana coming out of the toilets, what's more he can hear some kids fucking in there, sounds like more than one lot, they're comparing notes about how they're going. He waits until he's down on the beach before blowing his nose and wiping his eyes. It's probably got something to do with the end of the trip as well, but he shouldn't fool himself, he always has a howl round about now.

Stan sets off along Ninety Mile Beach. It's not ninety miles long, but it's a great name. The elbowed curve of the bay where the kids were rooting in the toilets is supposed to be where the souls of the dead have a rest before finishing their last journey to the Cape, where they descend into the underworld. Maybe that's what the kids in the toilets were, really – souls resting. McCahon painted jets heading off across the Tasman, apparently the paintings were about the last journey of one of his friend's daughters who had cancer and was going to Sydney for treatment. But Stan always imagines them flying up Ninety Mile Beach, these souls, jetting out. McCahon painted *Boy am I scared* and Stan thinks of the extent of Ninety Mile Beach as a huge stride, a step your soul would take knowing this was it. End of the trip. No wonder you wanted to have a last shag before that. This was when you'd go down, finally, out of the world you'd got used to looking at and seeing every day of your living life. No more Ahiparas that looked just like what they always reminded you of and no more sea that always surprised you by reminding you what it was. You were scared shitless because soon, looking was going to be a different kind of experience altogether and because you had no idea of what you were going to see at the end of the jetting out, at the end of the walk, the big stride, the last one.

Stan senses the dark mass of Ahipara behind him as he strides along the hard, wet sand where the tide's going out. Ahead of him the great, gradual curve of the beach disappears into greyish mist. The mist's a mixture of sea spray blowing up off the breakers, sun haze and the cloudy white-out of distance. The black specks of dogs become three immense Rottweilers shining with sea and heat – they circle Stan with their huge tongues and their dopey, affectionate grins, before running on. Their owner's a Maori guy with long dreadlocks hanging down his back. He pursues the dogs on a fat-tyre quad bike to which is strapped a surfcaster and a wet sack. He and Stan communicate with chin tilts and the sight of the cigarette in the man's mouth makes Stan light up a fresh one.

The weight of Ahipara seems to lift after about an hour's walking and it's only then that Stan turns around and looks back. The hill's almost lost in the same mist that had hidden the far north of the beach when he set out. The tide's a long way out and it's this moment that Stan has come here for.

His footprints make a lonely, skinny-soled track towards him from the place he started out from, together with the tyre tracks of the quad bike. He can see how he's pressed down hard with his big toes to keep his stride going. The big dogs have run in the wet or in the shallows and their tracks only occasionally show up in the flat vista of the beach. There are many bird tracks, though, and splatters of white, limey shit where they've gouged the sand for shellfish.

Stan stands looking back along the beach and the signs of his own beach walk on it. He has a sense of the distance — his chest's hurting from the combination of walking, smoking and salt spray. This is the bit he likes. There's a distance back the way he's come which his walk's measured and which the almost-disappearance of Ahipara marks. It's a distance into the far-away, the kind of distance that makes far-away things smaller — it's perspective. But then, all the walking way along that perspective, there's been the sea at his left shoulder — the dry sand sometimes, then the wet, then the thin receding water, then the scum of the last wave, then the deeper water, then the tumbled yellow and brown of the sandy waves and their backwash, then the white of waves breaking in deeper water and the greeny bluish colour of the sea itself, then the big white breakers further out and the green-blue sea extending up to the sky, a different band of blue, then the sky whiting out into the glare of sunlight and above that, finally, the grey-and-white pile-ups of cloud.

Stan looks at this. He looks at it by facing out to sea and seeing it piled up in front of him, looking brand-new but also just the way he knew it would as he walked all the way here along the beach in the direction the departing souls take. This is what they've had at their left shoulder the whole way, scared shitless, jetting or walking, the same but different all the time, this view that always replaced itself, that was always in the process of replacing itself, never stopping. It began when time did and it would stop when time stopped, when you went down into the underworld where you didn't know what you were going to see. It was always the same and always different, always there and never there in the same way, always itself and always the ghost of itself at the same time, always haunted by itself.

That's what you saw, here, when you looked at it. And it's what you'd know was always there, at your right shoulder this time, when you walked all the way back, the beach-walk, back the way you'd come, to finish the trip.

Keshamoni and her elder brother are watching the beautiful videos of New Zealand scenery. They are watching them using the big plasma screen that Biswas bought on his way home through Kuala Lumpur. It is something they like to do together, now that her brother is blind.

Keshamoni describes the scene she has selected on her brother's laptop. Although she knows them all by heart, they still play this game. 'Big pointy black scary mountain.'

'Mitre Peak,' says Mohammed Biswas, seeing it quite clearly in his mind, where its image seems to have left an impression that lights up when Keshamoni turns on the screen. 'G1A attraction. World Heritage.' He does not tell her about the phone call from Khulna on the night of the day he saw the famous peak. When he thinks about that night and the voice from Khulna on his cellphone, his mind always makes an image of the black fang and he cannot remove the horror of it, nor can he any longer simply shut his eyes and not look at it. What he sees now and what he does not see have nothing to do with looking. Before the glass of the lighting appliances blinded him it was looking-but-not-seeing. But now.

'Geyserland,' explains Biswas, telling Keshamoni again the story of the moonlit lake and its strange hot water and the people throwing empty cans at him, but not the story of the filthy men in the hot pool. When Keshamoni chooses *Geyserland*, Biswas cannot stop his mind from making a picture of the fat man's purplish tongue creeping thickly from his mouth as his head is pushed down into the hot, sulphurous water. He has to wait for her next choice to make the bloated face go away.

Some of the videos are very bright, for example the Mueller Glacier one that Pat took looking straight into the sunlit ice-glare when the CTI team went up the Hooker Valley. These ones Biswas believes he can sense against his eyes, a light that is often different from the picture in his mind. There is a globe of love in the heavens, sings the Baul singer Biswas under his breath when he senses this light – where is the owner, the proprietor? Who knows whom I can ask about this?

He associates the light with the money that comes from Krishna's milkmaid friend in Los Angeles, but he does not tell Keshamoni about this either.

Sometimes, Keshamoni puts her thin, warm hand against his face and over the skin of his eyes and then he is seeing her very clearly. She is little and dark, she keeps her hair clean and shiny and her face is bright with excitement, a true daughter of shonar Bangla. But he no longer sees the Keshamoni on his cellphone screen, knock-kneed, with filthy hair and eyes that begged him not to see her. He sees the black fang and the pool filth's disgusting tongue and some other pictures in his mind, but he does not see the Keshamoni on his cellphone.

'*The Chasm*,' says Mohammed Baul Biswas, the brother of Keshamoni, hearing the unruly thunder of the barsa rains overwhelm the house's spouting and crash into the yard below their room. It will clean the dusty yard and the alley where black crows hunt and it will run away into the brown, backwater arm of the Buriganga that reaches up to but does not touch their home in Bakshi.